A SPY FOR
HANNIBAL

A SPY FOR HANNIBAL

A NOVEL OF CARTHAGE

ELISABETH ROBERTS CRAFT

Bartleby Press

Silver Spring, Maryland

Battle descriptions come from Polybius, the ancient author.

Printed in the United States of America

Published by:

Bartleby Press
11141 Georgia Avenue
Silver Spring, Maryland 20902

Library of Congress Cataloging-in-Publication Data

Craft, Elisabeth Roberts, 1918-
    A spy for Hannibal : a novel of Carthage / Elisabeth
Roberts Craft.
        p.   cm.
    ISBN 0-910155-33-X
    1. Hannibal, 247-182 B.C.—Fiction. 2. Carthage (Extinct
city)—Fiction. 3. Rome—History—Republic, 265-30 B.C.—
Fiction. 4. Punic War, 2nd, 218-201 B.C.—Fiction. I. Title.
PS3553.R213S68   1996
813'.54—dc20   95-13835
                                                          CIP

To my friend, Mary Niven Alston

1

*H*anno hated his uncle Hasdrubal. From his hiding place among the tall dark cedars, the fig trees, the oleanders, and the flower-strewn shrubs that created a border between the temple courtyard and the surrounding walls, Hanno watched sullenly as Hasdrubal paced back and forth on the temple portico. Small for his eleven years, Hanno felt confident that his uncle would not see him squatting in the bushes.

In fact, Hanno was quite familiar with the bushes. They had been a source of security since the day when, at the age of four, he had been left at the priestly school. He had wanted his mother. That day, scrunched down behind a flower-covered bush, he had listened to the young priests scurrying around, searching for him, calling his name. When a shadow had fallen across him, he had looked up, straight into the unamused, night-gray eyes of his uncle. Hasdrubal was high priest of the goddess Tanit. Hanno still remembered the terror of that confrontation, though nothing drastic had happened. His uncle had given him warm, fragrant, dripping, sticky honey cakes which he had stuffed into his mouth until his mother came to get him.

Today, he had positioned himself carefully. He wanted an unobstructed view of the square sandstone temple across the paved courtyard and the triple mazelike walled entrance on his left. Why he watched, he couldn't say. He had been dismissed early from school to go to his sister's house. Instead of leaving, he had stalled until the courtyard was empty then rushed from the long, spread-out school building, flown across the front of the temple, casting a wild glance at the door of the high priest's house, and jumped into the bushes. If discovered, he would be punished, but he continued to vent his rage by glaring at the figure of the high priest.

His uncle was cruel, cruel, to members of his own family.

Plenty of others were available. Gisgo didn't have to be chosen. Besides, Hanno fumed, why was Uncle Hasdrubal still wearing the sheer, unbelted linen robe and the high cone-shaped hat that he had worn all day instead of his formal ritual robes?

The high priest swerved from the portico and started toward the great bronze statue of the goddess. Hanno slid the conical cap from his head, at the same time shoving the thick, unruly black curls from his forehead. He crouched lower. That Tanit faced the temple and was closer to the maze than to the large sacrificial animal altar in the center was probably his salvation. His uncle wouldn't walk around behind the statue. Hanno shuddered. His uncle's turned-down mouth meant trouble for somebody. To Hanno's relief, the cold, hooded eyes that recorded every movement within the temple were fixed on the marbled pavement and not sweeping around, spying into corners.

The high priest squatted in front of the statue with one graceful motion of his thin, agile body. What was he doing? Hanno popped his head from behind the sheltering tree trunk and as rapidly withdrew it after he cast a terrified glance at the entrance.

Anyone could walk in at any moment, and Hanno knew it. The Temple of Tanit had been built on the main road through Carthage. The road ran from the oblong commercial port with its string of crammed dockside warehouses, past the two-story blank wall of the military port and the equally unperforated walls of multistoried apartment houses. Further along, this empty sameness was relieved by an arcade of trading shops, eating stalls, fragrant spice closets, and open vistas of the forum.

To international travelers, the Carthaginian forum lacked the symmetry of the Roman or Athenian forums, but was pleasingly unified by the magnificent sandstone building at the far end that housed the senate.

After the crowds and the business of the day, the forum rested, silent and empty in the bright, silvery light of the heavens. Carthage was not a night city.

From the forum, the road continued along the enclosure of the Temple of Tanit on the left, the Byrsa hill, solid with buildings, on the right, then between more apartment houses until it reached the massive defense wall that surrounded the city. It ran out through the gate toward Megara, an area of palatial homes set among deep green cypresses, flowering bushes, and riotously colored gardens. These homes gave way to elegant houses attached to orchards and fair land where the rich and fertile fields supplied the tables of the city.

As they passed along this road, sailors, finding no god of their own in times of stress, sought the great statue of Tanit; women with problems known only to them came to the temple to pray; men who were financially strapped by losses at sea laid their worries before her. All kinds of people with all kinds of difficulties found their way to the Temple of Tanit at all times of day. Hanno had reason to be wary.

Seeing no one, he peered around the tree. Another glance at the entrance assured him that no shadow approached. He stood up. Clasping the cedar, he leaned sideways, twisting his neck this way and that until he had a clear view. Ugh! His uncle was rearranging the kindling laid by one of the lesser priests. Fighting the urge to vomit, the boy dropped onto his belly. He pressed his face into the dirt. When those kindlings flamed up, they would—

The sound of creaking bones made him look up. With long, barefooted strides, the high priest headed toward his living quarters. His home, a two-story stone building on one side of the temple, had originally mirrored the school building on the other side in perfect symmetry. Part way, he stopped. He stood, his chin raised, his head slightly tilted.

Hanno fidgeted. There's nothing to hear, he thought. Go on! Any second, the priest who nightly lit the lamps would start round with the amphora of oil. Hanno didn't want to be caught in the temple precinct.

The moment Hasdrubal reached his door and disappeared, the boy scrambled up, yanked his long brown robe to hip level, jumped over the shrubs, and dashed out, clapping his hat on his head.

Despite his nervousness, he shivered in delight as the warmth of the late afternoon sun struck him. The breeze was soft against his skin. The air smelled like moist earth.

Again, he shivered. Before long, the vines that coiled their long tendrils around each dark green cedar would be covered with purple blossoms. The walls of the temple and the private houses would be covered with pink, white, and purple flowers. Their sweet fregrance permeated the whole city. The air even smelled good mixed with the pungent odors of vegetables cooking in oil, spiced eggs, chickens roasting on spits, the stink of uncured animal hides. He hesitated when he reached the forum.

The one pleasure of his life was to wander along the wharfs of the commercial harbor. Ships from Rome and Athens and Tyre and Sidon and Rhodes and Alexandria and Hispania were tied to the docks. Near-naked, sweating slaves and dockhands, bent double with the loads on their backs, labored up the slanting boards that stretched from the dock to the decks. On the decks and on the wharf, overseers yelled instructions or swore when part of a load plunged into the water.

Russet or mud-colored warehouses, jammed close together, stored the skins, copper ingots, amber, gold and ivory, heavy wool carpets, and bolts of fine wool cloth. Traders, sailors, and slaves from all over the Mare Internum passed through the doors.

At intervals along the dock, proprietors of food stalls sold hot bread and lentils. Men in litters called greetings to passersby. The occasional horseman tightly reined in his animal or hurt someone in the crowd.

Usually, Hanno walked across the swinging bridge between the commercial harbor and the round military harbor to the docks and warehouses opposite. He gazed in agony at the ships. He wanted to be on one.

Walking back, he peered into the military harbor. The round island in the middle was completely covered by roofed slips for warships. The harbor side of the surrounding wall was also lined with slips. He never saw any of the warships or the slips, but he heard the hum of moving tackle, hammers, and oars slapping water. High above the central building, the admiral sat in a small room. From there, he directed traffic. A trumpeter sounded his orders.

Hanno's glance lingered on the road to the harbors before turning to the forum. Near him, a portico sheltered tiny shops, selling gold jewelry and alabaster lamps from Egypt, purple cloth from Tyre, pottery from Athens, swords and bronze helmets from the eastern edge of the Mare Internum, and spices from as far away as India.

Luxuriantly bearded Carthaginian men in dark woolen capes and conical hats conducted business. Slaves in earth-colored work garments hurried to do their owner's bidding. Sailors gawked at the buildings and the people. Women hovered around the shops. Friends stopped to greet friends. Men gathered in groups of two and three to talk quietly while others swirled around them.

Hanno's hesitation was momentary. He was already late. Thought of the coming ritual made him grind his teeth and curse his uncle. He started to run again, dodging through the crowd. As he veered from behind an old man with a cane, he cut too close in front of a dark-skinned slave shopping for her mistress. The woman yelled after him to watch where he was going. Hanno barely heard her. He crossed in front of the senate building where two young lions, chained at either end of the broad steps, growled at each other. He slowed, out of breath, at the foot of a steep and curving street. The great temples of Melkart and Eshmoun dominated the top. Just under them, nestled against the hill to catch the sunlight, and crowned by a cistern, stood his sister's five-story pink row house. He started up the hill at a dog trot, swerved to avoid colliding with a boy racing down and did a jig behind two sauntering men in noisy argument. The minute an old veteran on crutches passed him, he dashed around the men. He cleared each set of three steps in one leap as he came to it and, out of breath, arrived at his sister's door.

Planning to casually make his presence known from the security of his bedroom, Hanno slipped into the vestibule. He faced his mother. Her unsmiling black eyes met his without rancor, but he knew he had offended her. By Tanit, he said to himself, I don't care. I don't want to go. He shifted his feet guiltily.

Without raising her voice, Saphonisba said, "You are late, Hanno. You barely have time to bathe and change. We have already eaten supper."

Hanno opened his mouth to protest that he was hungry. Her gentle, luminous eyes met the defiance in his squarely. Under their steady gaze, his faltered, then dropped to the floor. Closing his mouth, he banged through the vestibule. He turned into the main part of the house, and scowling, disappeared up the stairs. Slowly, Saphonisba followed her son. She understood how upset he was. They all were. However, they knew their duty, and they would do it. She would see to that. Loyalty was paramount and had to be upheld. Hasdrubal had spoken.

Walking toward his private quarters, Hasdrubal increased his pace with the rapidity of his thinking. If that nephew of mine thinks I did not see him, he is mistaken. He should be severely disciplined, but under the circumstances, I will say nothing.

Hanno was a thorn in the flesh of every instructor. He assimilated what was taught without paying attention and was uninterested in what he learned. Yet, he was slated to become high priest of Tanit, an inherited position of great honor. As the only direct-line male in the family, he was obligated. He must be high priest, at least until another male was produced and reached maturity. Hasdrubal was adamant; only to himself did he admit that Hanno was ill-suited for the priesthood. This disturbed him. The succession was important to the family, yes, but in his view having a capable man run the temple was also important.

What caused the high priest even more worry was that Hanno knew what his father had done in a similar situation. True, Bimilcar had been two years older and had had a purpose in running away. He wanted to be a soldier. If Hanno ran away, his only reason—as far as Hasdrubal could tell—was to escape school.

Hasdrubal shook his head. With all the talk of a war with the Roman Republic, Hanno might attempt to follow his father to Hispania.

Thus preoccupied, the high priest reached his door. As he crossed the threshold, thoughts that had preyed on his mind all day returned to haunt him.

"Have the barber come to me immediately." Hasdrubal passed his prostrate Numidian slave without looking at him, but felt a rush of air as the wiry, athletic man sprang up and ran out.

In the bathroom, Hasdrubal removed his bronze, silver-inlaid razor from its case, laid it on the washbasin, fetched the chair he kept in the bedroom, positioned it the way the barber liked, and sat down. Only then did he remove his conical cap. He felt the top of his naked head and chin for stubble. Not bad. He had last been shaved at sunrise, but for a ceremony of this significance, he wanted to be perfect.

The barber, a young temple slave, was checking his scalp for invisible growth with sensitive, barely moving fingertips when the Numidian dropped to one knee in the doorway.

"The potter is here with the vase you ordered."

"Bring him in." Hasdrubal gestured for the barber to stop.

With bowed head, the heavily bearded potter knelt. His scanty clothing were splattered with clay. With both hands, he raised a vase the height of a man's finger spread. It was round and plump of body. Delicately fashioned of thin clay, the vase was painted with a red ocher crescent and disk—symbols of the goddess Tanit—on a polished cream slip.

Humbly, he said, "The work I did myself, sire, according to your instructions."

He mentioned neither the great pains he had taken nor the

many hours spent while his apprentices tended the narrow, dingy shop, molded the utilitarian pottery, packed and fired the kilns.

Hasdrubal examined the vase, turning it round and round, upside down and right side up. He ran his finger along the surface and felt the slender handles that curved from the lip onto the body. Satisfied, he handed the vase to his slave. "Pay the fellow his price plus half."

"Thank you, sire. Thank you." On elbows and knees, the potter wiggled backwards from the bathroom.

"Abdmelkart," Hasdrubal called out to his Numidian slave, "when my niece comes with her child, bring the boy to me and leave us."

The high priest leaned back and submitted to the barber's finishing touches.

Dressed in heavy, immaculate white linen, Hasdrubal adjusted the wide embroidered band that fell from his shoulders to the hem of the robe. Sandals, and the ever-present cap completed his formal dress. He selected a silver drinking cup from a wall niche and set it beside a pitcher of pomegranate juice on a small, portable, table. He looked around the room: two ebony chairs and a table imported from Euboea; more furniture than most Carthaginian homes contained.

The chair where he sat to eat his solitary meals would do. Cautiously picking up the table so as not to unseat the pitcher, he placed it next to the chair. Then, he emptied a thumbnail-sized packet of white powder into the silver cup. He filled it slowly with pomegranate juice, stopping repeatedly to rotate the liquid until the powder grains were taken up and dissolved.

The door opened partway. A child of four ducked in, ran to the high priest, and flung his arms around the man's legs. Hasdrubal caressed the boy's black curly hair and golden skin, the color of ambered honey. He picked the child up and kissed him.

"I'm going to a ritual," Gisgo said. "I can stay up late." His dark eyes sparkled.

"Yes!" Hasdrubal tried to match the child's joy. He put Gisgo down and passed a trembling hand over his own eyes.

"Oh, pom-pom juice!" Gisgo pounced on the cup.

Hasdrubal's glance sought the cream urn and returned to the boy. "Drink slowly, darling. Do not gulp."

"I love pom-pom juice." The small, rosy mouth was stained purply red around the edges.

"And Uncle Hasdrubal loves you." He settled himself in the chair and watched the child.

"I'm sleepy." Gisgo crawled into Hasdrubal's lap and nestled against him. After a few moments, the boy's eyes closed and his body relaxed. Hasdrubal rose, holding the child. He laid his face against the soft ringlets, remained still, then kissed the baby mouth. A movement of his arms shifted Gisgo's face into the fullness of the linen. The high priest left the room.

"Everything is ready, sire," the Numidian said from where he crouched by the door.

"Did you ask the priestesses of the orchestra to play with particular vigor?"

"Yes, sire."

Rigidly, resolute purpose in each step, the high priest crossed to the temple. As he left the seclusion of the main portico, he pinched Gisgo. The child slumbered, motionless. The second pinch was hard, twisting the flesh. Again, no objection from the boy. He drew himself to his full height, tall for a Carthaginian, and moved with the assurance and dignity of his office toward the statue.

The courtyard was alive with light, music, and people. On the side by the garden, ten priestesses rattled sistra, plucked lyres, and banged cymbals; all sang, while dancing an attenuated, complicated step. Flares blazed, their smoky flame seeming to sway with the long gowns and high headdresses of the priestesses. Even the dark purple robe on the goddess seemed to sway. A noisy, friendly, expectant crowd walked around. Others sat on carpets or cushions that they had brought, laughing and talking to their neighbors. Still more poured through the entrance, adding to the excitement.

Hasdrubal pressed his lips into a taut, straight line. He hoped to heaven his sister-in-law had given her daughter a sedative so the girl wouldn't cry out in agony. He did not want his own family to break the law by weeping on this joyous occasion. Without looking directly at them, he observed that all three sat stoically in front of the goddess, Saphonisba in the center, Batbaal and Hanno on either side.

Saphonisba held her spine straight, her shoulders back, her head up. She had pulled one end of her long, gauzy himation from her shoulders to drape it over her head and across the lower part of her face. She is superb, thought Hasdrubal, an intelligent woman who accepts the tragedies in life with the same calm equanimity as she does the joys. Her behavior will be a credit to her position in society.

Batbaal's back was as straight as her mother's. How alike they were. His eyes narrowed. She looks as if the slightest puff of wind would blow her over. Drugged. Just as well. The light from the flares blurred the edges of her topaz-colored himation. He noted that the fabric, though wound tightly around her body, was wrapped high to hide her mouth. Dear girl; nobody will know if your lower lip trembles.

Quickly, he looked at Hanno. He was hunched over, his chin resting on one hand. Hasdrubal followed the upward tilt of his head. In deep contemplation, he was gazing at the face of the goddess.

After making obeisance to Tanit, the high priest laid Gisgo in her arms. As he withdrew his hands, using a knife concealed in the statue, he deftly slashed the little boy's throat then stepped back to see if the blood was dripping properly onto the firewood in the trough at the goddess' feet. Satisfied, he nodded. A young priest pushed a lighted taper beneath the kindling. A bright orange flame sprang upward, hissing at the bloody trickle. The high priest passed behind the statue as the dancers whirled from the sidelines in wild leaps and turns. Round and round Tanit, they danced to an insidious loud beat.

Hasdrubal took hold of a thread he had rigged to the hands of the goddess. At the moment the fire was the hottest, the dance the wildest, the noise the loudest, he yanked the thread. Gisgo's lifeless body toppled into the flame.

The new orchestra priestess from Tyre dropped out of the dance as it swirled alongside the plants. She threw up behind an oleander bush. Seeing her, he ground his teeth. She would have to be punished in the morning.

The fire had spent its fury. Following the letter of the law, as he had throughout the sacrifice, he turned the ritual over to his principal subordinate. Holding his head high, his face a mask, he walked sedately to his residence. His slave, squatting in the dark, jumped to open the door.

"Take a bowl," he said, looking directly ahead, talking into space, "and watch from the portico. When everyone has gone, collect the ashes."

The door closed soundlessly behind the slave. Turning, Hasdrubal stared, unseeing, at it. By degrees, his ceremonial mask crumpled, around the eyes first then the mouth and chin. He collapsed into a chair and buried his face in his hands. A few drops of water seeped through his fingers. The sensation of moisture made him spring into a tense, upright position. No living being must catch him weeping. He had carried out his part of the ritual to perfection. It was completed. Surely, the goddess would forgive this momentary weakness. He attempted to rise.

"I cannot," he moaned, sinking back. If only I had died instead of the child. His whole life was before him. Mine is over.

2

asdrubal slumped back into his chair. Alone, shut off from the world, he surrendered to the stillness. Slowly, his eyelids closed. Restlessness sucked at his mind. Funny, he thought, the way life turns out. I would have liked to travel. The only place I have been is our family's vineyards and cattle-grazing land on the peninsula across the bay. I was not supposed to be high priest. It should have been Bimilcar.

How well he remembered that day. Bimilcar was seven, and he was five. Their nurse had taken them for a walk in the orchard behind the house in Megara. Falling blossoms carpeted the ground. They had run, laughing and kicking at the pink and white petals. On the way back, Bimilcar said, "I'm going to be high priest."

In silence, they turned the corner from the vestibule into the main part of the house, crossed a cool, statue-filled foyer and stepped into the central garden. Hasdrubal was pouting. He didn't know what a high priest was, but he intended to find out. Why was Bimilcar going to be one and he wasn't? He looked around for his mother and spied her at the far end of the garden.

She sat in the shade of the covered walkway, a large, dark-skinned woman in flowing draperies. Three women sat at her feet. Distaff in hand, she was showing them something. He ran through the garden, along the edge of the pool. Sun-sparkled water winked invitingly. Any other day, he would have stripped and jumped in. Not today. He flung himself onto his mother's knees.

"What's the matter, son?" She scooped him into her arms.

Nestled on her broad, comfortable lap, soothed by her caresses, he looked up at her, quizzical bewilderment on his round, chubby face. "Why aren't I going to be high priest."

"Dear child, Bimilcar is older than you are. Your papa is high priest now, and someday Bimilcar will be."

"Papa is high priest?" His eyes widened.

"Yes. You've been to the temple to see papa. He showed you his house and the school building. Remember? Soon, you'll go to school there."

"Will Bimilcar live at the temple like papa?"

"Yes. But you can do all sorts of things. You could be a senator and work in that big building where the lions are. You could be a trader and travel to foreign lands to sell all sorts of beautiful things. You could join our army and become a great general. Don't you think one of those would be nice to do?"

He looked up at his mother's lovely smile and thought maybe all of them would be nice.

Hasdrubal, the man, ruefully shook his head. Strange. No sooner was Bimilcar enrolled in the priestly school than he began to complain. First it was the length of time he had to sit cross-legged on the floor. Then it was learning the formulas for the religious festivals and the numerous administrative duties. Papa, for all his gentleness, was a hard taskmaster. If Bimilcar was to be the next high priest, he had to learn the rituals of Tanit and how to run the temple.

Because papa wanted me to have a good education also, I was included in Bimilcar's training sort of as an adjunct. I was my brother's confidant, his sounding board, the recipient of his whispered unhappiness. Initially, the inactivity frustrated him because he learned quickly. The real complaining started after he decided the army was more worthy of his energies.

Night after night, he kept me awake, talking about the army and the glorious feats he hoped to perform. He put forward one plan of escape after another, most of them the silly aberrations of children.

Hasdrubal thought about the bedroom they had shared—the two beds placed end to end, a tiny oil lamp on the floor beside each bed. He had blown out his lamp. The other one flickered, bathing the room in dim light. He lay on his back, hands under his head, fighting sleep, as he listened to Bimilcar.

Bored, he blurted out, "Tell father you want to be a soldier."

"Oh, no." Bimilcar sounded shocked. "I'm the one directly in line. Papa would never agree." He got out of bed and stood over his brother. In the faint light, they stared at each other. Hasdrubal's heart thumped. Something important was coming; he knew.

"I'm going to run away," Bimilcar whispered.

"No," cried Hasdrubal, sitting up.

"Sh!" his brother hissed. "I'm going to join Hamilcar Barca's army."

Deliberately, Hasdrubal laid aside the coverlet, swung his legs around, and stood up. Face to face with Bimilcar, he demanded, "When?"

"Don't you tattle."

"Of course, I won't. But when?"

"I don't know exactly; soon. Before I'm initiated into the priesthood."

Hasdrubal nodded. Then, for no reason, he flung his arms around Bimilcar, hugged him and jumped back into bed, turning his face to the wall. Suddenly, a hand squeezed his shoulder. Seconds later, the lamp went out.

The high priest sighed. Bimilcar was thirteen at the time. Even at that age, he had written extensively. The scrolls had started the moment he found Hamilcar. Long, detailed, and stilted, they told of the ebb and flow of war as the Carthaginians and then the Romans suffered defeat at the hands of the other. His chronicles expressed his amazement that Carthaginian power would be challenged by the young, upstart Roman Republic. They extolled the courage of Hamilcar when, surrounded by the Roman enemy, he refused surrender on unacceptable terms and ruled the remains of the army from Mount Eryx in Sicilia. They described Hamilcar's joy and the joy of the entire army at the birth of the first Barca son, named Hannibal. Later, Bimilcar wrote of his friendship with the child.

Their father, despite all the scrolls, never recovered from the blow dealt by the runaway. His eyes always retained an aggrieved sadness because his first-born son had shirked his duty to the family.

How well I remember the day papa summoned me to his personal audience hall. The corners of Hasdrubal's mouth twitched, the extent of any smile that ever lighted his solemn face. The eyeballs beneath the closed lids moved rapidly as he watched the strutting twelve-year-old boy outside his father's house.

At the doorway to the audience hall, he hesitated. The beautiful room was intimidating in its simplicity. The walls were covered with painted scenes taken from the life of Tanit. No furniture or other decoration disturbed the room's subtle tranquility. But today, two chairs had been carefully placed on the polished stone floor. His father stood behind one.

With formality, father, as the high priest, came forward and seated me. Then, in his mild, kindly manner, he told me that I was to become high priest in place of my brother; I must study hard and learn humility because an exalted position and much honor were to be mine.

We spent a long time together, Hasdrubal thought. Some of what he said, I now only vaguely remember. But when I left his presence, my head was high. I was proud of the faith he had in me, proud that he was my father, proud of my heritage, proud of being a Carthaginian, humbled in my determination to do the best job I could. Over the next few years, father and I became close. I understood the fineness of his character, the strength beneath his soft manner, and sensed the depth of his sadness. I always wondered whether Bimilcar's defection contributed to his early death. He was younger than I am now. The shock had been devastating. How inadequate to the task I felt, moving into this house; how small, lying in the bed where he had lain. His death could not have come at a worse time for me, though now that I think back, suddenly having to run the temple took my mind off Dido somewhat.

A groan escaped Hasdrubal as the figure of a beautiful girl floated into his mind. Her dark ringlets danced, her lips smiled in uninhibited pleasure, adding sparkle to her eyes and a glow to pale skin that had the texture of satin.

"Dido, Dido, how could you?" he murmured aloud. "After what we were to each other."

"I love you, Hasdrubal," she seemed to say.

"Lies, all lies. Together, that sunny afternoon in the garden while your nurse slept on a stone bench, we passed through the gates of paradise. Yet the night before our wedding, you ran off with the wealthy son of an Athenian shipping merchant. Do you call that love?"

Still smiling, the figure raised a hand in protest, and faded. He started to stay her departure, but changed his mind. Now in his forty-first winter, he could see that she was a superficial, uneducated, silly girl. But at seventeen, life had come to an end. He had withdrawn from society, turning into a bitter, cynical man who bottled up his feelings, refused the advances of excellent families with marriageable daughters, and immersed himself in his work at the temple.

Scarcely had the funeral rituals for their father been completed than a ship carrying Hamilcar Barca was wharped into the harbor. Ships bringing the remnants of the army followed. With them were escaped slaves, Roman prisoners, Libyans, Spartans, peoples from the far corners of the known world who rested their hopes of wealth and prestige on their beloved general. Hamilcar walked off the ship holding the hand of his five-year-old son Hannibal. Behind them walked Bimilcar.

Hasdrubal straightened in proud affection as he saw the image of his brother. Bimilcar had left Carthage a beardless sapling and had returned a powerful man. Life exuded from every inch of him, from the curling beard to the rippling muscles as he moved. That night, the high priest contemplated his own thin body, found it wanting, gestured indifferently, and went on running his temple.

Bimilcar spent much of his time at the Barca palace in Megara. One day, while visiting Hannibal and his sisters, he saw Saphonisba, the sedate young daughter of Elibaal, the suffete.

Hasdrubal needed little effort to bring that scene before him. He had been sitting in his study reading when his brother burst in.

"Hasdrubal," he begged, "please go to Elibaal and ask for his daughter. I would take her for wife." He grabbed his brother's shoulders. "I can't live without her."

Since Hasdrubal did anything Bimilcar asked, he consented. Dressed in his most formal robes, the high priest of Tanit went to Elibaal. One of the two highest elected officials of Carthage, he was a widower whose home life revolved around his only child. Elibaal hemmed and hawed, but eventually agreed. The wedding was a lavish event. Great feasts were held on public porticoes, and baskets of food were distributed to the city's poor. Elibaal made sure nobody was forgotten. Nine months later, Batbaal was born.

Bimilcar frequently brought his daughter to the temple, often accompanied by Hannibal. The inquisitive, active boy found himself confined to the Barca palace because of the daily civil strife instigated by remnants of the army. Trips to the temple were a welcome change for him.

Soon, Hannibal began to visit the temple in the company of his Athenian tutor. His excuse was that his older sister was a priestess of Tanit, but he spent his time with the high priest. Laughter was in his eyes, his face open and intelligent. Underneath lay a quietness, a vision, something Hasdrubal couldn't fathom, something that tied him to Hannibal with bands of iron. Many times, they sat and talked about life and places and people. Then one afternoon, they talked about death. Hannibal had been eight.

"I don't like it when people die." Hannibal sat on the floor, sober-faced, his eyes wide. "Some go away and never come back. I've seen others. They're so still. But it's not like sleep."

Hasdrubal leaned toward the boy. "What is so different about it?"

"They look funny. They're skin's so white. They don't breathe. People stand around and cry."

"Does that make you feel bad?"

"It hurts right here," Hannibal said, taping his chest.

"Those who loved them feel sad for a long time."

"My papa said he had killed soldiers. He was sorry, but he had to win the battles. It's awful to have to kill them and make people sad."

"Yes." Hasdrubal understood what lay behind the discussion.

The veterans of Sicilian Mount Eryx revolted. Carthage had not lived up to their hopes. The senate had given them little, if any, money. Living in a camp outside the city was hard. They were not accepted by the Carthaginians. They became resentful. Revolt spread as fire before a wind until the hinterland under Carthaginian control was aflame. The senate, at its wit's end, recalled Hamilcar Barca to put down the rebellion. Throngs flocked to him, and Bimilcar rode from the city at the general's right hand.

Hamilcar confronted the rebels, both slaves and free men. He tricked them into a blind ravine, and captured them. That ended the uprising. But the senate, in panic, appropriated money to build a defense wall around the city. Afterwards they ordered the prisoners paraded through the city and then crucified. Crosses were erected on both sides of the main roads leading into Carthage. Here the captives hung, to die slowly, sweating during the heat of the day and shivering during the cold of night. Hannibal saw this, saw men who had played with him on Mount Eryx, men who had taught him horsemanship and warfare, men who loved him. Death was terrible, and the battles that caused it frightening. Yet what was the choice? War was war; boys and men died, women and babies suffered, rape and pillage occurred. He understood this necessity, but nevertheless, he gave his heart to the victims.

A year later, Hamilcar, taking his family with him, sailed to Hispania to found New Carthage. The day of their departure was the last time Hasdrubal had seen Hannibal. That nine-year old was now twenty-eight and supreme commander of all the Carthaginian troops in Hispania.

Hasdrubal followed Hannibal's development through his brother. Bimilcar did not choose to transplant his family to Hispania. Instead, he made frequent trips home to Carthage. He reported in intimate detail Hannibal's reaction to the death of his father at the hands of hostile tribesmen. The murder of his brother-in-law who had led the army after Hamilcar Barca drew the same intense, but controlled, grief.

Later, Elibaal had been in Hispania as a representative of the government at the time Hannibal was raised to supreme commander. He gave Hasdrubal an enthusiastic, graphic description of the wild cheering after the announcement.

Hasdrubal understood the troops' loyalty and devotion. He gave it himself willingly and in full measure. He had no doubt Hannibal was a genius. The high priest sighed. Soon, that genius would come into play on a grand scale. As for himself, he had Saphonisba and her children to look after.

At the thought, Saphonisba's face emerged before him. He noted her lustrous black hair and olive skin, the perfectly applied kohl around her black eyes. Her small, perfect features matched her diminutive, elegant shape.

"My dear," she said, "a good-looking man like you—you should have accepted one of those overtures of matrimony. You'd have had children of your own. You should have, you know. You'd make a wonderful father."

"Perhaps you are right. You are the one who made me realize that not all women are perfidious and double-dealing." He hesitated. "And it is true that I have been lonely. That hurt remains in my heart like a knot. I do not want to be hurt again."

"My dear, Bimilcar and I have had peace and joy all our married lives. You could have had the same."

"If I had married, my grandchild would have died tonight instead of Gisgo, but the line for the priesthood would have been secure."

The high priest clutched his chest at the memory of Gisgo.

Bimilcar's stern face appeared, startling Hasdrubal. Dressed in battle readiness, as he had been the day the flotilla sailed from the military harbor, he was very much the commander of his troops.

"Brother," said Bimilcar, "much as I loved and honored Hamilcar Barca, I love and honor his son Hannibal more. Hannibal is the most brilliant leader Carthage has ever had. Fortune smiled on us when he assumed command. My place is with Hannibal. I must serve my country in the coming war. Care for my family."

"I will. I will."

At the forceful sound of his own voice, Hasdrubal blinked and looked around the room. He was alone. Was he losing his mind? It must be his extreme fatigue; he had to watch himself. Bimilcar was right, though. No one needed a specter to know that there would soon be war with Rome. It was bruited about on the wharf by foreign sailors and discussed in the markets by shop-keepers haggling over grain.

As soon as anything happens, the high priest thought, I will get a letter from Bimilcar. His reaction had been spontaneous, but he winced. Yet, somehow he knew that the evening sacrifice had not been in vain. He would hear from his brother.

In the meantime—Hasdrubal stood up—he had better try to sleep. That priestess had to be penalized in the morning. Why had he accepted her? She had appeared like thunderheads in a clear sky and asked for admission without offering any credentials from her mother temple. That was what? Three months ago. Three months, and still an orchestra priestess at her age! She must be at least twenty. Outrageous. She had been placed there at her own request, but with the understanding that she would be moved as soon as he decided what work at the temple best suited her abilities. To his annoyance, she had resisted all attempts to find out her background, her interests, her talents. She faced any probing question with a polite, genteel, but firm refusal to divulge information about herself.

She was delicately bred. He instinctively sensed that. Other-wise, he knew only that she answered to the name of Elissa and claimed Tyre as her home city. He often corresponded with Ahiram, high priest of Baal in Tyre, about temple matters. Many times he had considered asking about her and had not done so. Now that she had disgraced herself and must be dealt with, he wished that he had inquired. He needed more knowledge on which to base his choice of punishment.

Why did she irritate him so? It was as if she were deliberately trying to goad him into being cruel. He had always made a point of dealing fairly with those under him. He never overstepped the boundary between fairness and cruelty, though at times his pronouncements had been harsh. He was well aware that his evenhanded, efficient running of the huge complex had earned him the respect of all, from the most lowly temple slave to the great priest immediately under him.

Enough of this. He had been indulging himself too long. With repeated warnings that he must not let her rile him, the high priest headed for his bedroom.

3

"You wanted to see me, sire?"

The high priest, studying some scrolls on his office work table, raised his head. In silence, he inspected the poised and graceful priestess standing in the open doorway. Though heavily made up, her skin showed none of the usual Phoenician tattoo marks; her features delicate and finely sculpted. Not beautiful, but passable, he thought. A belt cinched the voluminous robe that was too big for her small-boned, slender body. Even covered by a himation, her black hair, curled high in the latest fashion, bobbed as she bowed low.

Athenian. All the women copied Athenian fashions; only the men carried on the Phoenician tradition. His niece and her mother wore their hair the same way. He didn't like the craze for copying the Athenians, but was helpless against the onslaught.

The priestess was older than he had at first thought. She was possibly in her mid to late twenties. And, while her bearing contained exactly the correct amount of humility and obedience, there was nothing humble about her.

His eyes narrowed into catlike slits. His observation missed not one fraction of her from curled head to bare feet peeping from beneath the linen robe. He pushed aside the temple accounts received from the chief scribe, folded his hands in his lap, and steeled himself to act impassive and cold.

"You made a spectacle of yourself last night at the most sacred ritual of our goddess and, by so doing, broke the law. You understand, do you not, that your actions might bring the ire of Tanit upon us and ruin the benefit of our great sacrifice?"

She again bowed low, but not fast enough to conceal the rocketing jet of anger that sprang from her eyes.

"What punishment do you think you deserve?" Careful, careful, he said to himself.

"None."

"None!" he shouted. "You shall be whipped until you atone for your transgression."

"Whipped like a slave? No!" The cry had an hysterical edge. Half lowering her lids and contorting her lips in scorn, she said, "I forgot this is Carthage where the punishments you mete out are as cruel as the way you treat your children."

"Obviously you have not been in Carthage long enough to know that our children are well cared for and loved."

"Ah, yes." The priestess flung back her head in derision. "Just the way you treated that little boy last night."

"Do you find that more cruel than the way the Hellenes and Romans expose their unwanted children on the hillsides? Perhaps you prefer their living flesh be torn by wild animals or pecked by scavenger birds. Or is your choice leaving them in the market-place for slave traders to take?"

Angry color flamed in her cheeks, moisture erupting from the hot skin. She glared at the high priest. "Everyone substitutes lambs or baby goats for young children—except Carthage. The whole civilized world is revolted by the hundreds of tiny graves."

"We carry on the traditions of the true faith."

"My father in Tyre will hear about last night and your treatment of me." A sound much like a sob escaped, nothing more.

"Whoever your father may be, in this temple, my word is law, and you will obey," said the high priest with authority. "Dismissed."

Deliberately, the woman turned her back and started toward the door.

"At your age, you should know how to leave the presence of the high priest." The icy tone caused her to freeze.

"Do it correctly."

Red-faced, Elissa turned, dropped onto one knee, bowed her head, rose, bowed at the waist, and backed out the door.

Repeatedly, soundlessly, he hit the table with his clenched fist. However, a few minutes later when he ordered a muscular, elderly priest to whip her, he said, "I want no marks left on her body. You can do that. But beat her until she screams for mercy. She is never to forget this whipping."

The old priest grinned. "I'll be gentle, great priest but she'll scream and holler and think she's going to die."

4

*T*he high priest gave Elissa time to regain her composure. Pale orange tendrils foretelling the rising sun had barely colored the horizon, but life in the compound hummed. In front of the temple, five priestesses, carrying small musical rattles called sistra, bowed shyly as they edged past him. Just inside the entrance of the administrative building, young priests awaited the chief of sacrifices. Two or three, here and there, were already in grave discussion. After the chief appeared, they would proceeded to the pillared audience hall to discuss ancient rituals and the value of performing them correctly. Hasdrubal himself intended to participate later in the morning.

In a room further along, Hanno and his classmates sat cross-legged on the floor. Hanno looked worn and discouraged, different from his usual sullen attitude. The high priest castigated himself. In his preoccupation with Elissa, he had neglected his brother's family. Batbaal needed all the support he could give her. Undoubtedly Saphonisba was still with her, not having returned to her own house in Megara. All three needed Bimilcar, except, in a way, Hanno. Hanno had an independence about him reminiscent of Bimilcar. If only he were not so immature, thought the high priest. Anyway, time must be made later in the day to visit Saphonisba. It must. It had to be. He shook his head. There was never enough time.

Ah! Drawn by the lilting voice of the head priestess, he peered into a small, square room. It was devoid of furniture. Two eleven year olds stood contritely before a seated Asherat. On seeing the high priest, the girls dropped to their knees and touched their foreheads to the floor. A tranquil, gray-haired woman, whose prodigality of flesh spilled loosely over her hips onto the floor, acknowledged his presence by a slight bend at the waist and a lowered head.

How fortunate he was to have a woman of her character and background. Not only was she from one of the old, established Carthaginian families, but she had brought up children of her own. She knew how to handle the young priestesses. He had had no trouble with them since she came to the temple after the death of her husband.

"I wish to talk in private," he said.

She addressed the priestesses. "Go now. Remember what I said. There will not be another warning." The pale blue tattoo covering her upper lip and chin quivered in emphasis.

Side by side, like puppets on a string, the two backed out, bowing prodigiously.

"What have those young ladies done?"

She sighed, a mixture of amusement and annoyance in her black eyes. "The usual problem with young people, though these two are starting early with a different twist. It's not just boys, but will they get suitable husbands who'll treat them well and make them happy. Since when was that subject for women!"

She threw her hands above her head and dropped them back into her lap. "I don't understand it."

She looked directly at the high priest, who chose to consider the question rhetorical. "Where would priestesses their age get such notions? Is it limited to these two? I leave you to discover that; I would speak of Elissa."

Straining to get her legs where she could roll onto her knees, she gathered in one hand the folds of the linen gown which she always wore unbelted. A heavy gold ankle bracelet scraped the floor. "Is your desire to go to my rooms?"

"No, no." He extended a flat palm to stop her struggle. "I will sit here with you."

In three quick steps, he reached the door, closed it, and returned to seat himself comfortably on the floor facing her. "Did the woman from Tyre take her whipping in the proper spirit?"

"That is hard to tell. Though opinionated, she keeps her deepest feelings to herself."

"She is behaving normally and performing her duties?"

"With her head high as if she were above it all."

Hum! he thought. She is hostile to the Tyrian woman. I cannot blame her. Elissa is arrogant. Pulling thoughtfully on his lower lip, he said, "Strange that we have had no communication from the temple in Tyre."

"She says she announced to her superior one day that she was leaving. If true—and I'm not sure I believe her—there's not much to communicate. She gave the high priest no reason for her defection."

"Did she tell you why she left?"

"She does not approve of temple prostitution. She chose Carthage because we have none."

Hasdrubal examined the mid-distance behind Asherat's head. He thought, those two young priestesses she disciplined are members of the orchestra. The stuff they are prattling could come from Elissa. She is old enough to gain their confidence and mother them.

His eyes narrowed. I thought that was what Asherat was supposed to do.

While mulling that over, he said, "You did not hurt her?"

"Only her dignity. You were most magnanimous considering the seriousness of her crime."

"She did not show sadness during the ceremony. We think we know why she disgraced herself, but do we really know? Hence, I chose to be lenient." He rose. Asherat knew nothing more. Of that, he was certain. He was also certain that there was more to Elissa's leaving Tyre than prostitution, and he intended to find out. First, he would immediately inquire of Ahiram.

Striding along the corridor, he was already composing the scroll in his head when he saw Elissa. He caught the flash of recognition, and saw the panic, the eyes darting to the right, then to the left, as though hunting a place to hide.

"Elissa," he called gently.

She came unwillingly and bowed before him.

"I would like to see you in my office." He quickly calculated—a day would be enough for Asherat to find out where the orchestra priestesses were getting their ideas. "Come first thing in the morning two days hence."

"To reprimand me more?"

"To find out what temple employment interests you."

"You mean away from the public so I won't upset your equanimity?"

"If that is your attitude, we have nothing to discuss. I had hoped to learn something of your abilities. In this temple, people work at what they do best. Everyone pulls together for the good of the whole. If you are not prepared to do that, you do not belong here. The choice is yours."

As he left the building, he wanted to kick the door. Violence was his usual reaction to contact with her. He scowled. Why? Violence wasn't his nature. He prided himself on his cool assessment of all that went on in his temple. Well, his anger must not show. Certainly, she must not see it. That would undermine his control. He walked quietly to his quarters and mounted to his comfortable second-floor library.

Rage flooded through Elissa as she watched his departing back. She was a mature woman—she flung up her chin—a sophisticated woman. Yet, he always made her feel like a naughty child. She could never prick that calm superiority. Like a coin twirling out of control, she spun on her heel and rushed aimlessly along the rambling, intersecting corridors before tears forced her to stop. Blinking rapidly, she shook her head and sniffled. She had reached the small room used by priests prior to a major sacrifice. Today, the room was empty. In relief at the silence, the emptiness, the privacy, she laid her forehead against the wall and gave way to sobs. The arrogance and confidence she had exhibited before the high priest evaporated. Fear, stark and pervasive, lurked beneath her unrestrained anger. This man had absolute power over those in his temple. He was like Ahiram. She had fled to Carthage as to a mother city, but had found neither warmth nor acceptance.

First, she had to contend with that horrible woman. She stamped one foot. The old hag. What business was it of hers if she chose to remain an orchestra priestess? Asherat was nothing but a busy-body with her personal questions: Why did you leave Tyre? What happened at the Baal Temple? Where are your introductory letters? How is it that you travel alone? If Asherat asked her any more, she would strike her. Before Tanit, she swore she would.

Now, by sheer accident, she had run afoul of that contemptible priest. She hadn't been feeling well. The sight and smell at the sacrifice had been too much for her.

I was lucky to get behind the bush. I could have thrown up right in front of him. That would have upset his equanimity, she thought with a wry smile. I would have enjoyed it, too. The punishment would have been less unfair.

She shivered at the memory of the beating. She had ground

her teeth and not given them the satisfaction of hearing her scream. Afterwards, locked alone in a room, she had been unable to examine her back. Later, she had decided not to look. It would just upset her more. Her back had been shredded. The scars branded her. No man suitable to her family would accept her as his wife.

Anyway, she wouldn't find a husband in this temple. They were all traders like the high priest's family. She dismissed Carthaginian men with a scornful movement of her shoulder. She had dug herself into a pit and couldn't get out. With that, she succumbed to self-pity.

After a time, the tears abated. She used her himation to wipe her face. Crying wouldn't help. She had to get control of herself. Decisions had to be made.

She sighed. Her eyes and cheeks were hot. If only she had water to splash on them. Oh! Yes. She perked up. There was water in the animal trough near the sacrificial cattle pens. After drinking from the fountain, the chosen animals were led directly to the high alter in front of the temple. Perfect. The temple would be cool and quiet inside. She needed to think. No matter what her personal feelings, to stay here, she would have to get along with Asherat and the high priest.

She drew her himation almost completely across her swollen face. With lowered eyes and a silent prayer that she meet no one, Elissa left the sanctuary of the room.

As she walked along in the sunlight, she heard the happy chirping of birds. She looked around. The air was fragrant and felt good. A smile poked at the corners of her mouth, and her chin jutted forward. This city, she thought, was founded by a royal Tyrian princess named Dido. She broke with tradition to live her own life as she wished to live it. I will also do what I believe to be right, whether given approval or not.

5

*I*n cloistered silence, surrounded by the scrolls of his library, Hasdrubal wrote at length to Ahiram. He dripped melted wax on the edge of the papyrus scroll. It smelled spicy, herbal. He sniffed delightedly. When slightly cooled, but still soft, he rolled the tiny carnelian cylinder seal across its surface. The impression emerged sharp and clear from the wax. The figure of Tanit dominated. Beside her, upright, sticklike, stood the diminutive figure of Baal, her husband. The high priest of Tanit, presenting an offering, knelt before the divine couple.

Satisfied, Hasdrubal placed the seal back in its carved ivory box. He had a personal seal, but enjoyed using this ancient one that had come down to him from time immemorial. Ahiram was a worthy recipient and would appreciate the seal.

"Abdmelkart," he called.

The Numidian was immediately beside him. "Sire?"

"Take this scroll to the wharf and find a trader who will deliver it into the hands of the high priest of Baal in Tyre."

Swift and silent, the Numidian darted away. Only then did Hasdrubal push the subject of Elissa from his mind. The moon might return to fullness at least once and maybe more before he could expect an answer. In the meantime, he must visit with Saphonisba and Batbaal.

Despite his good intentions, the afternoon was well advanced before his duties allowed him to leave the temple.

An old family nursemaid greeted him. "Master, how could you! My baby. My baby." Tears blurred her nearsighted, wizened eyes and dribbled across the wrinkled brown cheeks.

Gently taking her shoulders in both hands, he pulled her to him. So many times as a child, he had been comforted by her, and he loved her. There was nothing to say. She knew as well as he did that in dire circumstances the only way to be sure that the goddess would hear their plea and look favorably upon their request was through human sacrifice.

And Carthage was in dire circumstances. The men on those ships represented a whole generation. Their loss would deal the city a mortal blow. As high priest, he had had no choice. The more precious the child, the better the chance of success. He had had to cross the abyss to the heart of the goddess.

He held the old woman and patted her for a bit, then said, "Where is your mistress Saphonisba?"

"By the fountain."

She led him to the house's square enclosed court. Water tumbled from the mouth of a small bronze satyr and splashed cheerfully into a marble basin. Birds twittered among the deep red poppies. Sunlight played on the marbled floor. Despite the late-winter chill, Saphonisba was seated in the sun beside blooming yellow hyacinths. Tired lines drooped from the corners of her mouth. Dark blotches, visible in spite of the heavily applied kohl, circled her eyes. The rouge only emphasized her paleness and the small tatoo on her chin.

"You are not sleeping?" he asked, seating himself in the chair placed for him.

"No."

"And Batbaal?"

"She is resting now. I have kept her sedated." The black eyes that met his were dulled with pain. "That was a dreadful thing, Hasdrubal; such a lovely child."

He thought, she is not sprinkling her speech with "my dear." She is tense, measuring her words.

He reached for her hand. "If we, one of the leading families in Carthage, are not willing to sacrifice our own to the goddess, how can we ask others to do so? Our men are headed for Hannibal's army in Hispania. High seas and severe storms have plagued our ships. No word has come. What else could I do? Nearly every household is represented on those ships."

"I understand your reasoning, but it's terrible, terrible. First her husband. Mago has been in Tyre for months, as you well know. That in itself is hard on her. Now this. I - I can't—" She caught her lower lip in her teeth.

A chest pain stabbed Hasdrubal. He pressed his free hand over the spot.

Saphonisba said, "Rather than grieving for Gisgo, I ache for his mother."

"What do you say to sending her to Tyre?"

Startled, Saphonisba tried to withdraw her hand. Hasdrubal tightened his grip. "It is best. She needs another baby." And the family needs another male for the priesthood, he thought to himself.

In the silence, a nearby bird joyously puffed out his breast and sang. When Saphonisba spoke, she said, "Who would take her?"

He released her hand and relaxed; she was willing.

"There are a number of traders of excellent reputation and fine character in the city. We could send Batbaal with one of them. She would be accompanied, of course, by her own women and bodyguards."

"So be it," she said softly. "I will prepare her, though I don't know what Bimilcar would say."

"He would agree." His glance swung to the sky without taking in its sailing pink clouds.

"My brother would be more concerned about his son," he said, bringing his eyes back to rest on her as he spoke.

"My dear, what about Hanno?"

He noted fear in the sharp question. "Hanno does not want to be high priest."

"What has not wanting got to do with it? He will be high priest." Her head rose magisterially. "That is what he is being trained for. Few people in this life are afforded the opportunity he has. He should be proud. A great honor is to be handed to him," she spread her arms before her, "without any effort on his part."

"It does take a lot of study." He observed the placid way she expressed her emotions. This calm, juxtaposed with her intense feelings, was always a source of fascination to him.

"My dear, he would have to study anyway. If that is your reason, time should straighten him out. We both admit he is immature. The important thing is that the high priesthood not pass from the family. Bimilcar would not allow it."

Hasdrubal's snort was short and ironic. "Hanno is well aware of his father's performance in the priesthood. I am afraid that he will run away, too. That is the reason I need your help." Hasdrubal heard Saphonisba gasp. He pretended to studied his hands. "If he does," he said slowly, "there is no one to follow me."

He raised his eyes and met hers. For a short time, their gaze locked.

Saphonisba sighed and looked away. "Do you have any idea what he might be planning?"

"No. Or if he is planning anything. He does not confide in me."

The high priest watched a bird on the edge of the fountain. "I simply sense something coming. Would you talk to him?"

"I could." She was thoughtful. "Actually, I think having my father talk to him might be better. Hanno is very fond of his grandfather."

"As you wish." He added, "We need to know his interests to judge what move he might make." Both remained silent, lost in their own thoughts.

"I do not think," the high priest picked up the conversation, "he envisions joining his father in New Carthage."

Visibly paling, she said, "Do you think my beloved husband is with Hannibal?"

"I firmly believe," he said slowly, "that Bimilcar will find Hannibal before the war starts."

"The war has all but started. Father tells me that Rome has sent new envoys. These men are of a very different caliber than the ones who came from New Carthage."

Amusement crept into Hasdrubal's eyes as he remembered the Roman envoys. He hadn't thought of them in a long time. Almost a year had passed, but he could still see the forum on that hot, bright day.

Sword-wielding Numidian troops had paraded up and down to keep the center of the forum clear. The Romans were coming from the harbor. Rumor had spread that the senators, led by the suffetes, would meet them in the open at the forum. The entire city had turned out to watch. Good-natured and noisy, the people bantered with the troops until the Romans appeared at the south end of the forum. Absolute silence prevailed.

The city's two suffetes, resplendent in caps and gold-decorated purple robes, appeared on the top step of the senate building. With theatrical, measured tread, they descended. The senators, inching forward like a formal dance, followed behind in an ever-widening triangle.

The beardless Romans moved disdainfully forward, their white wool togas gleaming in the sun.

The lions, chained on the flat stone arms of the steps, kept their heads lowered and their yellow eyes sweeping around. City mascots, they seemed to reflect Carthaginian feelings. Now, they padded restlessly in the limited space the heavy chains allowed. What was going to happen?

Slowly, the senators advanced toward the oncoming Romans. The crowd held its breath. Were the senators going to walk right up to the Roman delegation? That would be awkward. What were they waiting for? The crowd became uneasy.

A Roman stepped out of formation. Was that a signal? All eyes swung to the Carthaginian senators. In one united motion, the senators prostrated themselves, their arms stretched straight up above their heads, toes curled into the packed dirt. The lions raised their heads and roared as the crowd sighed in delight.

Saphonisba saw his mind leave her and saw the small spark of mirth. Mirth at this time? How could he! It was out of character for someone usually so solemn.

"Do you find something funny?" She sucked in her breath. She hadn't meant to sound irritated.

"Sorry. I was thinking of the stupidity of those envoys, demanding that we turn Hannibal over to them."

She agreed. "Even the senators who thought he had been stirring up trouble between the people of Saguntum and the local tribes got annoyed at the envoys' complaints. What kind of reception did they expect?"

"According to the envoys, they were waiting in New Carthage when Hannibal arrived with his troops to take up winter quarters. They said he was arrogant and short with them."

"I don't believe that. Do you?"

"Of course not. Hannibal is the most gracious of men. He would listen and weigh their arguments."

"The envoys apparently asked Hannibal not to harass Saguntum since it was in their zone of influence. That is a deliberate untruth."

"Saguntum is about a mile north of New Carthage." The high priest shifted his body to seat himself more comfortably. "Some years ago, there was a treaty between Carthage and Rome stating which parts of Hispania were to be dominated by Carthage and which by Rome. The Ebro divided the two parts."

"I looked at some maps father had here one night. Saguntum is quite a bit south of the Ebro."

Hasdrubal nodded. "According to the treaty, Carthage was to have responsibility for everything south of the river."

"Rome was wrong to claim Saguntum was in their part."

"Being wrong makes little difference to Rome. When Rome wants something, Rome takes it regardless."

Hasdrubal inspected the water jet in the fountain before continuing. "Rome certainly must shoulder some of the blame. The Romans are as interested in war as Hannibal. They want all of Hispania for themselves, and will stop at nothing, particularly when our wealth makes them jealous."

"Hannibal claimed that he was protecting the people of Saguntum because the Romans had killed some of the town's leading citizens."

"From what I understand, the town was split. The group favoring Rome drove those favoring Carthage out of town. Naturally, they wanted to get back in so they joined forces with some local tribesmen. Was Hannibal aiding and abetting this? Probably. Rome was undoubtedly doing its share of skullduggery."

After a silence in which they both watched the shifting sunlight, he said, "The Saguntines themselves are not exactly innocent. They kept Rome fully informed of Hannibal's every move. When some of them defected to the local tribes, the others were afraid."

"That they'd lose their power."

"Of course. They appealed to Rome for help."

"Is that when Rome sent the delegation to Hannibal? I mean the one that came here to complain about their treatment."

"Yes. And as soon as the delegation left Hispania, Hannibal started the siege."

"Why?" Saphonisba puckered her brow. "The envoys didn't threaten war. They just asked him to leave Saguntum alone."

"He knew Rome's intention was to control all of Hispania. Saguntum was just the first move." For some moments, the high priest was thoughtful. When he spoke, he said, "If we did nothing, Rome, in effect, would control Saguntum. Another of our cities would be next. Hannibal had to stop the onslaught."

"That siege has only just ended. Seven long months. I've heard descriptions of the sickness and starvation when they surrendered. That anyone lived is a miracle."

Hasdrubal raised his arms slightly in a helpless gesture. "Saguntum was an exceedingly rich city, judging by the shiploads of jewelry, gold and silver plate, ivory and bronze Hannibal sent here."

"He showed great political astuteness by sending all those valuable things to Carthage."

Hasdrubal exhaled noisily in derision. "Gold certainly changed the minds of the senators who were against the siege."

"Such greed! I hear some of the senators ran to the military harbor to finger the stuff. The suffetes had to order everything locked up. Otherwise, some of the most valuable pieces would have found storage in private homes rather than the state warehouse." Saphonisba wobbled her head in indignation.

"Unfortunately," Hasdrubal said, "too many of our senators use their position to become rich."

"Do you think Hannibal kept all the coinage to finance the coming war?"

"Is that what your father says? That is also politically astute."

"Those who survived the siege went into slavery as payment to our troops."

He nodded. "An even division of spoils. Everyone was satisfied. Now Rome has their war, Hannibal has his war and—Bimilcar is with Hannibal."

Saphonisba turned her face from him. With one hand, she covered her eyes. She laid the other on his arm. "My dear, you have been such strength to me in my weakness. What would I do without you!"

Hasdrubal gave her hand a little squeeze. "When is your father expected back in the city?"

"Tomorrow. I'll ask him to invite Hanno to Megara for supper. Hanno loves to go to his house."

"No wonder. It is such a princely place."

"It's small for the area, but you're right, it is quite perfect. Father has his houseboy set the dining couches on the patio." She laughed. "Hanno lies back as if he were a senator and becomes quite talkative. Perhaps that will do the trick, and we'll find out what we need to know."

"Let us hope. So we can put a stop to undesirable notions."

Saphonisba nodded agreement.

"As for Batbaal," the high priest continued, "have her write to Mago immediately. We need his consent to send her to Tyre. I will find out which of our traders might be sailing there in, oh, about thirty days. The seas should be more dependable then."

After her brother-in-law left, Saphonisba remained absorbed in thought. She dreaded the day Batbaal would leave her. She pictured it: The commercial harbor, the blared order to drop the chain at the mouth, the ship warped out the right-angled channel. She shuddered. Returning alone to the empty house. Of course, she'd move back to the Megara estate. Hanno didn't need her. He was living at the school.

In one short year, her warm, noisy family had disintegrated. First Mago had been posted to Tyre. She had urged him to leave Batbaal and Gisgo in Carthage because young Antiochus, four years on the throne of the old Persian Empire, was preparing to march against the coastal cities held by Egypt. Who could tell what Ptolemy IV, the young Pharaoh of Egypt, less than a year on his throne, would do? She had argued that both wanted to prove their valor in war.

Add to that, she had said, the unknown quantity of Philip of Macedon. He is nineteen and wants to emulate his famous ancestor, Alexander.

Her arguments had won. Batbaal and Gisgo remained in Carthage. What irony! She shook her head. Now that Batbaal was to sail, Antiochus and his army were again preparing to attack the Phoenician coastal cities. Ptolemy had torn himself away from his women and was readying to lead his army east across the desert. Antiochus wanted Tyre. Batbaal could arrive right in the middle of the fight.

And her beloved Bimilcar was in the middle of another war. Her heart contracted, and she breathed deeply to steady it. The ships had left long before the winter storm season. Who could know that the storms would start so early or be so severe? As a result, little Gisgo, the darling of the entire household, had given his enchanting life for that of his grandfather.

That Batbaal should follow her husband was just and right. She belonged with Mago. Saphonisba vowed to the combined pantheon of Carthaginian gods and goddesses that her daughter would never know how much she would be missed.

Carthaginian women were strong, strong like their men. Whatever had to be faced, she would face. Saphonisba rose heavily, sadness in every motion of her body. Right now, she could relieve her daughter's desolation a little.

Batbaal was sitting on the floor of her bedroom, resting her forehead against the bed. The piled black hair, so carefully dressed earlier, tilted left. Unruly, wet strands lay across her cheek. Tears welled from her eyes and inched down her gaunt, kohl-streaked face. They dropped unheeded into the folds of her lavender wool gown.

Saphonisba paused. How thin her daughter had become. Batbaal's flesh had melted away in the days since the announcement of the sacrifice.

"My dear," her mother said quietly, "I have something to tell you."

Batbaal turned her head. She had been spoken to, she was used to responding, but she met her mother's gaze without interest.

"Your uncle thinks that we should send you to Tyre."

The catch in Batbaal's breath brought a smile to Saphonisba's lips.

"To Mago!" Batbaal flew off the floor and threw herself into her mother's arms.

For a moment, Saphonisba held her tight. "Run along now and write him"—she made an instant decision—"that we will send you with the first suitable trader leaving for Tyre."

Hurrying from the bedroom, Batbaal was unaware of the pleading in her mother's outstretched arms.

6

*T*he next morning, Hasdrubal carried a carefully wrapped bundle to the Tophet, the ancient graveyard near the commercial harbor. He shifted the heavy bundle several times from one hip to the other. Twice, hurrying laborers offered to carry it for him. He declined. He didn't want strangers around while he did what he had to do.

Inside the Tophet grounds, he walked along the rows of little tombstones, decorated with the sickle of Tanit. He noticed the occasional startling white of marble among the small slabs of graying stone, the bits of mica flashing in the sun. Few of these tiny mementos of great danger had been placed since his rise to high priest.

The new grave had been dug along here somewhere. He should have had the family come, but Batbaal was in no condition to watch the ashes placed in the ground. Saphonisba certainly didn't need to be dragged through another service. He would tell Batbaal where the grave was. When she felt able, she could sprinkle a handful of grain over it.

Ah! There was the hole, fresh dirt piled beside it. Kneeling down, he placed the bundle on the ground and undid the wrapping. A small redware pot, the cheap variety generally used in graves, sat on an oblong piece of sculpted marble. Fresh, brightly colored flowers surrounded the pot and tumbled across the curved end of the stone. He picked up the pot and laid it in the hole. It contained the ashes of a newborn kid. Gisgo's ashes rested in the cream urn in the wall niche at his house.

He partially replaced the dirt, held steady the marble tombstone engraved with the crossbar and upright arms of the goddess, and finished filling the hole. Using his hands, he tamped down the dirt. He rose, planted one sandaled foot next to the stone, and shifted all his weight to that foot. The soft dirt trickled onto his toes, but compacted beneath. He worked his way around the slab, hardening and smoothing the dirt. The stone secure, he draped blossoms, which Abdmelkart had strung together, over the marble. He remained for several minutes, touching the flowers, overpowered by his own emotions. He left the Tophet rapidly, looking neither right nor left, and returned to his workroom in the administration building.

Abdmelkart awaited him. "The head priestess wishes to speak with you."

"Ask her to join me," he said.

She marshaled her bulk through the door. Deliberately, she laid her hands on the table and leaned forward. Her face level with his, she stared into his eyes.

Immobile, resting against the chair back, hands flat on his thighs like an Egyptian statue, he returned her stare. He saw joy, ebullient, dancing joy. Amazing, he thought, this short, fat, quiet grandmother. Just before hers faltered and dropped under his intense gaze, he saw beneath the joy something that startled and repelled him.

"I have discovered," she said solemnly, raising veiled eyes, "who is responsible for the nonsense babbled by every child in the orchestra."

Asherat hesitated, hoping for comment, but the high priest remained motionless, his eyes half shut. She knew that look, knew that she had his total attention. "The Tyrian priestess, Elissa, has been filling them full of heretical ideas. If you will excuse my saying so, my lord, that woman doesn't belong in this temple, let alone the orchestra."

Hasdrubal drew in his breath. So, his guess had been accurate. That could be dealt with easily, but her continued unacceptable behavior tried his patience.

Asherat's glee also disturbed him. He would not tolerate friction between the two women. It jeopardized the smooth running of the temple.

He studied the head priestess. This was his first inkling that she allowed her personal likes and dislikes to influence her rule. He had expected—indeed, he had assumed—she would treat those under her with the same impersonal, even fairness that he used in his dealings. Sad. He had thought her the perfect head priestess. Now he questioned his judgment. But he was unaware of discension among the priestesses.

Most of the priestesses were considerably younger than Elissa. Apparently none of them defied the lady's jurisdiction.

"I commend your rapid solution to the problem," he said, with a single dip of his head.

She smiled deprecatingly, waiting, hopeful that he might cast out the Tyrian, though she knew that he never made snap judgments.

Signaling dismissal, he said, "I will inform you as soon as I have reached a decision about her."

Asherat smiled broadly. She scooped up the folds of her garment as though to bow from the waist, but merely inclined her head. I want, she thought as she backed from his presence, that woman out of this temple. She'll destroy my authority. But with his reputation for doing what is best, I can't be sure he'll dismiss her.

Waddling along the corridor, she tried to duplicate the way the high priest might reason. What has the woman done to make her valuable to us? Nothing. Has she been a good orchestra player? Yes, but he doesn't know that. Will she break more rules in the future? Yes. Will she ever be of use to us? No. Has she been open and fair with us? No. Is there any reason to be fair with her? No. Where can she go? Back to Tyre.

Asherat licked her upper lip, savoring her triumph when Elissa would be told to go elsewhere.

At his desk, Hasdrubal shook his head. Undoubtedly, the priestess had been thrown out of the Temple of Baal in Tyre. If eventually I force her from this temple, where will she go? Any place along the African coast is impossible. I cannot recommend her. Hispania? Not likely with that country soon to be overrun with Roman soldiers. Athens? That temple has sacred prostitutes. I will not force her to join them. Rome? Possibly.

Much as he disliked her, he sensed her vulnerability and was unwilling to turn her out. But she had to be removed at once from the orchestra. What job in the temple was suitable? He picked up a stylus and absentmindedly tapped it on the table. She should work alone or with the priests, having as little contact as possible with the priestesses. The chief of sacrifices? One priestess was already working with him. Another could be trained. Assisting at the altar was also a possibility. That involved proximity with himself. No. He might really resort to violence. What was it about her? For a minute he considered the woman, not the priestess. She was an attractive young woman, but hostile. For his own composure, she better work elsewhere.

Administration meant being able to read and write. Could she? He didn't know. He opted for sacrifice. That involved bloodletting, and apparently she was squeamish. Well, so be it. Let her get used to blood. He would sound out the chief of sacrifices.

Alone in his living room that night, Hasdrubal idly toyed with the meager supper he allowed himself—bread, some fruit, water. He was still thinking about Elissa. The chief of sacrifices was willing. All that remained was to tell her in the morning. But he was dissatisfied. Was it best? How would she react?

With much indecision, he chose a plum from the fruit bowl. A flustered Abdmelkart knelt before him. The plum dropped from his hand and rolled to the edge of the table.

"Senator Elibaal arrives momentarily," breathed the Numidian.

Rising so quickly that he nearly knocked his slave over backwards, Hasdrubal said, "Take this table of food away. Bring a tray of choice fruit and some wine."

Although a small, wrinkled man in his early sixties, the senator filled the room with his commanding presence. From the tip of his conical cap to his shoulder-length gold earrings and heavy, carefully combed beard, to the bottom of his purple woolen cape, he radiated authority. The high priest bowed low and cautiously sniffed. Elibaal was using lovely, expensive perfume.

"Senator Elibaal, you do me great honor."

"Only for the sake of the family." He sat on the edge of the proffered chair, his back straight, his face grim. "I shall never forgive you for the other night, but I must bury my sorrow and go on with my life."

Hasdrubal humbly lowered his head. Nothing more was said.

Moving like a wraith, Abdmelkart placed a table bearing a tray of fruit, a bottle of sweet-smelling, dark red wine, and goblets between the two men.

"Exquisite," said Elibaal, helping himself to a sectioned orange. He sniffed delicately as the fragrance of the wine permeated the air. "Rome has named Quintus Fabius Maximus as envoy to Carthage."

"He is a most honorable and just man. The Romans must be worried."

"Not of the negotiations. The outcome is cast in bronze. But Rome doesn't want the same reception their last envoys were given."

"They were shown great formality," said the high priest, a slight sparkle visible in his eyes.

The senator's eyes twinkled, scrunching together the laughter lines. "We did that deliberately to irritate the Romans. They don't understand that we consider prostrating oneself a form of politeness. They think it servile and humiliating" Turning sober, he said, "When Fabius and his companions arrive, they will be escorted directly into the council chamber."

"Do your sources say whether they have left Rome?"

"No. Some of my cohorts in the chamber think he will leave soon. I think he will wait until Rome has a clearer idea of Hannibal's next move, which could be months."

"What will Fabius ask of us?"

"He will demand, as did the others, that we surrender Hannibal. Naturally, we will refuse. Then he will ask if Hannibal's destruction of Saguntum was our policy. Even though Saguntum lies in the territory administered by us, Rome cares little for the niceties of diplomacy." Slowly tilting his goblet to see the color of the wine, he said, "Actually, the so-called treaty was never ratified by either the Roman senate or the Roman people. Rome wants war and demands the surrender of Hannibal because of his aggressive leadership."

"And when we refuse, they will declare war."

"Fabius will try to make Carthage the instigator. He will claim to be giving us a choice of peace or war, but we will let Rome choose."

The senator drained his glass and set it down decisively. "Saphonisba tells me you want me to talk to Hanno. Why?"

"To find out whether he has a strong interest the way his father did for the army."

"And if he doesn't?"

"Get an idea where to hunt for him if he succeeds in running away."

"Run away!" Elibaal exploded. "My dear fellow, Hanno isn't going to run away. He'll soon settle down. He's rapidly becoming an adult. Being high priest of Tanit is his duty."

"Agreed, my lord. It is my fervent wish that he be high priest of Tanit. But in the meantime, I need a foundation on which to base my judgments. Hanno has stopped confiding in me. He still talks to you. Will you do this?"

"Yes, of course, since both you and Saphonisba desire it, though I think the whole thing ridiculous. Duty is duty. The sooner he learns it, the better. And speaking of duty, you are still young enough to marry and sire a son yourself."

"No."

"You owe it to your family to secure the line for the priesthood."

"No!" rang out.

Elibaal looked Hasdrubal up and down at least three times while Hasdrubal looked at his lap.

In taking leave, the senator said, "You, too, have to let bygones be bygones."

Left alone, the high priest paced back and forth, back and forth. Having that old scandal brought up disturbed him. He did not agree that he was still of an age to be siring sons. True, some men did. He didn't know any suitable woman. Also, he wasn't sure whether he wanted his life disrupted by a woman. His existence was rather peaceful, except for the small emergencies that cropped up at the temple. Bimilcar was the one who had the excitement. He himself had been left behind. But it no longer mattered. He had done his duty to the family by taking over the temple, and he had been content with his lot. Now, he was getting too old for change. The rest of his life could proceed at its own slow, day-by-day pace.

I am too restless to sleep, he thought, removing his conical cap and sliding out of his sandals. I will read. In his library, he chose a scroll and sat down. The skin lay on his lap while he thought. Occasionally, he picked it up, read a few sentences, laid it down again. Finally, in disgust, he placed it back in the niche. I will work in the school building for a while.

Upon reaching the courtyard, he realized that the lamps around its edges had long since been extinguished. Even the small lamp at the temple door had been put out. No matter. He knew the complex well.

Closing the door of the administration building, he observed a dim light. Cautious, he sought the bend in the wall used as a work station by his second in command. From there, he could watch and not be seen. The light grew brighter. The figure of a woman holding a flare emerged from his office. Hasdrubal bit his tongue to keep quiet. With gliding step, silent as the tomb, Elissa passed him and left the building. As silently, he followed. The flare moved inexorably toward the exit. Was she leaving the precinct at this hour! Alone? In spite of his anger, he realized he had to protect her. Trailing outside the circle of light, he could see well enough, without making her aware of his presence.

Like a sleepwalker, upright, ethereal, she crossed the maze. Catlike, alert to danger, he shadowed. In the street, her step quickened. She walked resolutely toward the wharf. Thinking she had taken leave of her senses, he pursued as close behind as he dared. They had reached the warren of dirt streets behind the temple compound when a whoop stopped Elissa. He noticed her hesitate and then saw the sailors.

"Ho, ho," shouted one, "a priest." He held his flare high for a better look. "Without his hat," he yelled gleefully. "Let's get him."

Four sets of powerful arms pushed him against a building front. Hasdrubal was aware that Elissa had started to run. Amidst coarse laughter about what they would do to a eunuch, the sailors yanked up his robe and ripped off his scrotal reinforcer. One roughly probed his genitals while the others held his shoulders and legs against the wall.

Finally, the sailor bending over Hasdrubal said, "So you're not a eunuch, priesty. How about a little play," and roared at the instant reaction.

"Knock it off, Phestos," said another. "You've made us lose the woman."

"What a lousy town." And three strode off, taking the flares with them.

The fourth, his hands still busy with Hasdrubal, gave him a sucking kiss and followed.

Hasdrubal trembled like a bark in a roily sea. He leaned against the building to keep from falling. Far from protecting Elissa, he hadn't even protected himself from this base indignity. He didn't know how.

It was a long time before he trusted himself to walk back to the temple. He moved slowly, staying close to the blank fronts of the buildings. Every noise terrified him. Suppose he was recognized, the high priest of Tanit, without his cap and his clothing torn. The sound of footsteps and quiet male voices caused him to flattened himself against the soft brown building. Motionless, he waited. A group of men carrying flares hurried along the street. Absorbed in themselves, they passed him. He crept on. At last! He stepped inside the maze and crumpled against the wall's familiar blackness and security. Later, he made his way to the inner sanctum of the temple and flung himself face down before the curtain covering the holy place.

7

*H*asdrubal, the man, was tired the following day. Hasdrubal, the high priest of Tanit assumed his duties as efficiently as always. He sent a priestess to summon Elissa.

There was no longer any question of assigning her to the chief of sacrifices. She had to leave the temple. However, he would place her elsewhere rather than allow her to drift. At Vasa, a rigorous, elderly priest administered a small temple with one assistant. He pressed his lips together. She wouldn't have much chance to cause trouble there.

Glancing around his cubicle, his eye fastened on the empty niche where he kept a small red and black glass bottle. The name etched on the glass indicated that the bottle contained a mixture of poppy juices. In emergencies, Hasdrubal cautiously doled out minute amounts. So that's what she had taken. Why? How did she know what the bottle contained? Hasdrubal sat down. He realized that she was able to read and knew something about drugs. That cast a new light on her. But that bottle! If she were in pain, why did she take the bottle into the city? And where was she?

He stood up. As he started toward the door, the priestess returned, upset and apologetic. She couldn't find Elissa.

"Thank you," said the high priest. "You may go." He sat back down, rested his elbows on the desk, and put his face in his hands. When the men attacked him, she had been left unprotected. He supposed he would have to comb the neighborhood, looking for her. Fortunately, he was on good terms with most of the families who lived there. Anything could have happened in those narrow, filthy streets. A faint noise made him peep through his fingers. Elissa, bottle in hand, was slithering along like a snake, watching him with cold, unblinking eyes. Soundlessly, he dropped his hands, his even colder eyes boring into her.

She let out a yelp, jumped and subsided into statuelike stillness. "You wanted to see me," she stuttered.

"Return the bottle to the niche." He kept emotion from his speech.

With undue care, Elissa set it in the niche. She returned to stand quietly before him, her head bowed.

She was, he observed, a different woman than the one he saw the previous night. Under red-rimmed eyes, dark circles spread down her cheeks. Her mound of hair looked as if birds had nested there. She had aged at least ten years, and her disarrayed clothing had—he looked closer—blood on it.

"Begin from the beginning," said the high priest. "I wish to know why you took that bottle and what you have been doing. At the moment, you are not a credit to the temple."

In a soft, despondent voice that matched her dejection, she said, "All night, I have been attending a girl of twelve who is already in a life of prostitution. It was her first baby, a long and difficult birth. The baby is dead; the girl will live to have another."

What difference does it make, she thought. What difference does anything make? He's going to dismiss me, and I have nowhere to go.

Hasdrubal was glad that Elissa was keeping her eyes focused on the floor. He didn't trust his own expression. In all the years that he had been going into the crowded hovels that stretched to the waterfront, he had never done more than help with food and money. This slip of a woman had risked her life and her reputation by doing something concrete. Amazing. His eyes softened as he observed her. Perhaps she would talk openly if his questions were discreet.

"How did you know the girl had need of you at that particular time?"

"She sent her younger sister to the temple where I was praying. The child knelt beside me and whispered, 'The hour has come.'"

"Why you? Why did she send for you rather than some neighbor?"

With a nothing-matters gesture, Elissa raised her shoulders and dropped them. "I have been trying to teach the pregnant girls how to care for themselves."

Was she all that despondent? Would she snap at him?

"Not very wise to go out as a priestess of Tanit and risk a scandal, was it?" He deliberately barked his question.

She was too exhausted and too discouraged to fire back.

His voice returned to a flat monotone. "Are you able to read the label on that bottle?"

"Yes."

"How did you know its use?"

"It all started," she said with a sigh as if there were no point in holding back, "at the temple of Baal in Tyre. A woebegone girl, no more than a child, poured out the litany of her sad life. She was promised to the god at birth, had little training and no education. On physically becoming a woman, she was thrown into the temple pool. Terrified, defenseless and pregnant, she sobbed in my arms. I managed to shield her from further mistreatment and had her baby sold in the slave market. After that, the other sacred prostitutes started coming to me with their complaints about the men they serviced, the demands made upon them, their weaknesses and sicknesses. So I asked Ahiram to put me in charge of them. He was amazed, but said if I thought I could do anything with them, I was welcome to try. Then, he simply walked off."

The passion in her last sentence surprised the high priest. She had said everything else matter-of-factly. Very few did care. Life was structured that way. He himself was out of step with his society because he showed concern for those under him. In front of his desk stood a woman like him. His interest was also tantalized by her admission that she used go to Ahiram and make requests. What had been her position in the Baal temple?

"But I showed him. I went to a doctor, a friend of my father, and asked him to teach me sufficient medicine to take care of the priestesses. The doctor thought the whole thing a joke, I suspect he even thought I was crazy, but he agreed."

Hasdrubal reassessed his decision. She might, after all, fill a needed post in the temple.

"I got the girls cleaned up," she continued, "and tried to help them prevent the men from engaging in the wild, orgiastic sex that left them physically bruised and many times mentally deranged. That's when Ahiram flew into a rage and made me play with the musicians."

So, she hadn't played in the orchestra early on. Unusual.

"When the girls continued to come to me, crawling into my bed at night to whisper through their tears, Ahiram forced me to leave the temple."

The high priest pursed his lips. Elissa spoke familiarly of the high priest of Baal. She was extremely presumptuous. Ahiram was a member of the Tyrian royal family.

"My parents had objected to my entering the temple, but they were furious when he threw me out."

So, she had entered of her own free will. Possibly, she had not been one of the prostitutes.

"That's when I ran away." Elissa glanced at him and again dropped her eyes.

With slitted gaze, he observed her. She wasn't telling the whole truth. Of that, he was sure. He was also sure that what she withheld was what he needed to know.

At that moment, Abdmelkart's frantic face appeared in the doorway. "Master, master," he cried as he flung himself to the floor.

Elissa leapt to one side, and Hasdrubal rose to his feet.

"Hanno," the slave said.

Every muscle in the high priest's body became rigid. His lips hardly moved. "What about Hanno?"

"I was bargaining for the most beautiful fresh fish at the commercial dock when I heard groaning and saw Hanno, all bloody, lying near the edge of the dock."

"Where is he now?"

"In your bedroom."

Hasdrubal was out the door. He scarcely heard Abdmelkart say, "I put him on a mat." He certainly didn't see Elissa dive for the bottle of painkiller and rush after him.

Transparently pale and still, Hanno looked already dead. His face was streaked with blood, and his clothing was caked with dried blood. Unable to control his weak knees, Hasdrubal dropped to the boy's side. He looked anxiously up and down the prone body.

Elissa dropped to a squatting position opposite. Setting the bottle beside her on the floor, she shifted to her knees. With knitted brow, she leaned over the unconscious boy, felt his forehead, shook her head, slid her hand to his cheek and along his arm, noting the rapid rise and fall of his chest. "His skin is cold and damp," she said. With strong fingers, she ripped his priestly robe to the point where dried blood made the fabric adhere to Hanno's body. "Bring some warm water," she ordered.

After Abdmelkart complied, she gently proceeded to loosen the cloth and clean the boy's wound.

Hanno groaned.

Grabbing the bottle of poppy juice, she raised it toward the high priest. "My lord, please give him some."

Without comment, he poured a little bit between Hanno's teeth, turning the boy's head, careful not to gag him.

Finally, when Elissa saw the wound without all the blood, she said, "He's been stabbed."

"Stabbed!" exclaimed the high priest, almost letting the bottle slip from his fingers.

"From the cut's position, it doesn't look deep. Hanno must have jumped sideways and twisted because the gash is at waist level. It starts in the back, runs around to the front, and ends with a scratch near his navel." She began to clean the boy's face with the soft, wet cloth. "He must be quiet so he doesn't bleed any more."

"Abdmelkart, send one of the young priests to Alcibiades, the hunchback doctor from Delos, and come back here immediately."

"There is nothing more I can do," said Elissa. "Keep him warm."

Hasdrubal pulled the cover from his bed and laid it over Hanno as Abdmelkart returned. "Watch that he does not move," said the high priest to the slave. Gesturing to Elissa to follow, he headed for his audience chamber. Like lightning, the solution to her placement had come to him. Exactly right, he thought.

"Elissa," he said when the two stood in the middle of the empty room, "I am going to make a suggestion."

A suggestion! To her wonder, his tone of voice was reasonable. Be careful, she warned herself, you are overtired, he has had a shock, but is heartless. She compelled herself to look steadily at the inlaid floor. If she kept her face expressionless and didn't look at him, he wouldn't know how deeply he hurt her.

"Elissa, look at me."

Unwillingly, she met his gaze. It bore into her. Straightforward, unclouded, it made her feel weak. She couldn't remember ever looking directly into his eyes. What she saw was not unpleasant.

"First, I absolutely forbid you to go alone into the streets at night."

The terror she had felt at the approach of the group of sailors assailed her. She shifted her gaze.

"I want your word on it. There is to be no backsliding."

"Yes, sire. I will obey, sire." That must mean she could stay.

What was he planning with his suggestion? Punishment, undoubtedly, which would be horrible, but she would survive. Her chin went up a fraction, and she looked back at him.

He caught the chin movement. Ah! he thought, she is starting to behave normally. The barbs will flow. Elissa, Elissa, you have simply got to stop that. We cannot work together with this constant hostility.

"In Carthage," he said slowly so that each word would have an effect, "we have a particularly fine physician, the one I sent for, Alcibiades of Delos. I propose to send you to him to receive instruction."

Her eyes went wide and round. Rather than the expected harshness, he was offering her the one thing in life she wanted most. As she was a woman, either he was exceedingly stupid or in desperate straits. She didn't believe either one.

He hid the quiet mirth caused by her expression with a particularly unyielding facial mask. "Many workers come to our temple each day. Between the metal workers, woodworkers, glassblowers, dyers, stonecutters, priests and priestesses, the school, and the slaves, something is always the matter with somebody. You would not be expected to deal with the more serious problems." He looked intently at her. After a short hesitation, he said, "This is a long-term commitment. Are you willing?"

In answer, she dropped to her face on the floor.

Strange, he thought, but why not? Women doctors exist in Egypt and women high priests in some of our minor temples. Why not a woman doctor here? Anyway, he had found her place. She would cause him no more trouble.

"You may go," he said quietly. "Say nothing of this for the moment."

Elissa watched his feet leave the audience chamber before she struggled to a standing position. Ridiculous. She was thinking kindly of him. She just needed sleep.

The sleeping area the priestesses shared was deserted. She stretched, then scratched her back. Instantly awake, she realized that she had never looked at it after her beating. With gentle, exploratory fingers, she searched every part of her back that she could reach. She felt no remaining scabs or raised portions that might be scars. Using her mirror and twisting her body, she looked. Nothing. No mark showed, not even redness. Her back was perfectly smooth and clear. She moved to a better light. Still nothing.

Incredible. Slaves had been whipped in her presence. Bloody welts were always the result. With great deliberateness, Elissa threw herself on her back on the bed. Not even a twinge of pain. That priest who had beaten her probably felt sorry and had been careful. No. Being honest with herself, she had to admit everyone did the high priest's bidding. If she were not lacerated, he gave the order. He—She slept.

8

*H*asdrubal was busy. Alcibiades arrived, awkwardly carrying his hump over his short body and long legs. His head, bearded in Athenian fashion, was a handsome replica of the God Zeus with twice the intelligence. He confirmed Elissa's diagnosis. The knife had cut cleanly, though not deeply. "Whoever wielded that knife fumbled the job."

He sewed the wound together carefully, but the high priest, holding Hanno's shoulders, winced each time the needle pierced the soft flesh. Alcibiades commended Elissa's work.

"She is by instinct suited to the job," Hasdrubal said. "You can see for yourself that her abilities are considerable."

Alcibiades threw him a queried look. What was this leading to?

"She has matured beyond the silly, young-girl stage," said the high priest, "and could treat the minor ailments of the priests and laborers with impunity." He stopped, struck by his unexpected eloquence.

The doctor laughed, his nimble mind grasping the implied question. "Send her over in the morning," he said. "We'll see. If she shows promise, I'll train her."

Next, Saphonisba walked into the house, followed by slaves. Eight cautious hands eased the bundled Hanno onto the litter they had brought. Two Numidians, stripped to the waist, raised it. Their oiled dark skin glistened in the sun. Saphonisba positioned herself by Hanno's side. Resting a hand on his shoulder to prevent jarring, she instructed her slaves to keep the street crowds at a distance. Every few seconds, as they crossed the temple courtyard, she said, "Easy, easy."

At that rate, Hasdrubal thought, they will not get to the top of the Byrsa until way past dinnertime. "Abdmelkart," he said, intuitively aware that his slave was behind him, "ask the soothsayer to read the entrails of a chicken concerning Hanno's recovery. I must arrange for the sacrifice." He strode off toward the administration building without a backward glance.

Abdmelkart hesitated and scowled before running toward the maze.

The high priest searched through most of the workshops behind the school building. Speaking by name, one after the other, to the workers he passed, he finally found the nearly naked and perspiring chief of sacrifices. He was in the fiery heat and clanging noise of the metal workshop, huddled with three equally grimy and wet men around a dirt drawing of a drain pipe section that needed replacing at the sacrificial altar. Pulling his chief aside, Hasdrubal explained the need for a sacrifice.

"I think Hanno is too old for a pure white goat."

"Agreed," said the chief, brushing droplets from the end of his long nose and his sharp, beardless chin. "I suggest a young adult male, gray and white, a third of the meat, including the haunches and the best cuts, to feed the priests, as well as five silver coins from the Carthage mint."

Hasdrubal kept nodding his head as he listened. "See to it," he said when the chief stopped talking.

Walking back to his quarters, he was met at the temple entrance by a smiling Asherat.

"My lord," she said, "a thousand apologies. I will only keep you a minute."

"Do not apologize. I am at your disposal." He bent his head attentively, marshaling his thoughts, not quite ready to reveal Elissa's change of assignment.

"Now that the priestess Elissa has disgraced us and stirred so much unrest among the priestesses, I wish your approval of some changes I intend to make while awaiting your decision." If only, she thought, he'd let slip what he intends to do about her, I'll have a better idea of how to act. "She'll be removed from performances and reduced in status. I also intend to isolate her from the young priestesses. I need your permission to arrange sleeping space. My suggestion is the storage area next to my room so I can keep a close eye on her."

"Your concern is admirable," said the high priest, "and your suggestion of separate sleeping quarters is excellent."

Asherat bit her tongue. So Elissa was not to be dismissed. Too bad.

"I shall have to determine where we put her," he continued. "She will need something larger than that storage area for what I have in mind."

From the corner of his eye, he saw Abdmelkart return to the house. Ah! By tomorrow, the soothsayer will have divined the will of the gods.

"You will know my arrangements before the day ends. She will not trouble you again."

Asherat left the high priest, a sly smile playing around her lips. She knew what to do. He was right, the Tyrian would not cause trouble again.

Hasdrubal followed her erect, waddling form with his eyes. In removing Elissa from the orchestra, he had also removed her from Asherat's control and placed her directly under himself. His lead priestess would harbor insult on two counts. First, because he was championing someone she disliked, and second, because he had reduced her authority.

He drew in his breath and let it out. That Asherat was capable of fomenting trouble when she disliked a priestess was wrenching. He pressed his lips together. One problem was solved, only to give rise to another. Lost in disquieting thought, he turned toward home.

Just inside, he faced Abdmelkart groveling on the floor, a scroll in his hand. Hasdrubal's heart thumped wildly.

"Master," cried the slave, "when the scroll was delivered, there was no time to give it to you. Beat me if you wish."

"I am not going to beat you," snapped Hasdrubal. "When have I ever beaten you!"

His hand trembled a bit as he took the scroll. Nobody else used a seal like the one that closed the skin. It was Bimilcar's.

"I will be upstairs in my library," he said. "I am not to be disturbed."

In the library, he threw himself on a pile of cushions stacked on the floor. He moved one behind his back until it was positioned just right against the wall. Relaxed, he turned the scroll round and round in his hand. The hardened wax showed the imprint of their father's ring, a gold seal, that Bimilcar always wore on the middle finger of his right hand.

Carefully, Hasdrubal inserted his thumbnail under the edge of the skin scroll and cracked the wax.

The first sentence was: I salute you from the headquarters of Hannibal.

Hasdrubal swallowed hard. If Bimilcar was with Hannibal, others of his troops were too. Gisgo had not died in vain.

Hasdrubal read rapidly straight through to the end:

The goddess has been good to us in spite of our reverses. The flotilla seemed under an evil spell from the start, though the twenty-five quinqueremes sailed at the time the soothsayer pronounced propitious.

At midday, three days after the new moon, we passed through the channel connecting the military and commercial harbors. The trumpet from the admiral's roost sounded for the chain at the mouth of the commercial harbor to be dropped, and we were warped out. In acceptable Carthaginian fashion, we hugged the coast of Africa. Naturally, the square linen sails on the short masts were easy to see. Most of the time, the ships were close enough to see the long oars as they rhythmically cut the water to the beat of the flute player in the stern. Because the ships were lightly built with shallow, flat bottoms, we beached them before dark rather than navigating by the stars as do the commercial ship captains.

Late the following afternoon, under a clear sky, the ships started to pitch. I was writing in my bunk and was thrown to the floor. I staggered onto the deck. Black storm clouds, pushed by gale winds churned the sea into hissing towers of water. Men had hold of the sides, the ropes, each other, to save themselves from being hurtled overboard or into the gaping, undecked hold in the middle of the ship.

The next day and the next were the same. At times, we seemed to go backward instead of forward, alternately battling wind and heavy seas or rain, wind, and sea. We were weeks reaching the narrow stretch of water where we crossed to Hispania. The wind, funneling through the Pillars of Hercules, separated our ships and blew some beyond New Carthage toward the Balearic islands.

Nine of our ships followed my lead into the harbor of our colony at Ebusus. With the consent of the townspeople, we lashed ourselves together into a compact group. As day after useless day dragged by, the troops grew restless. Incidents occurred, drunkenness and rape. Supplies dwindled. The once-friendly islanders became sullen and hostile. Fights broke out. I'll say no more about that.

On the first day possible, I gave the order to depart. Townspeople lined up on the wharf to watch as one after the other, our ships moved slowly through the breakwater. Joy was short-lived. A storm approached from the east, leaving chaos behind from the hurled lightning bolts to the waves that struck the ships.

Of those ten quinqueremes, mine and one other, heaving and crashing together, were flung upon the Hispanian shore. Leaping into rolling surf, the men struggled onto the beach. Archers and slingers, unencumbered by heavy armor and weapons, snatched at foot soldiers when, weighted by bronze breast- and back- plates, they started to sink beneath the surface and pulled them to safety. I was managing on my own, my sword and shield held above my head, when two men grabbed me and carried me ashore.

A wet and disorganized crowd ranged along the beach, some with, some without, their weapons, some rescuing swords and shields that were bouncing around in the breaking waves. I was readjusting my bronze armor, my shield on the ground, my sword stuck into the dirt. Howling men, wearing antler helmets, carrying round shields, and waving swords, rushed at us from the surrounding forest. A giant helmetless warrior, his hair short and plastered back from his forehead like a horse's mane, a golden torque around his neck, dealt me a nasty sword slash on my shield arm. An instant later, the shield would have been in place. Though the cut affected my grip on the shield, I fought him. Weakened by pain, I began to lose ground. Any small hole to twist my foot as I inched backwards could have toppled me.

Instead of pushing his advantage, the warrior vanished into the forest as unexpectedly as he had come. As I stared after him, my eyes played tricks. The surrounding trees seemed to move. Not trees, but fresh warriors rushed toward me. Unable to pull up the shield that had slid down my arm, I threw it on the ground. Die, I must; I could no longer fight. Imagine my feelings when those around me broke into excited yells. The men bearing down on us were Carthaginians. I recognized a slinger from my own command who had been on one of the quinqueremes I thought sunk. All around, men were laughing and yelling and hugging each other.

Somebody poured stinging sea water over my arm and bound the wound.

I learned that the other fifteen quinqueremes were forced back to Africa and stayed there until a few days before our meeting. Near the coast of Hispania, the ships ran into another storm. The men beached immediately, and were marching toward New Car-

thage when they heard the noise of battle. Scouts reported our peril, and the approach of the troops had caused the Celts to withdraw.

By the time campfires were lit, the rest of our Ebusus cohorts joined us. They had been cast ashore around a spit of land. Overall, only one ship was lost. For the great and marvelous deliverance from the many misfortunes, I ordered the entire camp to give thanks to Tanit.

Seeing Hannibal was a great joy. Since our last meeting, he has married and sired a baby son, born during the siege of Saguntum. He talks of sending Imilce, his wife, and the baby to Carthage before the campaign starts.

His two secretaries go with us as he is a prodigious correspondent. Thus, I shall be able to use the same couriers to carry my scrolls to you and Saphonisba.

Hasdrubal's mind kept repeating, safe, they're safe. The scroll slipped from his hand. His head slowly fell forward, and his body slumped sideways. In the softness of the cushions, he slept.

9

*H*asdrubal chose to interpret positively the enigmatic message that came from the soothsayer. Relieved, he went up the Byrsa to see Hanno. Batbaal, in a red gown that put color in her face, and tinkling ankle bracelets, led him up the stairs.

She seems more like herself, he thought. The prospect of going to Tyre must have helped.

His niece, ahead of him, turned and said, "In the confusion yesterday, Mother forgot to tell you that we heard from Mago. He's coming home. He said by the time we got the scroll, he'd be on his way."

"Which means he did not receive yours before leaving."

"And you don't need to hunt for a ship." She smiled at him.

Mago must fear major destruction, Hasdrubal thought. The Seleucid King Antiochus wants those cities along his coast, and the Egyptian Pharaoh Ptolemy means to prevent him. Understandable. Tyre and Sidon are rich cities.

They reached the top.

"Mother's with Hanno. I'll see you in a bit," Batbaal said, and ran back downstairs.

Hanno lay still, flushed and unresponsive. His mother sat beside him on the floor. Her face was tired and puckered in worry.

Noticing the rolled bed mat against the wall, Hasdrubal said, "You spent the night here?"

"Yes. I would not do otherwise." Surprised that he should ask the question, she stared at him with sad and sunken eyes.

Hanno groaned. Instantly, she bent over him, brushing back his damp hair, adjusting his body so that he wouldn't lie on the wound.

"I will sit and watch," said the high priest. "Go rest a while."

Her shoulders sagged in a gesture of thankfulness. She smiled gently. "You will call me if he takes a turn for the worse?"

"Yes. But he is not going to, according to the soothsayer."

Hasdrubal sat by the bed all afternoon. If Hanno moaned, he laid a calming hand on him, changed the boy's position, and felt his forehead. He seemed to be getting hotter and hotter. He was becoming restless and babbling nothings.

Hasdrubal summoned a slave. "Send for Alcibiades." At last, though hating to disturb her, Hasdrubal roused Saphonisba.

"Hanno has developed a fever," he said. "The doctor is with him."

She rushed ahead of him to her son's room. The two of them stood quietly to one side while slaves bustled about at Alcibiades' command. Water was brought, herb poultices made, unguents applied, and medicines administered: Alcibiades used every treatment his facile brain could think of.

I'm overdoing, he admitted to himself.

Being a strong, healthy boy, Hanno mustered his defenses. He began to look around him, at the blue stucco walls of the tiny room, the changing face of the person near him. He opened his mouth obediently when warm, good-tasting liquid was poured down his throat. He was hungry. He talked of school, of classmates, of teachers, of what he saw while walking through the city, but the minute the talk turned to why he was at the wharf before dawn, he was evasive. He made up all sorts of stories. None rang true. For the time being, his uncle stopped asking.

Two weeks later, sitting with his nephew in the garden, the high priest returned to the subject. Hanno, wearing a sulky expression, sprang to his feet.

"Hanno, come back here and sit down." Hasdrubal picked up the blanket Hanno had thrown off and tucked it around his reluctantly submissive nephew. "I want you to tell me as accurately as you can, what happened the morning you were stabbed."

Hanno pouted.

"Sooner or later," Hasdrubal said, "you are going to have to talk about it."

In silence, Hanno looked around the garden, his gaze dwelling on each object. The high priest waited, observing the boy through slits. Finally, Hanno said, "I was almost out, quite near the gate, when I heard a man call that I was crossing the courtyard. There was a little light by the temple, so I started to run."

"Could you see any people?"

"No. It was all too fast. I heard a woman say, 'Stop him,' then running feet. But I got outside and ran toward the port."

Hanno showed no inclination to continue. "What happened next?" urged Hasdrubal.

"There were no stars. It was very dark and hard to see. People were moving about; I could hear them. Nobody was near me. Suddenly, it was like—I can't express it."

"Try."

"Like—no noise—like somebody is there. Everything's like it was, only you know somebody's there. It was scary. The back of my neck felt creepy. I jumped away just as someone stabbed me. I screamed and put my hands over the spot. I screamed some more and covered my face. Then my eyes felt sticky so I shut them. I banged around and remember falling, but that's all. I don't remember any more until I heard my name like from a great distance, and somebody picked me up. That's all until I knew people were around me and things were happening to me, but I didn't know what. And I began to feel warm again." He made a face and shuddered. "I had been so cold. It was funny because it wasn't cold, just me."

"Think hard," the high priest broke in. "Did you recognize the woman's voice?"

For a long time, Hanno sat, resting his head against the chair back, staring into space. Gray miniature cloud shadows on the ground surrounded the two still figures and drifted on. Hasdrubal watched the changing light patterns on his nephew's face. No longer drawn, Hanno's face still looked thin. Long, dark lashes curled across the gray circles under his eyes. The prominent, high nose was a family characteristic. It shaded lashes and cheek on one side. The lovely curve of the full lips came from his mother.

Hanno's eyeballs moved with the intensity of thought; twice the lips and brow tightened. When he finally spoke, he said, "The head priestess."

"Thank you, Hanno. You may be right. She frequently goes early into the temple."

After returning to the temple, Hasdrubal sent for Asherat.

"I have asked you to come," he said, once they were seated in his rooms, "to see what light you can throw on my nephew's stabbing. He seems to remember hearing your voice call 'Stop him.'"

"He certainly did. I was just waiting until you were less rushed to tell you about it."

"I would be most pleased to hear what you have to say." He sat back and folded his hands in his lap.

"Elissa and I had been praying in the temple," said Asherat.

Immobile except for a half-closed eye flicking over her, the high priest waited. As far as he knew, she had never lied to him before, but he couldn't be sure. Sadly, he could never be sure of her again.

She went on placidly. "My male slave was with us. Elissa and I were proceeding along the edge of the portico. My slave was ahead, lighting our way with a taper. All of a sudden, he cried, 'Hanno nears the gate.' I cried 'Stop him,' and the three of us ran down the steps. In the confusion, the taper went out. The sky was overcast, as you may recall. Elissa said, 'I can't see in the dark.' I said I couldn't either. We weren't able to do anything. As best we could, we made our way back to our rooms."

Hasdrubal thought, does she mean to insinuate that Elissa had sneaked out to stab Hanno? The flaw in her nefarious scheme is that she does not know that Elissa was out all that night.

He was fully aware that Asherat had been indignant when he informed her that he was assigning Elissa to a suite of two rooms, one for herself, one to be operated as a clinic. Asherat had turned deep red and refused to look at him until she had controlled her feelings.

His head priestess was adamant in her desire to have Elissa thrown from the temple. She is hunting a means, he said to himself. Much as Elissa and he had clashed, he never would have suspected her of the stabbing.

He scratched his eyebrows. Elissa had been down by the wharf that morning. In her despondency, had she vented her hatred toward him on Hanno? He did not believe it. Any knifing would have been unpremeditated on her part, and she wasn't prepared. All she had been carrying was the bottle of anesthetic.

Why did the head priestess hate the Tyrian so? The answer escaped him. It was most peculiar; Elissa was no longer defiant, no threat to her authority, and had no regular contact with the priestesses. Yet, according to Asherat, nothing Elissa did was right. Undoubtedly, Asherat had noticed the change for the better in his dealings with the priestess.

His mind dwelt on Elissa. She was conducting herself admirably. Of her own free will, she was reporting her progress, discussing quietly and sensibly what she was doing. No barbs issued from her mouth. She even smiled at him when they passed each other around the school building. He quite enjoyed her changed attitude and looked forward to her reports. Interesting. She was an intelligent young woman. Alcibiades sent glowing summaries, and she had been with him only a short time.

Well, more than likely, Hanno had seen something on the wharf best unseen. Corruption was so flagrant through every stratum of the city's society, the grasp for money and power so overwhelming, that hiring a thug to dispose of a nosy boy had no more meaning than wringing the neck of the dinner fowl. But at that hour! That bothered the high priest. Who would have known that Hanno was on the wharf just before dawn? The sailors on some ship? Perhaps this was an attempt on his nephew's part to run away. Maybe in making arrangements to board a ship, he had seen something best unseen.

As far as he could judge, this was Hanno's first attempt. He was positive the boy would make another. The stabbing had prevented Elibaal from issuing the dinner invitation. But using Hanno's recovery as an excuse, the senator had suggested a celebration. The spark of amusement crept into Hasdrubal's eyes. Hanno's joy was instant. He told everybody who would listen.

He is like I was the day Father invited me to his audience hall, thought Hasdrubal. But Hanno was apt to leave the party more hopeful of not being high priest if Elibaal succeeded in getting him to talk.

Hasdrubal sighed. Hanno's hopes would soon fade once he was back in school. The problem was keeping him there.

10

*U*nhappy and morose, Hanno resumed his place among the male students in the priestly school.

Hasdrubal and Saphonisba dined with Elibaal a week later.

"He expressed interest in six fields that I remember. There may have been more. He jumped from one occupation to another. The only thing he was positive about was the temple."

"He doesn't want to be high priest," Hasdrubal said.

"He has to be," Saphonisba sounded sad.

"He hates school," said Elibaal.

"My dear, lots of boys his age hate school," Saphonisba said.

"But they don't try to run away," said Hasdrubal.

"Hanno is immature," Elibaal said. "He'll settle down in time."

Seated on the cushions in his library, a skin scroll in his lap, Hasdrubal mulled over the conversation. Elibaal could very well be right, but in the meantime, a potential runaway was unsettling him. Feeling caught in the middle vexed the high priest. If he were too severe with the boy, he was insuring another attempt to run away soon. If he were too lenient, Hanno would become more and more difficult to handle.

Throwing down his scroll, he informed Abdmelkart that he was going for a walk.

On soundless feet, the slave followed his master to the bedroom. The high priest didn't take these incognito walks unless something bothered him. What? The master was pleased with the priestess Elissa. It was something else. Hanno? The boy had been subdued and despondent since his return. But while that might concern the high priest, it was hardly sufficient to bring on one of these walks. Abdmelkart took a carefully folded pile of dark blue Carthaginian woolen garments from the large pithoi clothing jar in the corner. He sniffed the fresh, clean smell, and reached for the wig and false beard in the niche above the jar. The head priestess? He cast that thought aside. While he was wary of her and her slave, the master trusted her, and he had nothing positive to go on. He watched them cautiously from his side of the temple, storing the information in his head.

Abdmelkart didn't know his age. He had been in his first manhood when he was captured in battle and put on the slave block. His purchaser had been a youth dressed in the robes of a priest. The Numidian had sneered. He was a warrior; he would soon twist the little eunuch to his own liking and make him regret his purchase. That was twenty summers ago. His treatment had been kind, but firm. His duties had not been arduous, but instant and perfect compliance were expected. Within a short time, Abdmelkart found himself reduced to mental as well as physical slavery. His master, no eunuch, commanded the profoundest love and respect.

He couldn't put his finger on when he began to worship the high priest of Tanit, but the day the heavy sculpture in the stone-cutters' yard was accidentally knocked off its base and just missed falling on his master, he realized that he would give his life for him.

After tying on his beard and fitting his wig, Abdmelkart watched the high priest leave the temple precinct.

Hasdrubal let himself out a small door in the wall directly behind his home. Perhaps a look at the water level of the city's cisterns or the inner city's fortifications would clear his mind. Better still, Elibaal had casually mentioned one afternoon that Hannibal had sent thirteen thousand Hispanian infantry and twelve hundred cavalry to Africa. Though most of them were stationed up north along the coast, a few had been assigned to defend Carthage. Intrigued by Bimilcar's description of the barbarian, he hoped to obtain a look at these Celtic tribesmen.

On the broad main thoroughfare, he turned left toward Megara. The Byrsa hill with its lower reaches of multistoried mercantile buildings, terraced to catch the light, rose on his right. On his left, there were apartment houses. Among them, one private home, like a giant bud, nestled in the midst of dark green trees and blossoming plants. By the open gate, a slave held a jug. A water carrier filled it with sweet water from one of the pitchers carried in great plaited baskets which hung on the sides of his sloe-eyed, patient donkey.

Beyond were the fortifications. The massive bastion, fifty-seven feet high and twenty-eight feet wide at the base, had been hewn from stone. The four-story towers, protruding outward every 195 feet, had been built in his lifetime, after the slave uprising. How well he remembered! Prisoners had hung crucified, starting just about where the wall was and stretching out way beyond. As Hasdrubal walked, he saw, first, one of the towers off to his right, then the main structure came into view. Twenty thousand infantry were housed within those walls, along with four thousand horses and three hundred elephants.

The highway was crowded with Phoenician traders, the litters of wealthy women, Greek chariots with sleek, prancing horses driven by foreign merchants, laborers from Cush in the far reaches of the Nile, Egyptian soldiers, plodding caravans. The camels always had such a pungent odor, unlike the elephants. Their handlers constantly bathed them. With ponderous steps, their trunks swaying from side to side, five war elephants came toward him. Their leather armor gleamed in the sun. Atop each animal sat a mahout. A thrill of pride swept over the high priest. The whole world passed along Carthaginian roads. This was his city, a city that had surmounted great difficulties. Carthage had grown to equal and even surpass the great cities of Greece and even the mother Phoenician cities. After all, he was a Phoenician. His heritage was steeped in the ages. He walked along, his head high, looking like the aristocrat he was.

The troops were quartered on the other side of the city. Hot and wanting to rest, he turned off the boulevard to the public fountain. When the wells were all brackish, the city was fortunate to have this fresh water fountain, the only one in Carthage. Water bubbled from deep in the cliff hill and flowed quietly from the cave's mouth near the sea. He had no intention of going into the cool, hewn passage where the water issued from the rock. He simply wanted to rest near the water flow, to see the women who came to fill their jugs and gossip, and to watch the old men under the trees who played the Egyptian game of senute.

Hasdrubal savored the tranquility of the scene. A horseman, probably in his early twenties, approached at a slow, walking pace from the direction of Megara. Clean shaven, the man had tightly waved black hair. He wore Athenian dress. Dismounting, he handed the reins of his magnificent animal to a small boy.

Obviously a Hellene, thought Hasdrubal, but dark complected

like Phoenicians. Probably from one of the islands. Then he blinked two or three times. He wanted to make sure that the sparkle of sunlight among the leaves had not affected his eyesight. His imagination must be playing tricks on him. He looked away to clear his vision. It was no use. The sensation of looking at himself as a young man, the way the body moved, the tilt of the head, made his skin prickle. The man was probably twenty years younger, but he looked exactly like him.

Had anyone else noticed the resemblance to the high priest of Tanit? Hasdrubal scanned those around the fountain. No one seemed to be paying any attention to the man. Using cupped hands, he was drinking from the water flow. Hasdrubal observed every movement as the Hellene finished drinking, tossed a coin to the urchin holding his horse, mounted and rode off.

Who was he? Where did he live? How long had he been in Carthage? Where did he claim citizenship? Profoundly agitated, the high priest hurried back to the temple, all the while mapping strategies to obtain answers.

Again dressed in priestly robes, he was crossing in front of the statue of Tanit when the sound of running feet coming from the maze made him turn around. A priest flew by him. Alcibiades followed, his skinny, long legs moving rapidly. Knowing that something serious had occurred, Hasdrubal chased after them. They ran to the room he had given Elissa for the temple sick. A woodworker lay on a mat, his right foot bound in a bloody bandage. Elissa, on her knees beside him, stroked his forehead.

"Hold him while I unbandage the foot," ordered the doctor.

"I've given him something to dull the pain," she said, laying one arm across his hairy chest to firmly grip the muscular body.

Alcibiades, nodding approval, cut through the bandage. As it fell away, the high priest winced. The man had nearly severed his foot.

Removing the stopper from a bottle, Alcibiades poured evil-smelling liquid over the cut. The worker screamed. Alcibiades grabbed his leg to keep him from drawing it up, while Elissa threw all her strength into controlling the man's shoulders. Hasdrubal flung himself beside her and grabbed both legs. Alcibiades, released to keep the foot from further injury, flashed a look of thanks.

The screaming stopped. The man seemed to collapse. Every muscle went limp and every pore opened, bathing him in perspiration. He lay still, his eyes closed, his face above the black beard drained of color, but he was breathing normally. Elissa mopped his face with her himation. The high priest inhaled in a short gasp as he looked at her. During the struggle, their shoulders and arms had touched. A thrill had gone through him. On his feet, standing back a bit, he watched her from under lowered lids. She was so efficient, so alive and, yes, so lovely.

Fires that he thought were dead flamed anew. He scolded himself. The woman was young enough to be his daughter.

Do not be a fool, he thought to himself. You will go from an old scandal to being a laughingstock. She no longer is aggressively hostile, but she hates you. Nevertheless, the incident left a nugget of happiness deep within him. He counted the days before she might report again.

Alone with her patient, Elissa covered him with a blanket she kept folded in a corner of the room. Then, sure that he slept, she went to the temple. She sat down behind a pillar, hidden from the view of anyone entering, and leaned against the wall. It was dark and cool. From her first days at this temple, she had made the spot her own, a place where she could rest and think without interference.

The touch of his arm had passed through her like a rod of bronze, hot from the kiln. Nothing like that had happened to her since her youth when she had been so desperately in love. But this high priest! Ridiculous. She hated him. Actually, did she hate him? He had been extremely generous with her, she had to admit, when she hadn't behaved very well.

He was feared rather than loved by many of the lowest workers, but that was normal. All were loyal. Everyone she talked to, even people like Alcibiades, sang his praises, both as a man and as an administrator. She was the only one out of step. At first, she had voiced her feelings, but of late she had kept them to herself. Upon reflection, she realized that she didn't hate him. When had she stopped?

She laughed silently. That high priest wasn't going to look at her. He never thought of women except as servants for his temple. The best thing to do was to stay out of his way. True, she gave him reports of her progress, but that was her own doing. He hadn't asked for it. Their paths didn't usually cross. She could easily avoid him. That's what I'll do, she thought.

Ready to leave the temple, she remembered the spring festival, the music, singing, dancing and feasting all day. She didn't want to miss that. He would be there in full regalia, performing his role perfectly. All day long, she would have to see him. In the dimness, her eyes widened. She loved him.

11

*T*he spring festival was a time of joy, celebrating the escape of Baal from the netherworld and his return to the mountaintop. The earth burst with renewed energy. Flowers in brilliant hue sprang from the parched soil. Trees budded and turned green. Goats produced young. Cattle calved. Baby lambs jumped on spindly legs. The whole world rejoiced.

Long before dawn on that day, the priests lit fires in the animal area and secured sheep carcasses on spits.

Other priests washed the sacrificial bull as the sun rose in a cloudless sky, and a cool breeze blew from the sea. A sleek and powerful black beast, the bull had been fed with mounds of sweet grass and clover mixed with dried stalks and pods, his drinking water carried in jugs from the cistern and emptied into a special stone basin. The priests scrubbed his thick neck, his powerful flanks, his sturdy legs, then laid a garland of white flowers over his head and tied a long woolen cord around his neck.

The chief of sacrifices, in special festival robes, bowed in the formalities of ritual. Taking the cord in his hand, he led the bull along the winding path to the altar in the courtyard. In a euphoric mood, chanting priests and priestesses followed in a double line. The procession moved slowly behind the lumbering bull. The animal had bellowed as the garland was placed around his neck. Surely Baal looked favorably on the sacrifice.

Hasdrubal, in ceremonial robes, waited at the altar. The garlanded line of worshipers reached him, their chanting stopped, and they fanned out into a semicircle. All eyes followed the chief of sacrifices. Leading the bull behind the altar, he gently guided the massive horned head onto the altar's flat top. The worshipers knelt, touching their foreheads three times to the ground. Seeing their movement, the bull flared his nostrils.

At the corner of the altar, the high priest recited the festival verses while his chief performed the blood sacrifice. Afterwards, Hasdrubal signaled specially assigned priests to remove the carcass. He led the others into the temple. Shadows created by the flickering wall lamps danced across the floor. The fragrance of incense rose from the many burners placed around the walls and in front of the holy place. Small wisps of smoke curled upward and dissipated. Members of the orchestra positioned themselves on either side of the curtain shielding the sacred stone as the last few stragglers crowded into the temple.

The high priest stood before the curtain, scanning the priestesses. Elissa had not been in the group at the altar. She wasn't in the temple. Where was she?

In spite of his own pleasure and excitement, he began to chafe. The temple door was closing. All were inside. The ritual was about to begin. He must keep his mind on his performance.

Ah! There she was. Way in the back, looking rather shy. He wanted to take her in his arms. Instead, in a sonorous voice, he intoned the opening lines of the long poem he had written for the occasion.

Toward the end, towns people were allowed to join those standing in the rear. They brought their children to see the holy stone when the curtain was drawn. The high priest was suddenly aware that the man he had seen at the fountain was standing near Elissa. His stomach contracted. He was reaching the high point of the whole service and almost stumbled. Steeling himself, he went on. The words came. To his relief, no facial muscles near him twitched. Many in the temple listened intently, sometimes he thought, to catch him in mistakes. He must pay attention. He could not afford to slip again. He refrained from looking toward the back of the temple.

After reading the verses he had written in praise of the festival, he walked slowly to the edge of the curtain. Priests and priestesses raised their arms in praise, and began to sing. With a snap of his wrist and a few quick steps, he flung the curtain aside as a scream, high pitched and terrified, vibrated above the singing. That was Elissa's voice. He knew it. He maintained his composure and his position of obeisance beside the holy place. From the corner of his eye, he was able to observe scrambling near the door. Women huddled together, their faces bent toward the floor. Men bobbed up and down in general chaos. Elissa was gone, and he couldn't see the Greek.

Somehow, he finished his part of the ceremony, sprinkled the wine and closed the curtain, indicating the start of dancing and feasting.

Asherat hurried towards him.

"You have such a glorious voice," she said, "and you read those glorious verses with such emotion. The ceremony was glorious."

He thanked her, but found himself wishing she weren't so effusive. Still, if she thought his performance good, it must have been satisfactory. She had been in the front row of priestesses and would have caught any mistake.

"What a tragedy that the ceremony was marred," she continued. "As usual, the troublemaker was Elissa. Such noise and banging at the most holy moment. Really, Hasdrubal, if you'll excuse my saying so, you overlook all the evil she does. Does she have some kind of hold over you that you can't get rid of her?"

He was stunned. How dare this woman question his judgment? As high priest, he knew what was best for the temple. She had overstepped her bounds. One more outburst like that, and she would be dismissed out of hand. No one would question his decision. He pulled himself up to his full height and authority.

Asherat fluttered her eyelids and pulled back her ears. "Abject apologies, my lord. Forgive me, please."

He thought she was going to drop to her knees right there in front of the High Place. Slightly inclining his head, he said, "Today is a day of rejoicing, priestess. We will say no more about it." With perfect grace, he moved off to talk to others. She, too, moved off, intense, flashing anger making her head throb. He had crossed her once too often. She laid a hand across her breast to still her furiously pounding heart. If she weren't so anxious to see the play, she would go to her room to lie down. Later when she was calm, she would make plans. There was no need to rush.

The temple priests and priestesses were starting to mime the play. A priestess, taking the part of Baal's sister Anath, pretended to journey to the netherworld and plead with Noth, king of shades, for permission to lead her brother back to earth. Only with Baal's return would the world spring to life again.

Hasdrubal searched the crowd for Elissa. Slowly, he walked around the edge of the audience and peered at the face of every priestess. She was not in the temple.

By nightfall, the feasting over, quiet spread through the compound. Tired participants sought their beds. The high priest sat alone at his desk in the school building. He had walked passed the clinic door. It was closed.

Why had Elissa screamed? Perhaps he should have questioned some of the townspeople. But after Asherat's outburst, he had avoided mentioning the interruption, letting it be forgotten in the pleasure of the day. There was time enough later to find out from Abdmelkart.

Was she ill? For any other priestess, he would have personally rapped on the door of the room where the priestesses slept and asked. Not Elissa. He shied away from drawing attention to his interest. He fretted and waited. For what, he knew not.

Then, there she was, cowering on the floor before him, her face hidden, her voice agonized.

"Sire, sire, beat me, punish me any way you want, but don't send me away—please."

Send her away! He wanted to gather her close. To cover his emotion, his voice was cold. "Stand up, Elissa."

She obeyed.

Though she hung her head, he saw the red and swollen eyes, the full red lips drawn in and caught between her teeth.

Smitten, he cleared his throat and said gently, "Tell me what happened."

"An asp suddenly slithered across my shoulder and arm." At the memory of its flicking tongue, she covered her face with her hands. She didn't see Hasdrubal start.

"My himation was folded over my arm, and my robe was made of heavy linen so the bite didn't break my skin. I don't know where the snake came from. I screamed. Then I wanted to die. This is the second time I have ruined your ritual. The noise, the people scrambling around after the snake—" She gulped.

"You left the temple?" He had to know if she left with that strange Greek.

"A man who was standing beside me helped me out. He insisted on getting me water. He walked me over here even though I assured him I was all right."

"Very kind." A pang of jealousy passed through him. Head down, she stood before him wringing her hands. In a voice so soft that he had to strain to hear her, she said, "I was so ashamed, I couldn't come back." Her voice became urgent as she lifted her swollen eyes to meet his. "Don't send me away—please."

"Elissa, the incident was very unfortunate, but couldn't be helped," said Hasdrubal, stepping around his desk. "Go to bed now. I think you need some sleep before you meet Alcibiades in the morning."

Like a crumpled rag, she sank to the floor and kissed the hem of his garment. His hand, following the lines of her body, caressed the air above her. Without looking at him again, she crawled out backwards and was gone. He stood where she had left him.

That Hellene. Who was he? He must know. In a flash he thought; I do not want him hanging around Elissa. That last reflection was so strong, he wondered if he had said it aloud. What business was it of his? The Hellene was closer to her age. Yes, Hasdrubal and Dido all over again. But Elissa certainly was not another Dido, shallow and greedy. He held his breath, his whole body tense. As usual, he was harping on his own hurts. The question was, where did that snake came from?

She had said an asp. Asps weren't usually found in the city. The poisonous reptiles preferred a warm, drier climate. They weren't native to Tyre either. Was it really an asp? How did she know? Judging from the commotion around her, others apparently had had the same idea. He reviewed the scene. Abdmelkart, barely taller than Elissa, had been standing behind her, a step or two to the side, along with Asherat's Celtic slave. He was always noticeable in his towering blondness. Right behind her had been some men and women whom he recognized from the industrial area of the Byrsa. Did one of them have the asp? Had some family member Elissa treated died? Was this revenge? Hasdrubal decided to find out what Abdmelkart knew about the affair.

The Numidian squatted in the cool air on the opposite side of the temple. From that vantage point, he could see everything that went on in the courtyard. When he heard the whisper of the high priest's step on the temple portico, he sprang to open the door.

Hasdrubal went to the table where the slave had laid out wine and poured himself some. Keeping his back to Abdmelkart, he said, "What do you know about the business of the snake this morning?"

"An asp suddenly went across the arm of the priestess. A man from the city found and killed it."

"How do you know it was an asp?"

"When I was a boy, we had these snakes where I lived. They are very dangerous. The bite is deadly, but the death is painless."

"Did you see the snake?"

"Yes, sire. I saw it drop from the priestess' arm."

"Where did it come from?"

"Somebody had it, sire." Abdmelkart thought, best keep my suspicions to myself.

"The stranger in Greek dress?"

"I don't think so, sire. He was on the other side of the priestess."

Someone who knows her then, thought Hasdrubal.

"Thank you, Abdmelkart. That will be all tonight."

The slave hurried off to his kitchen bedroll, leaving his master to pace the living room. Up and down, back and forth, around in a circle, he went, his mind going over and over the same bits of information. Instinct told him the snake had not been accidental. First Hanno, now Elissa. Could the two be connected?

He had considered whether someone wanted the honor of being high priest of Tanit. With Gisgo dead and if Hanno were murdered, there would be no male in the family to fill his position after him. However, if the attempt on Hanno and this incident with Elissa were related, succession could not be the issue.

His eyes narrowed. No breath of scandal had ever come from Asherat's family. Of her six children, the first, a daughter, had died in infancy. The second little girl had died of some childhood disease soon after Asherat gave birth to her first son. Her family had been devastated.

There had been two more boys, then the last child was a daughter. All had grown to adulthood except the middle boy. Sickly since birth, he died at eleven. Hasdrubal knew the eldest son. He was in the senate and had a brilliant political future. Her other son was in business in Rome. As his life in Carthage had been a continuous stream of dinner parties, their paths had seldom crossed.

On the rare occasion that Hasdrubal had been in their home, he had been aware of the devotion that enveloped the whole family. That was one reason he had been so pleased to accept Asherat's overture after the death of her husband. As far as he could tell, the priestesses in her care adored her. True, she disliked Elissa, but an asp! Somehow an asp wasn't in character.

In spite of Abdmelkart's comment, he wondered about the

Hellene. Elissa apparently didn't know him. Or did she? Perhaps she had met him in the course of her work with Alcibiades. He could have struck up a speaking acquaintance with her as a priestess passing back and forth across the city to treat patients. Her statements hadn't sounded as if she knew him. Was she deliberately obfuscating? If she did not know him, why was he in the temple? Greeks did not worship Tanit.

How he wished for word from Ahiram, some clue to Elissa's background. In the meantime, he would have to protect her. He wouldn't be able to live with himself if she met with an accident while walking to Alcibiades'. Starting the next morning, one of the young priests would accompany her. He gave himself the task of tracking down the Hellene. This caused him some trepidation. He looked so much like him that any inquiry on his part might cause talk. He would have to frequent the forum, he concluded.

For the next few days, Hasdrubal made daily trips into the forum, hoping for a chance encounter. He walked past the great library, the beautiful small building from which the two suffetes administered the affairs of government, the Egyptian-looking building that housed the Council of One Hundred. All were dominated by the sandstone senate building at the end. He never failed to observe that although the forum wasn't symmetrical, it was aesthetically attractive.

Wherever, whenever he walked, his observation missed nothing. On these forays into the forum, his senses were even more acute. He sought the man, but at a distance. He wanted to follow, not confront, him. Useful bits of information were necessary before confrontation. To no avail. He fought discouragement, shaking his head in disbelief.

If the stranger were doing business in Carthage, the forum was the place to be. Any Greek knew that. Just residing in the city, sooner or later, every man came to the forum, to hear the latest news, gossip, meet friends, see and be seen, savor the heartbeat of the city. The Greek did not appear.

12

*T*his is pointless, Hasdrubal said to himself after a long, aimless stroll in the forum. I have better ways to spend time than pretending to be enjoying the afternoon sun and talking with family friends. I will have to devise another tracking method. Right now, I will pay a call on Saphonisba, see how Batbaal is faring, and then get back to my own business.

He turned abruptly and headed for the walking street that led to the top of the Byrsa.

His niece was in the garden with her mother. She was thin, but her natural vivaciousness was slowly reasserting itself, a smile here, a titter there, an arm flung out in excitement to match a sudden sparkle of her black eyes. Like a thrilled little girl bursting with news, she jumped from her chair and tripped toward him. "We have another skin from Mago," she said. "He hasn't left yet, so he received our scroll."

"You could have waited until your uncle sat down, my dear, before you told him," gently admonished Saphonisba.

"Never mind," said the high priest, giving Batbaal's arm a pat. "Tell me what Mago said." He steered her toward her seated mother.

"He said everything is in flux. Both armies are converging on Tyre. At first, he wanted to close the business and come home until the fighting was over. But he has decided to stay." Batbaal was smiling and chatty.

"What made him change his mind?" Hasdrubal smiled at the houseboy bringing a chair.

"He says the people of Tyre like King Antiochus. They know him; he has been in the city before. They expect his army to arrive any day. When he comes, they will open the gates and receive him. There won't be any fighting or any pillaging."

The high priest shook his head. "Do they think Pharaoh Ptolemy is going to allow that? Tyre belongs to Egypt now."

"If the pharaoh's army reaches Tyre, the king will meet them on the other side of the causeway. Tyre won't be harmed," she finished triumphantly.

"Well, that remains to be seen. More importantly, what did he say about you?"

"As soon as King Antiochus controls Tyre, you are to send me on the first available ship. Mago will let us know."

To Hasdrubal, remembering the stricken, drawn expression of the past weeks, Batbaal looked happy at the prospect of joining her husband.

"Mago seemed to think that would be soon," said Saphonisba.

"I would not be surprised," said Hasdrubal. "Antiochus is showing great promise as a ruler. He is wise enough to give the cities under him a certain amount of leeway. Naturally, the citizens like that and are loyal. Whether Ptolemy puts up a fight for Tyre is what we don't know. The Egyptians are good fighters once they make up their minds."

The old nursemaid appeared and announced that the young mistress was needed. After Batbaal left, Saphonisba cocked her head and said, "My dear, I'm glad she was called away. I want to talk to you."

Her voice and attitude struck him as secretive and slightly disconcerted. How unlike her, he thought. He prepared himself for disagreeable news.

"I spent a few days at our estate in Megara. I wanted to discuss the new grape vines with the overseer and the weaving with the women in the work rooms."

Why exclude Batbaal from a decision concerning the estate? He contracted his brow in puzzlement.

"Late in the afternoon," she continued, "as I was experimenting with some wool, I walked to the edge of the pool then nearly toppled in when I saw you standing at the other end—you as a man of, what, twenty-three?"

Hasdrubal stopped breathing. Stillness settled over him. It was the Hellene. She also saw the resemblance.

"He apologized, saying that he hadn't been able to rouse anyone and was looking for the two slaves from the estate down the road. He knew they worked in the weaving room. Then, he said a strange thing, Hasdrubal. He said he was living in that house and that his mother was Dido, a Carthaginian." She stopped and gripped the seat of her chair. She leaned toward him. "Are you all right? You are as white as your robe."

"Yes" was barely audible. Then, in a flat, far-away voice, he said, "He is my son."

Saphonisba's eyes bulged. After a moment, she said, "My dear, you must not have understood me."

"I understood you very well," he said calmly, aware of his surging pride in this handsome young man. "If he says his mother is Dido of Carthage, then he is my son."

"My dear, you can't be serious," she insisted. "He claims Diodorus of Athens as his father."

"The fact that he believes Diodorus is his father does not change the truth." The high priest rearranged the long bands of his scarf across his legs.

Saphonisba shook her head. Silence lay between them, each lost in thought. Finally, she said, "Have you met him?"

"No."

"Then how can you be so sure?"

"I saw him once at the public fountain near the main road. Like you, I thought I was seeing myself twenty years ago. It was eerie. Then on the day of the spring festival, he showed up at the temple." The high priest examined the fingernails of his right hand. "I have been haunting the forum, hoping to run into him. The resemblance was too great for me to start asking people questions."

"He is living in that house. His mother left it to him." So this was part of that old scandal, Saphonisba thought. Dido must not have known she was pregnant when she ran off. Poor Hasdrubal. What a shock. No wonder he turned white. He was living the whole sordid mess over again in that instant.

"Dido is dead?"

"I assume. He didn't say specifically." What kind of a woman was Dido to do such a thing? Her mother had been considered superficial and greedy. Was Dido? Hasdrubal had been in love for the first time; his judgment on her character would be slanted. She herself was so young when it all happened that she had no independent opinion of Dido. She only vaguely remembered the scandal. What characteristics had she imparted to this exceedingly attractive young man? What did he have of Hasdrubal, beside looks?

"Dido must have taught him something about our goddess," said Hasdrubal after a long silence.

"Because he came to the festival? Maybe; maybe not. Festivals and great parties under public porticoes are the only forms of entertainment we have. And the parties are given by politicians looking for votes. This is a hardship for the fun-loving Hellenes."

He brushed that off. "If he shows any interest in Tanit and our rituals, he could, as my son, become high priest."

Saphonisba bridled. Her son was to be the high priest of Tanit. "My dear, you can't just walk up to him and say, 'You're my son; be high priest of Tanit.' He wouldn't believe you. And he probably worships Athenian gods. You don't know what he's like or anything about him."

Gently, she continued. "Besides, Hanno is the son of the oldest son. He is going to be high priest."

Hasdrubal felt as if he had been hit in the gut by a iron bar. Saphonisba, Senator Elibaal, Bimilcar, all were determined that Hanno be high priest. As long as there was no other family male, he also agreed. His hope was that Batbaal would have another son. If so, he would educate Hanno and prepare him for another life's work. The others either couldn't or wouldn't see the boy's unsuitability. Besides, he thought, his son had as much right as Hanno. Bimilcar gave up the first right of his progeny to inherit when he ran away.

Instantly, he felt ashamed. His concern should be for the best interests of the temple. Saphonisba was correct; he knew nothing of his son, but promised himself he soon would. Skirting further discussion, he asked with diffidence, "Will you arrange a meeting?"

"If you wish. A small dinner, I think would be best—just the two of us, Batbaal and Aristide."

"Aristide! Is that his name?"

"Yes. I'll invite him, then say at the last minute that you are joining us."

13

*F*our people, smiling under the glow of wall-socket flares, lay on couches in Batbaal's dining room with its frescoes of musicians. Two of those people had dressed to make an impression. Hasdrubal emphasized his role as high priest of Tanit by arranging a wide embroidered stole across his shoulders. Its intricate patterns in many colors suited his purpose. All eyes instantly slid unseeing across his face and focused on the exquisite workmanship.

Aristide wore an expensive white tunic in the height of fashion, deliberately caught with a gold pin so that the draping fabric showed to advantage his perfectly proportioned young body. No color distracted the eye of the viewer from traveling back up his torso to rest on his handsome features and brilliant smile. Aristide's manners matched the perfection of his form, and he used every nuance to enhance the impression he made. Even his slightly accented language added to the impression.

With instinctive sensitivity, Saphonisba had arranged the dining couches so that she sat next to Aristide, Hasdrubal across beside Batbaal. That way, Batbaal wouldn't look at the two men, her gaze casually shifting from one to the other, then sharpening as she found this or that feature similar. As it turned out, the only comment on their resemblance was made in offhanded delight by Aristide.

"Isn't it amusing! The high priest and I have the same type of large nose."

Everybody looked around and laughed, except the high priest who allowed the corners of his mouth to curve upward. Yes, wasn't it strange.

The conversation turned to Dido. "Mother," said Aristide, allowing a faint longing to creep into his voice, "was a very beautiful woman."

A shudder passed through Hasdrubal.

"She was tall and a bit heavy with black hair and serious black eyes." Aristide hesitated. "Occasionally, if I surprised her, I saw something in their depths I couldn't fathom."

The black eyes that I knew, thought Hasdrubal, sparkled and danced. Did you regret, Dido? Did you think of me? Darling girl, I would have devoted my life to keeping that sparkle in your eyes. And our son would have been trained from childhood to take the reins of the temple. We would have had others. The succession would have been secure. Wave after wave of the consuming love he had felt for the young Dido enveloped Hasdrubal. Through the years, he had gotten over the emotional intensity. With maturity, he had understood more of Dido's true character. Now, watching and listening to their son, his love for her flooded through him, making him flushed and hot. Moisture erupted on his palms. He surreptitiously rubbed one in the folds of his robe.

Feeling Saphonisba's eyes, he shifted his gaze from Aristide and met her look. It warned him to take care.

The high priest picked up his wine goblet. Without actually drinking, he took some into his mouth to moisten his tongue and let the coolness of the liquid wash around his lips.

Aristide was looking at Batbaal.

"Her clothes were always midnight blue and the green you have on tonight," he said, smiling at her.

Batbaal lowered her head slightly, her face alive, acknowledging his implied compliment.

How attractive and charming you are, my son, thought Hasdrubal, your mother's olive skin, her height, and my curly hair, if I let it grow. And you are clean-shaven. It becomes you well.

"If the himation that floated behind her was one color," said Aristide, "her dress was the other." A sad expression crossed his face, and he looked ruefully at each one around the table. "I miss her."

If only I could tell you that I loved your mother, thought Hasdrubal, that it is I who am your father. Someday, when the time is ripe, when we have become friends, I will. You are a Carthaginian. The high priest's full heart overflowed and sang with joy as he watched his son.

"I'm sure you miss her," said Saphonisba. "You take your good looks from your mother."

"She must have been very proud of you," Batbaal said, leaning toward Aristide.

He colored at their praise. "My mother loved Carthage."

"She taught you our language, didn't she?" Batbaal smiled.

"Yes, but I didn't speak it much until I came here. When I grew older," he said, moving the conversation away from himself, "I understood that she regretted not being in this place. What else was behind those stony eyes, I don't know and guess I never will. When she was sad she would caress me tenderly, differently. Once, I mentioned this to her. She just laughed and said it was my imagination."

Blood pulsated behind Hasdrubal's eyeballs, but he calmly took a piece of bread from the table placed beside his dining couch. "What caused her death?"

"An accident. I was feasting with friends at home one night when my father came rushing—"

I am your father, thought Hasdrubal.

"—out of their bedroom yelling 'Get a doctor. Your mother has had an accident.' Naturally, we all scattered. My father is a stern, bitter man. He kept mother confined to the house the way Athenian women are, and he wouldn't let me see her."

Ill feeling exists between the two, thought Hasdrubal. How deep? Was it true dislike or just generational differences? And why?

"The doctor arrived." Aristide sighed. "When he came out of their room, his lips were pressed tight together. He gave my father a hard look, said 'She's dead,' and left."

"How tragic, dear Aristide," said Batbaal.

The high priest suddenly felt sad. But, he thought, I can listen to talk of Dido without that deep anger. He found it hard to believe. So quickly. All because he realized that Dido had continued to love him. His eyes sought those of Saphonisba. In her subtle way, she communicated encouragement.

"Then we went into the bedroom together, my father and I. She lay on the bed, her gold chains carefully straight and a sheer dark blue veil over her face. We both cried. But I don't know exactly what happened. Nothing was disturbed in the room."

Her mother's daughter in every way, Batbaal offered instant sympathy. "Dear Aristide, I'm so sorry. If you ever need company or just want to talk, you are welcome in my home. Mother and I would be pleased to receive you."

"Thank you, lady," said Aristide, neatly covering his surprise at the freedom of Carthaginian women. "You are most kind."

Strange, thought Hasdrubal. In spite of his gracious response, somehow he doubted Aristide would become a frequent visitor.

Aristide turned to the high priest. "And I should like to visit your temple again."

"Any time." Hasdrubal showed genuine pleasure.

Saphonisba's eyebrows rose slightly as she contemplated what was behind her brother-in-law's delight.

"How long do you plan to stay in Carthage?" asked the high priest.

"I'm not sure. Maybe forever." Aristide laughed.

Sobering, he added, "When I expressed an interest in seeing the house mother left me, father arranged for me to oversee his business here."

"What a generous thing for him to do," said Saphonisba.

"Thank you, Saphonisba." Aristide inclined his head.

Though his response and demeanor had denoted the very essence of courtesy, Hasdrubal's eyes narrowed. His son disliked Diodorus. It could even be deeper than dislike.

Again addressing the high priest, Aristide said, "How is Elissa, that lovely priestess? She had no aftereffects from her contact with the snake, I trust."

"No, she is fine." Hasdrubal did not encourage further conversation. Somehow, he didn't want to discuss her with his son.

The son persisted. "I should like to know her better."

"Forgive me for being blunt, but the priestesses in my temple do not receive gentlemen. We do not have temple prostitution."

Aristide's left eyebrow went up, giving him a quizzical look.

"My abject apologies, sire. That was not my meaning. However, I thought all temples connected with Baal had temple prostitution. The one in Athens does, and she was there."

The high priest ground his teeth, trying to keep his anger from showing. Was Aristide making up a story to cover his slip? Elissa had never said anything about being in Athens. But he had addressed her by name. Hasdrubal returned home determined to pry the truth from Elissa before he retired for the night.

Darkness shadowed the temple. The high priest secreted himself behind one of the pillars. He had discovered by accident that Elissa went late into the temple, and he intended to confront her there. He didn't have long to wait. The soft glow of a small lamp appeared at the other end of the portico and lighted Elissa's features as she turned into the entrance. She seemed to slip in as if she didn't want anybody to see her.

Something's wrong, thought Hasdrubal. Asherat? Alcibiades? I can't believe she is having trouble with Alcibiades. Is she in love with him? He drew down his mouth in distaste as understanding flashed like a comet across a starlit sky. You old fool. You are jealous. First, Aristide, now Alcibiades. Any man who mentions her name. Next, you will be spying on them.

At the picture of himself spying on Alcibiades, he gave a low, derisive burst of amusement. He was acting like a seventeen-year old. He had to help her if he could, if she would let him, but leave his own emotions out of it.

For a short time, he remained where he was, talking himself into the proper frame of mind.

Elissa headed straight for her secluded corner of the temple. Setting the lamp down, she curled her legs under her body and leaned against the wall. She had to hide her feelings about the high priest. But how not to let it show? If she stayed in Carthage, she would see him. She could not avoid him totally. Seven days had passed since she last reported to him. He would wonder. She must go to his office and report, simply and matter-of-factly as she had always done in the past. The trouble was, if she went to his workroom regularly, she might reveal her feelings. That would so mortify her that she would have to leave Carthage.

She leaned forward to move her lamp. She jumped. Sandaled feet had appeared beside her. She grabbed the lamp to raise it as a familiar voice said, "I didn't mean to startle you, Elissa."

The high priest dropped to her level. "May I sit here beside you?"

"Of course," she made a feeble gesture of acquiescence.

Ignoring her reticence, he said, "You have come to the temple late these last few nights. Is something bothering you?"

Did he see everything that went on in the temple or was he spying on her? She had done nothing. He had no reason to distrust her. She was slightly annoyed. Besides, she wanted to think about him, and here he was in the darkened, empty temple, sitting next to her. Withdrawn, she said, "I came to pray and think about how best to treat my patients."

"In that case, I will keep you but a short time. I have something I would like to discuss with you."

He sounded ominous. Two little worry lines formed on her brow. She sat still, an internal stillness that anticipated destruction.

"Do you know the young Hellene who helped you the morning of the festival?" His question was abrupt.

"No." She raised her eyes to his, amazement spreading over her face.

"He says you were in the Baal Temple in Athens."

She gave a little cry and ducked her head, turning her face from him.

"The time has come for you to tell me the truth."

Clasping her hands tightly in her lap, she continued to hang her head and say nothing.

After a minute, he said, "I am waiting, Elissa. Now."

"It's true," she began and swallowed. "I was in the Baal Temple in Athens for two years, but I never saw that man."

"Then how did he know you were there?"

"When he was so kind to me the day of the festival, I mentioned it. He's Athenian. I had been in Athens. It was just a remark."

"I find it strange that you, a Phoenician, would babble that to an Athenian stranger, but not tell us—unless you had something to hide."

"I have nothing to hide," she said defiantly. "I have told you the truth."

For a few minutes, he looked at her. Maybe she was telling the truth.

"Go on," he said. "I want to know what you were doing there. Why did you leave? And I want to hear the truth about why you left Tyre."

She drew up her legs and rested her chin on her knees. "My parents wanted me to marry a wealthy admiral, a friend of my father. But I loved a beautiful young man. We managed to avoid detection and spent one night together."

Elissa wanted to die. Why had she told him that! It had popped out. Now, he would think she had been one of the sacred prostitutes. Quickly, she tried to cover herself.

"We wanted to marry. I persuaded my grandfather to intervene on our behalf, and finally my parents consented. Before the wedding, he was killed in battle."

So she loved, too, thought Hasdrubal. Their lives had parallels. Had there been a scandal? Was that why she left Tyre? Did she have a child in Athens? His eye flicked over her. No, he decided.

"After that, I didn't object when my parents betrothed me to the old admiral. I was numb inside. If the marriage made them happy, fine. But he died before the marriage took place. That's when I went into the temple."

So, he had jumped too fast in searching for parallels.

With a sigh, she said, "My parents weren't happy about my being a priestess. They wanted me to marry. I think what they really wanted was grandchildren. But, anyway, when I had trouble with Ahiram and was thrown out, my father was furious. I thought he was furious with me. I didn't realize Ahiram was the one he was angry with. I was devastated. One night, taking an old slave with me, I ran away and boarded a ship for Athens."

She stopped.

Folding his hands, Hasdrubal maintained that position in silence.

"Now, I realize how preposterous my actions were, but at the time, I didn't care. I stayed at the Baal Temple in Athens until the pressure to join the sacred prostitutes became too great. I simply walked to the harbor one day and came here."

She threw up her arms. "That's all."

They sat side by side, each wondering how to cope with new love. Elissa wildly desired to brush against him, to experience the wave of physical excitement that she had felt the time they touched accidentally. What would he do? Probably move away. His voice broke into her fantasy.

"Asherat says you were with her in the temple the night Hanno was stabbed."

Elissa's mouth dropped open. "But I wasn't," she cried, rising to a kneeling position and facing him.

Even in the lamplight, he could see her flush, blotches of red on her cheeks and neck. By tensing all his muscles, he restrained himself from pulling her into his lap.

Her words came fast and furious. "If you are asking me if I stabbed Hanno, no, of course not. How could I possibly know he was there? I had no reason. He's just a boy." Collecting herself, she said, "I was caring for the pregnant girl until just before I saw you. The family will tell you."

"Sit down, Elissa. I believe you. Do you have any idea why she would say such a thing?"

"Please," she said, subsiding against the wall, "I don't like to tell tales."

"I want a direct answer to a direct question."

"The head priestess constantly tries to cause me trouble. No matter what I do, she twists it to put me in the wrong. She whispers innuendos to the priestesses, making me feel awkward. But it doesn't matter. I can live with it. I know why she hates me."

"Because of your behavior when you first came here?"

"Yes."

"Do the other priestesses get along well with her?"

"I think so. The ones she likes. She mothers them. The ones she doesn't like have learned to stay out of her way."

And you mother them, thought Hasdrubal.

Elissa added, "Hanno hasn't learned that. And for some reason, she hates him."

The high priest started. The day seemed full of pronouncements that had thrown him off balance. He needed to think. "I will leave you, Elissa. In the future, tell me the truth. I don't like finding it out from strangers." He stood up.

Her ears picked up the words "in the future." She had told him details of her life that she had told no one else, and he went right on treating her as evenly as always. Obviously, he didn't care what she did; his feeling for her was no different than for any other priestess in his temple. As long as she cared for the patients well and kept out of trouble, she could stay. Well, she would make him proud of her, she would report to him at stated intervals, she would fade quietly into the background, and he would never know how much she loved him.

Hasdrubal looked back. She had not moved. What an enigma she was. Even the things she had said tonight whetted his appetite. If only the word from Ahiram would come and throw some light on why she did the things she did.

Instead of going to bed, the high priest went to his library. He sat deep in thought for a long time. If Elissa's comment was right, the attack on her and on Hanno might be related. In that case, they came from inside his temple. He found it hard to accept what his instincts were telling him. He needed to talk to Hanno.

14

By late afternoon the following day, the dissimilar pieces were starting to come together—a snake, a nephew, a stabbing, and a priestess—but too many extraneous bits of information were insinuating themselves into his thoughts.

To clear his mind, Hasdrubal walked swiftly to the forum, his robe flapping about his ankles, the breeze striking his face. The physical exertion revived him. I should do more of this, he thought. His mind got dull dealing with the same thing day after day. The peninsula across the bay might be a good diversion. The crops should be planted on the temple estate, the livestock ready to give birth. Our family estate should be in the same condition. I cannot remember when I rode over last. Those estates are the basis of our wealth; it might be a good idea. Though, fortunately, the goddess has favored us with excellent overseers.

In the forum, he slowed down, commensurate with the dignity of his office. He looked at the buildings, the colorful dress of the crowd, the number of foreigners. He greeted acquaintances, even stopped to talk. He reached the foot of the senate building. Wondering whether to go in and tell Elibaal about his conclusions, he heard a well-known childish voice.

"Uncle Hasdrubal! Uncle Hasdrubal!"

Before he could turn, Hanno, his eyes bulging, breathing heavily and chattering gibberish, banged into him.

"Calm down, Hanno." Hasdrubal laid a firm, steadying hand on the boy's shoulder. "Now," he said when Hanno began to breathe more normally, "what happened?"

"Somebody tried to get a cloth around my neck. It hit my forehead, and I pushed it off." Both hands went to his forehead and gave a jerking shove through his hairline, knocking off his cap. "Somebody's trying to kill me." The worried little face gazed up at Hasdrubal.

"Pick up your hat, and we will walk back to the temple."

Hanno swept up the hat and rammed it on his head. "Somebody's trying to kill me," he repeated.

The high priest's arm reached across his nephew's shoulders and drew the boy to his side. They started along slowly.

"Hanno," Hasdrubal said, "why does the head priestess dislike you? Do you know?"

"Oh, that old priestess." Hanno sneered.

The high priest slitted his eyes. "Are you doing something to annoy her?"

Hanno looked up at the blue sky, the sun, the lovely day, and skipped.

"It is a beautiful day, Hanno, but that isn't going to distract me. I want an answer."

Silence. They continued to walk along, the man's arm still across the boy's shoulders. When they got close to the temple grounds, a small voice said, "I put snakes in her jars."

The high priest continued to place one foot calmly before the other. He ground his jaw and coughed. When he could, he said, "What kind of snakes?"

"Just little garden snakes."

"Why?"

"One day when I was passing by her workroom, I saw her bending over a box talking. I snuck in when she wasn't there and peeked. She had a little snake in the box. It almost got out. I clapped the lid down and hurried out of the room as fast as I could."

Hasdrubal gulped in his breath and held it. When he let it out, he said, "Hanno!" and gripped Hanno's arm so hard, the boy looked at him in fear, "we will go to my library."

As Hanno had never been invited to his uncle's library, he knew the matter was serious. He found himself propelled rapidly to the temple grounds and through the maze before his uncle's grip relaxed. Hasdrubal cast a swift glance around. Two minor priests were at the altar. Otherwise, the courtyard was empty. He knew that Asherat usually rested after the noon meal, and he assumed that her Celtic slave was either doing the same or was outside the temple. Of course! How stupid. The slave had been in the town.

"Abdmelkart," he said when the Numidian opened the door, "take my nephew to the library. I will follow in a minute."

Standing just inside his door, he watched the courtyard entrance. Seconds later, a wisp of blond hair, then a blue eye peered cautiously around the edge of the maze opening. Satisfied, Asherat's slave entered, looked neither right nor left, and walked with a sly, obsequious movement toward the administration building.

In his library, Hasdrubal dismissed Abdmelkart. Hanno was lying atop piled floor cushions.

Hasdrubal said, "The snake you saw the head priestess talking to was not the kind you put in her jars. It was an extremely poisonous snake. Its bite doesn't show. Do you understand me? You might have been killed without realizing you had been bitten."

He stopped to assess the effect of what he had said. His nephew paled, swerved to a sitting position, his feet together and his hands clutching his head.

"You are to stay as far away from Asherat as possible. You are also to avoid her slave. Go out of your way to avoid them. She apparently thinks you have a better understanding of her behavior than you do and so she doesn't like you."

Hanno's eyes got round and wide. "She doesn't like the priestess Elissa either."

The high priest looked at his nephew for a few moments. "I misjudged you. You understand the situation perfectly."

"I could leave and not be high priest."

"That is not necessary. This current situation will not last long. In fact, it may come to a head very soon."

"Will I die?"

"No. You will not be involved this time. But, Hanno, being high priest is a lifetime position. One day, you will be very proud to hold such a position in our city. You are restless now, I realize, but you will get over that and settle down."

Hanno's eyes slanted to the side as if he weren't sure.

"Would changing your assignments in the temple make you more accepting? I can do that. But as there is no other eligible person"—he hesitated—"at the moment, you will be high priest. And I know you understand that."

He gave Hanno an opportunity to express a wish, but the boy simply looked daggers from under lowered lids.

"You may go now." Hasdrubal laid an affectionate hand on his shoulder. "And remember what I said. Be extremely careful."

The boy bolted down the stairs. The high priest stood, his curled fingers pressed against his mouth, staring down the staircase. Then he turned, took writing materials from a niche, a skin from the stack, and wrote extensively, pointedly, to his brother. When he finally descended, Abdmelkart was waiting at the foot of the stairs. The slave fell to his knees, a wax tablet in his upraised hands.

"Sire, a slave from the hill has only now delivered this note from Saphonisba."

Hasdrubal took the tablet then looked questioningly at his slave who had not moved.

"And a scroll came this morning while you were gone," Abdmelkart said.

"Where is it?"

The Numidian darted across the room and lifted a scroll from beside the cream urn.

At a glance, Hasdrubal knew his answer had come from Ahiram. Grasping the papyrus scroll and the tablet, he returned to his library.

First, he read the wax tablet from Saphonisba.

My dear Hasdrubal, two things: We have heard from Mago. Tyre is in the hands of Antiochus. The Tyrian king sits on the throne as his vassel. We are to send Batbaal. I have checked the roster of ships leaving for Tyre. A suitable one departs two days hence with the noon tide.

Excellent, thought the high priest. The sooner the better.

Secondly, Aristide is most anxious to see more of you. He asked if he could visit you. I assured him by all means.

Hasdrubal laid the tablet aside for Abdmelkart to flame and smooth the wax. Aristide was not as anxious to see him as Elissa. Nevertheless, he did want his son to come to the temple. He hoped Aristide would understand the worship of Tanit, reverence temple functions, and accept the high priest's great responsibility to the community. Then one day, they would have a quiet talk, and no other person would stand between them. But in the meantime, he would keep Aristide away from Elissa.

The high priest broke the seal on Ahiram's scroll.

Dear friend, how delighted I am to hear from you and also to know the whereabouts of Elissa.

Let me apologize for the long delay in answering. As you know, all has been in flux here, but is now happily settled.

You ask about Elissa. I will admit to grave concern as we have heard nothing from her since she left Tyre. Shortly afterwards she sent word that she had entered the Baal Temple in Athens. I wrote to her there of her mother's death and again, recently, of her father's decline. Being with you, she has obviously not received my last scroll. Her father keeps asking for her. May I humbly pray that you tell her this!

You may wonder about our concern. Ordinarily what happens to a headstrong, runaway priestess is of no importance. But Elissa is a member of the royal house of Tyre.

The papyrus trembled, then was still. That does cast a different light on a lot of things, thought Hasdrubal. Her arrogant outspokenness, for one.

Elissa's mother, my half sister was the the most beautiful woman I have ever seen. She was my father's daughter with a minor concubine. When she came of age, our father, the king, married her to his favorite admiral, the son of an old aristocratic family. Elissa was their only child, the pampered darling of the entire court—particularly of my father who could deny her nothing.

Elissa was espoused to a young army man. None of us thought the marriage suitable, but after much begging on her part, the king, consented. My father was at the end of his days, tired and frail. I personally thought he consented to keep her quiet. Before the wedding took place, the man was killed in battle. The family promptly arranged a marriage we all thought eminently satisfactory. Elissa agreed to it, but I don't think she realized the import of what she was doing. She walked around in a dream world. My heart ached for her.

The betrothal was conducted at court with great ceremony. The intended groom was a widower, a man older than I. He also died but a handful of days later. She showed no feeling one way or the other. She was still grieving for the young man. When she expressed an interest in becoming a priestess, I arranged that. Against the wishes of her father, I must say.

That was autumn. By spring, I began getting complaints

about the priestesses offered to the god. They were refusing the men who came to the temple. I discovered that Elissa was lecturing them on their bodily functions and urging them to refuse the more violent men.

Hasdrubal whistled under his breath. What a novel idea.

We called the priestesses together and informed them that they were women; they had no right to refuse. They would perform their sacred duties or be sold in the slave market. Elissa was put in charge of the orchestra priestesses. Soon, those girls were all stirred up about getting married.

That sounds familiar, too, thought Hasdrubal.

I suggested she leave the temple. Perhaps she has told you why she chose to leave Tyre. I am not sure I fully understand why. She certainly created a furor here, and her father blamed me, I think unjustly.
Your temple is administered differently than mine. Elissa may not cause you those problems. However, I certainly would not put her in charge of any priestesses.

Ahiram was right about that. But the problem no longer existed.

The scroll concluded with a political discussion. The citizens of Tyre were thankful to be in Antiochus' hands. Ahiram added that his older brother was acting for Antiochus.

Hasdrubal let the scroll drop. Did he have to tell Elissa that her mother was dead? Perhaps she might be interested in going to Tyre with Batbaal. She could visit her father, then return to Carthage. At least, he hoped she would return.

Was she opposed to marriage? Assuming she would look at him, would she consider being his wife?

Rising abruptly, he called Abdmelkart.

"Ask the Priestess Elissa to come to my audience chamber."

He was standing in the middle of the chamber, thoughtfully pulling at his chin, when she arrived.

"Elissa," he said gently, "a scroll has come from Ahiram with some sad news."

He saw her tense.

"Your father is failing rapidly. He is asking for you."

Pain crossed her face, and she lowered her eyes.

He continued. "Did you receive a scroll from Ahiram while you were in Athens?"

"If you mean about my mother, yes."

He took a step toward her then stopped and put his hands behind him.

"In two days, my niece sails for Tyre. Would you like to go with her?"

She looked up quickly. There were tears in her eyes. "Are you sending me away?"

Before he could stop himself, he said, "My dear, I will never send you away. I meant," he said coldly, "for you to see your father and return to Carthage."

Her ear caught the endearment, and her heart skipped a beat. Oh, foolish girl, she said to herself, that's just a figure of speech. He means nothing by it. Notice how indifferent he was afterwards.

"You don't have to decide this minute. Let me know by tomorrow so I can make the arrangements." He added, "You may stay here if you want to think."

Hasdrubal went to his library and flung himself on the floor cushions. How could he have made such a stupid slip? She would get the idea he cared. That was also stupid. He did care. If she went to Tyre, he would have time to get hold of himself and reassess the situation. Maybe he would ask her if starting marriage negotiations with her family was acceptable to her. He was a Phoenician aristocrat; Ahiram was an ally. There should be no objection to his suit. As for Elissa herself, she, too, had been in love once. She might be willing to settle down with him. They weren't a bad match.

Elissa walked to the closest wall of the audience chamber and laid her heated forehead against the cold plaster. Fortunately, she had told the high priest the truth that night in the temple. Ahiram must have given him a general outline because the high priest hadn't mentioned her actions, only her father.

She vividly remembered the last time she saw him. It was in the garden of their palace. He had fallen asleep on the cushions laid for him. His beard, filled with gray, lay on his chest, and his mouth was slightly open, deep red in the mass of black and gray.

He had looked so peaceful lying there with the slave standing guard nearby and the insects humming in the flower beds.

That was the memory of him she wanted to keep instead of the rage he had flown into when she told him that she was leaving the temple. His face had turned muddy red as he screamed at her and at the slaves. Thinking that his anger was directed against her, she had run, crushed, to her rooms. She was sure that if she had been beautiful like her mother, he would have shown more sympathy. With tears still damp on her cheeks, she started to plan her escape.

While he slept, she had stood watching him a long time. She so wanted him to speak to her, give her some little indication that he loved her, but he did not wake up. She had blown him a kiss with her hand and stolen away.

What good would it do now to go back to Tyre? He might be dead before she arrived. And then there would be Ahiram. Elissa made a decision. She would not go. Ahiram might try to keep her in Tyre, and she couldn't live without being near the high priest.

She would write to Ahiram, telling him she wouldn't come because of her duties, and to her father. She wanted him to know that she loved him, how she had misunderstood and been hurt by his anger. She would ask for his forgiveness. If only he lived long enough to receive her scroll! She wiped the corner of her eye with her himation. If not, she would at least have made contact with Ahiram. Her life was here in Carthage. The high priest had said he would never send her away, and she believed him.

Holding her head high, Elissa left the audience chamber.

Asherat, coming from the temple, saw Elissa leaving the high priest's house. Instinctively, she drew back into the temple. She didn't want Elissa to see her. Hasdrubal, she thought, is getting much too involved with that female. He lets her do whatever she wants. It's too bad.

15

*A*bdmelkart announced from the open workroom door that Aristide awaited him. Much as Hasdrubal wanted to spend time with his son, this afternoon was not the time. Batbaal sailed the next morning, and he had a number of chores to accomplish.

He had already spent too much time at the ship. The captain, a native of Tyre and part owner of the vessel, came highly recommended, but Hasdrubal had wanted to talk to make his own judgments.

Well satisfied after the interview, he had asked to inspect the accommodations set aside for his niece and her attendants. The captain apologized, saying that the cramped quarters were the best he had. Hasdrubal brushed it off, "No ship has better." The Tyrian bowed at the compliment.

"And you personally will hand her to her husband."

"I will, sire."

With relief, the high priest had settled himself at his desk. And now this interruption.

With a frustrated sigh, he set aside the instructions that he was writing to the overseer of the temple estate across the bay. Pressures seemed never ending.

Keeping his head down, his eyes on the ground, absorbed, he made his way to his private audience chamber. The minute he set eyes on Aristide, his annoyance evaporated, replaced by joy. This fine man was his son. He was young, he would have many children, the succession of the priesthood would be secure. How he longed to call him son, to speak of religion, to help him follow Tanit, to tell him what an important and worthy future could be his as high priest. Training at such a late stage in life was not the best approach, but his son was intelligent.

Aristide was examining the frescoes. His head tilted to one

side, he stood in front of a rendition of Tanit as the wife of Baal. She was offering her husband a bowl filled with the produce of the earth, the blooming that he created year after year on his return.

Hasdrubal cleared his throat.

The young man swiveled around. His face lit up as he greeted the high priest. "These are superb, you know," he said, waving his hand to take in the frescoes. "Carthage has so little good painting and sculpture. Everything that I've seen like this is probably done by Hellenes."

"You are quite a connoisseur, my—boy." The high priest bit his tongue. "These were done by an Athenian at my father's behest. He was a collector of Hellenic things. All of the furniture in my home is Hellenic."

"I was brought up surrounded by beautiful statuary and painting." He shrugged and smiled. "It's practically on every street corner. I find Carthage pretty sterile, you know. Not just your art; your young men. There aren't any parties. What do they do?"

"They work. Don't young Hellenes?"

"Not my class," sniffed Aristide. "I'm at a loss here and thought maybe you could help me."

"Involve yourself in the work of one of the temples—this one, for instance. We have lay priests. There is much to interest a bright young man such as yourself."

"There certainly is." Aristide laughed.

The laugh contained an unsavory note. Brushing the wisp of a warning from his mind, Hasdrubal said, "If you will walk with me, I will show you the extensive workings of our temple."

They started along the side of the temple building, reversing the path the sacrificial animals took to the high altar. Brilliant shafts of light danced on the whitewashed administration buildings. They took their time, talking companionably, one questioning, the other explaining. Aristide bubbled with enthusiasm; Hasdrubal smothered his happiness. They arrived at the water trough in the large animal yard. A group of novice priests led a regal black bull to a pen across the yard.

Aristide stopped short. "I have never seen such a fine animal," he said. "The short, sturdy legs, the long back, the haunches, the black head. Do you breed them around here?"

"They come from the temple estate as do our sheep and goats. We keep one or two of the larger animals here so we have them ready for festivals or unexpected emergency sacrifices."

"My mother told me that the landed aristocracy had great estates." Aristide sounded excited. "That's where you get your tremendous wealth from."

"That and trade. Don't forget, Phoenicians are traders."

"My mother's family were traders, you know. I knew them. They came to Athens to visit us and were lost at sea when they went back. Mother cried and cried. After that, my parents got along even worse than before. Somehow, I think it had to do with me, but—" He lifted his shoulders and dropped them. "Well, my grandparents objected to my being so fat. They said I looked bloated."

"I find your being fat hard to believe," said Hasdrubal.

"I lost it after mother died. She always said she liked me fat and plied me with sweets. I rarely eat them anymore. I don't even crave them."

Was keeping her son fat Dido's way of masking his features?

"How old were you when your grandparents came to visit?" Hasdrubal asked.

"Sixteen. It seems ages ago. I'm going to be twenty-four, you know."

Hasdrubal raised an eyebrow in fake surprise. Of course, he knew; he had worked it out with care.

"Let us look in on the shops," he said, leading Aristide through a small door in a wall.

They entered an inferno of a courtyard. Heat from a blazing open oven and white-hot metal competed with the afternoon sun. A horde of muscular, naked, sweaty, hairy men tended the oven or shaped the glowing metal. Their sight disgusted Aristide. It's a wonder, he thought, that they didn't strike each other as they swung those heavy mallets. The noise was appalling. He watched the high priest stride into the center of the narrow shop, speak by name to the men around him, and pat one on the shoulder. Ugh! How could he!

Hasdrubal beckoned him. He showed Aristide metalworkers fitting pipe, woodworkers, glassblowers, stonecutters, until Aristide's head swam.

"Is this normal in Carthage?" he asked as they entered the school building. "Temples in Athens don't have all this activity."

"Many here do not. My great-grandfather added the metalworkers and glassblowers. He expanded the woodworker and stonecutter areas when he enlarged the school building. Now, our temple is like the great temples in Egypt. Originally, this building was exactly like my home, creating perfect—"

A sudden gasp from Aristide caused the high priest to look at his son. Aristide's eyes bulged, hard and bright. In them, Hasdrubal saw fascination, disbelief, admiration, desire, in rapid succession. He didn't need to turn to see why. He knew, but turned anyway. Elissa was visible through the open clinic door, Elissa in profile. She was splinting a child's arm. As she bent over, her robe billowed forward, outlining her lithe body. The white fabric clung softly to every curve.

Aristide saw her slim hips and rounded buttocks. With the fullness in front, he couldn't see her breasts, but pictured them as high and pointed. I'd like to get into her, he thought. This rigid old high priest insists there is no sacred prostitution in Carthage. What an innocent! She isn't even from Carthage. She'd give a man a good ride. I'll bet anything she was a prostitute in the Athens temple.

Hasdrubal's voice interrupted his fantasy. "You have already met our temple doctor." He moved along, drawing the unwilling Aristide with him.

"I didn't know she was your doctor." After a slight pause, Aristide said, "Now I know where to come if I'm sick."

"No. There is a fine doctor in our city, Alcibiades of Delos. You should go to him."

"I would much rather have Elissa treat me." Aristide smiled at secret animal pleasure and enjoyment.

No, no, my son, thought the high priest. This woman is mine. Yet if Elissa chose the younger, handsomer man, he would be helpless. By her own admission, she liked handsome young men.

In misery, Hasdrubal finished showing his son the school building and escorted him to the maze. As they parted, Aristide said, "I wish to know more about your temple and religion. I shall come again, if I may."

"Of course." Hasdrubal voiced his assent with a twinge of reservation. Two sets of feelings raced through him, tripping over each other, mixing and separating, pulling him in different directions. He hoped Aristide would replace Hanno, leaving Hanno in reserve, next in succession, until there were other male children in the family. But if Aristide were around the temple, how could he keep him from Elissa?

As he watched Aristide disappear through the maze, Hasdrubal told himself in no uncertain terms that the succession came first.

16

"Your ship is just beyond the ivory warehouse," Hasdrubal called out. They were part way down the wharf beside the commercial harbor, Batbaal and her mother each in a litter. "It is good sized and sturdy," said the high priest. Walking between them, he adapted his strides to the smooth pace of the litter bearers.

Batbaal had seen ships all her life, but she observed this one with close attention. Though the three banks of oars were drawn up, she could make out the rowers already in place, ready to maneuver the ship through the harbor. The large square sail, tied securely around the cedar of Lebanon mast, swayed high above the dock. Sailors lounged over the rail at the prow, scanning the crowd. A stern beaching ladder hung down the vessel side. Planks had been laid from the deck to the wharf for laborers loading the ship. Twittery and excited, Batbaal felt the urge to pat—for good luck—the ship's turned-back sternpost. It looked like a goose neck. But she resisted, not daring to risk comment from her uncle.

He had tried and tried, unsuccessfully, to get her and her mother started for the wharf early. The fault had been hers. What with last-minute packing, saying good-bye to the servants, reapplying kohl after her tears, she just hadn't been able to get away. Now there wouldn't be much time for her mother and uncle. She hadn't even seen Hanno yet. Oh, dear! They were already at the gangplank. For all her joy at going to her husband, Batbaal was upset to leave these dear people who meant so much to her.

Holding her hand to steady her as she alighted from the litter, Hasdrubal thought Mago would be pleased with his wife's appearance. Her cheeks bloomed, and she had gained some weight. She was sweet and submissive, but she had inherited her mother's strength of character. She would have no trouble managing a household in a strange land.

"My dear, where is Hanno?" asked Saphonisba, surveying the dock. "He knows his sister is leaving Carthage."

"He is expected here."

Time did not allow for more. The captain greeted them at the top of the gangplank. "We sail shortly," he said with a deep bow. "Please follow me." He took them to his quarters and graciously left them.

Hasdrubal handed his niece the neatly wrapped bundle that he carried. "A child's precious ashes," he said.

Batbaal's hand flew to her mouth. Her eyes widened. So the grave in the Tophet where she had placed offerings didn't contain her son's ashes.

"May the gods give you another son," he said as she dropped to her knees, her eyes glistening. He glanced at Saphonisba. Hers had the same shine. Leaving them alone, he idled along the deck. Women's tears made him uncomfortable.

His sister-in-law soon overtook him. Together, they stood on the wharf giving last-minute instructions to Batbaal who clung to the rail, flanked by two serving women and a broad-shouldered Egyptian slave.

Sailors untied the ropes holding the ship to the dock and scrambled up the beaching ladder. With minimum pulling and backing on the oars, the crew slowly maneuvered the ship out into the harbor. Mother and daughter waved. It might be years before they saw each other again. Saphonisba would not only miss her daughter, but the babyhood of any grandchildren. Much as he sympathized, the high priest hoped the tears that glittered on her lower lids wouldn't trickle down.

When they could no longer see Batbaal, Saphonisba beckoned for her litter. Hasdrubal brushed perspiration from the cap edge above his ear. The day had turned unusually hot.

"My dear," she said, "you could have used Batbaal's litter instead of sending it back to the Byrsa."

"Me! Ride in a litter! Because the sun is a little warm! Really, Saphonisba, I prefer to walk." He strode at her side. They were silent while the bearers maneuvered the litter through stacked copper ingots ready for loading.

"I didn't know that you had kept Gisgo's ashes," Saphonisba said.

"I thought it advisable." His eyes met hers. "The kid's ashes will serve as a memento in the Tophet."

"As usual, my dear Hasdrubal, you are kindness itself in your care of us."

He flushed slightly at her praise. Perhaps it was the heat. The sun beat down on him in his priest's robe. He noticed how its light glanced off the bodies of the Numidian litter bearers and the sway of their light-weight wool skirts. It sparkled on the gently lapping water of the commercial harbor, and covered the roof of the three-story central island drydock in the military harbor with golden light. The Admiral, sitting on top of the building in his lookout post, must be hot. As the bearers walked, their shoulder muscles rippled. They moved in rhythm, a smooth flow of body, like a woman carrying a jar on her head. Light-reflecting globules of perspiration formed patterns along their foreheads and over their noses. The oily faces of laborers loading heavy cargo on various gangplanks showed the same sweat patterns.

Summer weather had arrived with a vengeance, though it was only late spring.

"You did allow Hanno to come, didn't you, my dear?" Saphonisba cut short his reverie.

"I gave him leave to go up the Byrsa so he could accompany you to the ship."

"He never came. I thought you were keeping him at the temple for some reason."

"I will find out," was all the high priest said. Was she worried about another attempt on Hanno's life? She didn't know about the second attempt. He had thought it best not to tell her. To his surprise, she said, "My dear, do you suppose he has run away?"

Running away had not even entered his mind. He half expected to find Hanno's lifeless body at the temple. However, if Hanno had run away, the timing couldn't be better. He was excused early. There was confusion at Batbaal's home. Saphonisba had no opportunity to stop and fuss about Hanno's whereabouts.

The high priest discovered a number of facts by surreptitious inquiry at the temple. Hanno was excused early in the day by the chief scribe to go to his sister's. A number of priests saw him leave the compound. Asherat was concerned about the health and business of her son in Rome. She was with the chief of sacrifices all morning. Her slave was with her.

Hasdrubal sent a message to Saphonisba: yes, apparently, though he couldn't be sure quite yet, Hanno seemed to have run away.

Days went by with no sign of Hanno. Saphonisba was distraught. The high priest put out a notice all over Carthage: had anyone seen a short boy in priestly robes in the city four days back? That was the day that had turned so hot. Please report to the temple of Tanit.

A sometime trader, who drank too much and hung around the docks, produced the only lead. He had seen Hanno running along the wharf with two sailors. The sailors' country of origin? The man's eyes glazed and stared blankly at the high priest. Well, that is that, thought Hasdrubal. Although, if true, I fully expect that Hanno will inform us of his whereabouts once the ship lands. He motioned Abdmelkart to reward the fellow and cast aside the information.

Ironically, right in the middle of searching for Hanno, a thin skin scroll came from Bimilcar. Hasdrubal turned it over and over. His brother, he thought, had not had time to receive his last communication and reply. Halfway up the stairs to his library, he stopped short, one foot already on the next rise. Had Hanno gone to his father? Impossible. Where else would he go?

He took the remaining steps two at a time. In the library, he dropped heavily upon the floor cushions and unrolled the skin. Bimilcar had never before plunged right in without a greeting.

My wife tells me that you think Hanno may run away. By this age, he should have some sense. Apparently he doesn't. What he needs is strong discipline. You are too easy on him. If he ever turns up in camp, I'll send him back to you in chains. He will be high priest of Tanit. It is his duty to his family. He must be made to understand that. And that is my last word on the subject.

"Just the way you became high priest of Tanit, brother," whispered Hasdrubal. "You are not the one to talk about family duty." Though, he thought, Bimilcar certainly had learned duty after he got what he wanted as his life's work. Hanno wouldn't be bound by tradition any more than his father had been. Nonetheless, there was a difference. Bimilcar had left him to take over the priesthood. Hanno left nobody—except possibly Aristide.

Here in New Carthage preparations go on. Hannibal has dismissed the local troops to return to their own cities. This is to leave them well disposed toward him. He has arranged for the defense of

Africa. Hispanic troops are already stationed there, as you know, having written me that you hoped to see them. He has given his younger brother the administration of Hispania, leaving him infantry, cavalry, and naval forces for the defense of the country.

Imilce, his wife, pleads with him daily to let her come on the campaign instead of being sent to Carthage. He told me he will not allow it. I agree. Having her along would worry him, as does leaving her in New Carthage. Everybody knows the brutality of the Romans toward prisoners. What the outcome will be, I don't know. It will be settled soon because, by the time this reaches you, if all goes well, we will have set out toward the north.

Hasdrubal laid the letter in the niche beside the others. Bimilcar had been of no help whatsoever on the question of Hanno's whereabouts. Would Bimilcar's attitude change when he received his most recent letter? Hasdrubal headed for the stairs. His brother's wishes were after the fact and, therefore, unimportant. Hanno had taken things into his own hands. Until they knew where he was, all they could do was wait.

17

*E*ager and full of questions, Aristide became a frequent visitor at the temple. Nothing was too minute for his interest. He even helped Elissa with particularly difficult patients. At first, Hasdrubal bridled, jealously watching. But the contact seemed innocuous enough. There was no dallying. On the other hand, his relationship with Aristide seemed to blossom—an understanding glance, the sensed sameness of feeling and purpose, like father, like son. Deep, pervasive joy greeted his waking body each morning. To his surprise, his attitudes were changing. For the better, he realized. A priestess, no more than a child, smiled as she passed by him in the school corridor. She didn't look scared.

Hasdrubal emerged from the temple into a cool, dark night. Broaching the subject of parentage occupied his thoughts. A small light moved near the entrance to the school building. "Stop!" he called and swiftly descended on the bulky shadow. Aristide stood holding a lamp.

"I cut my foot," he said. "I was looking for Elissa."

"Come to my audience chamber," Hasdrubal said, his speech calm and quiet, but with anger building like suppressed thunder. Taking Aristide's arm, he led him across the courtyard.

"Abdmelkart," the high priest said, "bring a chair for our guest. Help him while I go for the priestess Elissa."

Hasdrubal returned, not only with Elissa, but with three husky young priests. They stood discreetly to one side, watching Elissa clean and bandage Aristide's foot.

"You can walk on it, Aristide," she said. "Take the bandage off in a couple of days."

"You do it," he wheedled.

"No."

He pouted, trying to conceal his irritation.

"You three," said Hasdrubal to the priests, "carry him and put him on his horse."

"I can't go back to Megara tonight." Aristide sounded surprised.

"You should have thought of that before you came."

"I was already here when I hurt myself."

Hasdrubal's eyes became slits. "Your horse is outside, is it not?"

"Yes," meekly.

Between them, the three priests lifted Aristide.

"After you get him on his horse," Hasdrubal called out as they disappeared, "wait for me at the maze."

He turned to Elissa. "Granted I am a novice in such things, but that looked to me more like the kind of cut you care for yourself and forget."

Elissa nodded and gave him a peculiar look.

"What are you thinking?" The high priest was sharp.

"It seemed self-inflicted."

"My feeling also." He nodded his head. "I believe it was a ploy to see you."

Her eyelids fluttered. A bit astonished, he realized the thought was new to her.

"We will discontinue all Aristide's assistance to you and limit his visits here." He couldn't tell whether she was pleased with his decision.

"Abdmelkart, take a flare and walk the priestess to her room." With that, the sadness and austerity of years descended. For a short time, they had lifted. Now, like a box placed over his head, dropping, dropping, until it enveloped him completely, his hurts returned. Elissa was the reason his son had been so attentive to the temple's work. His happy daydreams of a successor lay shredded before him. The chrysalis with which he had surrounded a flawless Aristide ripped from top to bottom. A different man emerged: still beautiful, but with a cold eye, a lustful satyrlike smile. Stop it, Hasdrubal lectured himself. He was exchanging one extreme for the other. Sighing, he shook himself, starting from his head, like a wet dog.

The high priest followed the others out of the audience chamber. The priests were just coming back into the courtyard when he reached the maze.

"He objected to our setting him on his horse," they said. "But we got him up and saw that he rode away."

"I suspect that he may not stay away," said the high priest. "You are to remain here all night. Take turns, two of you watch, one sleep. Alternate. He is not to be allowed in. Report to me in the morning."

Hasdrubal was barely out his door in the gray dawn when they hurried to him. "Aristide walked in without limping," one said.

"He claimed he dropped his purse," chimed in another.

"We found it just outside the maze," said the third.

"I held his horse," said the second priest. "They stood right in front of Aristide, shoulder to shoulder. ready to help him."

The first priest snickered. "He mounted by himself. I slapped the horse's rump and said, 'Don't come back.'"

"Well done," said Hasdrubal.

Praise from the high priest sent the three tired youths off to their chores with happy hearts.

Hasdrubal castigated himself. How could he have been so blinded by his past love for a woman, and by the handsome man who was the product of that love? His normally astute judgment of character had failed. Last night, Aristide acted outrageously. He had been planning to take Elissa by force.

The more Hasdrubal thought about Aristide, the angrier he became. Other acts coursed like a torrent through his thoughts, behavior that he now interpreted differently. His son appeared to have inherited little of him and all the worst of Dido. He huffed derisively. Well, Aristide's free roaming in the temple compound was at an end. For a time, at least, he would order the entrance blocked at night. The head of the metal shop would see to that. For how long, he would decide. Over and over, he agonized—if only Aristide had come honorably. Aristide could have asked for Elissa. But, no, his son simply wanted her as a plaything.

Everything seemed to go wrong. One intrusion after another interrupted the flow of the ritual verse he was composing. His stylus lay idle, his sheet of skin pushed aside.

First, Saphonisba requested his presence, mainly to have her spirits bolstered. He assured her that Hanno would write soon.

"You feel sure he has run away?" she asked for the umpteenth time.

"Yes, I am sure."

"I think, my dear," she said, sensibly, matter-of-factly, "I will move back to Megara. I am needed on the estate. I must supervise the weaving rooms and choose the grape cuttings now that the growing season is upon us."

"Excellent, but I shall miss you."

"Megara is not far. You were always an excellent horseman."

"I seem unable to find time to ride," he said with a wry twist of his lip.

"Now, my dear, you will have an excuse," she said sweetly and went on to talk of other things.

No sooner was he back at his desk than Asherat asked permission to speak to him.

"Of course, my lady. Anytime." What now! All she did lately was complain.

The sun poured through the window he had had cut in the wall behind him. Asherat couldn't observe him without shading her eyes, which she considered impolite. But as she said to herself, what did it matter if she observed him if he remained immobile, a stone statue with hooded eyes?

Dripping honey, perfected over years of practice, she said, "I have discovered that Elissa is going into all the filthy, pestilential places surrounding the temple, places that house sailors, laborers, loose women, good-for-nothings—unconscionable behavior for a priestess of Tanit."

His head twitched.

Ha, ha, she thought, that got to him.

"What does she do in these places?" he asked coldly.

"Apparently she doctors them. Imagine!" Asherat made Elissa's actions sound indecent.

"How do you know?" He tried to appear natural. Impossible! Was Elissa not keeping her promise to him?

"A child came to me when she couldn't find Elissa. She said her sister was sick and Elissa had delivered a baby." Asherat hesitated. "I didn't understand whether the baby was the sister's, if it had just been born, or what the circumstances were."

So, the head priestess was putting snippets of information together, and embroidering them.

"Forgive me, my lord, for burdening you with all these things. She is no longer in my department. She is haughty and ignores me, so I must come to you. Ordinarily, I would solve these minor difficulties myself."

"You do right to come. She has no reason to be haughty, as you put it. She will not ignore me." Elissa, Hasdrubal thought,

probably ignored Asherat as the only way to cope with this domi-
neering woman.

"She takes charge of the priestesses when they are sick and
makes them stay in bed without consulting me." The pale blue
design on her chin quivered.

"My lady, her duty is to care for them when they are sick."

"Sometimes it upsets my plans." She sounded petulant.

Was she intimating that the priestesses feigned illness? "Do
you think they are not sick?"

"Perhaps."

Preposterous. She was searching for minutiae to hold against
Elissa. "I assure you, my lady, the priestess would not keep them
in bed unless they were sick. If it will help, I will order her to
inform you whenever she decides a girl needs to be confined to
bed," he said, thinking that Elissa probably did so anyway.

"Thank you, my lord." She hurried off, glad to escape the
strong rays of the sun. Her skin felt damp and hot. She sliced
through an inner court, close to the wall. In the dimness of the
covered walkway, she swirled her garment around her to trap the
cooler air underneath. It could evaporate the droplets of perspiration that seeped along the crevasses of her flesh.

If he knows what's good for him, she thought, he better
come to his senses soon. I've about had enough.

Hasdrubal understood perfectly that his lead priestess would
not be satisfied until Elissa was out of the temple. Asherat faulted
him for siding with the Tyrian. He had to play a waiting game,
albeit a dangerous one. The moves were hers.

Had he somehow offended his goddess? The thought that he
might be the object of Tanit's ire frightened him. Before she became any angrier he had better figure out which ritual had offended her. His tears for Gisgo? He hadn't known he was crying
until he felt the wet. He would offer a personal sacrifice, something larger than the usual chickens and baby lambs. A big, beautiful, perfect goat.

He consulted the chief of sacrifices. Only afterwards was he
able to tackle the liturgical verses he had to write.

By the time he left the building, it was late. The myriad
flying insects, birds, crawling things that added their thousands
of tiny noises to the day were silent. He was uneasy. Giving into
his feelings was not like him, but he left the shadows of the temple
portico and walked across the courtyard. Abdmelkart sprang to

open his door, flooding the master's last few steps with light. How silly, he thought. With all the undercurrents swirling around here lately, he was beginning to imagine things.

Two days later, he knew his instincts had been right. Dressed in the clothing he wore when walking incognito through the city, he stooped over a bundle of rags. It contained the inert form of a baby girl. The dark, bare hovel smelled of excrement and food. Beside him, a weary, woman clutched the piece of meat he had brought.

"She didn't move all morning," said the mother. "No crying. She didn't take my breast."

Hasdrubal stroked his bushy false beard and pulled at a ringlet of his wig. "The child is weak. Try to pour a little of your milk through her lips." Sad, he thought. The infant will not live out the day. The mother understood; she had already lost other children. The high priest was more concerned for the three naked, runny-nosed youngsters hanging around the woman's legs. So far, only the youngest was infected with the eye disease that blinded so many children. Their parents went to sorcerers instead of to doctors.

Alcibiades scoured these slums behind the temple. He dispensed medicine. The doctor had prepared a stick of salve for the woman and had shown her how to use it. If she did as told, the results had been minimal. The child would lose his sight. His skin stretched over his little bones with nothing to buoy it up. The woman wasn't much better off than her infants. Yet, year after year, she spawned these wretched children.

In the past, the misery of the city's poor used to overwhelm him. Hasdrubal questioned whether he should continue his efforts. Compared with the need, his aid was so small that it didn't seem worthwhile. All it did was let the poor drag through another day. What they really needed was to build up their strength.

Few of his class tried to help. Most considered these people no more than animals. They threw them the waste from their banqueting tables to watch, laughing raucously as they pushed and shoved, caterwauled, and bloodied their fingernails over a bit of food.

With a helpless gesture, Hasdrubal moved toward the door.

The woman whined that her milk was poisoning her baby. His glance swept through the open doorway and scanned the street. It was a short street; not many people passed up and down.

Some children chased each other in the middle of the road. A blond slave who gave the impression of being in mid-flight from somewhere to somewhere darted from behind a structural pillar of the public bath. He stopped to watch as one child grappled the legs of another, bringing him crashing to the ground.

"The slave at the corner looks familiar," he said. "Does he live in this neighborhood?"

Shifting her body, she stared at the man, dressed in a short, mud-colored skirt. "No. Never seen him."

"I prefer he not see me. Is there another way out?" His eye fastened on a low door in the back wall.

"That's to a shed. Then there's a wall. The children'll show you how to get through." She looked at a girl of five. "Can't you?"

The child nodded her head.

"Go." The mother snapped her fingers. The girl darted toward the closed door. After a quick glance at his mother, the two-year old was at his sister's heels. Still hugging the meat with her elbow, the woman picked up the third child as Hasdrubal disappeared through the small doorway.

He found himself in a lean-to. He stumbled over rags, bits of metal, a cooking pot, some kindling, pieces of ceramic, miscellaneous objects begged or stolen. He recognized the sandstone wall that formed one side of the shed. It was part of a series of public structures started by some senators with the idea of becoming rich. For years, the project had languished. Originally, stone archways allowed passage through the long wall. The archways had filled higher and higher with refuse. Some had been deliberately mortared over to form the rear wall of a dwelling. The passages had become clerestory windows that only permitted light. Occasionally, at ground level, there was a tunnel in the refuse just large enough for a medium-sized person. Hasdrubal's fastidious nature cringed. The choice was his: this or being forced to defend himself.

The narrow alley on the opposite side of the wall was no more than a footpath. It led to the sea on one end and the forum thoroughfare on the other. He hooded his eyes as was his wont when annoyed.

The girl removed some meshed twigs plugging the shed and popped out. The boy, with two-year-old caution, crawled through the outlet. On his hands and knees, Hasdrubal followed them into a damp, musty space just large enough to hide a chariot. The sky was barely visible, hemmed in by shacks precariously perched on top of shacks. Stinking refuse, animal bones, dead rats, and human waste surrounded the exit. His stomach heaved. He swallowed with determination, dropped to his knees, and wormed his way through the opening. On his feet in the alley, he patted the children and sent them back to their mother. He hurried toward the forum road, revolted by his own filth.

He had to walk among a stream of people, horses, and chariots before he could reach the narrow road skirting the rear temple wall. A bend in the wall contained a well-camouflaged entrance to his home.

Emerging guardedly onto the main highway, he glanced right then left. Just the normal crowd. The slave must still be stationed behind one building or another. Hasdrubal strode to the door in the temple wall.

As he stepped into his empty audience chamber, he started to strip. "Burn those," he ordered a wide-eyed Abdmelkart, "then scrub this floor."

Hasdrubal lay in a perfumed bath and seethed. He had enough to worry about without being cautious on his own behalf. For days, he had been aware that an attack was imminent. He hoped he would survive it. The attack could come from any quarter at any moment. But until Asherat struck, he saw no way to avoid the inevitable.

18

The news swept through the city like fire. Quintus Fabius Maximus, the Roman envoy, had arrived. His ship crept into the gulf, weighed anchor, and dispatched a small boat with only one passenger, a messenger to the Carthaginian senate. Carthaginian boats surrounded the Roman ship; Fabius himself appeared on deck, wearing a knee-length, narrow-waisted tunic and broad-brimmed hat to protect his pale skin. He persuaded them to withdraw and wait for an answer from the senate.

Hasdrubal sent Abdmelkart to find out what was to take place and when. The survival of Carthage as a power in the Mare Internum lay in the balance. Through jealousy and clouded vision, the senators could chose not to support Hannibal. If so, Carthage would lose the war. If Elibaal's coterie were able to persuade the majority to back Hannibal, the city might remain a great power and master of the seas. Hasdrubal voted for Elibaal.

"The senate receives Fabius," reported Abdmelkart, "three hourglasses hence. An escort will guide him from the dock to the senate chamber."

"I will have a look at this Roman as he passes through the forum," said Hasdrubal.

At the appointed hour, he walked casually but cautiously past one of the forum's lions. The beast was resting, crouched catlike, his massive head dormant on limp paws. Every once in a while, an eye opened, glanced around, and closed again. Small knots of men stood talking as if nothing in particular were happening. Most pretended to examine cursorily the aristocratic, blue-eyed Roman in the formal white wool toga and his three companions as they crossed the forum. Led by the guide, the four mounted the steps between the indifferent lions and disappeared.

There is no nonsense in that man, thought Hasdrubal. Fabius will speak his piece, the suffetes will speak ours, and all will be over. The envoy will return to Rome where the senate will order the doors of the Janus Temple opened, showing the face of the war god to the citizenry.

The high priest looked around. People were suddenly noisier, calling to each other or leaving. Everything seemed to have exploded. Little of the calm before the Romans' arrival remained. What was the point of waiting? Hasdrubal knew that as soon as Elibaal could, he would come to him with details.

Toward evening, the senator was announced.

"Well," he said, settling into a chair with great aplomb, "Fabius presented Rome's demands." His laugh was short, sharp, cynical. "What else, but the surrender of Hannibal and his staff? We gave an emphatic 'no.'"

He fingered a heavy gold chain that hung over his chest.

"Fabius asked if Hannibal's attack on Saguntum accorded with the policy of the Carthaginian senate. We replied that the treaty between Rome and Carthage made no mention of Saguntum. Furthermore, the treaty was never ratified by the Roman senate, nor, for that matter, by the Roman people. Therefore, Saguntum was not, and could not, be an issue. Then, we invited him to state what was really on the mind of the Roman Senate."

As though expecting comment, he peered at Hasdrubal before continuing.

"Quintus Fabius Maximus stood alone before us. He drew himself up to his full height and said, with great dignity, 'We bring you a choice of peace or war. Choose which you prefer.'"

Elibaal gazed at the ceiling. The scene was so clear in his mind. "My senior requested permission to confer with us. Fabius assented. Carthalo wanted to be sure we were agreed that Rome was the one to declare war. Whether or not to back Hannibal was never mentioned. After we filed back into the chamber, the suffete said, 'Rome can choose.'"

"'War,'" said Quintus Fabius Maximus.

"We said, 'So be it.' That was all. So simple. But as a consequences Rome or Carthage will be destroyed. Let us hope it is Rome," he said soberly.

Hasdrubal had been holding his breath during Elibaal's last few sentences. It came out in a whoosh, almost like applause. Elibaal's clique had won. Carthage would be the final victor.

Elibaal clapped his hands on the arms of the chair. He pushed himself up. "I must go. I promised to spend the evening with Saphonisba."

That night, Hasdrubal became entangled in the temple's financial accounts. By the time he left his workroom, even the small lamp at the temple door had been extinguished. The night was overcast, the air oppressive.

He stopped abruptly, tensed, flung up his right arm and brought it down hard. The arm caught an object that gave way beneath the blow. Something cold crossed his thigh. The next instant, a man screamed.

"Abdmelkart," Hasdrubal called, "hurry."

The Numidian flung open the door. Light from the room made the corridor visible. The high priest stood erect, his head turned expectantly toward his illuminated doorway. At his feet lay Asherat's slave, a knife protruding from his leg. Abdmelkart darted to his master's side.

Ignoring the painful slash on his own leg, the high priest said sternly, "Rouse the temple. Have the chief scribe and the chief of sacrifices personally escort Asherat here."

Abdmelkart stared hard at the high priest's bloody robe before running off. Hasdrubal observed the slave at his feet. His face was contorted in terror, his shifty, frightened eyes pleading. Blood oozed around the edges of the knife blade. It dripped onto the pink inlay of the white floor, making dark spots that spread on spidery feet. The high priest looked at his own wound. A line of blood crept along the fibers of his garment and made it stick to the cut. When he flung down his arm, he had apparently struck the arm of the slave. He had shorted the blow to himself, but the force had sent the knife into the muscular thigh of his assailant.

"Bind him." Hasdrubal indicated the slave to the priests.

Elissa was among the first priestesses to arrive. Seeing the blood on the high priest's clothing, she began to tremble. The competent physician in her soon overshadowed the lovelorn girl. Blood wasn't spurting onto his robe. He was on his feet. She turned to the three priestesses with her.

"Bring a basin of warm water."

"And you," she said to a second priestess, "get clean rags from my office and bring them to me."

Hasdrubal kept his eyes on the priests as they bound the arms of the slave behind his back, but was achingly aware of

Elissa's every movement.Lights began to appear, moving along the portico and the courtyard, toward the high priest's quarters. The chief of sacrifices and the chief scribe with Asherat between them stepped into the circle around the prostrate man. Seeing her slave, Asherat turned the white of the pavement.

Hasdrubal was judicial. "Your emissary was unable to carry out his assignment. He did not kill me any more than he succeeded in killing Hanno. You did not choose well when you enlisted him."

Asherat lunged toward the slave. Faces stark with shock, the two chiefs restrained her. The high priest motioned them not to interfere. She knelt beside her slave and said, "When I found out about your criminal activity, I told you to discontinue it or I would sell you. You disobeyed me."

"He did not disobey you," Hasdrubal interrupted. "In fact, he carried out most of your orders extremely well, including placing an asp to bite the priestess Elissa."

A startled cry came from the circle. They all looked at Elissa who stood transfixed, her mouth open. Asherat had tried to kill her? And Asherat had tried to kill the high priest, her high priest. Elissa shook. Another priestess caught her around the waist and drew her into shadow so Elissa could collect herself.

Asherat's eyes widened as she looked at the high priest.

The priests and priestesses stared first at the head priestess, then at her slave, and back again, slowly closing their circle as if proximity would broaden their understanding.

"The greater penalty is yours," intoned the high priest. "You will stand before the citizens, in the forum, as a murderer."

"No," screamed Asherat. She snatched the knife from the slave's leg and plunged it into her own breast. The priests and priestesses watched in numb horror as she coughed and slowly tilted onto her left side across the slave's body. Blood gushed from her mouth, staining his bare chest. He whimpered.

The chief scribe knelt and turned Asherat's head around. "She's dead."

"Take her body to her son and guard the slave until morning," said Hasdrubal. "I will take him before the Court of a Hundred Magistrates for judgment."

The priests, workmen, and slaves cleared a path for the high priest. He started toward his open, lighted door. Elissa, holding a basin of warm water, extricated herself from the knot of priest-esses and followed. He tried to walk normally, but movement made his leg hurt and blood ooze. The others, busy and jabbering, didn't see it, but Elissa was immediately at his side.

Switching the basin to one hip the way a woman carries a child, she supported him with her other arm and shoulder. "Sit down," she said, maneuvering him in front of a chair in his living room. "I'll wash and bind the wound." In spite of his pain, he tingled at her touch.

Abdmelkart shut the door behind them. Hasdrubal dropped into the chair on his left buttock, extending his right leg.

"Master, master," wailed the slave.

"It is not a deep cut, just a bad spot." Discomfort in his groin was fast reducing the pain in his leg. He feared an exhibition. "Clean the mess in the corridor while the priestess takes care of me," he said, concentrating his attention on the slave.

Abdmelkart shifted his weight uncertainly.

"I am all right, Abdmelkart," said the high priest. "Do as I say."

Unwillingly, he went.

Hasdrubal caught his breath as a warm, wet cloth touched the cut. He looked at Elissa. Tears were spilling down her cheeks.

"You could have been killed," she said.

"Would it have mattered?" He wondered what made him so bold.

She continued washing his leg. Without looking at him, she said, "Yes."

Reaching over, he took her face between his two hands. She raised her eyes and lost herself in the blaze of his.

"I love you," he said simply.

"I have loved you for a long time," she whispered, radiance spreading across her face. When he tried to gather her into his arms, she shrank back. "You are my patient," she said with a little laugh. "Let me finish washing and binding your leg."

Unable to leave her alone, his hand kept caressing her shoul-der as she worked. Once, she laid her cheek against the stroking hand. True to her profession she continued to tear and twist the rags tightly around his leg until she was satisfied. In complete abandon, she flung her arms around his neck. He gave a happy chortle and caught her.

At last, between kisses, he said, "Will you be my wife?"

"Yes" was all she managed as his lips and tongue covered her face.

Presently, he slid her off his lap so that he could stand up. Burying his face in the massed curls, he said, "I cannot believe that such beauty and such joy is mine." She pressed against him. He reached for her hand. He drew her to his bedroom where he picked her up and laid her on the bed. He closed and bolted the door.

Once, a hand rattled the knob. "Master," called Abdmelkart.

"I am all right. I was sleeping," lied Hasdrubal. The door was still bolted the next morning, later than usual, when fists pounded on it. Elibaal's voice called, "Hasdrubal! Open up. Why have you bolted the door?"

"Lie here," Hasdrubal said to Elissa. Getting out of bed, he slipped a robe over his head and picked up his hat. Before putting it on, he stooped to kiss her. "I will return shortly." He pulled back the bolt, opened the door, and shut it as he stepped out to face a puffed-up and angry Elibaal. Behind the senator stood a frowning, worried slave and behind him the barber.

Elibaal glanced over the high priest. He took in the leg bandage. "Abdmelkart said you were wounded in last night's melee. How badly?"

"Not very." The anxiety on Abdmelkart's face smoothed out.

"Thanks to Tanit for that," snorted Elibaal. "You have terrified your staff."

Hasdrubal's eyebrows rose. "Unintentional, I assure you, my lord." He indicated the two chairs that were always placed together. "Please sit down, Elibaal. We have much to discuss about last night."

To his barber, he said, "Return when the hourglass has emptied."

This was hardly the right moment to speak of Elissa, but he could not leave her trapped in the bedroom while he had a long discussion with Elibaal. At least, the barber had disappeared.

"Allow me a minute, my lord, and I will join you."

Elibaal strode toward the chairs. Hasdrubal, his hand on the bedroom door handle, motioned for Abdmelkart to draw near. "Bring the priestess Elissa fruit and some goat's milk," he said in barely audible tones. A smile curved his lips as Abdmelkart eyed the bedroom door with astonishment. The high priest disappeared inside.

Minutes later, he rejoined Elibaal. Immediately the senator began. "I was crossing the courtyard when your barber and your slave rushed at me in great excitement, babbling about murders and suicides. I would be pleased to know what this is all about."

"It goes back to Hanno's stabbing, senator." Hasdrubal went through the whole thing: from the attacks on Hanno, Elissa, and himself to his discovery that Asherat—the upright, respected, pillar of Carthaginian society—had a secret life in which she did away with all who opposed her.

Elibaal sat rigid, staring at the high priest, an occasional flick of his eyelids the only movement. "I'm surprised and yet not surprised."

"Explain yourself, please, sire."

"Years ago, Asherat's husband and I were good friends. He told me once that she was determined to have her first child be a son. She was beside herself when the first two were girls. He felt their deaths were not natural, but that was just between the two of us. The family jumped to her every command. I thought they were motivated by fear. But, again, I had nothing to go on."

The high priest heard the bedroom door open. Elibaal's eyes bulged. Elissa gracefully crossed the end of the room and left the quarters. In silence, Elibaal's eyes followed her.

Hasdrubal laughed. "My lord, that is the happy result of last night's fiasco. As soon as negotiations with her father are complete, the priestess Elissa will be my wife."

Pleasure spread across Elibaal starting from his toes. "My dear man, that is good news." *The man laughed,* he thought. *Hasdrubal actually laughed. One night with a woman, and warmth and joy are emerging from under that shell.*

"I hope you will do us the honor of being present at the sacrifice."

"With great pleasure. I wouldn't miss it. But you must put off your wedding for a time."

"My lord, forgive me for being dense. Why? I want no scandal surrounding Elissa. I want to marry within a fortnight." *Negotiations would just be a formality. Ahiram would back him. The specific time of the ceremony really depended on the soothsayer.*

"Please excuse me. I didn't mean to interfere." Elibaal sounded sincere. "My reason for coming was to tell you that Hanno is in Tyre."

"In Tyre!" cried the high priest.

"Saphonisba received a letter from Batbaal. He stowed away on the ship carrying her to Mago. My daughter begs you to fetch him. I have checked, and a ship leaves—" Elibaal hesitated, hating to destroy Hasdrubal's happy plans—"tomorrow morning."

Inwardly, the high priest groaned. His voice was steady. "Elissa will travel with me. You and Saphonisba kindly present yourselves in my audience chamber immediately before the dinner hour. I will send to the soothsayer. I hope that the portents are favorable. Otherwise," he humped his shoulders, "I have no choice. We will be married today."

His voice was low and calm, his mind sorting out all the details.

Elibaal didn't like his precipitous action. Hasdrubal had not yet contacted her family. He owed the courtesy of a big wedding celebration to the priests, priestesses, and workers of the temple. Besides, the wedding should be announced publicly. A man of his position in the community should see that necessity. A great feast needed to be given. And the report from the soothsayer—well, that was Hasdrubal's affair.

Rising, Elibaal said, "We will be here."

Hasdrubal hastily scribbled a note to the soothsayer. "Deliver this," he said to Abdmelkart, handing him the wax tablet.

"Send Elissa to me instantly." He emphasized the last word, making Abdmelkart jump and rush toward the door.

"My lord, what is it?" asked Elissa breathlessly as she hurried into the room.

He caught her two hands in his. "My dear one, change of plan. Only a change," he insisted as fear crept into her eyes. "I must leave for Tyre in the morning to bring back Hanno."

Her face fell before she could control herself. He wouldn't marry her. Like the first time, she would find herself alone and abandoned. She hung her head, trying not to cry.

"We will be married in my audience chamber tonight," he said quietly. He kept tight hold of her hands. "I will not go without you being my wife."

Her face came up to meet his. She fell forward, drawing his arms around her. He released her hands and crushed her against him.

"Together, we will meet your family," he whispered into her hair.

Elissa extricated herself sufficiently to search his eyes. "My lord, to be your wife, yes, with all my heart. But if I go with you to Tyre, we will not be able to come right back. My family will want to celebrate our marriage. We would have to consult the soothsayers. Ahiram would insist on finding the appropriate moment for our wedding, and we would have to be married again. The soothsayers alone can take time."

Hasdrubal's mind flashed to the local soothsayers. With his whole being, he willed a favorable omen.

"The receptions and ceremonies would be elaborate and long." While her excuses were true, Elissa admitted to herself that she didn't really want to see her father. He had written to her, but his papyrus scroll was querulous, irritating, full of gossip and slights. He had always been such a vital man. She wanted to remember him as he was.

"Garments would have to be made for me. Our stay could extend for months, and that would make you unhappy."

Hasdrubal frowned. She was right. He could not afford to be away for long, especially now after Asherat's death.

Sensing what was passing through his mind, Elissa touched his cheek. She said, "I do not do well at sea. Let me stay here. I am happy and busy. I shall miss you, but you will return quickly. And I can be of help with the priestesses."

Everything she said made sense. He conceded unwillingly.

"Will you stay in the administration building or move over here?"

She smiled. "I will move. Surrounded by your belongings, I'll feel closer to you."

He kissed the end of her nose. "I will ask Saphonisba to send a woman for you and a man to watch over the house. I will take Abdmelkart." Straightening his conical cap, he said, "I hate to leave you here, but it is probably for the best."

Arrangements went forward hurriedly. With apologies for the haste, he asked his second in command to perform the ceremony. "In my audience chamber," he said. The elderly priest raised an eyebrow, but Hasdrubal had already turned.

A jarring message came from Saphonisba: Of course, my dear, I shall be there. I rejoice for you both, though I worry at its abruptness. Wouldn't it be best to wait until you return and have the marriage performed properly?

How like her, Hasdrubal thought. However, she was right. It would be better. But under the circumstances, he had no choice.

With a repressive motion, he scraped a thin layer of wax off the surface of the tablet.

The soothsayer's report, while equivocal, was more negative than positive. It said: The day looks favorable, but requires much caution.

In spite of the pressure to put the temple in perfect order before his departure, he sat at his desk for many minutes considering the report, its pros and cons. Anger of the goddess! He had chosen the finest ram in the pens to sacrifice. Failure to negotiate with Elissa's family! Her father was in no condition to negotiate. Ahiram, yes. Ahiram would understand and plead for them before the king. If he drowned at sea! That thought sealed his determination. Elissa must be his wife before he left. They had spent a night together. Suppose she, like Dido, had become pregnant? He wanted his son—he hoped it would be a son—brought up to be high priest of Tanit. He picked up the stylus to finish what he was writing.

Blissfully, he arranged the service and the festive dinner as though in a dream. To his amusement, he found Abdmelkart on his hands and knees scrubbing the bed-chamber floor. "Don't you have enough to do without this?" he said. "The room is always immaculate."

Abdmelkart ignored him, and just before the guests arrived, he placed fresh flowers in the chamber, transforming the plain, white-washed room into a colorful, fragrant bower.

At dusk, a small group assembled in Hasdrubal's brilliantly lit audience hall. Saphonisba brought a middle-aged female retainer, a personal slave for Elissa. She also brought a strong young male to do the heavy work and guard Elissa.

Elibaal arrived, driving his chariot. He swept in, his elegant, deep-purple dress cape billowing behind him and his long jeweled earrings dancing. Abdmelkart completed the company.

Hasdrubal's efficient second married them.

Holding Elissa's slim hand, Hasdrubal pushed an emerald and electrum ring firmly on her index finger. With Alcibiades' help, she had managed to buy a plain gold band. The ring stuck at his knuckle. Elissa struggled, turned a bright pink, and looked helplessly at him. He smiled gently. With a quick twist, he sent the ring home. "Perfect," he said, his eyes full of joy and love.

Taking her by the hand, he led the way to the dining room and the marriage feast that Abdmelkart had so hurriedly prepared. A succulent roasted lamb knelt in the middle of a table. The smell was delicious. Ewers of red and white wine, like sentinels, stood at both ends. Lentils, artichokes, tender greens, mounds of sweet dough, pomegranates, figs, apples and grapes lay on small tables. Three lighted flares cast a soft light. "My dear," sighed Saphonisba, "Abdmelkart is a marvel."

The dinner conversation naturally turned to Hanno.

"When I bring him safely back in Carthage," said Hasdrubal, "Elissa and I will hold a marriage feast of magnificent proportions. Everyone in the temple, down to the lowest laborer, will be invited."

"Along with half the city," laughed Elibaal.

"The courtyard will overflow," Saphonisba said.

"And I shall present you with a much more beautiful ring, one I can get on your finger." Elissa smiled shyly.

"My darling," Hasdrubal bent toward her. His laughter was gentle and loving. "For the high priest of Tanit who wears no jewels, this plain band is best. It is dear to me."

Elissa looked skeptical, but accepted his judgment.

It was an enchanting evening of geniality, warm affection, wit and laughter. The high priest sat at the head of the table, smiling and nodding, his wife beside him. To Saphonisba's delight, he joined in the banter.

"As punishment, I will make Hanno assist the priest at our public wedding."

"Do you want to be married properly?" Elibaal guffawed.

"He would only make a little mistake," said a broadly smiling Saphonisba.

Hasdrubal chuckled. "I will train him well."

The time came for them to be escorted to their bed chamber. Saphonisba took Elissa's hand and led her from the dining room. Smiling, Saphonisba returned and sat down. All eyes turned to Elibaal. The senator rose ceremoniously and conducted Hasdrubal to the closed bedroom door. Elibaal chortled. Clapping him on the shoulder, he said, "You have already tasted; enjoy."

With happy anticipation, Hasdrubal entered the room. Elissa lay on his bed, her skin dusky pink in the soft lamplight, her dark hair tumbled on the pillow. She smiled. He pulled his formal robe over his head and dropped it on the floor. Still smiling, love in her eyes, she held out her arms.

The following morning, Abdmelkart insisted that the high

priest and Elissa eat his specialty—a hot, liquidy mush of various grains—and some fruit. "I won't be cooking for the priestess for a while," he said, bowing before Elissa.

Hasdrubal procrastinated as long as possible before tearing himself from the arms of his wife. He and Abdmelkart left through the back wall door, hurried to the wharf, and boarded the ship for Tyre.

19

*T*yre lay before him. Hasdrubal watched the ancient Phoenician city's ever-changing skyline. In the afternoon light, rowers maneuvered the vessel along the port's massive stone breakwater and through the crowded waters of its north harbor. He could barely see the mole between the island and the mainland. It seemed strange that a hundred years ago—before Alexander, the great conquering king of Macedonia—the Tyrians had to take a boat to go to the mainland.

Ions ago, his own ancesters had come from Tyre. They were part of a small band helping the princess Dido flee Tyre to escape her brother's cruelty. They settled on the southern coast of the Mare Internum and named their colony Carthage. The colony flourished. It became a great city. Now, its ships ruled the Mare Internum and even sailed out through the Pillars of Hercules. Tyre had become a pawn, fought over by the Egyptian Pharaoh and the Seleucid King Antiochus.

Hasdrubal scanned the turreted battlements. They would not be easy to scale. Perhaps the improved battering ram could breach them. Above the defense walls, narrow houses jammed close together, rising tier after tier until they reached the palace. On the other, higher promontory stood the Temple of Baal.

Imitating the temple's large pillars, the houses had small pillars on either side of the entrance door. They had two or three stories instead of the Carthaginian four or five. Miniature palm-shaped columns supported the balustrades of the top-story windows. They were decorated with palmettos or lotus buds in bright colors. Hasdrubal thought they looked like flower beds topped by slowly waving fans. Interesting, but incongruous, he thought.

His niece and her husband lived in one of those houses. Maybe he would find their home, maybe not. A few hours of daylight remained. He could always go to Ahiram for help. He

would order Abdmelkart to wait on the wharf with their belongings. He looked around for the Numidian. To his surprise, the
slave was trying to carry on a conversation with a Tyrian seaman
who was busily straightening piles of rope.

What was this all about? It was not like Abdmelkart to make a
nuisance of himself. Could he not see that the man was occupied?

Scowling, the high priest gave his attention to the landing.
Sailors were easing the boat to the wharf side. Half-naked laborers lined up on the dock, waiting to unload the ship's cargo. Others,
with outstretched arms to catch thrown ropes, yelled at workers
on the ship.

"Sire," said Abdmelkart, at the high priest's elbow.

Hasdrubal turned his head.

"The Tyrian knows the city well. He explained to me how to
get to where the Carthaginian traders live. Then we just have to
ask for Mago."

"Good," said Hasdrubal. "You lead; I will follow."

Abdmelkart swung the sack containing their possessions onto
his back. They turned upward, moving slowly through the narrow, twisting streets of pounded earth. Hasdrubal reveled in each
twist and turn, savoring the multicolored, continually changing
crowds. Litter bearers trundled their unseen burdens. Horses carried richly appareled and bejeweled men. The fragrance of perfume on the passersby mixed with the odor of gutter filth and an
overall, pervading smell of cooking spices. How like Carthage it
was. Yet, it seemed livelier. He could not put his finger on how,
but he sensed it. Batbaal would feel at home here. No wonder
Mago enjoyed Tyre and wanted to stay.

The Numidian slowed. After calculating the distance they
had come, he turned off the main thoroughfare into a quiet street
with rows of narrow, brightly colored homes.

"Which is the house of Mago, the Carthaginian?" he asked
four little boys who were playing with a ball.

The children gave the strangers a peculiar look. One of the
bigger boys pointed to a house. "Number five down."

They stared after Abdmelkart in silent curiosity blended with
fear. How odd, thought Hasdrubal. Abdmelkart was already near-
ing Mago's house. Hasdrubal forgot the children and hurried.
Their appearance on the doorstep would be a complete surprise
to Batbaal and Mago, deliberately so. Hanno would not have time
to disappear again.

Abdmelkart pounded on the door. For a few minutes, his raps brought no response. A crack appeared and widened enough to show a man's nose and a shadowy eye.

Hasdrubal announced that he was high priest of Tanit in Carthage, uncle of the mistress of the house.

The door shut abruptly. Abdmelkart raised an arm to pound on the wooden panel again.

"Wait!"

Mago suddenly flung the door wide. He was a shocking Mago, without his hat, his thick curly black hair and beard in disarray, the snap gone from his eyes, his face tight. Hasdrubal had just absorbed Mago's appearance when a tearful Hanno catapulted toward him. He braced himself for the impact.

Mago quickly drew the high priest and his slave into the house, closed, and bolted the door.

Leaving Abdmelkart in the dark entrance vestibule, Hasdrubal followed Mago's bright blue garment into the main room of the house, wondering why there were no lights. Little daylight entered from the walled courtyard where gray shadows foretold the coming night. He bumped into a chair. Feeling the delicate, carved back, he remained standing with his hand gripping it.

Somewhere ahead of him, Hanno sniffled out of control.

"Stop it, Hanno," said the high priest. "Both of you sit down. Tell me what this is all about. Why is Batbaal not here?"

Hanno let out a howl.

"Hanno," snapped Hasdrubal. "That will do." He couldn't see Hanno, his eyes only slowly adjusting to the dimness. To his right, a dejected Mago slumped in a chair.

"The guards of the king came this afternoon. They took Batbaal away. We have no idea where she is." Mago's voice broke. "Or why they took her." He gulped a few times, fighting a breakdown.

Hasdrubal's stomach bounced. Squaring his shoulders, he clapped for a servant.

"Sire!" The voice came from close behind him.

"Do you allow your master to sit in the dark? Bring some light." Hasdrubal commanded instant obedience.

Light filtered through the room as the servant brought in lamps. The high priest saw Hanno crouched in a corner.

"Everybody in this house," he said to the servant lighting wall flares, "is to carry on as usual at this hour. See to it."

"Yes, sire." The servant touched his head to the floor.

"And show my slave our quarters."

He glanced around the small room: An expensive carpet, the usual chairs and small tables of the well-to-do, and handsome, woolen floor cushions. A bit overcrowded, he thought, but all arranged with Batbaal's good taste.

"Now," he said to Mago "I will write a note to Ahiram, high priest of Baal and brother to the acting king. Have the note delivered into the hands of the high priest and no one else. Then, we will have our evening meal and talk of other things until we receive an answer from Ahiram."

Mago, a trader, knew when decisions were necessary and actions had to be taken. He got up and bowed low before the uncle of his wife. He clapped his hands. His slave appeared. "Bring a wax tablet and stylus for the high priest. And have your assistant prepare to go to the high priest at the Temple of Baal."

Mago, solid and stocky, moved with such rapidity that his garments seemed to sail behind him as before a wind. He left the room. Almost instantly, he returned, bearing the tablet and stylus himself.

"The house slaves are doing as you ordered," Mago said.

Hasdrubal wrote quickly, succinctly outlining the situation. He asked a prompt response from his friend.

Mago called the young male house slave. "Go swiftly and return to us with the high priest's answer. Give this to the high priest himself, no one else."

"Yes, sire." He bowed and was gone.

"Shall we," said Mago, the gracious host even though his black eyes, anxious in his heavily bearded face, lacked their usual luster, "have a little food on the patio? My servant has set out lamps. The evening is warm and beautiful. Our flowers are in full bloom. We may as well enjoy their color and fragrance until our messenger returns."

"I'm hungry," said Hanno.

"Then come," said Mago, leading the way.

For a while, time passed as pleasantly as possible under the circumstances, but the slave didn't come back. More time passed. Hasdrubal caught Mago surreptitiously biting his nails. He tried to distract him even though he himself was beginning to worry. Hanno, he observed, ate a tremendous amount. The boy was acting as if he need no longer concern himself since they had Hasdrubal's firm hand to guide them. In a way, thought the amazed high priest, good philosophy. He tried to calm his own nerves.

At last the messenger knelt before them.

He said that he had gone to the Temple of Baal. The high priest was not there. According to his instructions, he had insisted on knowing where the high priest was. "He was eating the evening meal in his wife's apartments at the palace," the slave reported. "He made me wait. I sat at the door a long time before he came himself and read the tablet. He said to tell you that he would go right away to his brother, and that you will receive an answer tonight."

This time, the wait was short. Ahiram had not found out much. His brother was feasting with dignitaries from Antiochus. The feast would go on most of the night.

My wife tells me that she was in court this afternoon when my brother said something she couldn't completely hear about a pot and demanded to have the person who owned the pot brought to court. I think it would be best if you come to the temple in the morning. I will request an audience with my brother for the high priest of Tanit.

Sparks erupted from Mago's eyes. His beard quivered. "The pot! Your pot," he said to Hasdrubal. "The one with"—he hesitated and stumbled over the name—"Gisgo's ashes. She thought the pot was beautiful. She told me she had been showing it to a group of ladies."

"The one who's married to the chief royal potter saw it," said Hanno.

Two heads swiveled as if one. He met their gaze for a moment. Looking embarrassed, Hanno lifted his shoulders insouciantly. "She did."

The two men looked at each other. "And word of it got to the king," said Mago. "Or the royal who passes as king."

"But to arrest Batbaal and not—" The high priest broke off. Strange that the king would not order the pot brought to him. "Was she ordered to bring the pot or is it here?"

Mago blinked rapidly. "I think it's here." He jumped up, ran into the house, and returned. "Yes, the pot is on the stand in our bedroom."

Suppressing his anxiety, Hasdrubal said, "We can do nothing

more tonight. I intend to retire and suggest the two of you do the same."

Everyone was up long before the normal hour, dressed and ready to leave for the Temple of Baal. The problem was how to occupy themselves until a reasonable time. Hasdrubal wrote to Elissa, saying that he feared his return would not be as soon as hoped. Mago did figures for his business. Rechecking them, he always came out with a different answer. He tossed the work aside and joined Hanno. Both wandered aimlessly about the house.

The high priest appeared at the top of the stairs. Hanno and Mago, anxiously patrolling the bottom step, watched him.

"Have you two nothing better to do?" Though sharp, Hasdrubal's words were without bite.

The two, with solemn, upturned faces, continued to watch him.

"Let us go, then," he said.

The men walked up the hill to the temple, Hanno tagging close behind. The high priest turned to his nephew.

"This is a very, very old temple, Hanno, a relic of the time hundreds of years ago when Tyre was the greatest power on this coast. Look carefully. You will never see its like again."

Hanno, looking up the narrow street, saw sunlight on a roof. The next minute, he gaped, rooted to the earth. Bathed in morning light, the Baal Temple reflected misty pink with deep shadows of purple. It was small, square, weathered old stone. Two columns at the entrance, one jade, one gold, cast a glitter. For an instant, Hanno shielded his eyes.

Gently, Hasdrubal touched the boy's shoulder. "Come along."

They were directed to an adjoining building. In a sunny carpeted room, they found the high priest of Baal. The swarthy, clean-shaven man, sat on the floor reading. Rainbow colored cushions piled beneath and around him emphasized his elaborately embroidered white woolen robe and ever-present cap. The cushions make him look fleshier than he was.

The high priests, on their knees, bowed low.

"My dear friend," said Ahiram, rising stiffly, jangling his heavy gold bracelets and long gold earrings, "this is indeed a pleasure, albeit under unhappy circumstances. My brother is expecting us."

Ahiram led the way. The high priest of Baal explained that the original palace was old. It had been burned and rebuilt many times. Now, it had six entrances, and it rambled over the entire top of the hill. He and his wife had an extensive apartment in the new part.

A message was sent in of their arrival. Word came back that they would be received in the throne room.

"You are an honored guest," Ahiram said, smiling at Hasdrubal.

Two uniformed soldiers bowed deeply and opened the door. Hanno stared at the short swords thrust through the waist band of their knee-length pants. Ahiram and Hasdrubal stepped in together. A richly dressed courtier, on his knees before the king, said, "The king's brother, the high priest of Baal, and his honored friend, the high priest of Tanit."

Hasdrubal heard Hanno gasp. He cast a swift glance around, noting the red murals on the wall, the gold leaf on the pillars right up to the painted capitals. Light from flares bounced off the gold. The whole room sparkled. A small man dressed in purple linen bordered with gold sat on an ebony and ivory throne. A purple cap worked with gold was on his head. Priests and courtiers surrounded him.

Mago, Hasdrubal, and Hanno bowed, lowering their faces to the marble floor.

"Rise," said the king. "We are pleased to receive the high priest of Tanit from Carthage."

"Sire," said Ahiram, stepping forward, "we come with a plea. We would know the whereabouts of the Carthaginian woman and the reason for her arrest."

The king's face clouded. His bushy eyebrows contracted. "Of what interest is that to you?"

"She is the niece of my counterpart, high priest of Tanit, and newly arrived in this city to join her husband who is a trader here."

Hasdrubal modestly stepped beside Ahiram. "I beg you to tell us what she has done and how we can atone for her crime."

Ahiram, observing his brother, read the telltale signs.

"She brought into this city," said the king, "a vase more beautiful than anything we have in the palace. That is not permitted."

Hasdrubal could see the set of the jaw even under the heavy beard. The mean little eyes looked arrogantly from beneath the jetting brows.

"Majesty," he said humbly, "the vase is mine—"

"If you expect me to arrest you instead, on that trumped-up

statement, you are mistaken." The king was working himself into a temper. "The fault is the woman's. She will pay the penalty." Jumping up unceremoniously, the king swept from the room.

"Take the boy and go to your home," Ahiram said to Mago.

"The vase is the high priest's. I will bring it," said Mago.

"No. Do as I say. When the time comes, you will be told what to do with the vase."

Mago bowed, motioned to Hanno, and walked to the door. It silently opened before them and as silently closed behind.

"We will go to my quarters," Ahiram said to Hasdrubal.

Neither spoke until they were seated facing each other in Ahiram's study.

"Sire, I designed the vase in question. I can easily have a more beautiful one made," said Hasdrubal.

Ahiram shook his head sadly. "My friend, when or how my brother saw the vase is unimportant. The vase is an excuse."

Hasdrubal's eyebrows rose like two question marks over widened, guarded eyes.

"Carthaginians, and many Tyrians—certainly I am one—are monogamous. Unfortunately, my brother has taken on some of the eastern trappings brought here by the conquering Alexander. The king has seen your niece and decided he wants her in his harem. If necessary, her husband will be killed."

A cold numbness enveloped Hasdrubal. He closed his eyes. He couldn't think, he couldn't breathe. With returning sensation, his brain cried: safety; send them to safety.

"I will put Hanno and Mago on the next ship leaving port. They can transfer—wherever." He waved an arm agitatedly into space.

"There's no rush at the moment. The woman is your niece. Because of that, we can assume that nothing will happen too soon. My wife has access to my brother's women. I will have her find out where Batbaal is. Maybe his legitimate wife will help us protect the girl until we obtain her release."

Ahiram was thoughtful. "He thinks he hoodwinked us by talking about the vase. It might be wise to offer it to him. Let him think we believe his story."

He clapped his hands. A slave girl appeared.

"Send to the home of Mago in the street of the Carthaginian traders. Ask for the vase of the high priest of Tanit. Say the high priest of Baal requires it."

Ahiram said, "I shall have his favorite courtier take the vase to him with your compliments."

Hasdrubal nodded in agreement.

"Until we see his reaction, and know what my wife gleans, there is nothing more we can do." Ahiram spread his hands wide on his knees.

"I would hope, my friend, that you would share my noon meal with me," he continued. "We can talk of other things."

"With pleasure," Hasdrubal said. "I have other things to talk about."

Ahiram raised his hands in mock horror. "Such as my niece."

In his joy, Hasdrubal burbled a few times. He broke into a laugh. Ahiram gave him an odd look.

"To come right to the point," Hasdrubal said, "Elissa is my wife."

Astonishment held Ahiram speechless. Married without negotiation, without contacting her family! He knew the girl was beyond the pall. But Hasdrubal! Not to follow the proper—unbelievable.

Sensing his friend's bewilderment, and more than a little embarrassed, Hasdrubal succinctly summarized the circumstances.

"My dear friend," cried Ahiram, "I am delighted. Her father will be, too. He has long desired her marriage. Unfortunately, he is near death. May I arrange an audience?"

"By all means. I can carry his last wishes to her."

Elissa's father agreed to receive the high priest of Tanit late in the afternoon, after his rest.

Ahiram led Hasdrubal through the palace. "Since the last fire, all the entrances were rebuilt except one. That is inaccessible. They are pillared with marble stairs leading to the courtyards. Sixty rooms surround these courtyards. Many rooms in the new section are paneled in cedar and hung with linens and wools. That includes all the rooms in the king's apartments. The furniture is inlaid with ivory or decorated with gold and silver viello work."

"Beautiful," murmured Hasdrubal.

Ahiram laughed. "It's a craze at the moment. The admiral has a chair. He'll be sitting on it. Otherwise, his rooms are plain. He lives on the third floor of an inner court in the old part of the palace."

They entered a lovely court, fragrant with flowers and a pool laden with lily pads.

Ahiram took his leave in front of the admiral's apartment. He promised that as soon as he heard any news of Batbaal, he would inform Mago.

Elissa's father, old beyond his years, was wrapped in blankets. His white beard was straggly and his eyes watery. Steam rose from a bowl beside him. Incense permeated the room.

Hasdrubal noted the extraordinary workmanship on the chair. But a whole room full of that furniture! No.

"Leave us," the admiral ordered the hovering female slave.

She reluctantly pushed aside a heavy fabric curtain, dropping it into place behind her.

Hasdrubal sat down on a large cushion placed in front of the admiral. The old man could see him without straining his weak eyes.

"I am pleased to meet the husband of my daughter. I regret that she chose not to see her father for the last time." The admiral kicked at the shawl that covered his legs and knees.

"She gets this too tight," he complained. A final kick released his right foot and exposed a pale, emaciated ankle above an embroidered slipper.

"Elissa ran away, left us alone, after all we had done for her." He closed his eyes and stroked his wispy beard. As if returning from some far-off, private retreat, he added, "She will be an enormously rich woman when I die. I am grateful that she finally has someone to manage her wealth."

Hasdrubal bowed his head. "I will do my best, my lord. Is there any message you wish me to take to her?"

"Like what?" he snapped. "I wanted grandchildren. Now I won't live to see them." His eyes closed again.

He is tiring, Hasdrubal thought. "I will tell her you love her." He pushed himself from the cushion.

The eyes flew open. "No, no," cried the admiral. The woman's head immediately appeared around the door drape. "Wait."

Hasdrubal hesitated. He sat down again.

"Fetch the case," the admiral called over his shoulder.

The woman's head disappeared. In a second, she came into the room, carrying a gold-inlaid ebony box with silver handles. She laid the box on the old man's lap and withdrew behind the curtain.

Slowly, with great ceremony, the admiral raised the lid. From where he sat, Hasdrubal could not see inside the box.

Elissa's father held up a heavy gold necklace studded with rubies. "This is part of a set I gave my wife on our wedding day." He dropped the necklace back into the box. He drew out a delicate gold ring set with a large ruby. "My wife wore this ring every day of our married life."

Hasdrubal envisioned how beautiful the exquisitely filigreed ring would look on Elissa's hand.

The ring was also dropped into the box.

"Take the box." The admiral gave it a weak shove.

The high priest set the box on his knees. He caught his breath. Jewelry of gold, silver and precious gems lay in a heap, filling the box to the brim.

"My daughter's wedding present," said the admiral with a wave of his hand.

"No," said Hasdrubal softly. "Elissa would not want all this right now. Keep it here for her. But if I may, I will take this ruby ring. The ring means much to you. It will to her, too. It is also something she can wear with her priestess' robe."

"As you wish. Everything will be left in Ahiram's keeping until the day you claim it for my daughter." The admiral closed his eyes. His obligation was completed. The interview was over.

Hasdrubal carefully tied the ring in one end of his high priest's stole. He clapped for the woman.

"Return this box to its place," he said when she stood before him, "and see to your master."

Thinking about what Elissa would do with the jewelry and the chair, Hasdrubal made his way to the home on the street of the Carthaginians. Mago met the high priest with a long face. In his haste to send the vase to the king, he had forgotten to remove Gisgo's ashes.

"I think," said Hasdrubal, staring over Mago's head, "that is a good sign. The child will intervene for his mother." His eyes returned to Mago's face. "We must await developments."

20

*M*ago came home with news. He found Hasdrubal and Hanno in the pleasant little patio. "There has been a death in the royal family. An old admiral who was married to a daughter of the late King died this morning."

How fortunate, thought Hasdrubal, that I was able to see him yesterday.

"Batbaal's release will have to wait until the ceremonies for the dead have been concluded," said Mago.

"Will there be a parade to the cemetery?" Hanno looked forward to a change from the surrounding stillness. He was bored, and yet for the first time in a long while, he wasn't bored. Thoughts were beginning to form in his head that would take some mulling over. He wasn't afraid, but he had to be sure he knew what he was doing.

"Probably," said the high priest. He saw no point in telling them that the admiral was Elissa's father. In the immediate concern over Batbaal, he had not mentioned his marriage. His own affairs could wait.

Thus, for many days, no word came from Ahiram or the palace. During those dragging, aimless days, alone in his bedroom, Hasdrubal turned the ring over and over in his hand. He slipped it on his little finger as far as it would go, and admired the beauty of the ruby, the delicate gold work. Elissa would wear it with such pride. It would become her. He secreted it safely away among his belongings and wrote to her without telling her of the ring. That would be a surprise. He wanted to see her expression when he laid it in her open palm. He wrote of seeing Ahiram and her father. After much thought, he decided not to mention his death, preferring to tell her in person when he could comfort her.

The high priest and Mago sat in the cool of the patio in the evening. On a number of occasions, Hasdrubal wondered aloud where Hanno was. The response was always the same. Hanno had gone to bed. Strange, he thought, at his young age to be spending so much time in bed. With nothing to do but sit and wait, perhaps boredom was the answer.

At long last, a message came from Ahiram. He asked Hasdrubal and Mago to come to the temple. Before leaving the house, the high priest went to his nephew's room. The boy was in a deep sleep.

"How can he sleep so much? I do not understand it," he said to Mago. "However, we will let him sleep."

Ahiram received them in his library surrounded by piles of open scrolls. He had a papyrus and stylus at his right hand.

"My news is both good and bad," he told them. "The vase was given to the king. He threw it on the floor then sent the shattered pieces and ashes to Batbaal."

Hasdrubal and Mago remained still with lowered eyes.

"My wife was sitting with Batbaal and the queen when a female slave brought in the remains. The slave dropped them at the feet of your niece. She let out a little cry, hovered over them on her knees, then scooped up the ashes in her two little hands. My wife thought she was going to cry. She looked at the queen. The queen took pity on her. She ordered a bowl brought to contain them."

"So my niece is with the king's women," said Hasdrubal in a low voice.

"Has he touched her?" Mago could hardly get the words out. His nails dug into his flesh.

"Not yet. At first, she was isolated and her clothes taken from her. She was given a sheer linen skirt pleated Egyptian style. Because she did not kick and scream, she was allowed in the main room with the other women." Ahiram was silent, thinking.

"I guess she went to the queen," he continued.

"The queen told my wife that Batbaal asked why she was arrested and talked of her husband and young brother. The queen befriended her. So when my wife went to the women's quarters, she was in a position to discuss Batbaal with the queen. They spoke of substituting a temple prostitute. My wife thought of bringing in a girl and leaving with Batbaal. But if they did that and the king realized the woman was different, not only would he kill the prostitute, but my wife and the queen would be in jeopardy."

Hasdrubal wondered if the substitute might be one of the girls Elissa had befriended.

"Forgive me, but I forbade that plan as too risky."

Hasdrubal interrupted. "No, no. Do not apologize. We could not allow harm to come to your lady or to the queen."

Mago sat disconsolately, leaving the negotiating to the high priests.

Ahiram continued, "The queen agreed to talk to my brother. I think today. She has a great deal of influence over him and may get him to release your niece."

"Do you think she will be successful?"

"My friend, I do not know." Ahiram threw up his hands, dropped them like stones into his lap. "What I do know is that if she gets out, all of you had best leave Tyre promptly. My brother is a far different man these days than he used to be. His decisions cannot be trusted. If Batbaal manages to escape, your lives would be forfeit."

Hasdrubal's throat constricted. In rescuing Batbaal, one or more of these good people would be endangered. Much as he loved his niece, he could not, according to his strict moral code, cause suffering to innocent people.

"My dear friend and high priest in the Temple of Baal," he said, "You have done all you can. We are grateful. We will talk among ourselves as to what we should do."

Mago couldn't believe what he was hearing. His wife's uncle was calling off the negotiations, leaving her to the lustful abuse of an old man.

Hasdrubal bowed low. Mago followed his example and backed toward the door. He heard Ahiram say, "I will keep you informed," then he was out of the room. When Mago looked up, he was alone. Confused, he waited.

Inside the room, Ahiram laid a hand on Hasdrubal's shoulder. Hasdrubal straightened. The two men stood eye to eye. "I was with the admiral when he died," said Ahiram. "He put into my keeping a casket of jewels plus much heavy gold, silver plate, and furniture. He asked me to give them to Elissa. What more of his estate I can save for her, I don't know."

Hasdrubal bent his head humbly. "From the depths of my heart, I thank you for all you have done. Hold them until you hear from her. She will decide how to dispose of them. Naturally, you are aware that as my wife, she lacks nothing."

With great formality, the friends parted.

Mago and Hasdrubal sat in the living room of the house on the street of the Carthaginians. Hanno danced around impatiently. "What happened," he asked before they could even sit down. Hasdrubal lowered his lids to slits. First Hanno slept all the time; now he was titillated and edgy. The high priest could only conclude that his peculiar behavior foretold Hanno's passage to manhood.

"Come out to the patio where we can be alone and talk," he said to Mago. "We must devise a scheme to rescue Batbaal without endangering the friends who have helped us."

"For days," said Mago, "I have been thinking up wild schemes, all too risky and untenable."

"I can get her." Hanno cried. He bounced from the floor and planted himself, feet akimbo, arms punching the air, before his uncle.

Amazed, Hasdrubal gazed thoughtfully at the boy. The works of the gods are strange, he thought. A stowaway to rescue his sister.

"Keep your voice down and tell us your plan."

The three drew their chairs close together.

"Remember how the high priest of Baal said there were six entrances to the palace? I nosed about, particularly the old ones. They all have marble stairs, except one. It's down an alley, close to the wall of a house. The steps are broken away. I had to climb up to get in. I discovered how to get into the main part of the palace. I've done it over and over. I can do it in the dark without a light."

A new appreciation for Hanno surged through Hasdrubal. All those nights they thought him sleeping, he had been in the palace.

"I found where the women live in the new part."

"Are they heavily guarded?" asked Mago.

"Two guards walk back and forth. Most of the time, they don't."

"Explain," said his uncle.

"They walk to the end of the balcony—it's on the second floor—and back. One leaves for a while then the other. Sometimes, they even squat against the wall and sleep. Nobody comes around."

Hasdrubal pushed back his chair, rose, and walked slowly

along the periphery of the patio. His head was lowered, his eyes on the stone flooring. He came to a halt behind his nephew.

"Hanno," he said, "I am proud of you. While the rest of us worried, you did something."

Hanno squirmed in shy delight.

Mago smiled in agreement. "Once inside the women's quarters, how will you find Batbaal?"

"I figured she'd be in the smallest room, farthest away from the door."

"Good deduction." Hasdrubal sat down and turned to Mago. "Find out what ships are leaving Tyre soon and for what port. We had best be prepared before Hanno makes his attempt. And we had best not try to enter the palace now while the moon is full. The next few nights will be dangerous."

"Batbaal," he said, after some thought, "cannot possibly run through the streets of Tyre clad only in a sheer linen skirt."

The vision of his wife thus clothed made Mago sit up straight. "Absolutely not. I won't allow it."

The high priest considered whether Mago would rather stick to their code of ethics or have his wife back.

"Hanno will have to carry some clothing." Mago looked questioningly at Hanno.

"I think," Hasdrubal said, "we had best dress her as a boy."

"I've thought that out," said Hanno. "Her slave made me some new clothes. They fit her. We dressed up in them one day. It was fun."

"Can you carry enough for her?" asked his uncle.

"Sure. Easy."

"Good." Hasdrubal rose, ending the conference. "In about ten days, the moon will hide herself. We must be prepared to act quickly." He left to write to Elissa, telling her approximately when they would leave Tyre.

21

Five days later, a priest arrived, a messenger from Ahiram. Hasdrubal was on the patio looking at the bright blossoms in the narrow flower bed. On a dainty orange bloom, a butterfly rested lightly, buoyed by slowly moving diaphanous wings. Nearby, deep inside an opening flower, a bee crawled, buzzing noisily.

A smile played about Hasdrubal's lips. He turned to greet the approaching messenger.

"My lord," the priest said, offering a wax tablet, "Ahiram, high priest of Baal, said that I was to deliver this into your hands. If anyone tried to stop me, I was to press my hand into the wax."

The high priest read the tablet:

My brother intends to act soon. He is having the husband watched. He knows Mago has been asking for ships leaving for Carthage. My friend, take care. The situation is dangerous.

Hasdrubal flamed the wax and dismissed the messenger. He didn't know where Hanno was, but assumed that he would come home for lunch. Mago was working in his shop, but would come home at noon for news.

Hasdrubal instructed Abdmelkart to tell them to remain at home until he returned. He left the house through a back alley used by the servants and hurried to the docks. There, he casually chatted with sailors, inspecting the cargos being loaded, acting like an interested visitor from another city. When he left the wharfs, he had a firm commitment for five places on a vessel sailing for Crete in the silent hours just before dawn.

Mago and Hanno were waiting when he returned. He took them to his bedroom. "Abdmelkart," he said to the lurking Numidian, "close the door and join us."

Hasdrubal laid his plan before them. Mago was to carry on as usual in the remaining daylight and come back directly. He was to be obvious about his movements. Hasdrubal told him to stand in front of his door a minute or two so all could see him before he went inside.

Hanno was to prepare his small bundle of clothes for Batbaal and make his way to the palace after dark. Unfortunately, the night would be bright, but they had no choice.

Abdmelkart was to gather whatever necessities they needed. Under cover of darkness, he was to transport everything to the ship. The Roman trader was the fourth on the left from the central point of the wharf.

He himself and Mago would make their way separately to the ship. He told Mago to dress as one of his servants.

Admonishing them all to be careful, Hasdrubal pleaded Tanit for success.

That final day was a nightmare. Abdmelkart, dressed in layers of clothing, went to the ship bound for Crete. Carrying a small bundle, he undressed there, leaving the extra clothing. Abdmelkart moved through the city as if doing family errands. He succeeded in transporting the clothing and personal nicknacks Mago didn't want to leave behind. As night deepened and the city quieted, the Numidian slipped out and did not return.

In the deepest part of the night, Mago and Hasdrubal hugged Hanno. They cautiously let him through the back gate. The two men faced each other. "May the gods go with him," whispered Hasdrubal.

When their turn came, Mago objected to leaving first. Hasdrubal flatly told him he must. They stood before the rear wall door. Hasdrubal said, "I will listen for any sound indicating that you have been discovered." A short time later, he left by the same servants' route. Hasdrubal walked stealthily away from the house. The sky was clear and brilliant. A great white moon cast strong light, making each stone visible. He kept close to the walls. Every few steps, he stopped and listened. All was silent. Nothing moved. Only when he emerged onto the main thoroughfare did he breathe easier.

On the wharf, he ignored the man he knew to be Mago. Shortly before sailing time, they met in a darkened warehouse doorway. Mago was nervous and worried, as was he. Did Hanno get into the women's quarters? What were his chances of success?

Hanno slipped rapidly through the city. The night was warm. Except for a few drunks or men coming from the evening's entertainment, he passed no one. Here and there light glinted through the cracks of closed shutters. Little sound broke the silence. He clung to shadows. He wanted no chance observer to mark his course to the dilapidated, unguarded entrance of the palace. Under his arm, he had tucked a new full shirt, a skirt he had worn a few times, and a conical cap. Batbaal would have to wind her hair under the cap. At least from the back, she would be taken for a man; from the front, a beardless youth.

Near the palace, he realized with some surprise that he was praying to Tanit for success. He wondered whether she would pay attention, much less help him. He had a clear memory of sitting in front of the goddess the night Gisgo was sacrificed, along with his mother and sister, staring up at her. What a stupid, silly child he had been. He had called her every nasty thing he could think of. Well, he thought as he clambered over the entrance debris, whatever happens, I'll do the best I can.

He quickly crossed the crumbling black corridors. He could follow them by dragging his hand along the wall. Hanno reached the courtyard that opened onto the extensive apartments of the king's women. He listened. Nothing. He peeped around the corner. The two guards, dressed in baggy trousers and loose, knee-length shirts, stood at attention before the door. He crouched down in shadow. Every little while, he cautiously looked around the corner, settled back, and waited. At last, he heard footsteps going away from him. One guard was walking toward the opposite corner; the other stood at the door. Hanno slumped back. He heard steps come toward him. He flattened himself on the floor and pulled his dark cape over his head. The steps came near, turned, and retreated. Silence. He crawled to the corner and carefully poked out one eye. Both guards crouched together on the far side of the door. He continued to watch. Soon, a snore sounded.

Staying close against the wall, he edged around the corner. As he inched closer, he saw one guard drop his head onto his bent knees. The other man was already asleep. Like a black streak, Hanno was at the door and soundlessly through it.

He stood against the door, gazing around. He was in an extremely large room. Two dim lights burned, one on either side of the room. A wide corridor extended opposite the door, to his left. On the right, he could see the opening of another corridor. The room itself was thickly carpeted and abundantly furnished with chairs, small tables, and floor cushions. Around three sides were sleeping alcoves, curtains drawn across them. Two had round globes of light shining through the curtains. Hanno decided that Batbaal would be at the end of the less impressive corridor on his right. He crouched low so the lamps would not cast his shadow and scurried across the room. Most of the curtains in the corridor were caught to one side to give air to the sleeper. He hesitated at each curtain. Any woman who was awake and facing the corridor would be aware of movement as his body blocked the light.

He reached a cubicle where a lamp burned. Gingerly, he looked around the curtain. The bed's occupant was turned toward the wall. Like a wraith, Hanno darted to the other side, and reached the last door. The curtain was also pulled aside, but he couldn't see the woman who lay on the bed. He moved closer to the curtain. A fragrance struck his senses. Batbaal always smelled like that. Jubilation made his heart pound. He had guessed right.

He knelt quietly by the bed. "Batbaal." He barely breathed. He was afraid she would wake with a start and cry out.

Batbaal had been awake for a long time, reviewing over and over the circumstances of her arrest. Her slaves had fluttered up and down the stairs in a steady stream between her bedroom and the front door where two officers of the king's guard stood ramrod, eyes glued on her. She had descended with hesitant step. In her nervousness, she had been afraid she would trip. With her left hand, she gripped the bannister to steady herself. The two guards had closed in on her as she reached the ground. They had not touched her. But with any unexpected movement on her part, they would have hurt her, maybe even knocked her down.

"I'll try to send a message to Mago," she remembered saying to her sobbing slave.

She sighed softly and turned on her side, searching for a cooler spot on the bed.

The guards had taken her through a menial servants' entrance at the palace and had left her in that tiny empty room. Faint light and little air had come from the door. She shuddered at the thought. And those guards stationed just outside—did they think she was going to run away? If she had tried, she wouldn't have known which way to go.

Her back to the wall, she had slipped to the floor, huddling there in misery with no way to judge the passage of time. She hadn't moved; she hadn't thought. She couldn't even think of Mago. She had no idea why she had been arrested.

Self-pity overwhelmed her. To be arrested for a pot was incredible. She rolled onto her back.

She didn't know how long she had cowered in the darkness and silence before she heard voices and saw a flickering light. Against the light, the outline of a tall man blocked the door. A long skirt was wrapped around his hips. Earrings dangled to his shoulders while his conical cap rose above his glistening hair.

He ordered her to follow him. The guards marched a few paces behind. She remembered that they seemed to have walked a long, long way, from the narrow, dingy, empty corridors where she had been imprisoned to wider, flare-lit corridors where people stared at her. Suddenly a door opened. She entered a marble-floored, bright-red chamber and was pushed onto her face on the floor. A small man dressed in a purple robe, a gold circlet of leaves resting on his cap, sat in a large ivory and wood chair.

She wondered who he was. A heavy staff hit the floor and a big, booming voice said, "The penalty for keeping a vase of such beauty instead of presenting it to the king is death." She would have fallen if she hadn't already been down, the shock was so great. She turned to ice by degrees, starting with her head. It was the strangest feeling as the cold crept down her body. In an instant, she turned boiling hot. She realized it was those women. She had shown them the vase. Among them was the wife of the chief potter. That woman had been the cause of her arrest.

The king said, "Stand up."

She scrambled up, not very gracefully, she was afraid. Her limbs trembled. Batbaal did not look at him again. The guards marched her off to this place. She hadn't been mistreated. She had the friendship of the queen. Still, she didn't understand. Why here when her arrest was over a pot? To protect her from the guards? No one would answer her direct question.

Then, Gisgo's ashes had been dumped on the floor at her feet. She had wanted to scream and scream uncontrollably. Why had the king done that? As many times as she had thought through the sequence of events, she could make no sense of them.

During the last couple of days, she had wondered if she were pregnant. The possibility gave her joy. Perhaps if she told the queen, she would be released. She heaved another sad little sigh and flung the thin covering from her. She fell into the never-never land between wake and sleep, thinking of Mago.

Her eyes flew open. She thought she had heard her name. She tensed, lay still and listened. She must have been dreaming.

Again, there was the whispered, tentative "Batbaal. It's Hanno."

The light from the lamp in the main room was almost useless at this end of the corridor. She could just make out the outline of a head at the level of her bed.

"It's Hanno," he whispered again, seeing her luminous eyes in the darkness. "Don't cry out." The tips of his fingers found her shoulder. "Listen."

Batbaal placed her hand over his.

"I have some of my clothes here. Put them on." Hanno pushed the bundle onto the bed. "Dress quickly; we don't have much time."

He sprang up soundlessly and stood by the curtain. He looked along the corridor toward the lamp in the main room. Nothing stirred. The light in the next cubicle still glowed. No sound came from behind him.

When she touched him, he whispered, "Did you get all your hair under the cap?"

"Yes," faintly.

As her brother started to move, Batbaal reached into the bowl containing Gisgo's ashes. She scooped up a handful. She breathed, "Guide us, little son," and left the cubicle.

With her right behind him, Hanno glided to the lamp-lit sleep cubicle. The girl was awake and facing them. He drew back and waited. An eternity seemed to pass. Suddenly, the girl sprang out of bed, and tried to push the curtain further back. Hanno and Batbaal hugged the wall and were as motionless as sleeping moths. The lamp went out. They could hear the young body hit the bed. In a flash, they gained the other side of the opening. After slow progress, they finally reached the main room. Hanno put his lips to her ear and whispered, "Do exactly as I do."

Crouching, he scuttled across the room and stopped at the door. She followed. He pushed her down behind a chair. She would only be visible to someone in the first cubicle or someone at the door.

He opened the door a crack. The sound of even breathing came from the guards. If he opened the door still further, either one awake on the other side would see a light. He closed it again. He hadn't foreseen this problem. He squatted near Batbaal and thought.

Earlier, both guards were asleep on the side of the door across from his path. If they were still there, he and Batbaal could get around the corner. If they were awake, he and Batbaal could still make it to the corner while the guards recovered from surprise. Once around the corner, he knew he could lose any guard. But could his sister run fast enough in her unfamiliar clothing?

He whispered, "You have to run fast." She clenched her teeth and nodded.

"We have to take a chance." When I open the door, run to the left. I'll follow. Surprise is our only hope."

Again, she nodded.

They stood up. Hanno laid his hand on the doorknob. They looked at each other. His mouth formed "Ready"?

Hers said "Ready."

He flung open the door. She was through it like a shot, and he after her. They were almost to the corner when they heard "Stop" and running feet. Hanno sprinted ahead of Batbaal. He caught her hand as he passed. They rounded the corner and darted into a narrow dark corridor.

He slowed to a fast walk. He used one hand to hold hers, with the other, he dragged a finger along the wall to give him his bearings. The running feet passed the corridor came back and stopped. Hanno's swift progress never halted. He knew that the guard had no light and guessed that the man was not familiar with these myriad little corridors.

No further sound came.Twisting and turning, they continued in silence.

At last, he said, "We're in the old part now. There are big stones and wooden boards all over the place. Try not to fall."

"Is it much further?"

"No."

In the starlight, they saw the exit. They clambered over a few blocks of stone. Hanno lept from the palace grounds to the alley. "Jump," he said, "I'll catch you." As she jumped, she thankfully released the remainder of Gisgo's ashes. Caught by the air, the ashes joyously kissed the gentle breeze.

Hanno scanned the sky. "We have to be at our ship," he said softly, "before it sails."

They hurried along single file, staying close to buildings, though the area around the palace was empty and still. Near the bottom of the hill, they met a few people beginning the day. A man leading two donkeys emerged from a side street. Further along, a trader was unlocking his stall. Hanno began to worry. The ship wouldn't wait for them. Mago had to sail. Would Uncle Hasdrubal or Abdmelkart stay behind? He had no money to book passage on another ship. He started to run. Batbaal, panting behind him, cried, "I can't go further."

He stopped to let her catch her breath. He could see lights in the harbor. "We must hurry," he said. This time, he walked and heard her light, quick steps behind him.

Acting as if they didn't know each other, Mago and Hasdrubal paced up and down the wharf. Finally, Mago beckoned the man he knew to be Hasdrubal into a doorway. Mago burst out, "What if they don't get here?"

Hasdrubal was all calm authority. "You sail with the ship. Abdmelkart is aboard and will go with you."

"I can't go without Batbaal."

"You must. Your life is forfeit. Wait for us in Crete."

They stared into the dark for any form moving toward them.

"We sail," called the captain from the ship's rail. "Where are your other passengers?"

"Here," boomed Hanno.

With a cry, Mago rushed toward his wife. Hasdrubal intervened before he could embrace her. "Get on the ship."

Mago felt as if he had been struck. He turned abruptly and marched toward the gangplank.

"Follow him," the high priest ordered his niece.

Without a word, she hurried after her husband.

"Hanno." Hasdrubal's hand squeezed his nephew's shoulder. He gave him a slight shove toward the ship.

Euphoric after his adventure, Hanno leapt after his sister.

His eyes slits and his face a mask, Hasdrubal crossed the gangplank, looking at Hanno. The boy has changed, he thought. Tonight, he became a man.

The four huddled together on deck. The gangplank was pulled away. The ship glided from the harbor in the freshening dawn as the rowers slowly picked up speed. No one spoke. Mago held his wife's hand tightly under the voluminous clothing. After

Hasdrubal's rebuff, he realized that she must continue to play the part of a boy until they were safely out of the king's reach. Batbaal shed a few grateful tears.

The ship cleared the harbor. Hanno heard his uncle speak to a sailor in a language he didn't understand. As soon as he could, he asked him what they were speaking.

"Latin," Hasdrubal answered. "My Latin is rusty. I hope to improve it by talking to these Romans."

Hanno's eyes widened. He didn't know his uncle spoke Latin. "Will you teach me?"

"If you wish. I can give you lessons after your regular classes."

Hanno scowled instinctively. In a normal tone, he asked, "Are you going to make me go back to school?"

Hasdrubal noted that his question was not hostile. Interesting, he thought.

"Whether you become high priest of Tanit or not, you must complete your education. Yes, you will return to school."

Hanno made no comment. Soon all four, weary after the tensions of the night, fell asleep.

During the trip, the slave waited on the other four. They remained close together in a sheltered corner, talking little. They disembarked in Crete in daylight. The captain took his first good look at them. The young man and two boys were probably sons of the old fellow who spoke Latin. One boy was pale and looked sickly. He had to be helped off the ship. He probably wouldn't live long.

The captain jerked his head around in amazement as the youngest boy bid him good-bye. He spoke the same provincial Latin as the old fellow.

For eight days the small group remained in Crete. They stayed in an area away from the wharf, avoiding contact with anyone from Tyre. They passed themselves off as a middle-aged Roman with his son, a barbarian slave, and two mute Hellene slaves. The Roman claimed to have been financially ruined by Phoenician traders. They had with them all he had been able to salvage from the collapse of his affairs. To any observer, it seemed niggardly. The older Roman was the only one who went out much. Occasionally, his son went with him. The slaves never appeared.

He booked passage on a ship from Rhodes sailing to Carthage, where he said he hoped to recoup his fortune.

22

*T*hey landed by mid-afternoon of a clear fall day. The sailors tied the ship to the wharf of Carthage's commercial harbor. Five motley passengers watched. All were silent, communicating their own personal thanks to Tanit for bringing them safely home. One, the oldest, was eager, longing to get his arms around the lovely woman who was his wife. On land, the two mutes suddenly became voluble; the barbarian discovered he knew a civilized language; and the Roman father and son spoke fluent Phoenician.

Hasdrubal sent Abdmelkart ahead to the temple.

"You," he said to Batbaal, "Hanno and Mago take my horses and ride out to Megara. You will find your mother there."

He turned to his nephew. "Hanno, spend tomorrow with her. I shall expect you at the temple the following day."

"Yes, sire." That was all. Simply, "Yes, sire," without a smile or a frown.

For a minute, Hasdrubal's eyes slitted as he looked at his nephew. Phenomenal, he thought. All in the space of those few hours in Tyre. He will be a fine man, but will he be high priest of Tanit? He wondered if Saphonisba would sense the change in him.

Hasdrubal hopscotched through the crowd, twisting this way and that to avoid slow-moving carts or clusters of people. He hurried to the small door in the temple wall behind his house. The ruby ring hung around his neck, firm against his chest. He touched it in anticipation as Abdmelkart opened the door for him.

"I sent a priestess for Elissa," said the Numidian.

"Then you may go."

Abdmelkart shot his master an understanding look and disappeared.

The high priest, counting every minute until his wife rushed in, ambled around the room. He looked at the beautiful pieces of pottery and silver in their niches. A strange sensation assailed him. The room didn't feel lived in. He looked in the bedroom. Elissa's powder and kohl jars, her perfume containers, were there. Again, he had the feeling that a long time had passed since they had last been used.

The woman from the Megara homestead, Elissa's personal slave, ran into the room and flung herself at his feet.

"Sire, sire," she cried in agitation.

"Where is your mistress?" His voice sounded stifled.

"Hasdrubal," she cringed on the floor as he stood looking down at her, "the priestess is gone."

"Gone!" ejected from the high priest, uncontrolled like lightning in a summer storm.

"I don't know where," she said, her lips close to the floor.

"You don't know where!" he repeated. Numbness replaced the fire in his brain.

"The young Hellene Aristide came one afternoon. They talked in front of the goddess in the courtyard. She went out with him and never returned."

"Are they at his house in Megara?" Hasdrubal managed to get the words out one at a time.

"No. He is gone, too. They have disappeared."

"You may go," he said, turning from her.

The slave got to her feet. She had known the high priest since he was a young man. Stretching out an arm toward him, her voice spilled with sympathy. "My lord—"

His back was to her. He knew her eyes would be sad and that she was trying to offer comfort. "I want to be alone," he said.

He collapsed onto his favorite chair. His hand shielding his eyes, he sat unmoving as the hourglass drained unnoticed. For the second time in his life, he had lost the woman he loved to another man. Like Dido, Elissa had professed love for him then she had run away. Why had she bothered to marry him? Why? Why? She had gained nothing except the emerald and electrum ring he had given her. While his mother's ring was valuable, she couldn't live on it forever. He didn't think money was her objective. Material things didn't mean that much to Elissa. She was rich now that her father was dead, but she didn't know.

Material things were very important to Aristide. Once he found out Elissa's wealth, he would force it from her. Apparently she had taken nothing. She had left behind her clothes and her creams. The whole thing was very strange.

His life disintegrated around him. He couldn't go on without her.

Something brushed his leg. Indifferently, he moved his hand and looked. Abdmelkart squatted on his haunches, his face level with the master's knee. The saddest expression Hasdrubal had ever seen confronted him. The slave held out two scrolls.

"From your brother," said the Numidian. "The other came from the high priest of Baal today."

Ahiram! Hasdrubal's mind whirled. Great goddess Tanit, he humbly pleaded, please let no harm come to Ahiram's wife or the queen. He took the two scrolls, observed the seals, laid aside the one from Bimilcar, and cracked opened the one from Ahiram.

That you, my friend, and the members of your family are safely in Carthage, I have no doubt. Here, all is confusion. No one can figure out how the woman escaped or how the husband, you, and the boy got away undetected. Batbaal's absence was not noticed until fairly late in the day, after it was known that Mago was missing.

When he did not come out of the house as usual and go to the Carthaginian warehouse, the men watching his home became perturbed. Their superior went to the door and knocked. A servant answered and said nobody was at home.

The king exploded in fury. My brother had planned to make an arrest that night. He ordered Batbaal brought to his chamber. When she could not be found, the queen and the other women were questioned. They all started screaming in fear, but succeeded in making the king realize that they knew nothing. It was total chaos. The night guards denied any knowledge. When they were tortured, they admitted seeing two boys run along the corridor. They pursued, but lost them.

My brother remains in a filthy temper. He takes his anger out on all around him. The queen, who usually has such success with him has been helpless. We all worry about him. In time, the tirades will pass. He will be himself again for a while.

Sometime, I should like to know how you managed to escape, but will leave that up to you.

At least, Hasdrubal thought, neither the queen nor Ahiram's

lady had been suspected of complicity. They should not be; they were not involved. The guards, yes. They did not perform their duty. He thought it best not to let Ahiram know what Hanno had done.

Hasdrubal glanced through the scroll again before rolling it up. He must, he thought, send immediately for the Carthaginian slaves who served Mago and Batbaal, lest the king spend his fury on them.

He picked up the scroll from Bimilcar. It began with a terse greeting and hope for his well-being and continued with his worries about Hanno.

My son the object of, not just one, but two murder attempts! And a runaway! You leave me staggered. He is my son, the seed of my loins. Yet none of the choices that present themselves please me. Undoubtedly fear of being killed caused him to run away, not dislike of the temple. Under the circumstances, assuming he comes here, I cannot send him back the way I threatened. But send him from here, I must. Any day now, the army marches out of New Carthage. I will not take Hanno on the campaign.

If, by chance, some prominent family in Carthage wants your position, I put my son in jeopardy by sending him to Carthage. Where do I send him? You hand me a terrible dilemma.

From your scroll, you seem to be leaning toward allowing Hanno to shirk his duty. That is not like you, brother, when there is no other male. If Batbaal produces another son soon, and you are still convinced Hanno is not suitable, we can consider passing him by, although I do not want to. My opinion is that he will eventually settle down.

Bimilcar went on in the same vein. Hasdrubal tossed it on the floor. Events had again moved beyond Bimilcar. Hanno was no longer under the control of anyone but himself. He would find his way, following neither the priesthood nor trade. Of that, Hasdrubal was sure. Likewise, he sloughed off the army as a possibility.

Hasdrubal sat staring into space. Noticing that Abdmelkart came and went anxiously, the high priest retrieved the scroll. He heaved himself from the chair.

"I will be in my study," he said to the Numidian. He wrote Bimilcar about the family's return to Carthage. He didn't mention the harrowing experience that had caused their hurried exit from Tyre. He dwelt on what Mago had said about the city's power, diminished by Egyptian machinations. The building of the great harbor at Bernice on the Red Sea had struck at the Tyrian economy. Trade from the Indian Ocean bypassed the city. Tyre was not the thriving metropolis of yesteryear. The Tyrians blamed Ptolemy and were happy to welcome Antiochus.

Tyre had surrendered to Antiochus without a blow, and Antiochus was heading south with his army to meet Ptolemy.

Hasdrubal dribbled liquid wax on the rolled skin edge and stamped the wax with the ancient symbol of Tanit. He suspected Bimilcar knew more about Antiochus and Ptolemy than he did, what with Hannibal's efficient lines of communication, but so be it. He gave the scroll to Abdmelkart to start on its journey. The high priest walked to his workroom, thankful for the temple. Bury his grief in work, he must.

Nevertheless, he lay sleepless each night. Elissa's defection pained him. His thoughts wouldn't behave. Way before dawn, he would dress and plunge into work. After all, he not only had to supervise the priests and all the laborers, but the priestesses as well until a new head priestess joined the temple.

Once Hanno was settled back in school, he told himself, he would pay a visit to Saphonisba. Her judgment was astute. Her sympathetic calmness led to revelations. Maybe Aristide had confided in her.

23

The high priest lay on his bed. Darkness hung like a shadow across the city, but the birds were starting to chirp. Dawn was right there, he could smell it. Any moment, the first faint beams would light the square window high in the wall. He stretched and wondered if Elissa were awake, wherever she was. Was Aristide's firm young naked body beside her? He thought of them locked in each other's arms and cringed. He had to put aside this continual thought of them embracing; it was tearing him apart.

Very few minutes of the day passed when he didn't think of her. She had been in the back of his mind while he was in Tyre. Then, his mental vision of her brought him peace and contentment. Now, a searing pain dogged his existence. During the day, he could fill the empty hours with work. In fact, he had done that well, enduring so much pressure during the ten days he had been home that he hadn't had time to go to Megara. Not entirely true, he admonished himself. He hadn't felt equal to seeing Saphonisba. If only sleep would come, he would feel better . . .

As he rolled over and stretched, he thought of their wedding night. He thought of her soft curves, the sweet smell of her body, her shyness and inexperience. She had wanted him as much as he wanted her. Or had she? Was it all an act? He pounded the bed with his fist.

The window was now quite light. He swung his feet off the bed and stood up. He crossed to the large pithoi jar in the corner where he stored his clothes. He must remember to have Abdmelkart remove Elissa's clothes from the jar. He could not stand coming upon them each time he searched for something of my own.

Abdmelkart entered, carrying a small table upon which was a bowl of steaming thin cereal and some dates. Hasdrubal knew that the barber would not be far behind. So even though he didn't want the food, he ate.

"Take one of my horses," he said to the Numidian "and ride to our estate in Megara. Ask Saphonisba if I may dine with her today."

Abdmelkart returned with the message that Saphonisba would be delighted to receive him.

The slave handed Hasdrubal a skin scroll. "From your brother."

Hasdrubal broke the seal. The letter plunged into facts without introduction:

We left New Carthage with ninety thousand foot, twelve thousand horse, and thirty-seven elephants, headed for the Pyrenaei. A number of tribes like the Andosini and the Barqusii fought obstinate battles. I mention only two as names mean nothing to you. We conquered all the territory between the Ebro and the mountains speedly, but sustained much loss in the fighting.

On reaching the Pyrenaei, Hannibal separated ten thousand infantry and one thousand horse from the main army and placed them in charge of the baggage with orders to follow. The rest of the army could then move rapidly.

He also sent home ten thousand foot and one thousand horse. I questioned his reason for doing this, but agreed when he explained that he wished men loyal to us left in the territory, and he wanted the remaining tribes to feel they had a chance of going home.

We are camped at the crest of the pass through the Pyrenaei and start our descent tomorrow with fifty thousand infantry and nine thousand cavalry along with the thirty-seven elephants. Hannibal's courier returns to New Carthage and will take my scroll. Continue to write me at New Carthage, care of Hannibal. His wife, Imilce, remains there and will forward them. Naturally, she is unhappy, but he was adamant. This camp, bedrolls thrown on the ground at night—Hannibal sleeps thus with the common soldiers—and fast marches is no place for a delicately bred woman and a baby. It was hard on him. Believe me, I know what it is like for a man of twenty-eight to leave his family, not knowing when or whether he will return.

What we need is someone in Rome to gather information on what the Roman consuls do and send the news rapidly to us. The

*many Carthaginians in Rome are known by the Romans and thus
would not be suitable subjects for our purposes. I have written
this to Senator Elibaal. From your position in Carthage and knowledge of the citizens, you could be of help to the senator. Discuss
it with him. Try to find someone.*

Hasdrubal scooped up the scroll and rerolled it. A spy in
Rome! The intricacies of gathering pertinent data would take a
special kind of person, one familiar with the political situation in
both cities. His mind dredged up individual after individual,
weighed their qualities, and rejected each. The man would have
to be unknown in Rome, act as a Roman, speak Latin, be close-
mouthed, and make Roman contacts. He would think about it
while he rode to his family's homestead in Megara.

He found Saphonisba sitting in a shaded corner near the pool.

"My dear Hasdrubal," she smiled broadly and gave him both
her hands, "I was afraid you had deserted me." How awful he
looks, she thought, so thin and worn. He has withdrawn into his
old dour manner. The desolation in his eyes made her heart ache.
Oh dear! He was coming to talk of Aristide, and she couldn't be
much help.

"The temple demanded my presence," he said, looking
around at the gardens of the old house.

Even this house, she thought, so near where Aristide lived,
causes him pain. Hum. She would make him think about something else.

"Let's walk through the weaving room. I want you to see
how I've rearranged it since I moved back here." She rose and
started slowly toward the door at the back of the atrium.

"Very well," said Hasdrubal, following her.

Oh, dear, she thought, so indifferent, so unlike him.

Ten years before, she had added the large, well-vented weaving room onto the original house. "I pushed the looms closer
together and installed three new ones," she said. At one end of
the room, a group of women clutched distaffs full of carded wool
under their left arm. They drew out and twisted fibers, attaching
them to a rapidly revolving spindle. Huge baskets of undyed
wool circled their feet.

The usually gossipy women were quiet as they covertly
watched the high priest. Even the women standing at the looms
watched. Their hands continued to pass the shuttle back and forth.

The room was full of upright looms and piles of dyed yarn. Hasdrubal had to step cautiously to avoid hitting the loom posts. He spent a moment or two at each small cluster of looms, talking to the women.

One woman attached weights to the warp threads that hung from the transverse beam holding the two posts together. As she let go, each newly attached weight pulled the thread straight and taut. Another woman loosened a knot that had formed in the weft thread. It wouldn't pass through the hole in front of the shuttle. Released, the thread spilled out, and she drove the weft up tight against the finished fabric by comb teeth.

Hasdrubal was proud of the weaving done on his estate. The women were assigned by the masters' of neighboring estates to work in the weaving room. He knew many of them. They produced finely worked, multicolored patterns in great demand by traders as well as the utilitarian cloth used by the household. Despite his melancholy, he soon questioned the women and assessed their work. It was good. They knew it and were proud of it, but were flustered under his praise.

The same with the vineyards. Instead of venturing out among the vines, Saphonisba sent for her overseer, asking him to meet them in the fruit orchard behind the house. The man was waiting when they came through the vegetable garden. He was in his middle forties, weather-beaten and stooped. He had learned wine making as a boy at Megara and had crossbred the vine samples that lay at his feet.

He discussed his experiments. "We'll know this year how good the wine from new stock. The yield promises to be large. From old stock, too. The year's good."

At Saphonisba's instigation, Hasdrubal agreed to give an expert opinion on the new batch. Pleased with her small victory, she steered him back into the house.

"Has Batbaal told you that she is pregnant?"

"No," he said. "I knew she thought she might be."

"Well, my dear, she is sure. With luck, we'll have another in line for the priesthood." She sounded eager. He nodded, likewise hopeful.

Dinner was long and relaxed. The dining room, the largest room in the house, had a marble inlaid pink cement floor. Its crimson walls were painted with scenes from Carthage. Saphonisba had had two of the dining couches moved from the wall into the center of the room so they could look out to the sunlit pool and the slaves could serve them more easily.

They ladled soup, heavily spiced to Hasdrubal's taste, out of a large tureen. They filled his plate with fish baked to perfection, plump tender pigeon, lentils, fresh artichokes from the garden. They replenished the wine cups with the best the estate offered before they were completely emptied.

Hasdrubal picked at his food. During the meal, Saphonisba spoke of gossip she had heard, politics, the yields of their vineyards, but inevitably the conversation turned to Aristide.

"My dear," she said, "I know little of Aristide. He came here only when Hanno was around, which wasn't often. Hanno didn't like him and tried to avoid him. He would never tell me why. Be that as it may, there are a number of things I wish to say. Since he is your son, you may not like what you hear."

She had been looking at the bunch of grapes in her hand and glanced at Hasdrubal to catch his reaction. He did not return her look and remained silent.

"At first," she continued, "I accepted him without question. He had great charm and beautiful manners. He was one of us. But my judgment of him and his character began to make me wary. I found no depth in him. His head was filled with images of wealth. I also began to suspect that his interest in Hanno was more than friendship."

She stopped and gave her brother-in-law a piercing look. She tried to assess the effect of what she was saying. His eyes were down; he did not move. He could have been asleep, though she knew better. She must choose her words carefully. Every one would be printed on his mind for future reference.

"Aristide never made one move that wasn't deliberately calculated to gain advantage. His main objectives in life are money and status. He found much gold in us. Fortunately, he did not know he was your son. If he had known, nothing would have stopped him from obtaining our wealth. And his sexual proclivities, to my mind, are not what I expect of a man, which makes me think it's odd that he ran off with Elissa."

"He was certainly interested in her when he thought she was a temple prostitute," Hasdrubal muttered between closed lips. He shifted his body on the couch to a more upright position. She was reinforcing his impressions of Aristide. "Not characteristics to be proud of," he said, keeping his eyes averted.

"No, they are not. He has your looks and nothing more. Where does he get his greed from? Was his mother like that?"

"Whatever I say is hindsight. Twenty-four years ago, I was besotted with Dido. Our family was wealthy, but lived rather simply in spite of this beautiful home. The Athenian man flaunted his money and dazzled her." He looked directly at Saphonisba and raised his eyebrows sadly. "Poor Dido. What good did the wealth do her if Diodorus kept her confined in Athenian fashion?"

Saphonisba agreed, but didn't really care whether Dido was happy or not. She was distressed by the deadened spirit in her brother-in-law's eyes.

"Did Aristide talk to you about Elissa"—Hasdrubal stumbled over the name. "Was she a willing participant?" How could she run off with him? Didn't she see what Saphonisba saw?

"My dear, one day, he came to say he was leaving. He gave me a long story about his father needing him. He had closed his house, and he didn't know when or if he would return. That was our entire conversation."

"So they have gone to Athens."

"Don't be too sure. Somehow I didn't believe a word he said."

"Not that I plan to search for them." Hasdrubal pressed the inner corners of his eyes with his thumb and forefinger.

"My dear," Saphonisba hesitated, "searching might be a good idea."

The high priest dropped his hand to pinion her with a look. "What do you mean?"

"Have you talked to Meridan, the Egyptian slave I gave Elissa?"

"No. I sent her back to you. After she told me Elissa was gone, there was no need to keep her at the temple."

She motioned for the slaves to remove the small tables. The room was cool and quiet; they were comfortable lying on the couches facing each other. She saw no reason to move to the patio.

"After you left, Elissa transferred what few things she had— mainly her clothing—to your house and lived there. She and Meridan talked. Elissa wanted to know everything about you and expressed her great love for you over and over. She radiated joy, and she was so happy living in your house where everything reminded her of you."

Hasdrubal fidgeted. Hearing about Elissa's love was a balm, but made his longing for her inexpressible.

"Aristide came to the temple two or three times. She refused to see him. On the day they disappeared, he told her that he had to see her urgently because he was leaving Carthage. Elissa did not give him entrance to your house, but agreed to meet him at the high altar in the courtyard. Meridan watched. They spoke briefly, then left the temple grounds together."

Saphonisba recrossed her ankles. Hasdrubal again had that still, deceptively sleepy look.

"This isn't the behavior of a woman who is running away, my dear."

His "no" was almost inaudible.

"I think you should search. Somehow, by some ruse, he has abducted her. She needs you, my dear—perhaps desperately."

The high priest's whole body shook.

"Saphonisba," he said in a falsetto, agonized voice, "so much time has elapsed. Elissa left about nineteen days after I did. I may not find any witnesses, but I will make inquiries. Elissa is well known, and she would have been wearing a priestess' robe."

Senator Elibaal supped with his daughter three days later. He frequently drove to her estate in a gilded chariot behind fast, prancing horses, his groom clinging to the sides as they took the bumps at high speeds. His driving terrified his daughter, but she held her tongue.

Dinner with her father was always fascinating. She learned all the local gossip along with what was going on in the government. They were hardly settled on the dining couches before he said, "I had a message from Bimilcar."

Saphonisba's spoon dropped with a clatter.

"I didn't mean to unnerve you." Elibaal tinkled in gentle laughter.

"It must be important, dear papa. Don't keep me waiting."

"He thinks we should have a spy in Rome."

"But there are plenty of Carthaginians in Rome."

"Bimilcar thinks we should have some man who does not claim to be Carthaginian. He could relate what the Romans were doing directly to Hannibal."

His daughter gasped. "My dear, that is impossible."

"Not at all. We just need to find the right man."

"You mean you would send someone?"

"Of course. If the man wasn't wealthy, I would finance him out of my own purse."

Her spoon stopped in midair. "And you wouldn't tell the senate what you were doing?"

He snapped, "My dear child, don't be so naive. The fewer who know, the better. If I told the senate, the whole world would know before midday."

"That is true," she sighed.

At the end of the meal, she mentioned that Hasdrubal had been there. "He has lost weight and looks terrible with great dark sockets where his eyes are."

She sucked in her breath and clapped her hands. "Papa, send Hasdrubal to Rome!"

Her father's eyelids fluttered in surprise.

"The high priest of Tanit? Don't be ridiculous."

"His second is a capable man. This is for the good of Carthage."

"He would never go."

"He might. He needs distraction. Besides, he speaks Latin. With a neatly clipped beard and short hair, who would know he wasn't Roman?"

"He is small for a Roman and dark skinned." He threw out objections, but his mind had begun to work the idea.

"He's almost as big as the Romans. Besides, many of the provincials are small and dark skinned. Look at some of the Etruscans who come here."

"Hanno could take over the position of high priest," said the senator.

"I don't know whether he's ready," she said with some hesitation. She had seen such a change in her son since his return from Tyre that she had drawn back to watch and evaluate him. Hanno was no longer an immature boy. He exuded an inner self-confidence and a purpose that had been totally lacking. At times, the boy reappeared, but never stayed. Just as surely as she knew he had changed, she knew he would range far beyond the Temple of Tanit.

Elibaal, immersed in the possibility of sending Hasdrubal, didn't absorb his daughter's changed attitude toward Hanno. "I'll sound out Hasdrubal."

As was his habit, the senator acted promptly. He sent word to the high priest the next day that he wished to visit.

Late that afternoon, Hasdrubal sat in his living room on a wool cushion of tapestry weight. It had been intricately woven at the shop supervised by his sister-in-law. Above him, were three small carved ivory cream and perfume jars that belonged to Elissa. After his talk with Saphonisba, he had placed the jars in the niche where he could see them. Hasdrubal sat cross-legged, his white robe pristine against the tawny earthen color of the cushion. At his order, Abdmelkart moved his favorite chair up against the opposite wall and set the sole remaining chair a bit removed from, but facing, the cushion upon which he sat.

Vaguely, he wondered what the senator wanted, then reviewed the only information he had been able to glean about Elissa.

In answer to his request for information, a number of people from the wharf, both laborers and traders, came to the temple to report that, yes, they remembered seeing the priestess Elissa and a slender Hellene with smoldering dark eyes board a ship. But no two people agreed on who owned the ship or where it was bound. Hasdrubal thanked each, gave some coins to the laborers, and found himself facing a blank wall. He took in a deep breath and let it out noisily. What to do next!

Abdmelkart interrupted his thoughts. "Senator Elibaal has arrived."

The senator's aura of energy and power invaded the room. Hasdrubal noticed his long gold earrings. They caught the slanting rays of the sun from the small, high windows. New jewelry, he thought, and his beard had more gray than since he last saw him.

Elibaal agreed with his daughter. Hasdrubal looked frightful, like a skeleton. And all over a woman.

"My dear man," said the senator, plumping himself in the chair as Hasdrubal bowed low before him, "I have come to tell you that I received a short scroll from your brother."

Hasdrubal nodded. "As did I." ˙

"Then he undoubtedly made the same suggestion."

"I imagine. And I actually think it's a good suggestion. Such a man might be hard to find."

Elibaal slyly ran his tongue over his lower lip. "Have you any ideas?"

"I have thought of a number of people and rejected them all." Hasdrubal named those he had considered. Elibaal's instinctive reaction was the same.

Hasdrubal said, "Who would you propose?"

"Hasdrubal, high priest of Tanit."

An instant passed before the impact registered. Startled, Hasdrubal got up and slowly walked to the other end of the room. He stopped before a table standing against the wall, his back to Elibaal. Placing his hands on the table, he leaned over them, his head bent forward. The temple was his life. Somehow, he could not let it go. Also, there was that humiliating incident when he had followed Elissa. If anything happened, he would be unable to defend himself. In all probability, the war would not last long, but if it went on for years, he would have to stay in Rome. He would live under the tensions of impersonating someone he wasn't, the constant lurking specter of discovery. He might never see Carthage again. But this was for Carthage, the Carthage he loved. He might even see Hannibal. But if word came from Elissa, he might not know it for weeks.

These arguments went back and forth in his head. Elibaal watched. There was no motion, no sign, no hint of which way the argument was going. That there was debate, Elibaal had no doubt.

The thought of Elissa clinched the argument for the high priest. No, he would not go. Yet, way in the back of his mind, something nudged him. Rome was a great metropolis, different from Carthage. The only place he had been was Tyre. Try it.

No.

Who knows, word of Elissa might come through Rome.

No. He shook his head and straightened up.

Elibaal marshalled his persuasive powers. This would take work.

Hasdrubal pointedly resumed his seat on the woolen cushion. "I am flattered at your confidence, but no."

The senator enumerated Hasdrubal's many strong points: his knowledge of Latin, independent wealth, anonymity outside of Carthage; all points that were essential for anyone undertaking the work. "Besides," he said, laughing, "nobody would recognize you with a beard."

The idea of a beard intrigued Hasdrubal. The only beard he had ever worn had been false. He rubbed his chin. The nudging continued, became more insistent. It offended him. He tried to submerge it. He admitted that the proposition was an interesting challenge. Instead of hampering him in finding his wife, he would have a chance to nose around the Hellene colony for Aristide. His family were traders. Somebody might know where he had gone.

Sensing Hasdrubal's weakening, Elibaal added, "With the

guidance of the excellent priest who is your second, Hanno would have no trouble as high priest." The senator smiled indulgently at the thought of his grandson.

Hasdrubal snapped, "No. If I go, Hanno goes with me," then could have struck off his tongue.

Taken aback, Elibaal coughed, a subterfuge he used to gain a moment's thought when changed circumstances required changed tactics. He had expected to spend the evening persuading Hasdrubal to go to Rome. Yet, in one offhand sentence, he had given tacit acceptance. But Hanno! Never. The boy was destined for greater things than being his uncle's lackey on a dangerous mission. What possessed Hasdrubal to make Hanno a condition? Hanno could ruin the whole enterprise.

Elibaal had not seen his grandson since his return from Tyre. He was both perturbed and nonplussed by Hasdrubal's outburst.

There was a troubled silence. Hasdrubal leaned against the wall and said, "I have forbidden the others to talk of the circumstances surrounding our leaving Tyre. This is for your ears and yours alone. I will tell you why I insist on taking Hanno."

When the tale was finished, the senator had changed his attitude toward his grandson. The pride he now had was for his accomplishment: he respected Hanno as a man.

"Saphonisba will object," he said, "But I will take care of her."

Elibaal began to pace up and down the room. Stopping before the high priest, he said, "On the pretext that you are ill and need a long rest, you will disappear. You will come to my villa with Abdmelkart. I assume you are taking him."

"Naturally."

"I will make all the arrangements from there."

"Much must be done here before I can leave."

"Agreed. However, the sooner, the better."

Thirty days passed before Hasdrubal was satisfied that he had left his temple well prepared for his absence.

In his formal audience hall, he watched Abdmelkart seal the last pithoi jar of his personal belongings to be stored in Megara. A young priest delivered a skin scroll. Hasdrubal saw Bimilcar's seal. He dropped down cross-legged on the floor to read. As usual on military matters, Bimilcar wasted no introductory words.

We are over the Pyrenaei, having paid off some of the tribes for safe passage and fought others. We march each day, along the coast by the Mare Internum.

Informants tell us that the Romans have put their legions into the field. They have sent Tiberius Septronius Longus to Africa with one hundred sixty quinqueremes. We do not know his destination. Publius Cornelius Scipio, in command of sixty ships, has been sent to Hispania.

They also tell us that Rome is colonizing Cisalpine Gaul. Two cities have been fortified, and 12,000 men are to report there within thirty days. Rome is foolish. The cities, Placentia and Cremona, have wanted to throw off the Roman yoke. Now they will do so and forfeit the hostages given as a promise of loyalty. They may have already revolted.

The scroll ended abruptly. Hasdrubal tucked it in his clothing, indicated his departure to the slave, and walked out of the maze.

24

*D*eep rose covered the horizon, outlining every tree branch and twig, every leaf, a crisscross patchwork in black against rose. A soft breeze caressed the rider cantering toward Senator Elibaal's villa in the early fall evening. The horseman in an all-enveloping brown cloak and a shawl wrapping the lower part of his face, scarcely noticed the beauty. Self-absorbed, he cantered on, missing the villa entrance, and had to backtrack.

Two slaves ran out at the sounds of his approach and were frightened when the stranger stared at them out of cadaverous sockets. What disease did he have? The master had said he was sick. Hastily, one led him to the two rooms and bath that had originally belonged to Saphonisba. At the far end of the house, the rooms embraced a small secluded patio, overlooking the sea.

Hasdrubal threw the cloak onto a floor cushion. He was fussing with the rest of his clothing when Abdmelkart hurried in, laden with a food tray.

"Senator Elibaal has taken complete charge of my existence, but I hope I am not expected to eat all that." Hasdrubal eyed the food with distaste.

On his knees, Abdmelkart held up the tray of attractively prepared grains and vegetables. "My lord, please, forgive your slave. You must gain some weight before we go. You are too thin."

The high priest inspected his slave, looked at the food, sniffed the enticing aroma. "Put the tray down and help me out of these clothes. I find their weight almost unbearable."

Abdmelkart placed the tray on the floor and ran to fetch a priestly garment. While he waited, Hasdrubal surveyed the room. Tiny, it contained one chair made of carved wood with ivory inlaid arms and back. Saphonisba no doubt chose the midnight blue wool carpet and the linen muslin cushions in deep pinks and light blue that were scattered around. A low table also inlaid with ivory was within reach of the chair. Even the wall fixtures for the flares were carved. Presumably the bedroom would be the same, a carved and inlaid bed against a wall and a pithoi jar for clothing.

Dressed in his normal thin linen garment, Hasdrubal felt better. He watched Abdmelkart lay the food on the table, stand back, and fold his hands across his body.

With a snort, Hasdrubal sat down. "Who is master and who is slave?" he demanded.

"You are always master for me, great high priest," Abdmelkart said humbly, assuming a crouched position on the floor. "But right now, you need care."

Hasdrubal lectured his slave. "The first thing you must learn is not to fall to your knees and touch the floor with your forehead."

The Numidian hopped up, but hung his head.

"Bow from your waist if you must and back away from my presence, but never go down."

In the days that followed, the high priest ate and slept and watched his hair grow and stubble form on his chin. His hair grew in thick and curly. To his chagrin, he could neither part it nor make it lie flat. Slowly, it became rounded like a bowl. He bade Abdmelkart trim it at the back of his neck so it wouldn't hang down. He also had it trimmed around his ears. He wanted it to hang only over his forehead.

He had no intention of wearing the full beard of his countrymen. He chose to have his follow the jaw line, clipped to about an inch. He gained some weight. His eyes lost their dull, tired look, becoming bright and alert as he studied the maps of Rome supplied by Elibaal. He spent hours with the senator, discussing Rome and its environs—the government, the customs, the living conditions, the means of communication. He hungrily snatched at every bit of information. In many ways, he was his old self, but always in the back of his mind was Elissa.

"Master, you are handsome," said Abdmelkart one day in admiration.

Elibaal likewise commented on the change.

"The time is drawing near for you to leave," he said. "I have invited Saphonisba and Hanno to dine tomorrow. We will see if they recognize you."

Saphonisba was unexpectedly late. Hasdrubal sat unconcerned and relaxed in a chair at the side of the door leading from the vestibule. Sparsely but expensively furnished, the room was vivid with colorful frescoes. Immobile against the wall, he could have been part of the scene if caught in the peripheral vision of someone entering the room. Elibaal waited hidden behind a door.

Needing no formalities, Saphonisba walked in unannounced. Seeing no one, she used the shining top of a small table to touch up her hair and straighten her diadem. She fingered the gold loops in her ears and readjusted the heavy gold bracelets on her arms before she smoothed her rose-colored gown. When she turned, she spotted the seated man.

"A thousand pardons, my lord," she said. "I did not realize that I wasn't alone."

Hasdrubal inclined his head to acknowledge her apology.

"I'm Saphonisba, daughter of Senator Elibaal." She smiled and approached the man.

"M. Manlius Paulus," he said.

She let out a little squeal and clapped her hands over her mouth.

"Do you think I will do?" asked Hasdrubal, rising and going to her.

"My dear, you are marvelous," she said, looking at his Roman garb.

"His dress is not too fashionable," said Elibaal, popping from behind the door. "He is from the provinces." The senator chuckled, delighted with their little game. "The same with Hanno. His clothes are not the latest fashion."

"Where is Hanno?" asked Hasdrubal.

"He'll be along, my dear," said Saphonisba. "He was trying on his Roman clothing when I left. I told him to ride one of the horses."

Elibaal suggested they go to the patio where he had ordered his slaves to set the dining couches.

Stretched on a couch, he discussed the arrangements he had made with a ship's captain for passage to Rome. Hanno bounded in and called a greeting to his grandfather. Hasdrubal stood where he could watch the changing blue of the sea and the sky, wondering how long it would be before he saw the soft color and felt the velvet breeze again. He turned toward his nephew.

Seeing the stranger, Hanno stopped in his pell-mell rush, embarrassed.

The high priest smiled. Wanting to appear easygoing and

approachable, he had secretly been practicing smiling before a hand mirror. "Do you think I will pass as a Roman, Claudius?"

"Uncle Hasdrubal!" the boy yelled and rushed over to inspect his new beard. "You're handsome," he said, stepping back.

Everybody laughed.

"I guess I meet with approval," said Hasdrubal as he straightened Hanno's conical cap. "You didn't even hear your new Roman name."

Hanno blushed. "I've practiced saying it over and over."

"Never mind. You will soon hear it enough."

After dinner, they went to Hasdrubal's rooms. "Abdmelkart," said Hasdrubal as the Numidian started to leave, "stay with us. Listen to the senator."

The slave sat on his haunches in a corner.

"All is arranged," Elibaal began. "You are a Roman who has been living in Hispania for years. Because of the war, you are returning to Rome with your son and a barbarian slave, a recent purchase."

He looked pointedly at Abdmelkart.

"Your household belongings, nothing luxurious, will go with you. Until you find a suitable house, you will stay in a guest house. I understand that they are not the most desirable, so you must waste no time in finding a house."

"Nothing showy," said Hasdrubal. "Somewhere in a slightly rundown neighborhood."

"Exactly." The senator nodded. "You are not supposed to be rich."

"Understood. And I will leave all information concerning the war at the address you specified."

"Your mail will come to you the same way."

"I will write often," Saphonisba said, "and tell you everything that goes on here."

Their departure arrived, on the day appointed by the soothsayers. Abdmelkart left early for the ship to supervise the loading of their belongings. Slaves came to the door with a litter for Hasdrubal. He didn't particularly like being carried in a litter, but this was part of his disguise. No self-respecting Roman would have walked to the commercial harbor. He had to admit the distance was considerable.

Senator Elibaal and the high priest stood by the litter quietly talking. A slave arrived from Saphonisba bearing a thick scroll from Bimilcar.

"How fortunate it arrived before you left," said Elibaal.

"I will read it on the way to the port."

Propped on his elbow in the litter, Hasdrubal broke the seal and unrolled the scroll.

Brother, this will be my last missile to you at Carthage. As instructed, I send it through Saphonisba. Future communication will go to Rome.

A chill is in the air. It will continue to get colder. We must reach the Alpes as soon as possible. I have never seen this thing called snow, nor have most of my troops. We understand it is dangerous. No one knows when to expect it. The uncertainty is worrisome to Hannibal. He says snow in the mountains will cause trouble if we don't get through the high passes in time.

Hasdrubal tried to imagine snow. Apparently, it just floated down from the sky in little round pellets so light in weight that they mounded up. He couldn't understand what was dangerous about it. Someone had said that if you put it in your mouth, it was cold, but it would melt away, leaving liquid which had no taste.

After finding a crossing point at the Rhodanus, we spent five days when we should have reached the base of the mountains. For two days, we built boats and collected anything that would float from friendly tribes.

While we were so employed, a Celtic force in war regalia gathered on the opposite bank. Hannibal refused to cross while admitting that staying where we were raised the specter of attack from the sides.

As a result, under cover of darkness, he sent part of the foot with local tribesmen as guides upstream to where an island divides the river. They were to cross by means of whatever they could build. On the other side, they were to rest a day and prepare for the coming battle. That accounts for two more days. Just before dawn the following day, they were to start downstream.

During our wait, Hannibal instructed the remaining troops. Light cavalry and the lightest infantry were to fill the boats, the man in the stern to handle three or four swimming horses by leads attached to their bridles. While this was going on, we could see the tribes crouched on the opposite bank, watching. Every once in a while, they would group together and gesticulate before they separated again to squat and watch. We speculated on their discussion, but knew that they had no inkling of Hannibal's ruse to keep them occupied so our troops could carry out his orders.

I and two others of the high command were with Hannibal when the smoke signal rose, announcing that the advance troops were nearby on the opposite shore. "Well done," he whispered and strode away, saying, "Order all boat captains to embark immediately and push out into the river."

You can't imagine the scramble. Men were yelling at each other, rocking the boats, jockeying for space. Horses were objecting and whinnying in the cold. In the river, the race was on. Jets of spray shot in all directions, blinding the rowers so the oars indiscriminately slapped the water. The horses were terrified. Their eyes bulged and rolled wildly, but the men controlling their leads held steady, calming the animals.

The barbarians added to the pandemonium by bellowing war cries and dancing up and down on the bank. When they were completely caught up in the action on the river, our forces torched their camp, leaving the wind to roar through, turning the sky bright before the flames were visible through the trees.

I was able to watch all this because my job of ferrying the elephants across couldn't begin until most of our troops had cleared the shore. As the unsuspecting, dancing, yelling, enemy were preparing to kill the first boatload of arriving troops, our army fell upon them from the rear.

Hannibal, as usual in the forefront, was among the first to land. He formed up the arriving men and joined the attack. Struck from the front as well as from behind, the Celts fled. Only then did Hannibal give the signal for the whole army to be ferried across and make camp for the night. Immediately, with the small crew left me, I prepared to ferry the elephants across.

I set some men to building solid rafts and others to binding two or three together. These were fastened securely to the bank. We waited until morning to bind the next group of rafts firmly to the first. As the day progressed, the pontoon extended further and further into the river.

At one point, I saw chieftains greet Hannibal, but didn't find out until later that they were the ones he expected from the plains of the Padus.

Rafts with towing lines were fastened onto the end of the

pontoon and dirt piled onto the entire structure until it looked like a wide pathway.

With everything in readiness, I instructed the mahouts to lead two female elephants onto the pontoon, knowing the others would follow. A bit nervous, I watched the two being guided along the footpath. Obediently, they plodded forward, trunks dangling, poking at the ground. The big males jockeyed into position, one behind the other, and followed. When six animals were in formation on the foremost raft, I ordered the men to cut it loose. The towing lines were fastened to a boat for the crossing. Another raft was quickly attached to the pontoon. I had to yell at the mahouts not to let the beasts see the water.

My attention was drawn to the opposite bank by excessive movement. The infantry was marching in one direction and the cavalry galloping off in the opposite. Before I had time to analyze that development, the elephants panicked. They screamed, turned, banged each other, lifted their feet over the water. The mahouts on their backs got control, and the beasts huddled together.

The next raft was cut loose. At once, a mammoth male became disoriented. He pitched and screamed. He unseated his mahout and jumped into the river. The mahout was not thrown clear. There was nothing I could do except urge on the raft crew and the drivers. After the fourth raft was cut loose, I spotted the animal struggling ashore on the opposite bank, without his driver.

When the last raft was in midstream, and my men already rowing toward the other shore, I pushed off in the remaining boat, elated that I had not lost an animal.

In the meantime, I could see Hannibal, dressed in the light armor he usually wore on marches, organizing the men as they landed and marching them off in double time. As my rowers neared the shore, Hannibal, leading two horses, walked to the water's edge while the few men who remained with him mounted. He handed me the reins of one horse and said, "The elephants and cavalry will form a rear guard against Roman attack." When I said I didn't know we were expecting Roman attack, Hannibal said that Scipio had discovered where we were. How he got there so fast remains a mystery. Through you we may not have these surprises in the future.

His reconnoitering forces met up with our Numidian cavalry, resulting in heavy loses. The cavalry acted as a covering force for our army as it marched away.

We are now in a place called "The Island," a corn-producing area, supporting a large population. No sooner had we arrived than we were confronted by a local problem. The king was hardly cold in his grave when the two sons started fighting over the throne. Hannibal, with his usual perspicacity, agreed to receive the older prince because, as he said to us, the growing year had been unusually good and the crop enormous. Hostilities would mean starvation for the people of the region. Faced with the combined strength of our two armies, the younger prince capitulated.

In thanks, the new king supplied us with corn, gave the soldiers new clothes and boots, replaced our worn-out weapons with new ones, and promised to guard our rear against attack through the territory of the Allobroges. Tomorrow, early, we take up that promise.

Hasdrubal pulled back the curtain slightly to see where they were. Hanno was to meet him at the Megara gateway of the city fortifications. He rerolled the scroll and stowed it in his clothing. Holding the edge of the curtain, he kept his face well away from the opening.

The gate where he had exited the day he first saw Aristide came into view. His hand instinctively touched the ruby ring that hung from a gold chain beneath his toga. The future was in the hands of the gods, but somehow Rome must yield up Elissa's whereabouts.

As usual, a swarm of people passed in and out of the gate. Two bearers holding a litter stood patiently to one side. He saw from the expression on their faces that they had recognized Elibaal's bearers and knew that they would continue their journey behind his own litter.

They passed into the inner city; the crowded, vibrant metropolis of one hundred thousand people; the private dwellings; the public buildings.

He felt strange, uneasy, melancholic, as they glided by his temple, wanting to go in, take up the reins, yet cringing for fear someone might come out the maze. No one did. They were past the temple. He could look at other things. On the right was the great sandstone senate building, and the portico with its many tiny shops. He smiled sadly when he saw the one where he had his sandals fixed. The few smaller buildings of the forum, buildings unimposing architecturally, were important to the government. And the library. His mind caressed it. The library of Carthage was well-known and contained a fine collection. When would he see it again?

Coming up on his left was the military harbor. The dry dock covering the central island of the round harbor must be in ferment. Longus was heading to Africa with a large flotilla. Which of the two hundred twenty slips with tackle and furniture magazines above were in use? The common entrance to the two harbors was seventy feet wide, and was closed by heavy chains.

For the first time since hearing of the Roman naval approach, he felt a touch of fear. Could this city so dear to him withstand an attack? There was the outer line of defense, a palisaded rampart with a ditch fore and aft, then the inner fortification, one gate of which he had just passed through. His musing ended. They had arrived at shipside. He got out of the litter and waited for Hanno. One behind the other, they walked up the gangplank.

Only once during the journey did Hanno slip. Fortunately, they were alone, eating the dinner Abdmelkart had prepared for them. Hanno started the conversation.

"Uncle Hasdrubal—"

The high priest quickly glanced around.

"Son, you have called me that once; you are never to do it again."

"Yes, father," meekly.

25

*T*hey disembarked at Ostia, Rome's seaport. Since it was late afternoon, Hasdrubal said, "We will rest here tonight and take the barge up the river to Rome tomorrow."

Hanno turned to him. "I thought you said this was just the port for Rome. It's a large city."

"Ostia may seem like a large city to a provincial boy, but Rome is much, much larger."

The boy's mouth opened wide in amazement. Seeing him, the high priest's lip twitched.

"All these people you see loading the ships and running up and down the wharf must have a place to live."

A half-naked dockworker bawled obscenities at a sailor who had thrown a rope short.

"Does he have to make so much noise?" Hanno clapped his hands over his ears.

His uncle eyed him through slits. "Best get used to it, son."

Hanno flashed a questioning look, but saw no anger or disapproval in his uncle's face.

"Yes, sire," he said, and continued to gape at the crowded harbor, the busy laborers, and Ostia's many warehouses.

"Abdmelkart," Hasdrubal said, "you and Claudius guard our things. I will get us rooms for the night." He strode off.

Standing side by side, Hanno and Abdmelkart watched him disappear between two whitewashed warehouses. The setting sun turned them to lavender. In the doorway of one building, four men gesticulated angrily.

Hanno snickered. It was much like home. After a while, he began to get restless. He stopped circumnavigating their piled furniture and spoke to the squatted slave. "Where is he? He should be back by now."

"As soon as he can." Seemingly undisturbed, Abdmelkart gazed into space.

Hanno moved off.

The minute the boy started around the heaped goods again, the Numidian's eyes darted in all directions. How long did it take to engage rooms? Not this long. Soon it would be dark. His master would get lost. He should have hired a local man to guide him. Abdmelkart was working himself into alarm when the high priest headed his way with serene, purposeful steps.

"Claudius," called Abdmelkart, "the master comes."

In two or three bounds, Hanno was beside the slave as Hasdrubal reached them.

"I have found an apartment."

"An apartment?" gasped Hanno. "I thought we were going to Rome tomorrow."

"We are, son. You would not have liked the rooms at the inns. I was fortunate in this arrangement. We will not need to store our furniture. Then, if we cannot find a suitable house in Rome, at least we have a place to sleep." He sensed his slave's approval. "Abdmelkart, hire some men to bring our belongings." He started off slowly, Hanno beside him.

"He doesn't speak Latin," Hanno said.

"You received lessons, so did he. He will manage."

Hanno glanced sideways at his uncle then looked back. The slave was scurrying from dock worker to dock worker, helping them load clothing bundles, furniture, cooking utensils, and dishes on their backs. Abdmelkart said something to one. The man looked up and caught Hanno's eye. Hanno turned around instantly and walked in silence.

Their apartment was in a four-story building, one of many, housing lower and lower-middle class workers. Each apartment had a balcony and windows to the outside. People hung over the balcony railings, watching the street scene below.

They reached their third-floor apartment. With delight, Hanno rushed to the balcony and peered down. However, he complained when he discovered that the building had no interior water supply. In all his young life, he had never been in such a mediocre dwelling and was not anxious to become more familiar.

"Son," said Hasdrubal, "stop that. This is a place to sleep. Do you think our army has much better? Tomorrow we will hunt for a house in Rome."

"Can we see the forum?"

"Finding a place to live is our first priority. As soon as we are settled, we will see the forum."

"Will Abdmelkart stay in this awful place?"

"Someone must watch our things."

Hanno swiftly turned away, but Hasdrubal caught his grimace. He chose to ignore it.

The barge ride up the River Tiber interested both Hanno and Hasdrubal. Blocks of apartment houses alternated with fields where goats and cattle grazed. The windows and balconies of these Roman houses looked out on the river. In Carthage, houses offered a blank wall to the passersby.

"Don't they want any privacy?" asked Hanno.

"There is not much privacy in those buildings anyway," said Hasdrubal. "Wait until we get to Rome. Homes there may be quite different—I hope."

They stepped off the barge onto the banks of the Tiber. Hasdrubal said, "Your grandfather suggested we look along a street called Vicus Tuscus west of the Temple of Castor and Pollux. The district was once fashionable. But the wealthy people have moved away, and the area has deteriorated. If we walk through this cattle market, I think we will come upon the Vicus Tuscus."

"How do you know so much about the city's layout?" demanded Hanno.

Hasdrubal smiled good-naturedly. "I memorized a map your grandfather gave me."

They found a house on a short street that ran into the Vicus Tuscus. It needed repairs which the owner was unwilling to make, and it had stood empty for some time. The house was small by wealthy Roman standards. Hasdrubal wonder if it had originally been part of an estate. Every other house appeared much larger. He questioned the owner, who told him that a young couple had owned the house until their family expanded. Since the house was small, it had not been broken up into apartments like the others in the neighborhood.

Hasdrubal was satisfied. The house would adequately serve their needs. Like Carthaginian homes, it faced inward. A door halfway down a passage led to the atrium. The square atrium, open to the sky, admitted light and air to the surrounding rooms. In the middle was a badly neglected garden. Both sides of the house were identical—two rooms and a spacious area. A portico running along three sides of the atrium protected these open areas. On leaving the atrium, the main passage ran through the functional part of the building and exited into a vegetable garden. A large dining room was on the right of the passage. From its doorway, a corridor veered at an angle to the kitchen behind it. Store rooms, bedrooms for the slaves, and two lavatories occupied the remaining space.

The high priest's Phoenician instincts came to the fore. He drove a hard bargain, buying the house at a much reduced rate because of its disrepair. The ex-owner promised to start cleaning that afternoon.

Relieved, pleased, and contented all at once, Hasdrubal returned to Ostia with Hanno and informed Abdmelkart of their good fortune.

"Tomorrow," he said to his slave, "take our possessions to Rome. Claudius will accompany you. I shall go up early to hire tradesmen. We need a drainpipe replaced in one bathroom. The roof must be mended in a number of spots, minor things improved by a carpenter, and, afterwards, the walls have to be refinished where the plaster has fallen. Put our furniture in the garden until we see what use we make of the rooms."

As darkness fell the following day, they completed their move to Rome. Hasdrubal chose one room for his bedroom. He sat down in the open area in front of it to survey their work. Hanno wanted the room opposite, but as one of its walls had to be plastered, he was using another room for the time being. He came from his bedroom, flung himself on the floor, rested his head on his arms, and waved his feet in the air.

"We will use," Hasdrubal said, "this area for our sitting room while the weather remains warm. Afterwards, we will move into the room where you are now sleeping. The plastering should be finished by then."

"We can put a little bench on the other side of it. Strangers can sit facing the front door."

"Your idea is good, but I am not so sure that is a Roman custom. We shall see."

"What will we do with the other room?"

"That will be my library."

Hanno wondered why they needed a library when they had brought no scrolls.

"You will take your lessons there."

Hanno had no time to express an opinion on that subject. Abdmelkart came into view. The slave started to bow.

"Once is enough, Abdmelkart," said Hasdrubal. "Walk up to me, bow, and wait to be acknowledged."

"Yes, sire." Abdmelkart would do as his master requested, but he really didn't think one bow showed sufficient respect.

"What is it you want?" Hasdrubal asked.

"Shall I serve dinner here or in the dining room?"

"I think here would be nice. Do you, Claudius?"

"Yes, let's," said Hanno.

"Which reminds me," Hasdrubal said when the Numidian left, "Abdmelkart has enough to do with the two of us and the house. I need to buy a middle-aged woman to do the cooking."

The surprised look on his nephew's face made him add, "Preferably one who is not Roman."

Hasdrubal visited the slave market in the morning. He found a pathetic-looking Macedonian woman whose price was low because she was deaf. He bought her without even finding out whether she could cook. She had no known name. They simply referred to her as the Cook. She was given one of the storerooms near the kitchen. He bought some inexpensive furniture for her room and endeared himself to her forever by giving her a little money for new clothes.

Two horses and a groom were added to the household. They were housed in an alley accessed through a locked and bolted door in the garden wall.

After purchasing them, Hasdrubal and Hanno rode out of town along the Appian Way. They hoped to find what purported to be an inn for travelers. Hasdrubal remembered the inns at Ostia with distaste. The rooms had been cramped and dirty with obscenities scrawled on the walls. When he had plumped the beds, insects had scampered for cover. Undoubtedly, this inn would be no better, but as it was his contact point for mail, he intended to visit with the proprietor.

"This is the inn," he said as they slowed the horses in front of a low, two-storied building. "We will go in and introduce ourselves. There has not been enough time for us to receive any news, but we must get on friendly terms with the owner."

The stench as they entered made Hanno wrinkle his nose. Women in various states of dress sat on a bench near the door, gossiping. Near them, a man was asleep on the floor. Hasdrubal caughed as he skirted him, an excuse to cover his nostrils against the smell of cheap wine.

He was surprised when handed a fat papyrus from Bimilcar. There was also a small skin roll for Hanno from his mother. Delighted, Hasdrubal paid the innkeeper handsomely. His intense, all-seeing glance surveyed the dingy room as they left.

A man sat against the back wall where the light was dimmest, apparently waiting for something. His horse perhaps? Was he a respectable traveler with no local friends to give him a night's lodging? Hasdrubal's eyes narrowed. The man was small boned with the full beard and thick hair of a Carthaginian. Under his right hand, half covered by his Phoenician clothing, lay a conical cap.

With a start, Hasdrubal realized the man was Palokart, Asherat's youngest son. What was he doing in this place? The high priest was fairly confident that he had not recognized him, with his new Roman look. Had Palokart recognized his speaking voice? Probably not, even if he had heard the conversation with the innkeeper. Palokart seemed lost in thought. Perhaps this was a chance encounter, but he couldn't risk meeting him again. He would let Hanno take care of the mail.

Seated in the bright, open space that he had furnished for his relaxation, a brazier under his feet, Hasdrubal unrolled Bimilcar's scroll. Seeing Hanno hurrying across the atrium, he waited.

"Shall I read this to you?" He looked at Hanno's eager face.

"Yes, please." Hanno dropped onto a cushion.

"He says:

We have climbed some of the mountains toward the pass in one of the worst experiences of my life. It started as soon as we reached the base of the Alpes, a march of ten days through the territory of the Allobroges. The king kept his word and protected our rear. No sooner had we camped than Hannibal announced that we would remain until further notice. Odd because he had been in such a hurry to get through the pass. It seems that he had been sharing the noon meal out of the same pot with a group of common soldiers when scouts came to him with the news that major forces of the Allobroges had gathered.

The way was narrow, steep, and so difficult that pack animals could cover the terrain more easily than some of the men, laden with weapons and armor. The enemy was so sure of us that they only maintained large numbers at strategic points during the day.

They withdrew to a town on the other side of the first rise at night.

Hanno said, "Pretty stupid of them."
Ignoring the comment, Hasdrubal continued.

That was all Hannibal needed to hear. He ordered the scouts to present themselves at his tent at sundown. Then, he sent for those of us who comprise his senior staff. When we were all in his tent, he said, "The enemy holds the pass. We will march the remainder of the day as if nothing were known to us of their presence and camp for the night at the base of the narrow section. You two," he pointed to me and the officer standing next to me, "have under your commands some excellent, swift, light-armed troops. Pick the best of them to accompany me. The rest of you see that fires are lit, the men are fed, and that they conduct themselves as usual. At daybreak, the column—soldiers, cavalry, elephants, pack animals—will start through the defile. Prepare the men for an attack. I do not know how or when or even if it will come. Tonight, the force under my command will make its way through the gorge and seize the abandoned positions. We travel by foot so send the horses up with your men."

We went to our stations, instructed our troops, and marched to the base of the gorge. As dusk closed in, our small group gathered near the lower end of the trail. On the heels of the Gallic guides, Hannibal led us into the pass. It wasn't easy to see, though the night was clear. Quickly, the ascent narrowed and steepened. Men stumbled and slipped on the rocks, but no sound came from them. They swore under their breath.

"Oh!," exclaimed Hanno, his face aglow, "I wish I could have been with them."
Hasdrubal looked at his nephew through slits. The darkness, the trail, the excitement of the unknown were what appealed to Hanno rather than the army.

Beginning approximately halfway up, Hannibal stopped every so often and counted off men with the order to hold the rise. At the top of the gorge, above which the ascent broadened out, the rest of us stationed ourselves on a flat rock jetting over the trail. Not much of the night remained. The men settled down,

wrapping themselves in their cloaks against the cold. Together,
Hannibal and I listened to every snapping twig, though he be-
lieved that the Allobroges wouldn't return until the trails were
visible.

Light filtered slowly into the gorge, but noise reached us through
the clear air as the head of the column entered it—the shouting of
men, the rattling of falling stones, the neighing of horses in the
cold. On they came with increasing noise. We knew the Allobroges
were around, but there was no sign we could pinpoint.

Finally, the column appeared way below, cautiously creeping
along the edge of a precipice. Hannibal frowned. We both knew it
was a bad spot if the Allobroges attacked. He said, "They have
been taken by surprise and are probably conferring, deciding what
to do."

As the sun rose higher, the wind died. Sheltered among the
trees, the men became warm and dropped their wraps. The light
armor glinted in the sun. At mid-morning, with savage howls,
the Allobroges attacked.

"Wow," cried Hanno.

Hasdrubal continued matter-of-factly.

From our position, we could see two areas of attack. We didn't
know how many attack points were below, but our ears told us
there were more, blocked from our view by the trees. Men dropped
to the ground. Wounded horses screamed in pain, wheeled, and
raced pell-mell down the slope, knocking men and animals over
the precipice.

It was terrible to watch. Hannibal chewed the inside of his
cheek and worked his fingers up and down his leg. He said, "If the
fight continues in this manner, our army will be destroyed. Our
only recourse is to strike. The confusion will be worse at first
because of the fighting ahead and behind."

Cupping his hands around his mouth, he shouted, "We at-
tack," and plunged down the slope. The rest of us, swinging our
swords right and left, flung ourselves into battle.

Hanno inhaled noisily. "My fa—he wasn't hurt because he
wrote us!" "At least not seriously," Hasdrubal said quietly, pretending to be absorbed in the scroll. He knew Hanno's face would
turn red with embarrassment.

*Hannibal's charisma is such that I could feel the renewed
courage in the troops. They sensed the presence of their commander in the worst of the fighting.*

*Before long, the Gauls were in headlong flight. Hannibal,
infuriated by the heavy losses of men and animals, asked for vol-
unteers to seize their town. So while the troops, groaning at the
steepness of the gorge and from the pain of their cuts and bruises,
continued to work their way upward, Hannibal led his Numidian
cavalry, on the theory that they would be fastest, to the enemy's
stronghold. I stayed with the main army.*

*When he returned, he said that they had found an abandoned
camp. I write you from that camp. The Allobroges were in such
a rush to leave that they left our captured soldiers behind plus
mules, horses, and a supply of corn and cattle. At Hannibal's
order, we remain where we are. The area is large and fairly level.
We need time to bind our wounds, seek the missing, count the
dead, and gird our-selves for the snow which we can see on the
mountains glittering in the sun. After all, it is the end of October,
and the weather has turned bad.*

Hasdrubal laid the scroll in his lap.

"How exciting," said Hanno. "I wish I could meet Hannibal."

"You very well may one day."

"And my you-know-who."

Hasdrubal smiled sympathetically. "Just refer to him as the
General."

"Right." Hanno hopped up. "I'll see what the Cook is making for lunch."

The high priest remained still, the scroll in his hand, his face
serious. So, the army was reaching the high pass. The feat was
extraordinary, the danger great. He would do his best to aid them
with information and pray to Tanit for their safety.

Hanno, returning from the kitchen, interrupted his thoughts.
"Father, now that we are settled, can we walk in the forum?"

"All right, after lunch," he said.

Morning was when all the city's business took place, and when
he would learn anything of use to Hannibal, but it might be a good
idea to visit the forum, get straight which buildings were which.
Perhaps he could spot some Hellenes, ask them if they knew
Diodorus or his son's whereabouts. Free Hellenes would be traders, though a recently captured Hellene might know of Aristide.

Hanno and Hasdrubal dressed in their formal togas, a requirement to walk in the forum. They entered the Vicus Tuscus and turned toward the Roman forum.

"What is this building with the portico and pillars," asked Hanno as they rounded the corner of their street. "Lots of different men go in and out."

"A public bath."

"A public— But I see well-dressed, well-to-do men go in there. Don't they bathe at home?"

His uncle smiled. "The public and the aristocracy do not bathe separately in Rome. They do not have our sense of privacy. They enjoy bathing in groups and use the baths as a club to discuss politics and city affairs."

"I would rather bathe at home," Hanno said in a low, disgusted tone.

"Agreed," said Hasdrubal and dropped the subject.

In the forum, the Viscus Tuscus ended in a perpendicular angle with the Via Sacra. Hasdrubal and Hanno stood at the intersection.

"This is the most sacred road in Rome," said the high priest, looking up and down the Via Sacra.

"It's crowded," said Hanno.

Though the day's business stopped at noon, men strolled about, talking to their friends. Across the forum, slightly to the left, was the Temple of Janus.

"The doors are open," whispered Hanno.

"Yes," said Hasdrubal. "Rome is at war." He looked at the temple. "Let us go over there. I think that is the Comitium and the Curia Hostilia just to the left of the Temple of Janus. If so, that is where I want to come in the morning."

They stepped around the Lapis Niger.

"This piece of black marble," Hasdrubal said, "marks where Romulus is buried."

Hanno shrugged, unimpressed.

"Is this where people meet to cast their votes?" He indicated the square open space behind the black marble.

"Yes. The building just beyond is the senate house. I would like to listen to their debates, but only the children of senators are allowed in."

They turned around, glanced at the imposing Temple of Saturn, and strolled down the Via Sacra. They looked at the Temple of Vesta, the House of the Vestals, the palace of the Pontifex Maximus, and the Temple of Romulus. Hasdrubal picked out many Hellenes among the strollers, but found no opportunity to speak to them.

However, the next morning, standing around the Comitium, he noticed a prosperous Athenian watching the people exit the senate building. Hasdrubal casually worked his way close to the man and struck up a conversation.

After they had talked for a few minutes, he said, "Do you happen to know a trader named Aristide of Athens?"

"Aristide of Athens," repeated the man thoughtfully. "No. There is no such trader in Rome."

"His father is Diodorus of Athens," Hasdrubal added, hoping for a different response.

The Athenian smiled. "Everybody knows Diodorus of Athens. But, no, not the son. Too bad. Diodorus is a brilliant, but ruthless trader."

Hasdrubal thanked him and backed away. His hopes plummeted. Aristide was so little known that even his name was unfamiliar to the trading community. How was he ever going to find Elissa?

26

*T*ranquility settled over the household, freeing Hasdrubal to spend each morning in the Comitium. In the afternoon, he took long walks through the city, sometimes alone, sometimes with Hanno.

One day they entered an unfashionable area. Hanno said, "I was here this morning. Some old men were sitting on that water trough over there"—he jerked his chin toward the trickling water—"gossiping."

Hasdrubal stopped abruptly. He looked at the trough, at Hanno, and back at the trough. The idea, as it struck, felt like a rock heaved from above. He unconsciously ran his fingers through his hair to make sure nothing hurt. "Let us go home," he said. In answer to Hanno's surprised look, he said, "I think I have the solution to your duties. We will discuss it."

They sat in his library, Hanno on a floor cushion. Hasdrubal said, "It occurs to me that knowing the various sections of the city well might come in handy."

Hanno nodded. "I can do that."

"More importantly, these old men around the city receive news through undercurrents no one else understands. Become friends with them."

Hanno grinned, his mind's eye constructing the scene.

"You are just starting to grow," Hasdrubal continued. "You can easily roam around the city like one of the street urchins. No one would question you."

To be in character, Hanno dressed shabbily and meandered in perfect freedom. He familiarized himself with the myriad little streets, types of homes, and people who lived in the different sections of the city. He befriended the old men who sat in the sun and talked of how the government should be run, of which senator was advocating what, and how much better they could run things. Hanno was in his element, eager, alert, and competent.

While Hanno wandered the streets, Hasdrubal walked slowly around the Comitium. He pretended to be thinking or resting, but in reality he was listening to those near him. Many scraps of information came his way. Most appeared to be the blown-up opinions of the speakers. One day, he stooped to fix his sandal near two well-fed, middle-aged Romans in quiet conversation. His ear had caught the word "Scipio."

"He got to the Rhodanus with his full force only to find Hannibal gone," said the taller of the two men. "He sent word that he couldn't believe what he was hearing. Instead of securing Hispania by conquering southern Gaul, Hannibal is about to cross the Alps."

"Absolutely foolhardy," pronounced his listener.

"The man is blinded by his hatred for us and will risk his whole army to satisfy his own desires. They will never get through alive."

Where have you two been, thought Hasdrubal. The crossing had been common knowledge for some time. He continued to fuss with the thong on his sandal, hoping they would say something of interest.

"I wish I could have been in the curia this morning," the shorter, clean-shaven man said in irritation.

"Scipio returned to Marseilles with his fleet, trying to decide what his next move should be."

"Why didn't he follow Hannibal?" interrupted the second man.

"That's impossible, my friend. He doesn't know where the enemy is." The taller man sounded very superior.

"What does Publius Cornelius Scipio intend to do? I hope not sit out the war in Marseilles." He sniffed.

"He has decided to send his fleet and most of his army to Hispania in order to secure that region for us."

"That's rather stupid." The man's voice was extremely irritated. "The Carthaginians are about to invade our country, and our general runs off to Hispania."

Hasdrubal stood up and moved off. Their conversation wouldn't tell him anything new. The information had already been conveyed to Hannibal. On hearing the news, Hasdrubal had instantly realized that if the Carthaginians lost Hispania, its base for supplies and fresh troops, Carthage could lose the war.

In his communications, Bimilcar had not mentioned Hannibal's reaction to the message, but the high priest reasoned that Hannibal would do everything he could to bolster his forces in Hispania.

He stroked his beard, wondering what group to listen to next. Scraps of conversation came to him from every direction. Three well-groomed, elderly men, standing a few paces on his left, mentioned Scipio. Hasdrubal edged toward them.

"Yes," said a gray-haired man in his seventies. "Before I left for Pompeii, I knew that Scipio had sailed to Pisae with the few soldiers he had not sent to Hispania. I take it, he has arrived."

"Not only arrived," said one who looked like a senator, "but marched through Etruria and took command of the legions on the frontier. He then advanced to the Padus Valley. He has pitched camp there and is waiting for the Carthaginians to arrive."

Hasdrubal hurried from the forum, dodging people as he went. I will send that information, he said to himself. He hoped that Hannibal already knew it. Scipio had accomplished his moves in a very short time. Hannibal had an adversary worthy of his genius.

As he emerged onto the Vicus Tuscus, he shifted his feet nervously, feeling edgy. Instinct warned him that he was being followed. Who would follow him? Why? A thief! Money! He had no money on his person. What should he do if attacked? It was broad daylight. People were around; quite a number, as a matter of fact. He turned left into a narrow, rutted street. He surreptitiously looked back. His heart stopped, thumped in his chest, then raced. Behind him was a man in Phoenician clothing. He recognized Palokart, the son of the late head priestess. Would Palokart turn into the street? Was his being here an accident? Very likely. Many people walked on the Vicus Tuscus. The high priest shivered when Palokart unobtrusively angled his body around the corner into the rutted street.

Turning right, Hasdrubal entered an alley which connected the street he had come down with another narrow street. No other way out was possible. He couldn't turn around and face the man. What an idiotic idea to have come through here. If Palokart chose to confront him, he was trapped. He walked faster. No sound came from behind him, but he knew Palokart was there.

Over his left shoulder, he heard, "Slow down, Hasdrubal. I would have words with you."

He kept on going. The other street wasn't far; perhaps he could make it. A firm hand grasped his shoulder and forced him to stop. Palokart was slightly taller and inclined to fleshiness. He moved around in front of him and looked intently into his face for what seemed an eternity.

"You are Hasdrubal, high priest of Tanit, in Carthage. One day, I saw you at an inn outside the city on the Via Appia. I recognized your walk, but couldn't place it. It took me a while to figure out who you were. The disguise is excellent. I have been watching you for some days. I know where you live, who lives with you, and can guess your activity." He waited.

With supreme authority Hasdrubal met Palokart's eyes squarely and said nothing.

"You can't have fled Carthage over the death of my mother. Her death was an out-and-out suicide witnessed by many people."

Hasdrubal held his tongue. He observed that his assailant was becoming exasperated and a little unsure of himself.

"If you think I'm going to hurt you because of her," Palokart said, "you are mistaken. I did not love her. I lived in terror of her. So did all the rest of us, including my father. That's why I left Carthage, a city I loved and still do, for Rome."

Should he admit his identity and solicit Palokart's help? They did not really need his help, at least not now, but they had to ally him to them so they would not be discovered. Could he be trusted?

"Hasdrubal"—desperation was in the tone—"I am doing what I can for Carthage, but I am well known as a Carthaginian. I have to move with care. I have bared my soul to you. If by chance you are a Roman, my life is forfeit."

"We cannot talk here," said Hasdrubal. "Follow me." He shifted one foot slightly forward. Palokart stepped aside, allowing him to pass. He walked normally, knowing that the Carthaginian was keeping his distance. When he came to his home, he glanced back. Palokart showed no interest. Hasdrubal left the door slightly ajar. He stood by the visitors' bench and waited. Soon the door pushed open.

"No one saw me," Palokart said, for the first time using the Phoenician language. Hasdrubal bolted the door.

They passed through the atrium. Hanno came from the rear of the house. Seeing the Carthaginian, he hesitated and looked uncertainly at his uncle.

"It is all right, Claudius. This is Palokart, son of Asherat."

"Lunch with us," he said to Palokart. "It will be more than the skimpy lunch the Romans eat."

"With pleasure," said Palokart. He added apologetically, "Do you mind if we talk about my mother?"

"Not at all. I thought you would." Hasdrubal led the way to the dining room.

"She pleaded with me to come home," Palokart said.

"She made me feel guilty when I refused. Now she's dead."

"I am so sorry."

Palokart's laugh was short and ironic. "Don't be. We all lived in mortal fear of that snake. Nobody dared cross her. She killed her first two daughters. We think she killed my brother." He hesitated. "I never knew whether I would wake up. She could slip in at night while I slept. You couldn't feel the snake bite. We all jumped the minute she expressed any wish."

"The snake was loosed on one of my priestesses," said Hasdrubal. "Fortunately, the bite did not go through her clothing. But I cannot imagine why your mother set her slave on Claudius, instead of the snake."

"I don't know how my father stood it all those years." Palokart shrugged. A sad little smile crossed his dark features. "As soon as I was old enough, I came to Rome. With mother dead, I can go back to Carthage. If it weren't for this war, I would. At the moment, I think I can do more for our city here."

"What are you doing," Hasdrubal asked. "You wear Carthaginian dress. You do not try to hide your origins. How do you gain information? Who are your contacts?"

"As an individual, I have no access to Roman secrets, but I have Etruscan friends. Etruscans hold high positions in Rome, and many of them are not wedded to her side. I get scraps of information now and again, a casual word here and there. It's not much. I pass it to Hannibal's network." He hunched his shoulders. "I can't be depended on; the risk is too great."

Hasdrubal and Palokart agreed to continue working separately on Carthage's behalf. Afterwards, feigning indifference, Hasdrubal asked Palokart if he knew of an Athenian trader named Aristide.

Palokart tilted his head toward the ceiling, then looked out the door, staring unseeing at nothing, and finally said, "No. How important is it?"

Hasdrubal hesitated. He kept his eyes on his tightly twisted hands. "He abducted my wife."

Blowing out his breath, Palokart said, "I'll ask among my Etruscan friends, but I can't offer you much hope."

Hasdrubal was unable to stop his spirits from dropping as a stone thrown into water. Aristide must have taken her to Athens, he thought, and until his services for Carthage were no longer needed, he could not go to Athens.

Dusk was heavy, the blue in the sky deepening rapidly to cobalt. The three walked across the atrium, and Palokart cautiously slipped into the shadowed street.

"Now that we have this new acquaintance," Hasdrubal said to Hanno, "I am free to canter to the inn. I shall relieve you of that duty tomorrow. He threw an arm over Hanno's shoulder and smiled at him.

Hanno smiled back. They walked on in silence, their close and strengthening relationship making talk unnecessary.

The next morning, Hasdrubal trotted along the Vicus Tuscus as the first faint rays of the new day crept up the sky. He had to go round the Palatium and meet the Via Appia. The cold penetrated. Hasdrubal pulled his wool cloak tighter. He hoped for word from Bimilcar. The army had been close to the final pass through the Alpes when his brother wrote last, and each day, he expected a scroll detailing their descent to the plain.

By the time the sun was fully up, Hasdrubal was in the dim, reception room of the inn. The room smelled of burnt cabbage and urine. He wrinkled his nose. Nobody was around. He banged on the counter. Slowly, the rear door opened. The grumpy innkeeper shuffled in. His uncombed oily hair stuck to his head. He snuffed and rubbed the back of his hand across his nose. Hasdrubal glanced away. The man was disgusting. He must have slept in that food-stained work shirt. Obviously, he had just wakened.

The proprietor growled, "Can't you come at a decent hour?"

Hasdrubal dropped a generous number of coins on the counter. The man's eyes sharpened. Good, thought the high priest. He handed the innkeeper the message to be forwarded to Hannibal. In return, the innkeeper gave him three skin scrolls: two for Hanno, stamped with the seals of Saphonisba and Elibaal; the third scroll, for him, bore Bimilcar's seal.

Hasdrubal stowed them in the folds of his cloak. He kicked his horse to a gallop until he reached the first apartment houses, private homes, shops, and temples where he slowed to a trot.

Abdmelkart answered his code knock on the back gate. "Bring

a brazier and some bread to my bedroom," he said to the slave, "and give these scrolls to Hanno."

"When he returns, sire. He has already gone out."

Abdmelkart set the steaming cereal and warm bread on a small table at his elbow. His feet on the brazier, Hasdrubal opened Bimilcar's scroll. He thought to skim it, waiting until lunchtime to read it when Hanno was present.

We are in Roman territory, having crossed the Alpes in heavy snow. At first, as we worked our way up, the snow was scattered. Men were fascinated. They kicked it, picked it up, threw it into the air, laughed as it fluttered down, tasted it. The mood didn't last. As cold and wet chilled them, laughter and play stopped. Wrapped in whatever clothing they had, the men plodded on.

Four days after our start up, the tribes surrounding the pass, carrying wreaths and branches of friendship, came to Hannibal. They had heard of the battle in the defile and the captured town. Rather than subjecting themselves or their families to similar treatment, they offered hostages as proof of friendship.

Hasdrubal, caught up in the detail, was reading every word.

Hannibal distrusted them, but did not want to anger them. He said to us, "We will take their hostages, have them act as guides and get cattle as from an ally. Unknown to them, we will prepare as for an enemy." Heavy infantry was sent to the rear to blunt any assault.

He was right. Three days later, taking advantage of a narrow gorge, they struck. Rocks were rolled down from higher ground on men trapped in the gorge, slingstones hurled at close range. The chaos in the rear was so great that the heavy infantry had difficulty at times telling who was with them and who was against them. As time passed, the defending troops became aware that they only faced each other. The Gauls had vanished into the wilderness.

Hannibal, along with half of our forces—including me and the troops under my authority—spent the night near a bare rock, offering only a modicum of shelter, to wait as the army and the pack train cleared the gorge. Groans from men and animals reached us continuously. At one point, Hannibal covered his face with his hands, heartbreak in the slump of his shoulders. Most of those

struggling, wounded, and dying men, he could call by name.
Their terror and suffering were his terror and suffering. And the
only thing we could do was wait.

Hasdrubal laid the scroll on his lap. Staring into space, he
tried to picture the snow, the gorge, the battle.

By morning, most of the Gauls were gone. Hannibal, along
with a few of us, his senior officers, led the advance. Small groups
still harassed us as we marched to the top. We counterattacked
with elephants. You should have seen the Gauls. They bolted in
mortal fear, knocking each other down in their haste. If the whole
performance hadn't been so tragic, it would have been amusing.

It took us nine days after leaving the base to reach the top. At
Hannibal's order, those of us who survived rested there for two
days, giving the laggards along the route time to catch up.

How can I adequately express to you the emotion we all felt
standing there in the cold and the snow, looking down on that
brown, sun-warmed earth? Longing was on every face, and every
face showed the strain of the constantly damp, dreary landscape,
and the cold. Always the cold. Looking, our eyes began to glitter.
Beyond the warm earth, we saw Rome and victory, untold wealth,
gold and slaves.

The descent turned out to be as bad as the ascent. Even with-
out marauders, many lost their lives. The trail was both steep and
narrow. A man or animal who stepped slightly off the traveled
path in the deep snow found nothing beneath his feet and disap-
peared. At night, the men huddled together in the wet, afraid to
move, afraid they would go over the edge. The elephants, driven
by their handlers, lumbered along, their skin hanging in folds.

Brother, be thankful you have never had to endure such agony.

There is other agony, thought Hasdrubal.

As the last straw, we reached a spot where a landslide had
carried away part of the mountain. What remained was too nar-
row for the elephants and pack animals, hardly wide enough for
men, with no definite footpath. Sending the men around, as
Hannibal intended, became impossible. Wet flakes started to drift
by, which rapidly became thick and deadening. We made camp as
best we could after clearing the snow from a ridge.

Sliding and skidding on the ice beneath the snow, the men pushed shovels full toward the edge, not getting close themselves, but sending the packed snow tumbling over. If a man lost his balance, he couldn't get up. His feet sank to the ice beneath the snow. Even his mates were of little assistance. They would catch him under the arms, and go down themselves when they tried to lift him. The animals did no better. The mules sank in up to their chests then couldn't get their legs out.

While the winter light held, I edged along the precipice, trying to find the blockage. An enormous rock had lodged across the path. After careful reconnoitering, I determined that by building a hot fire on it, then pouring sour wine over it, we could shatter the rock. Once shattered, men with pickaxes could send it into the valley. The path could be built up so that even the elephants could pass.

I presented my plan to Hannibal. Swiftly, he thought through all possibilities. He said, "Make your arrangements. I will throw my bedroll in with the cavalry tonight and be on hand when you start in the morning."

The dawn rang with the sound of chopping as trees were felled and cut into logs. The snow had stopped, and a strong wind blew, making the fire burn fiercely. When the rock was white-hot, I ordered buckets of sour wine thrown over it. The men jumped back from the scalding steam and yelled with joy at the hiss and crackle of the splitting rock. As soon as they could approach it, I had them tackle the mass with pickaxes. Huge pieces of rock went hurtling into the valley. Seeing it, the men started to laugh and then, as they worked, to sing. Excitement spread as the mass of rock disappeared. After the pickax wielders had cleared a patch, I ordered others to build up the path.

By the end of the day, Hannibal was able to lead the men, horses and mules across. He took them at once below the snow line and turned the animals out to pasture. After ordering the men to wait for him, he returned alone to where I was with the Numidian troops.

It took us three days, working in relays, to build a strong enough path for the elephants. Once we got those poor beasts to the grass and woods, we all rested. Three days after that, we were on the plain. Hannibal and those of us on the staff added up the time. It had taken us five months to get from Hispania to the foot of the Alpes. The actual crossing had taken fifteen days. We re-

*viewed our situation. The army had survived the ordeal, but all
of us recognized that before we could push our advantage of surprise, we, including the animals, needed rest and food.*

*We still have the elephants, but they are miserable, and we
undoubtedly will lose a few. I watched them in a wooded area
careening like demented beasts in their craze to get at the trees
and strip the leaves. At one point, three or four men rolled away
from a great charging male just in time. The beast saw nothing
except the young tree where the men were resting.*

*We are camped by a stream that bumps and gurgles over a
rocky bed. There are thick grasses where horses and mules graze.
Men lie on the ground or sit in clusters around cooking pots. Many
are dejected as a result of the physical exertion and privation.
Hannibal, therefore, placed his priority on the care of his troops and
animals. We will not move on until they are rested. Once that
comes about, I know not what our next objective will be.*

In slow motion, Hasdrubal rolled up the skin and put it in
the niche where he kept Bimilcar's scrolls. A great sense of relief
flooded him. The Carthaginian army had accomplished what no
other body of men had ever attempted. Now, the war would begin
in ernest. He didn't doubt that Carthage, led by Hannibal, would
be victorious.

By nightfall the following day, news that the Carthaginians
had crossed the Alps reached Rome. The entire city swarmed
into the forum, or so it seemed to the high priest and Hanno.
Excitement filled the air. The elegantly togaed men marveled at
Hannibal's exploit. But the conversation in the small groups
sounded worried, though the Romans had no doubt that their
legions would wipe out the intruder and bring Hannibal to Rome
in chains to be paraded, alongside his elephants. The animals
were another enthralling topic. The public had no idea what one
looked like.

After the initial excitement, life went on at the usual pace.
The war was far away and only affected the frontier. Brought up
in a staid Phoenician city, Hasdrubal was amazed by the Roman
nightlife. Noise never ceased in the metropolis. Moving torches
kept main arteries like the Vicus Tuscus bright. Fortunately, his
home was on a quiet, dark street with just the occasional torch-
bearing slave lighting his master's steps after the sun set.

27

*H*anno was crossing the atrium one morning when Hasdrubal called him. He retraced his steps and entered his uncle's bedroom.

"Would you walk through the well-to-do area behind the Palatium?" Hasdrubal asked.

Hanno raised an eyebrow.

Hasdrubal smiled. "A man named Galerius lives there. I think he is inciting the Celts to harass Hannibal. It might be useful to know who comes and goes."

"I'll do it first thing."

"His house is light blue set in a large garden."

Hanno easily found the house. He watched for a while. A slave went to market and returned. Nobody else went in or out. Sundown, he thought, would be the best time to watch.

He wandered around the neighborhood, looking at the houses. As he neared a white house set close to the street, a slave, carrying a tiny baby, rushed out. Hanno glanced from the slave to an agonized young woman in the doorway. Their eyes met. Her body leaned forward helplessly, and her mouth opened in a cry that never came.

"Close the door, fool." The harsh command from the house interior drowned any sound she had made. With a choked sob, the young woman backed up. An older woman, reaching from behind, slammed the door.

Hanno shifted his gaze to the slave. The man's steps slowed, and he bent, talking to the baby. They walked along like that. Hanno followed a short distance behind. A nursemaid shepherding three children and an old slave headed for market passed them. The children stared at the baby, but otherwise, Hanno and the slave walked unnoticed. After all, it was the height of the work day. Any man who was anybody, or wanted to be, would be in the forum.

Presently, they came to a place where buildings were widely separated, surrounded by small vineyards or empty fields. The slave found a flat rock and sat down.

Hanno stopped in front of him. "Your baby has no clothes on, and it's cold," he said in some surprise.

"I'm keeping him warm," said the slave, hugging the baby closer to his chest.

"Where are you taking him?"

The slave relaxed his arms and looked down at the baby who whimpered. He looked back at Hanno and said, "It's sad, but I have to expose him."

"What do you mean?" Instinctively, Hanno knew he meant something terrible.

"You're a big fellow not to know that," remarked the slave.

Hanno shrugged his shoulders. He remained standing in front of the slave.

"I'm going to put the baby on this rock and go home," said the man.

Hanno's eyes flew open. "But he'll die."

The slave nodded. "One way or another," he said as they heard a dog bark, "he'll die."

"But why?" persisted Hanno. He moved closer and looked down at the tiny, dark form. "There's nothing wrong with him. He's not deformed."

"No. He's a perfect little male."

The two watched the baby in silence. Shivering, the baby screwed up his tiny face, and cried.

"Oh," the unhappy slave pressed the infant to his warm chest. "The master is a hard, cruel man. He keeps the mistress locked in the house and guarded. He says this baby isn't his, and he won't have it in the house. The child was born while he was away taking care of business. He came home a few days ago. This morning when he left, he said the baby had to be gone by the time he got back. The mistress is in hysterics. Everybody is upset, running around and yelling."

"Can't you hide him?" Hanno's question sounded like a suggestion. "That's a big house."

"I'm just a Macedonian slave and have no people in Rome or I'd take the baby to them." The man heaved a deep sigh. "I hate to think what would happen if any of us hid this little one and the master found out."

"Give him to me. I'll take him home."

The slave stared at Hanno. This waif had a home! Probably some hovel, many mouths and hardly enough food. The boy looked healthy enough, though. Oh, well, better than dogs tearing at the baby's tender flesh. Without another word, he got up, placed the baby in Hanno's arms, and ran back the way he had come.

Astonished at the rapid transfer, Hanno gazed after him. The baby squirmed. Hanno looked down at the tiny form. The baby had light brown skin and black hair. His long-lashed eyelids flicked up, exposing black eyes, then closed again. Hanno wrapped the corner of his cape around the naked baby and hurried home.

He entered the kitchen from the dining room corridor. The Cook was chopping vegetables on a board Abdmelkart had attached by angles along the rear wall. Hanno felt rather sheepish and somewhat fearful. His offer to take the child had been spontaneous. He had given no thought to the results of his action. Uncle Hasdrubal had stressed over and over again the need to think through actions, particularly unnecessary actions, to make sure they did not betray their mission. Hanno was thankful the Cook was alone. He hoped she would take the baby, cuddle and clothe him before Abdmelkart appeared. Once she had the infant, he knew that Abdmelkart could not easily remove him.

He stood on the threshold, not wanting to scare the Cook by going right up to her. With the intuitiveness of the deaf and dumb, she turned around. Her eyes widened, and her mouth dropped open. With a guttural cry, she rushed to Hanno and stared at the baby.

He loosened his grip, holding the baby so she could see him.

She looked up questioningly. Hanno smiled encouragement. Gently, the woman took the baby in her arms and held him against her breast. She rocked from side to side, a radiant expression on her face.

Abdmelkart entered the kitchen from the corridor. The Cook's eyes became wary. Abdmelkart, who ruled his domain with the even hand of his master, said, "Where did that child come from?"

"He was to be exposed," said Hanno. "I—I—some dogs barked. I couldn't leave him." He faced Abdmelkart squarely, but nervously.

Abdmelkart looked from Hanno to the baby, to the Cook, to the baby, and again at Hanno. "I don't know what the master will say."

Neither did Hanno. While the Cook wrapped the baby and warmed milk for him, Hanno walked between the kitchen and the dining room, back and forth, back and forth. If his uncle told him to expose the child, he didn't think he could. Would he be allowed to pay someone to care for the baby? In the long run, that could endanger them. If only they could keep him. He was so cuddly and helpless.

The high priest entered the atrium. Seeing him, Hanno knit his brows and gripped his hands behind his back.

"What troubles you, Claudius?"

"I brought home a baby," blurted Hanno.

"You did what?" The thunderbolt made Hasdrubal stutter.

"The Cook and Abdmelkart are trying to feed him now."

"Let us have a look" was all Hasdrubal said.

They walked single file, Hanno leading the way, to the kitchen. The Cook sat on a bench, the baby in her lap. Beside her was a cup of warm goat's milk. Abdmelkart, keeping an eye on what the Cook was doing, stirred a pot hanging over the fire. The kitchen was warm and smelled delicious. The Cook dipped a finger in the milk and put it in the baby's mouth. With closed eyes, the baby noisily sucked the finger. Wrapped in clean rags, he appeared perfectly content.

Hanno ran his hand over the black fuzz on the baby's head. The Cook took her finger from the wee mouth and unwrapped the rags to show the baby's healthy body to her master.

The high priest of Tanit gazed at the small form. The baby whimpered. Quickly, the Cook dipped her finger and gave it to the infant.

Hasdrubal said softly, "That is a Phoenician child."

Turning to Hanno, he said, "Walk with me in the garden."

Hanno looked a little scared, but followed his uncle.

Hasdrubal stooped to examine some newly planted bushes. "Tell me exactly how you acquired that baby."

Hanno did in minute detail.

"Well," the high priest said at last, "we will keep the baby for the time being rather than let him die, but you are to pass by his mother's house regularly to ask anybody you see going in or out about giving him back."

After that, it seemed to Hasdrubal every time he wanted Hanno, he had to go to the kitchen where the Cook kept a large carrying basket as a bassinet for the baby. Hanno would be leaning over the sleeping child.

"Isn't he cute?" Hanno asked his uncle. Hasdrubal had just returned from the inn on the Appian Way. He handed Hanno his scrolls before looking at the peaceful little face. He loved the tiny button nose and little round red mouth. One minuscule clenched fist lay by his cheek. Suddenly in his sleep, the baby smiled, radiating the small face gloriously. Hasdrubal was transfixed. He stooped and caressed the baby's shoulder.

Hanno looked up at his uncle. "I'll never forgive Batbaal for having a girl. It means you still have to worry about the succession." His mouth curled in disgust.

"You infer that because the baby was a girl, you are the only choice." Though slitted, Hasdrubal's eyes were full of amusement.

"Humph," sniffed Hanno. "She didn't perform the right rituals for the goddess. I should have told her what to do."

"Get about your morning business." Hasdrubal turned quickly, smothering his laughter, as he headed for his library.

"Of course, she'll have a boy next," Hanno called after him.

28

*I*n spite of problems with feeding such a small infant, the baby gained weight as the days passed. The household seemed to revolve around him. Everyone cuddled him. Hasdrubal even unwound enough to sit on the bench, a cup of warm milk beside him, the baby in his arms. The man was gentle. The baby accepted his milk-dipped little finger without fuss. Hanno watched.

"He should have a Roman name," said Hasdrubal. "A short name, I think; he's so tiny. Do you choose Cato or Marc?"

"Marc. I like Marc."

"Marc, it will be." Hasdrubal handed little Marc to the Cook.

The Cook loved him as her own, spending a great deal of time caring for him. When her master tried to lighten her other duties, she would have none of it. Abdmelkart surreptitiously did what he could to help her. Palokart visited discreetly. At first he came to exchange information. Soon, Hasdrubal began to enjoy his company and Hanno treated him like an adored, newly found uncle. As their friendship blossomed, Palokart's visits became more and more frequent, but the three took care not to compromise the household off the Vicus Tuscus.

Working separately, they gathered the Romans' reactions to the presence of Hannibal's army in the north. At times, it seemed to Hasdrubal that every male in the city considered himself honorbound to proclaim his opinion in the forum. Likewise, Palokart, though more used to Roman excess than Hasdrubal, soon announced that his head was reeling from the onslaught. Hanno was both delighted and amused, reporting everything he heard with glee.

The senators' opinions were as easily obtained. Not content with orating in the senate chamber, they appeared on the speaker's platform in the Comitium, holding forth to the assembled crowds on what they were doing to protect Roman territory.

Hasdrubal sent a message to his brother:

The council has sent orders to Longus, who is at Lilybaeum, to return home immediately to defend the cities in the north. Every military tribune has been ordered to exhort a promise from the soldiers under his control to present themselves at a fixed date in Ariminum on the Mare Adriaticum.

There is not true panic yet, but the city fathers are close. Scipio with his forces has crossed the Padus. This has calmed matters somewhat. Their belief in ultimate victory is bound up with Scipio. He achieved the march from Massilia to Etruria in unusually rapid time and is ready for Hannibal.

The talk is that Scipio himself is impressed by Hannibal's achievements. He never expected Hannibal to cross the Alpes or, in doing so, succeed. Apparently both Hannibal and Scipio have profound respect for each other's abilities in the field.

Hanno delivered the scroll to the inn one evening. The following day, jogging past the inn while exercising his horse, his attention was on the threatening sky. Suddenly, he reared in the horse. He thought he had heard his Roman name. There it was again. Claudius. The breeze hung onto the end so that the sound was drawn out.

He pulled on the reins and turned. The innkeeper was jumping up and down, his arms flapping like victory banners in the wind.

Hanno, sure that a message of great import had come, wheeled the horse around and trotted smartly up to the inn door.

"A message came," said the innkeeper and disappeared inside.

Contrary to his usual slow-moving, disagreeable ways, the man was instantly back, scroll in hand. "It came yesterday," he said simply, "soon after you were here."

Hanno recognized the seal. "Thank you." He dropped coins into the man's open palm. Jabbing his heels into his horse's flanks, he galloped toward home, his mind on the scroll. Those in the street scrambled to safety, curses on their lips. Hanno was unaware.

Hasdrubal was in his library. The baby lay on his lap, solemnly looking at him with big black eyes. "You hold him," Hasdrubal said, handing Marc to Hanno, "while I read us the news."

Hanno tickled the baby's chin. "Goo, goo."

"It is short," Hasdrubal said in surprise. He unrolled the scroll to be sure nothing had been added. "No, that is all," he said and began reading:

> One tribe, the Taurini, was approached by Hannibal, who offered them friendship and an alliance. We had heard that they were suspicious of us. As our proposal was rebuffed, we captured their principal city and put to death those who had opposed us. Soon, the neighboring tribes flocked to our standard. We understood that many other tribes wanted to join us, but didn't. We didn't know why. Our foragers have now informed us that Roman legions have placed themselves between us and these tribes, preventing them from joining us. What legions these are and who commands them, we must find out.

"Probably Scipio's, but we will confirm that tomorrow." He looked at his nephew.

"Right. Easy."

Veiling his amusement, Hasdrubal continued:

> It is this situation that has induced Hannibal to try some action that will persuade the other tribes to throw in their lot with us.

"Is that all?" asked Hanno when his uncle stopped reading.

"That is all."

"He didn't say much," commented Hanno.

Hasdrubal assumed more scrolls would soon arrive. Each day, one of them rode by the inn, casually exercising their horses. The innkeeper, lounging at the door, would shake his head imperceptibly. One day, he nodded and stepped into the dark opening behind him. Hasdrubal slowly guided his horse past the door. With little observable motion, they exchanged money and scroll.

"Send Claudius to my library," he said to Abdmelkart, at his side the minute he entered the house. "And bring us some foot warmers."

Hanno curled on piled cushions facing him. Hasdrubal read aloud:

> Yes, the legions are commanded by Scipio. Eager for battle, we

advanced along the bank of the Padus. When our foragers informed us that we were close to Scipio's forces, we pitched camp. In the morning, Hannibal, riding at the column head, led out the cavalry to reconnoiter. I went with him. When we saw dust clouds on the horizon, we knew we had found the enemy.

In drawing the battle lines Hannibal placed bridled and heavy cavalry in front so that he could lead them straight at the Romans; Numidian cavalry on each wing. We charged. Scipio placed his javelin throwers in the front line. Our charge was so swift that they had no time to throw their javelins. They turned and fled before us. The cavalry fight was heavy and shifted back and forth. Finally, the Numidians were able to outflank the Romans, striking at their cavalry from the rear. That movement caught the javelin throwers in between. The Romans broke.

What we didn't know until later was that Scipio struck camp and marched to the bridge over the Padus. Hannibal had expected him to engage our infantry. When he didn't, Hannibal realized what was happening and rushed to the bridge. Too late. The Roman army had already crossed, pulling up the bridge planking behind them.

"He's left us hanging again," objected Hanno.

Hasdrubal's laugh was soft and short. "He is a military man. He is abrupt, though on occasion he gets carried away with his descriptions."

The following day, Hasdrubal heard that Scipio had received a sword slash in the battle by the Padus. Gossip was rampant in the Comitium. He immediately sent a note:

Scipio has been wounded. Because his injury needs attention and because the many wounded of his troops also need attention, he intends to remain at Placentia where he has set up camp until the men have recovered. He believes this position to be easily defended and, therefore, safe.

Hasdrubal read Bimilcar's quick reply while pacing in the garden.

We did not know Scipio was wounded. He and his army were way ahead of us. With the detachment we had captured at the bridge, we marched up the Padus, hunting a place to cross. A march of two days brought us to a spot where the river could be bridged. We constructed a floating bridge and crossed.

Hannibal gave audience to envoys from the Celtic tribes in the area, who waited on the opposite bank to offer their support. He received them warmly. They furnished us with men and supplies. We marched downstream searching for Scipio and the Roman army.

Arriving at Placentia, Hannibal drew his forces into battle order in full view of the enemy. Nothing happened. Finally, he ordered a withdrawal of six Roman miles, and we made camp.

The next morning, Celts arrived at our camp. They said that at morning watch, they had fallen upon the Romans sleeping nearby, wounded a number and killed many. They brought severed heads with them as proof.

Hannibal welcomed them and promised them rewards, then sent them home to tell their people what had happened and to urge that they join our forces. He thinks when the other Celts hear what their compatriots have done, they will come over to us. While they hate the Romans, they fear them.

Later in the morning, a delegation from the Boii arrived. They brought three Roman commissioners they had seized. These commissioners had been sent from Rome to partition the lands of the Boii. Hannibal thanked them for their goodwill and pledged them our friendship. He gave the three Romans back to the Boii envoys, and informed them that the Romans would be useful in negotiating the release of their own hostages.

"Abdmelkart," Hasdrubal said, "give this scroll to Claudius to read."

He took the baby to his library and settled into a chair. The next minute, he sat bolt upright. Marc had smiled at him; he was sure. He went to pieces, becoming the slave of this small toothless bit of humanity. To the Cook's consternation, he took the baby to bed with him that night. By the flicker of a small oil lamp, he watched the little one sleep. When he finally blew out the lamp the baby was nestled against the curve of his arm.

He handed Marc back to The Cook at dawn.

"Have you tried to speak to anyone from the place where you obtained him?" Hasdrubal asked Hanno.

"I have deliberately gone by the house. I want his mother to know he's well. But the house is always shut up tight; I never hear or see anyone."

"In that case, I will adopt him and bring him up as my own."

Hanno grinned happily. At last, another candidate who could replace him for the high priesthood. In spite of his relief, he remained true to his own rapidly developing principles of thoroughness and integrity. He walked by the house first thing the next morning. As usual, there were no signs of life. I don't understand it, he thought. There are people in there, probably lots of people. Don't they ever have business in the forum? Don't they go to the markets? He stood in front of the house and stared at the door quizzically. No response broke the deadened stillness. He walked swiftly away. What did he care? If the mother never knew that her baby was well cared for, it wasn't his fault.

He wandered to another area, a deteriorating section of Rome. His intuition told him that hanging around and listening might be worthwhile. A lot of old men lived there. They shuffled through the street or sat bundled up in the sun and talked. Hanno, acquainted with a number of them, spent the morning in their company. He knew how to worm information from them.

As a result, the next scroll sent north related how Rome had received the news of the cavalry action.

The people of Rome were surprised to learn that Hannibal had won. They do not understand how this could happen. They cannot accept defeat. All kinds of pretexts are put forward to persuade them that this was not really a defeat. At one moment, blame is laid to excessive fervor, and at the next to Celtic ill will. Regardless, as long as the infantry is unimpaired, everyone is sure Rome will win. Let us hope they are wrong.

Longus has not marched through Rome yet, but I understand that he is anxious to force a decisive battle. Scipio's illness will allow him to handle the situation according to his own judgment, which I gather is not the best.

Scipio, from what I hear in the Comitium, fears that the action you spoke of in your last scroll might influence all the Celts in the area to come over to our side. Wishing to forearm himself, in spite of his wounds, he broke camp just before light watch and marched toward the river Trebia. Apparently, there is high ground near the river. He felt that he could rely upon the

*ground formation for defense. Also, Scipio seems to think that
the Celts in that area are loyal to the Romans. He is camped on
the hills, having dug a trench and palisade to strengthen his
position. He intends to wait there for the arrival of Longus
while he treats his wounds.*

In reply, Bimilcar wrote:

*Native tribesmen came to Hannibal with news of Scipio's
move. The Numidian horse were sent in pursuit, and the rest of
the cavalry followed. Hannibal led the main body of the army
close behind.*

*The Numidians returned, saying that the Roman camp was
empty. They fired it. This upset Hannibal, but he said nothing to
them. Afterwards, he told me that the Numidian horse had done
the Romans a great favor. If, instead of burning the camp, they
had pressed on, they could have overtaken the rear, animals and
supplies, and destroyed it.*

*Without their supplies, the Romans would have been in dif-
ficult straits.*

A few days later, Palokart, preceded by Abdmelkart, bounded
into the dining room. Hasdrubal was teaching Hanno the rituals
of Tanit.

"Longus has just made camp outside the city," Palokart announced, his eyes sparkling. "He'll pass through Rome tomorrow
to make a grand show on his way north."

"Can we go?" In his eagerness, Hanno jumped from the
dining couch to stand in front of his uncle.

"Of course," Hasdrubal smiled broadly. "Even Abdmelkart
can go," he said, giving tacit permission to the slave who had
stationed himself near the door.

"Would you like to come with me?" Palokart asked Hanno.

"Oh, yes."

"Then meet me by the Temple of Saturn."

"Will that be the best view?"

"No, just a meeting place. They won't come through the forum
since it's not a victory parade. My guess, and it's only a guess, is
that Longus will symbolically try to march as close to the victory
route as possible." Palokart gazed around. "Victory parades end
with a sacrifice by the triumphant commander in the Temple of

Jupiter. What do you bet he marches along the Capitolium just as if he were already the noble, the plumed, the honored victor?" Palokart snickered.

Curling his lip into a sarcastic smile, Hasdrubal nodded.

"We can watch," Palokart said to Hanno, "from any of the porticoes where the street curves up to the Capitolium."

"You two are on your own," said Hasdrubal. He made it a point never to be seen in public with Palokart. What Hanno did was Hanno's business. No one would think of Hanno as a spy for Carthage. "Abdmelkart and I will watch from a little further up Capitolium."

The crowd was thick in the morning. Hasdrubal and the Numidian were lucky to get a protected spot to stand. Many behind them were getting jostled; some not so good-naturedly.

Long before the troops appeared, they heard the rhythmic tramp of feet. The soldiers came, led by a white stallion. A man sat regally on the horse's back. Hasdrubal's eyes narrowed. He observed Longus; a proud man with an arrogant, petulant mouth. He accepted the crowd's cheers with barely noticeable motions of his head. He was intent on presenting an elegant, victorious figure astride his horse.

Scipio, thought Hasdrubal, will have trouble with that man. Longus would not pay attention to suggestions. Determined to have his own way, Longus would deliberately use Scipio's physical incapacity to push for a major battle so that he could gain all the glory. He would help, not hurt, Carthage.

Hasdrubal looked at Abdmelkart to see his reaction. Their eyes met: the Numidian dropped his. Abdmelkart didn't think much of the Roman. He had seen too many Carthaginian commanders and could tell the difference between a military man and one who was playing soldier.

Hasdrubal thought the troops looked tired. He quickly calculated. After all, they had been marching for more than thirty days. By the time they reached Ariminum, it would be close to forty days without a stop. They needed rest before they could fight a major battle. And each day they rested brought Scipio closer to recovery. He hoped the forces met sooner rather than later. The advantage would be with the Carthaginians.

Abdmelkart became restless.

"Do you want to go home?"

"Yes. The morning passes."

"And you have work to do." Hasdrubal smiled. "Go. There will just be more of the same here."

The Numidian, pushing and squirming, wormed his way through the crowd.

Later, bored with the stream of tired marchers, Hasdrubal forced his way to the rear of the crowd so he could watch the citizens' reaction to the armed might of Rome. The crowd began to thin. He thought, their response is the same as mine. They have had enough. He moved again to see the marching men better. Suddenly, he found himself standing next to Aristide. At first, the impact of seeing his son staggered him. Then, unobtrusively, he maneuvered between people, quickly moving a short distance away, where he could watch Aristide unobserved.

No day passed when he did not think of Elissa. No matter what he did, or how concentrated his actions, she was always in the back of his mind. Now that he saw his son, a dull ache settled over him. Patiently, he waited. Aristide would go home at noon. If not at noon, later. Hasdrubal was determined to keep him in view until he found out where he lived. Abdmelkart would worry if he did not return at the expected hour. Hasdrubal shrugged indifferently. He dared not even look for Hanno. The only thing on his mind, like a brilliant light at the end of the road, was Elissa. Wherever Aristide went, she would be.

After a while, the line of foot-weary marchers came to an end. The crowd scattered. Proudly aloof, Aristide walked to the Lapis Niger and looked around.

Waiting for someone, thought Hasdrubal. He moved to the other side of the Via Sacra. Early in life, as a game, he had trained himself to observe everything. While appearing to rest, he noted every movement in the forum.

Aristide began to saunter slowly back and forth. He seemed anxious. He peered around and scowled. Even scowling, his son was an exceedingly handsome man.

A young Etruscan hurried across the Via Sacra. His fine wool toga was pinned at the shoulder by a beautifully wrought gold eagle. His skin was a pale bronze, and his dark eyes were slightly slanted. Moving with assurance, the man was clearly an Etruscan of noble breeding.

Aristide raised a hand in greeting and smiled. The two young men stood together and talked briefly. Then they started along the

Via Sacra. Acting preoccupied by his own thoughts, the high priest followed at a respectable distance.

Where were they going? They walked to the end of the Via Sacra, skirted the Palatium and headed for the fashionable area on the other side. The houses were large, prosperous, some pretentious, and separated by open spaces. He had to be cautious and keep far behind, but feared losing them if they suddenly changed course after rounding a corner. The two walked by a scrub-filled plot where someone had started to build a house. Hasdrubal stepped into the weeds and sat down. Amid the underbrush, he would not be so readily noticeable.

The two men reached the large house abutting the field. Aristide turned to face his friend. From his son's expressions and gestures, the high priest concluded that he was offering the Etruscan hospitality.

So this is the house where my Elissa is a prisoner, thought Hasdrubal. He had no doubt that she was a prisoner. He watched until they disappeared within the house before hurrying home.

As he and Hanno ate fruit and cold meat in the dining room, he said casually, "I saw Aristide today."

Abdmelkart, hovering over them to pour wine, let out a gasp before he could stop himself then apologized profusely. The high priest thought the slave was going to drop to his knees though expressly forbidden to do so.

Hanno laid down his bunch of grapes. His usually open expression became guarded. "He would recognize me."

"And he would recognize Abdmelkart." Hasdrubal indicated that he was through eating. "When dusk has descended enough to make things dim without being dark, we will walk to where we can see the house. Take careful note and avoid going near the house in the future. At least we can eliminate the risk of having Aristide walk out his door and into one of you."

At sunset, Hasdrubal and Hanno, trailed by Abdmelkart, turned left instead of right at the Vicus Tuscus, and walked around the Palatium in the opposite direction from which Hasdrubal had first approached the house.

"Do you know where you are, Claudius?" he asked when they neared Aristide's home.

"Yes. I followed the slave with our baby along this street. They came out of that house." He pointed.

Hasdrubal clutched his chest and went white.

"Sire, are you all right?" Hanno grabbed his uncle's arm, and Abdmelkart hurried to his master's side.

When he could speak, Hasdrubal whispered, "Aristide went in that door. Elissa is in that house." Disbelief spread across his face. "Marc is my child."

29

They sat close together in the library, Abdmelkart on the floor at his master's feet, Hanno in a chair that he had pulled right next to his uncle. They stared at the baby sleeping in his father's arms. Every once in a while, Hasdrubal drew a fingertip tentatively across the downy cheek. This bit of humanity was his, of his loins, his lineage.

Hanno, leaning over, gently brushed the baby's new hair. Hasdrubal turned to him and smiled. Profound wonder reflected in their faces.

Abdmelkart, too, sat in awed silence, though becoming uncomfortable since three braziers poured heat into the small room.

"We don't want him to catch cold," Hasdrubal said when he had appeared with only one. Abdmelkart thought three was overdoing it, but realized his master was not in a state to make the most lucid judgments.

When Marc woke and began to fuss, Hasdrubal jiggled him. For a moment, the fussing stopped, then started again.

"He's hungry," Abdmelkart said.

Without a word, the father handed him over. "Come right back," he said to the slave.

Lost in their own thoughts, uncle and nephew scarcely moved until the Numidian returned.

He squatted beside one of the braziers and immediately began to sweat.

"Put the brazier outside," said Hasdrubal. "It is hot in here."

The slave threw him a wily, sidelong glance and removed two.

When they were finally settled, Hasdrubal said, "This ruby was given to me by Elissa's father." He drew the ring from beneath his robe. "Somehow, we must get it into that house and into her hands. She would recognize it immediately."

"Why?" asked Hanno.

Taken aback, the high priest, who had been looking at the ruby, said, "To give her strength—tell her help is near."

Abdmelkart went to answer a knock at the door.

"Why don't we just rescue her?"

"We do not know how soon that will be, Claudius. We have to decide what to do. She probably feels abandoned. I think having the ring would be a great comfort to her."

Hanno nodded. Right. Understood. In his eagerness, he hadn't thought it through.

"Also," said Hasdrubal, "the ring would prepare her for whatever might happen, which could be useful."

Hanno shook his head, picturing the house's blank front and empty appearance. "You're right. But getting it to her might be more difficult than rescuing her. I can think of—"

Palokart's entrance interrupted him.

Abdmelkart produced a chair, and then Hasdrubal repeated the whole story.

"We must decide how to get this ring to her," he finished, dangling the ruby before Palokart.

"I can find out who the Etruscan was. There are only a few who fit your description. If it's the one I think, giving the priestess the ring is just the kind of game he would enjoy." Palokart rose, a conspiratorial grin on his face. "Give me a few days."

Hanno and Hasdrubal, in walking about the city, kept to major thoroughfares as much as possible. They mingled in crowds rather than being alone. Always, they watched for Aristide. Hasdrubal was less afraid Aristide would recognize him with his Roman haircut and short beard than his nephew. By the third day, the tension of being constantly on the lookout told on them both. Instead of sitting with his uncle to discuss the bits of information they had heard that day, Hanno flung himself on his bed right after dinner and fell asleep.

"I shall work here in the dining room," Hasdrubal said to Abdmelkart. The room was warm and the couch comfortable. He was soon engrossed in writing a detailed account to Elibaal, but sprang up with pleasure when the Numidian admitted Palokart.

"Whew," said Palokart, shivering. "It's cold and damp tonight. I've never gotten used to these Roman winters. I think it will snow before morning."

"That interests me very much," Hasdrubal said eagerly.

Palokart laughed. "You'll get sick of it after a while." He

added, "If it snows, there won't be much doing in the forum of importance to us. The Romans don't mind the stuff underfoot, but they stay inside while it's coming down."

A palpitating silence lay between them. Palokart broke it. "My friends know the Etruscan and introduced me. I told him what we wanted, and I let him think it was an assignation. He clapped his hands. As soon as he has the ring in his possession, he said he will set about delivering it to the lady. He's never seen the priestess, but he has seen her slave and thinks he can manage the affair discreetly."

Hasdrubal lifted the gold chain over his head. The ruby glowed brilliant red in the lamplight. Wadding up the chain, he handed the jewel to Palokart.

"She may want to wear the ring out of sight around her neck so take the chain too."

By morning, it was snowing—to the fascination of the three people from Carthage. Hasdrubal and Hanno laughed and ran about the atrium like children as the white particles floated around them. They kicked at the whiteness underfoot. It was cold. They tried to catch it, but it turned to water in their hands.

How could this fragile bit of weightlessness, destroyed by his touch, cause so much trouble? Hasdrubal scooped up a handful and threw it at Hanno who tried to catch it. The wet lump slipped from his fingers and hit the ground. At the edge of the atrium, Abdmelkart stood, his shining dark face uplifted into the flakes. A big one landed on the end of his nose. He automatically brushed it off then chortled in delight.

Amused and satisfied, Hasdrubal called for hot food. Afterwards, he went to the forum. Few men appeared. Most postponed their business. Those who came didn't stand around in clusters and talk, but kept moving, small clouds of steam whooshing from their mouths. Hasdrubal shugged off his worry about meeting Aristide. Reprieve was short-lived: the ground was still too warm; the snow melted, and Hasdrubal's tension returned.

Ten days went by before Palokart came again. Abdmelkart brought him to the library. Hasdrubal and Hanno were discussing the day's accumulation of news. The ring, he informed them, had been delivered to Elissa. He did not know how the priestess had reacted, but the Etruscan, laughing uproariously, had described how he had cornered the stupid, superstitious slave girl and told her that the goddess Juno, in person, had given him the keepsake for the mistress of the house. He told her that the ring would protect the mistress against cruelty; it had to be delivered in secret; and that if she ever told, Juno herself would strike her dead. "He said the girl trotted right off, pale and scared to death."

"Now," said Hasdrubal, "we have to devise a method of rescuing her. Let us discuss it."

"I think we can get her," said Hanno, having thought everything through with care. "We would need a lot of help." He glanced diffidently at his uncle.

"The Etruscans are always ready for excitement," Palokart said.

"What is your plan, Hanno?" Hasdrubal set down the wax tablet he had been holding.

"Build a big bonfire in the lot, close to the house. Yell, 'Fire! Fire!' and get everybody out. Aristide wouldn't know until too late that the fire wasn't really burning his house."

"He would come out with a tight hold on Elissa," Hasdrubal said.

"So we hit him in the back of the knees. He buckles and collapses," said Palokart. "He lets go; we grab her."

"We should have one of our horses ready to ride off with her the minute we grab her," said Hanno.

The plan seemed so sensible and simple that the three sat staring at each other as they ran the action through in their minds.

"I will hit him in the back of the knees," Hasdrubal said.

Skeptical, Palokart said, "We'll practice. You have to get it right the first time. And you have to get away before Aristide has time to recover."

Palokart's Etruscan friends sensed Hasdrubal's ineptitude. They made him practice, pretending the atrium garden was the street in front of Aristide's house. Laughing, tumbling, clowning, the Etruscans took turns being the victim. Amid the fun, they astutely judged how their new acquaintance, the Roman Paulus, wielded the stout round stick. He practiced until he could do it perfectly time after time after time under varying conditions.

Hasdrubal chose the night for the rescue with care. No moon appeared. Abdmelkart, on horseback, would catch her and immediately carry her home. Hanno was to bang on the door and yell "Fire! Fire!" Everyone else had to make sure the blaze was out before leaving. Under no circumstances was the house to be burned.

Heavy clouds hung low, tumbled listlessly by a light wind,

but enough to fan the flames. Hanno, left early hoping the rain, or, more likely, snow, would hold off. The wood they had surreptitiously collected and deposited around the empty lot next to the house was dry and would burn into a quick, hot fire. He didn't want the logs dampened.

The Etruscans filtered into the field. Quickly and with only the occasional tiny light, they built a huge pile of sticks and good-sized logs. The fire would be far enough from the house not to endanger it, but close enough to give that appearance. They also built a small fire at the corner of the house. Anyone exiting would see those flames instantly.

After the logs were laid to his satisfaction, Hanno checked his uncle and Abdmelkart. Hasdrubal was positioned in shadow near the house. Once the door was opened, he could see everyone leaving the house. Abdmelkart, also hidden from view, stroked the silky neck of his horse while keeping an eye on his master.

Hanno stashed unlit flares along the street for those who would leave after the fire was out. Hasdrubal ordered him to stay well away from Aristide and to go home as soon as Abdmelkart rode off with Elissa. Hanno grumbled. He could help extinguish the fire.

"Go home," Hasdrubal said, with slitted eyes.

"Yes, sire."

All was in order. Hanno gave Palokart and the Etruscans the signal to start the fire. The dry twigs sputtered and crackled exuberantly. Wind fanned the flame and the logs caught. The Etruscans glanced at each other smugly. They grouped behind the fire, ready to rush into the street and cause confusion when the occupants started running from the house. Palokart watched the fire from the street. Once it roared, he waived to Hanno. Hanno bounded to the door and banged on it with both fists. "Fire! Fire!" In his excitement, his voice squeaked and broke, but he managed to get out a few deep yells.

A slave opened the door.

"Fire!" cried Hanno, pointing toward the empty lot.

The slave dashed back in crying "Fire! Fire!"

Screaming house slaves poured from the house. Palokart shepherded them deliberately toward the flames. The Etruscans ran into the street, milling with the slaves, yelling "Fire! Fire!"

At last, Hasdrubal spotted Aristide hurrying toward the door. Far behind came Elissa. She held up her robe so she could run.

Seeing her made his head spin. He gritted his teeth and exerted a firmer grip on his club. Elissa caught up with Aristide as he reached the door. He stopped and arrogantly extended his arm to bar her way.

"You are not to go out," he said.

Elissa stamped her foot. "Kill me if you wish, but I am not staying here to be burned to death." Her stance was regal and her tone adamant.

Aristide looked down at her as at some slimy, unsavory crawler. He reached across her body and grabbed her wrist like a vice. Because of the awkward way he held her, he ended up dragging her as he left the house.

Instead of hurrying from the fire, as if mesmerized, he headed for it. Orange and yellow flames shot high into the air, lighting the street with glowing colors. Hasdrubal circled behind him, jockeying for position. Elissa was in the way. Abdmelkart watched, tensed, ready to guide his horse into the street the minute his master swung.

Aristide gave Elissa a vicious jerk. She stumbled, but regained her balance.

Hasdrubal swung. Aristide buckled and let go of Elissa. Palokart grabbed her and tossed her to Abdmelkart. With his heel, the Numidian nudged the horse toward the dark street beyond.

Hasdrubal dropped his stick and turned to make sure Abdmelkart had Elissa. He saw Hanno hand Abdmelkart a lighted flare.

He hesitated too long. Aristide was on his feet, confronting him.

"You'll pay for that," said Aristide in cold fury.

He pummeled Hasdrubal. Hasdrubal raised his arms across his face and over his head to protect himself.

Hunched over and gasping in pain, he stammered, "You can kill me, but Elissa is free."

The blows stopped.

"I know that voice. You're Hasdrubal, high priest of Tanit." He snatched Hasdrubal's arm, twisted it, and with a forceful yank spun him around and rammed his arm between his shoulder blades. Hasdrubal heard the bone crack and felt excruciating pain. Acrid smoke from the fire made him cough.

At that moment, a deep voice behind them said, "Let him go, Hellene, or this knife goes between your shoulders."

Hasdrubal's arm dropped and hung strangely. He cried out at the pain.

"Get moving, Paulus," the voice said.

Cradling his dangling arm, Hasdrubal hurried as best he could past the fire and into the darkness. As he did so, he heard the same voice say, "You get over there and help put out the fire."

He felt faint. Though he had learned the city well and had no fear of losing his way in the dark, faintness and nausea kept sweeping over him. He wasn't sure he could reach home. Rain spit then started in earnest, a cold, sleety rain. Blackness surrounded him. His bruised and battered body refused to move, but he told himself to keep moving. At least when he was walking, the icy rain cooled his hot face. He walked slowly, knowing that if he met a thief, he might be left unconscious in the gutter. The narrow streets were dangerous. Once he reached the Via Sacra, he would be safe. Romans with flares, coming from parties, from clandestine meetings, from who knows where, might light his way. He should have picked up a flare, but he couldn't have lit it, he couldn't have carried it.

He struggled along, wary of any dark shape that might be a robber. Twice, he had to stop and lean against a wall to keep from toppling over. When he began to shiver uncontrollably, he forced himself to move on. The left turn should be soon. He stared toward the Via Sacra, looking for the street opening between the houses. Suddenly, there was a light ahead. "Oh," he sighed, relieved. "The street—at last—and someone is coming—or going—which?" He tried to hurry, biting his lips with pain.

"Sire," he called, "please wait."

The light stopped bouncing. "Does someone call?"

"Help," cried Hasdrubal.

A light advanced toward him. He made out a tall, broad, liveried slave who carried his flare high, enlarging the circle of light.

"I have been beaten," whispered Hasdrubal. "My arm—" He strained to push it forward. The effort caused his whole body to sag toward the slave.

"He's in bad shape, master," called the slave, catching Hasdrubal from his good side.

A canopy held by two slaves drew near. "Where do you go," asked a well-dressed Roman, after assuring himself that he dealt with a cultured Roman.

"A small street off the Vicus Tuscus."

"We go to the Palatium. I will send my slave on with you."

"Many thanks," gasped Hasdrubal, through chattering teeth. Close to collapse, he leaned heavily on the strong, young slave. They fell behind. The slave lifted him with no more effort than if he were a sack of clothing.

"Sire," he said to his master, "the man is almost dead."

Turning, the Roman studied Hasdrubal who hung limply in the slave's grip. "Get him to his home as quickly as possible, Flautus," he said. "I don't want a dead man on our hands. Then come to my sister's house."

"I will reward you well," whispered Hasdrubal as the Roman hurried off. The torch lights around him faded from his vision. The next thing he knew, the slave had him tucked under one arm. They were moving swiftly along the Viscus Tuscus. He closed his eyes. They would soon be home.

Ignoring the cold, Elissa sat in a chair near her husband's bedroom door. She had refused to stay in the library where Abdmelkart first took her. She was free. She wanted to be where she could greet Hasdrubal as he returned. A brazier burned under her feet, her son lay in her lap. She was cuddling the cooing baby. She still found it difficult to believe that this was her baby. She had gone over every portion of his little brown form. His features were the ones engraved on her memory—the way one eyebrow moved up and down, the shape of his eyes, the compactness of his body.

During their ride, Abdmelkart had told her how they happened to have the baby. With what eagerness she had looked about the house as they crossed to the kitchen.

The Cook had gone to bed. The baby's basket was kept in her room at night. Abdmelkart had to wake her, and she hadn't been very happy about giving the baby to this strange woman. He had a hard time making her understand that Elissa was the baby's mother. Finally, she had fetched the infant, but indicated by hand gestures that he was to sleep with her.

Elissa said, "Never mind. It's just as well tonight. Then we will see what arrangements we will make." She carried him to the sitting area, aware that the Cook leaned against a pillar, watching from across the atrium.

When Hanno arrived, Elissa begged to hear how he had

gotten her baby. He told her how the woman at the door had called out to him.

"She's a good girl," said Elissa. "She hated Aristide for the cruel things he did."

Alternately petting and hugging her baby, she longed to see her husband. Where was he? More than enough time had elapsed. He should be home. "Oh, please," she whispered prayerfully, "don't let anything happen to him now." She shivered. Even with the brazier, the cold was penetrating. She was alone.

Hanno and Abdmelkart conferred out of earshot, moving under the portico of the atrium. The slave was worried. He suggested taking a flare and going to hunt. Hanno objected. "We don't know from which direction he'll come—or if he can."

Abdmelkart whirled on Hanno. "What do you mean?"

"I looked back when I lit my flare. I saw my uncle stare after you, and Aristide start to rise."

"He was supposed to leave right away."

"If Aristide beat him, maybe one of the Etruscans took him home. Some live near there." Hanno rapidly calculated which Etruscan homes he could contact.

"But if he has been attacked by robbers, he could be anywhere," moaned Abdmelkart. "The rain is coming down hard and—" he cried out in horror.

Hanno turned and saw a large, muscular slave holding his uncle as a father holds a sick child.

Abdmelkart was already across the atrium. He gathered his master into his arms.

"Reward the slave," Hasdrubal managed to say to Hanno. The Numidian carried him toward his bedroom. Hasdrubal said, "Where is Elissa?"

Elissa looked up when Abdmelkart approached with his burden. She saw the man's physical shock and broken arm.

"Let me help," she said. Calmly, she rose and laid the baby on the chair.

Hasdrubal had not seen her, but heard her voice and knew she had not recognized him. It was almost more than he could stand.

"My darling," he choked.

With that, Elissa screamed. She was on the floor, kissing the hem of his wet toga. Quickly rising, she ordered Abdmelkart to lay him on his bed and remove his clothing. She caught up the baby and flew to the kitchen.

The Cook, shivering with cold, had gone back to the warm kitchen. She did not know her master had been carried in and was working herself into a first-class rage. The strange woman rushed in and practically threw her adored baby into her arms. She could not understand what was going on. Abdmelkart had tried to tell her something, but he had been in too much of a hurry. She had never seen the household in such a pother. Clutching the infant, she shook her head in bewilderment. Elissa tried to poke up the fire to heat water. The Cook objected. Holding the baby on one hip, she pushed at Elissa.

In desperation, Elissa grabbed her by the arm and forced her along the dining room corridor to see the commotion in the master's bedroom. The Cook turned terrified eyes on Elissa, and rushed to the kitchen. She heated water, and ripped clean rags. She took braziers into the bedroom, and Hanno carried the large basin of warm water. Elissa had Abdmelkart pull the bed away from the wall so she could set and splint Hasdrubal's left arm without having to reach across him. With Abdmelkart's help, she wrapped rags around the arm until it was tight and bulky.

"We'll have to move the bed back and forth for a while. The wall gives him some support," she said to the Numidian. "Now, you bathe him while I get some hot broth."

Clean and warm, Hasdrubal swallowed the broth. He told the three hovering over him what had happened. Then Elissa sent the others away. After stripping, she lay close to warm him with her own body. She would keep him from floundering around during the night. Only then did she kiss him, a long, lingering, passionate kiss. He sighed. She shook her head at what happened to him.

"Not tonight, my love, much as I want to," she said, kissing him on the cheek.

"I don't think I could tonight," he said simply. She laid an arm and leg across his body, enveloping him in warmth. He twitched as his muscles relaxed, and he slept.

30

*L*anguidly, Hasdrubal turned his head on the pillow. His good arm lay wedged against Elissa's body. He tried to caress her. He succeeded in wiggling one finger. Dulled by sleep, shock, and pain, his mind stumbled. Am I dead? No part of him would obey. Do the dead feel pain? His arm! If only he could change the position a little! With supreme effort, he raised his legs to get some leverage on the bed.

Elissa instantly lifted the leg she had lain across his body. Leaning on an elbow, she bent over him. "Are you in pain, my darling?"

"My arm," he mumbled.

Cool air, pouring over his skin, replaced her warmth. The next minute, she knelt beside him, supporting his head as she held a cup to his lips. He drank and sank into oblivion.

Two hours later, a strong fragrance made him open his eyes. Elissa stood by his bedside holding a bowl and spoon.

"You're awake," she said and sat down on the bed to feed him. As she extended the spoon, the glow from the ruby on her hand struck his eye. He smiled and flashed a look at her.

She smiled in return. "I put it on this morning. I don't have to be afraid to wear it anymore."

"I want to know what happened to you, my love."

"And I want to know about my father and the ring. But first, sleep some more. When you wake up, I'll sit here with you, and we'll talk."

"Kiss me."

She did his bidding, his eyes, the tip of his nose, his cheeks, and his lips. Then she tucked the blanket under his chin, patted his chest, and left him.

He didn't wake again until late morning. True to her word, Elissa sat down beside him. He drew her hand to his lips, then locking his fingers in hers said, "Begin."

"You had been gone about three weeks—time enough for you to reach Tyre and write to me. It was close to midday. I was home looking for news of you when Aristide came. Every other time he came, I had refused to see him. This time, he insisted on seeing me. He said it was important. So I walked out to the statue of the goddess and met him there. He said that an Athenian ship captain whom I had once met through him had invited him to lunch. This man had specifically requested that Aristide bring me. I thought I knew which captain he meant. I had met him when he had a fever. Aristide had sent him to Alcibiades, and Alcibiades had asked me to treat him. After some hesitation, I agreed to go to lunch."

"Oh, my dear one." Hasdrubal's eyes became shiny. "And I thought you had gone of your own free will."

"Never!" In a second, she added, sorrow in her voice, "You should have known me better."

"Someday, I will tell you about my one experience with a woman, and you will understand." He asked her to continue.

"When we arrived at the ship, Aristide took me to the captain's room. The captain was polite, but busy. He was not the man I thought. He talked to us for a minute then excused himself. It was apparent to me that we would not have lunch very soon. Aristide took me to another cabin, a tiny one, and told me to wait. He left. Soon, I felt some motion and went to the door. We had left the dock. Aristide jumped from where he was sitting on the deck and forced me back into the cabin. I realized what had happened and started crying. I considered jumping overboard, but when he let me out, it was dark, and we were on the open sea."

Hasdrubal again drew her hand to his lips.

"Thinking that I would be safer with other people around, I insisted on sleeping on the deck. He slept there, too, near me. The ship stopped at Crete. Aristide found a big house and bought a lot of slaves. Up to that point, I had been relatively safe. He was occupied with making an impression on the local aristocrats. But the minute we were settled in the house, Aristide turned on me."

Elissa visibly shuddered.

"Darling, darling." Hasdrubal agonized.

"He came into my room late one afternoon. His laugh and the expression on his face were horrible. He started toward me. He said, 'We'll see how good a temple prostitute you were.' I could see his clothing jetting out where his organ was hard and erect. He grabbed my robe at the neck and yanked."

Hasdrubal twisted in the bed, his face flushed with anger.

"I screamed, 'I'm pregnant,' thinking that might hold him off. He just laughed at me. He said, 'We'll take care of that.' He pulled me against him."

Elissa covered her face with her hands and groaned. In misery, Hasdrubal flung his good arm across her. He held her as best he could.

"My clothes fell away, and I could feel him swelled against me. I screamed again, 'I'm not a temple prostitute. I'm married to the high priest.' His face went absolutely black he was so furious. He stuck his face up against mine and shouted 'married.' He fondled me for a few minutes while I struggled, but he couldn't get erect again. That's when he struck me in the jaw and knocked me down."

Hasdrubal growled and tried to move. Elissa put both hands on his shoulders. "You must stay still for a few days to give the bone a chance to fuse."

"I wish I had killed him."

"Shush! Nothing else happened."

Hasdrubal subsided.

"He stood over me, balling and unballing his fists, his face changed to purple and red. I wondered if he were going to kick me in the stomach." Elissa gazed into space. "I don't know why he became so angry when I said I was married. He knew I was living in your house." Her gaze came back to her husband. "He marched out of the room. I pulled up my torn robe, and I was trying to get up when two slaves came and helped me to my room. I didn't know that he had ordered them to make me a prisoner. We stayed in Crete, though I don't think that was his original plan. Of course, I didn't know that I really was pregnant." She smiled, remembering her joy when she had found out. "Aristide made me do everything he could think of to lose the baby. I began throwing up. It was an accident, but I threw up on him one day. He was so disgusted he didn't come near me for a week. After that, he kept me locked in my room."

Hasdrubal turned red and his grip on her thigh tightened until it hurt.

"Darling," Elissa said, easing his hand on her leg, "it's over now. I'm telling you because you wanted to know. Don't think about it. We are together, and by a miracle, we have our little son."

"Yes," he whispered when he could speak.

"I think Aristide was planning to take me to Athens to set me up as someone skillful in the healing arts and, incidentally, as his mistress. He had no intention of marrying me. He changed his mind when I began to show. As time went on, I got more and more depressed. I thought nobody cared. I told myself over and over nobody knew where I was."

Hasdrubal shaded his eyes. "If you had only known; you are my life."

"I know that now and will never forget it." She stroked his cheek. "I was far enough along to have trouble bending over when we left Crete and came to Rome. He bought that house where you found me. He again bought lots of slaves. He even gave me a little slave girl. Marita is her name. Just a child, really. The slaves were afraid of him. They guarded me like a captive. When my time was drawing to a close, he announced that as soon as the baby was born, it would be exposed. I was desperate and sick at heart, but I knew better than to beg him."

She stopped and played with the bedding.

"I think," she continued, "that turned many of the slaves against him. Marita opened her heart to me. We plotted, but having no one else to turn to, we could do nothing. Even if she took little Hasdrubal from the house—"

"You call him Hasdrubal?"

"I named him after you, my love. Is that all right? Did you give him another name?"

"We call him Marc. But that is only his Roman name." He smiled at his wife. He was enormously pleased. "We will call him Hasdrubal, then."

After a silence, he said, "I interrupted you."

"Where was I? Oh, yes. She didn't know anyone in the city. Being from way up north, she was afraid to get lost in the crowds. I had no money to pay for a woman to take the baby and nurse him."

Elissa again looked into space. "Aristide was in Athens when the baby was born. So the slaves didn't make a move to kill him." She grimmaced. "When he returned, he had three prostitutes with him and ignored me. But the minute he discovered little Hasdrubal, he had some of the slaves flogged. He stormed out, saying that when he returned, the baby had to be gone. I was hysterical. One of the guards tore him from my arms and left. Marita, as distraught as I was, followed him to the door, but was ordered back."

"She managed a strangled plea to Hanno who just happened to be passing by," said Hasdrubal.

"Fortunately. But I didn't know that then." She again smoothed the bed clothes.

"Anyway, I was hysterical. I couldn't eat; I couldn't sleep. I wanted to die. Everything valued in this life was lost to me."

"My poor darling." In his wretchedness, he turned his head aside.

"Then, like a thunderbolt, my slave dropped a ruby ring into my hand one evening. Marita's eyes were enormous, and she was white with terror. She said Juno had ordered that it be given to me." Elissa chortled. "Juno! I knew it could only have come from you. The sight of it stunned me into a peace I hadn't known since I had been taken from Carthage. You were near. I knew my father must have given you the ring."

"And much, much more, left in Ahiram's care."

"So, my father is dead." Her chin drew up as she pressed her lips together. Her eyes became slightly moist, though no tears fell. Their gaze turned inward. He gently patted her for a few minutes.

"Then," she took up her story again, "it was simply a matter of waiting for you to rescue me."

Hasdrubal caressed the curves of her body and smiled.

"Days went by," she said. "I didn't care. Whenever the signal came, I would be ready. The ruby hidden between my breasts gave me strength. When I heard the scream 'Fire,' I knew. I stood up to Aristide as I hadn't done in months."

She sighed happily. "And you know the rest."

He chuckled. "You were at peace; we were in ferment."

Elissa laughed and kissed the end of his nose.

"Abdmelkart told me on the way here how you found me. He also said that you and Hanno would follow on foot. He led me straight to the kitchen and made the Cook bring our baby. I almost fainted, I was so happy. I had to lean against the wall. Hanno walked into the kitchen, How he's changed. I could hardly believe it. He's so poised and confident."

Hasdrubal slitted his eyes, but a smile flooded his face.

"Abdmelkart wanted to light some braziers in your library, but I preferred to wait where I could see you." Again, she chortled. "I thought I could see around the corner." Laying her hand on his chest, she said, "Then to think I didn't recognize you." She flushed.

"You were not expected to," he said, rather pleased. "Nobody was." He became serious. "We are here on a mission, and you must learn to live accordingly."

She bowed her head in submission.

"When Claudius returns for lunch, the three of us will discuss it."

"Who is Claudius?"

"That is Hanno's Roman name. You must learn to call him Claudius so that there is no slip at the wrong time." He added, "I am Paulus."

Her eyes fastened sharply on his face. Slowly, she said, "I think I understand."

They were quiet, holding hands, looking deep into each other's eyes.

"Do you think Aristide will come here?" she finally asked.

"He does not know where we are."

Better not tell her that Aristide had recognized him. It would only worry her. He doubted Aristide would do anything, but he worried about it himself.

The third day after his beating, Elissa let him get up for a short time. Hasdrubal sat in a chair, his damaged arm across his lap. The splint extending below his fingertips was awkward. He realized that he was more comfortable in bed. But just to lie there was untenable. True, he was sleeping much of the time. But how long would that go on?

Elissa brought little Hasdrubal into the room. He was fussing. "He's hungry," she said. "I'm going to nurse him."

Overflowing with emotion, he smiled at the noisy smacking of the sucking infant. Elissa insisted that she had plenty of milk, she had kept it flowing, she would nurse her son, but should they buy a woman to take charge of the baby. "The Cook is surly and hostile. She snaps at everyone except you. This morning when I lifted him from her arms, she burst into sobs."

Hasdrubal's smile was compassionate. "My sweet, the Cook loves the baby dearly. She has cared for him like a mother. To take all responsibility for him away would break her heart. I suggest we make the Cook understand that she is to share his care with you—that you are his mother."

With his good arm, he touched his son's soft cheek, running his hand over the bit of silky dark hair. "Would you agree to that arrangement?"

"Of course," she said quickly, feeling a little guilty. "You run our home with the same perception and fairness you used in running the Temple of Tanit."

Still smiling, Hasdrubal turned his attention back to the baby. "He is so fascinating. I like to see him turn his head toward our voices. Every new thing he does amazes me."

"Wait. He's too little to do much yet except sleep and eat." Rome has been good for him, she thought. He smiles and his face becomes alive. He has mellowed without losing any of his force.

Abdmelkart arrived bearing two small tables. One, he placed right in front of his master.

"We need a table for Claudius," said Hasdrubal.

"He is with Palokart at the home of an Etruscan family," Elissa said. She handed the baby to Abdmelkart. "Take him to the kitchen and lay him in his basket. He will sleep."

Abdmelkart took the baby and returned with food which he set out for them. "Sire, the Cook needs some supplies. With your permission—"

"Go. I am just going to rest this afternoon," said Hasdrubal.

When they had finished eating, Elissa helped her husband back into bed and ordered him to take a nap.

"I don't know whether I am ready to sleep. What are you going to do?"

"I'll get some handwork and come sit with you."

He lay still, waiting for her to return and wondering why having his little son named after him had given him such pleasure. A movement caught his eye. He looked up and saw Aristide. His wildly thumping heart shook the walls of his chest. As usual in times of physical danger, he was helpless.

"How did you get in here?"

"I was watching outside and saw your slave leave. I walked in." Aristide sneered. "Since you're so curious, I'll tell you how I found you. I knew you would have your slave with you. I hung around the markets until I spotted him and followed him here. Much good may he do you now."

In one swift motion, Aristide jumped on top of Hasdrubal. His two hands, powerful and supple, squeezed the high priest's neck. His thumbs, with increasing pressure, dug into his throat. "You'll die," he cried, his face contorted in triumphant hatred.

With a gargled sound, Hasdrubal managed to gasp, "No— my son."

Flabbergasted, roaring in his ears like thousands of little

stones zinging around his head, understanding struck. Aristide released his grip. In the same instant, a knife drove deep between his shoulder blades, and Elissa screamed.

Aristide sagged to one side. With his legs, Hasdrubal managed to push him off the bed. As Aristide hit the floor and the knife twisted in his flesh, he let out a primordial cry of pain. Then "Son!" hissed venomously from his lips. "So that's what lay between my parents. That's why my father—" he was having trouble talking "—treated me so badly." Marshalling his energy into a vindictive effort, he rose on his elbow. "You bastard," he screamed and started to cough. Forcibly controlling his coughing, he stammered, "You disgraced my mother, cuckolded my father, ruined their lives. It's you who should die."

Dumbfounded, Hasdrubal tensed and lay rigid. Only his mind moved. Like a dropped coin, it skittered crazily. Aristide had no understanding of the truth. How awful. But Dido must have hinted. Aristide had realized what his use of "son" had meant. And Diodorus! What did he know? This man, blood of his blood, bone of his bone, was dying. A wave of agonized sympathy flowed from him, and he pushed himself across the bed toward his son. As he did so, Aristide's coughing started again, didn't stop. Blood flowed. Horrified, Hasdrubal and Elissa watched as he fell back dead. Elissa raised her eyes to her husband's. For an instant their glance locked before she turned and ran from the room.

Slowly, Hasdrubal got out of bed, careful where he put his feet. Holding his splinted arm across his body, he went searching for his wife. At the back of the house, he glanced around, turned right, and looked through each open door he passed. No Elissa. He found her in the kitchen, beside the basket of the sleeping baby. She was silently weeping.

"Elissa."

Her eyes traveled up his body. "What are you doing up?" she demanded.

He seemed to hang over her. The splint tilted him awkwardly forward. She jumped up and put her arm around him.

"I had to find you," he said simply.

"Your son." Her tears started again. "I killed your son. I didn't mean to. I couldn't help it. I—" She stopped. "That awful person your son! How can that be?" Her eyes looked sad and puzzled, "I don't understand a lot of things."

"Remember, I said I had a bad experience? Well, now is the time to tell you." He suddenly shivered.

"A short tunic isn't enough for this cold," she said.

"Let us go into the dining room until our bedroom can be cleaned. The couches should be comfortable. We will light the braziers."

In the dining room, she supported Hasdrubal while he settled himself. "I'll get a blanket from Claudius' bed," said Elissa. "I can't bear to go into our room." When she returned, she had a wool blanket and a fire to light the braziers.

She listened silently while he talked of how he had fallen in love with the vivacious Dido, the only child of his neighbors in Megara. He told her how he had begged his parents to allow him to marry her and how they had finally given in. "I never knew why they hesitated," he said. "They may have seen things in her character I did not and that only became apparent later."

He told her about the great wedding planned by Dido's mother, a showy, exaggerated affair way beyond the quiet desires of his own family. "The wedding was to take place in the morning," he said. "My friends and I were feasting late into the night when someone knocked at the door. A slave called me. Dido's father stood in the entry hall, having refused to come further. He looked pale. I was fearful, knowing something had happened, but my heart went out to the man. He seemed shriveled and so apologetic. He told me that they had found a scribe's note in Dido's room. She had run off with the son of a wealthy Athenian, a fellow who had been in Carthage but a short time. I had met him casually. Blackness formed before my eyes. I stumbled back into the house and informed my friends that my prenuptial feast was over."

He spoke of his mortification, of the months of depression and avoiding all those he knew, of burying himself in his studies at the temple, of the stolen afternoon in the garden a week before the wedding.

"I believed all women were evil until I met my sister-in-law. Saphonisba made me understand many things. But I never looked at another woman until you came to the temple." He studied his fingernails. "Even so, I could not bring myself to understand that such a lovely woman as you would be interested in me."

Elissa's lips curved in a sad smile. "And I loved you so. I thought you cared only about my value to the temple."

"Every time I saw you, I wanted to take you in my arms," he said indistinctly. "I was afraid you would notice."

"But Aristide!"

"I knew nothing about him until he appeared in Carthage. I saw him by accident. He was drinking at the spring. He looked exactly as I did at his age. In talking to Saphonisba—she had seen him—I realized that he was my son. I did not tell him. I was hesitant. He was attentive and seemed eager to work at the temple, but no intimacy developed between us. He showed none of my characteristics or those of my family. He was totally Athenian, naturally, since he was brought up in Athens. You would think," he mused, "that Dido would have taught him something of his Phoenician heritage." He returned to his recital. "Of course, when I got back from Tyre and you were gone, it was the same thing all over again: Dido had run off with Diodorus; you had run off with Aristide."

"Oh, no, no." Elissa gave an agonized cry.

Another cry, a howl, sounded over hers.

"Abdmelkart," yelled Hasdrubal. "Call him, please. He cannot hear me."

Elissa opened the door and called, "Abdmelkart!"

The Numidian rushed in and flung himself face down on the floor at Hasdrubal's side.

"Master, master," he blubbered. "I feared you, too, were dead."

"Get up, Abdmelkart." Hasdrubal touched the slave's bent shoulders.

Abdmelkart raised his body, but remained on his knees.

"My life, I would give for you, Hasdrubal."

Rarely did his slave call him Hasdrubal. Overwhelmed with emotion himself, the high priest said nothing.

"What shall I do with the body?" asked the Numidian.

"Late tonight, you and Claudius take him to the street near his own house. Leave him there so it looks like he was attacked by robbers and killed."

As Abdmelkart started from the room, Hasdrubal said, "Rearrange the furniture. Elissa and I will sleep in the library tonight."

31

*H*anno knocked on the library door. He munched on a large chunk of freshly baked bread.

"Come in," said Elissa. "We are up."

The room was warm from the brazier and lit by two lamps. Pale light crept in with Hanno. Elissa, fully clothed, stood by the bed.

"I'm going to Aristide's to see what's happening," he announced.

Hasdrubal, who was sitting on the edge of the bed, looked skeptical. "Take care, Claudius. I would hate to have to rescue you from the authorities and draw attention to our household."

"Trust me, Father."

Hasdrubal saw the muscles in Elissa's throat twitch.

As soon as Hanno disappeared, he said, "Does Claudius calling me father bother you? You know why I enforce the rule even in the privacy of our home." He took her two hands in his and insisted she look at him. "We have been all through what we are doing here. You know our need for caution. Actually," he said, dropping her hands, "had Aristide lived, he would have been a danger to us."

"Oh!" A second later, she said, "Forgive me, darling; I'm just touchy at the moment. I thought my son was the only son you had. Now what seems like a continuous stream of sons unnerves me."

"My love, your child is my only son. The one who lies in the street was really not mine. I just gave him life, a body. That seems to be all he inherited from me. His greed is his mother's. But cruelty!" He stared at the floor and shook his head. "It may be instinctively copying Diodorus, though I hate to think Diodorus capable of such cruelty. More likely, it stems from his upbringing." He ran his hand through his hair. "As for Claudius, while he is very dear to me, we both know our true relationship. He acts appropriately."

Abdmelkart appeared at the open door.

"We will eat in the dining room," Elissa said. "Help your master." To her husband, she said, "I will bring little Hasdrubal."

Hanno returned at lunchtime. Marita, Elissa's personal slave, was with him.

Hasdrubal's eyes narrowed. He sent Marita to the kitchen and requested Hanno's presence in the dining room.

"I listen," he said.

"When I got there, Aristide's body was still lying as we left it. A man was walking toward me down the street. So I just looked at the body and walked on. The man asked me if that was a dead man in the street. I told him it looked like it. He rushed over and pounded on the house door. I couldn't hear what he said, but a big slave ran out, looked at Aristide, and yelled at the top of his voice that it was the master. He didn't seem sorry, only scared. Then everybody started running out of the house. I counted ten slaves. They were all running around, some screaming, some dancing in joy. They really were." Hanno gave a little snort.

"A few people from neighboring houses came out to see what was happening. Finally, the slave who had answered the knock and who seemed to be the chief slave ordered the body carried inside. I heard him say that he must notify Aristide's father."

"So Diodorus will arrive," Hasdrubal said.

"The girl recognized me. I didn't realize that she was following me at first. We were walking around the Circus Maximus when she spoke to me. She asked about the baby and begged to come with me. She said her mistress had disappeared. Of course, I knew where her mistress was."

"Claudius, Claudius. Now we have a runaway slave on our hands. The authorities would cry foul so loudly that it would reach Jupiter. First the baby, then the mistress, now the slave."

Hanno's eyes widened. "How would they know to come here?"

"If Diodorus asks Aristide's Etruscan friends for evidence that might lead to the killer, the whole story of Elissa's rescue will come out. Palokart could be implicated in the business of the ruby. Palokart is Carthaginian."

Having adopted the habit from his uncle, Hanno's eyes narrowed as the ultimate conclusion flashed through his mind.

Late that evening, Palokart arrived with much news. Longus had arrived in Ariminum where the men bound by oath to come were to assemble. He had rested his troops and, after forced marches, linked up with Scipio. "My guess," Palokart said, "is that he will make a big point of holding conferences with Scipio, but he will take advantage of Scipio's present disability to gain a decisive victory for himself."

"In my judgment," said Hasdrubal, "any victory on his part will not be decisive. On the contrary, Hannibal may route him."

"My judgment, too," Palokart said.

Hasdrubal wrote his brother by lamplight the following morning:

> There is conflict of opinion in the Roman camp. Scipio believes that the legions need a winter for training and that the Celts will not stay loyal to Hannibal. He also hopes that when his wound heals, he can serve Rome along with Longus.
>
> According to talk here, he has suggested that Longus keep the situation as is. Longus wants to win the decisive battle himself and neither wants to wait for Scipio to recover nor for the new consuls to assume their commands, which is due to happen shortly. With Longus on the spot and in control, whatever transpires will be done with his own ambition in mind.

Bimilcar's reply to this was so fast that Hasdrubal could hardly believe his message had arrived much less a response come back. Bimilcar wrote:

> Hannibal's thinking is the same, but for different reasons. One, to do battle to exploit the warlike spirit of the Celts. Two, to engage the Roman legions while they have little battle experience. Three, to meet Longus before Scipio recovers. Four, to keep the initiative.

The days went by. Hasdrubal started walking outside the house. Abdmelkart was constantly beside him to ward off any collision with his cradled and splinted arm. The Numidian was nervous the day Hasdrubal insisted they go to the slave market. Crowds circled each individual offered for sale. Prospective buyers jostled to obtain the front spaces and jostled to leave. Abdmelkart feared that he could not protect his master. Hasdrubal brushed aside his remonstrances.

"We need a man for Claudius. He is rapidly becoming an adult and should have a slave to care for his clothing, help him dress, and wait on him. You have enough to do between looking after me and supervising our growing household."

Abdmelkart looked skeptical. The master was always so concerned about their mission being discovered, and here he was adding another person. The mistress' girl Marita was no problem. She was little more than a child herself, adored her mistress, had a sweet disposition and was rather stupid. She did as she was told and paid no attention to the rest of the household. He found her easy to deal with. But a healthy male! Abdmelkart didn't like it.

"I want a Hellene, preferably from some tribe mistreated by Rome. We will see to it that he is kept busy at home while Claudius makes his daily rounds, but he is always to accompany him otherwise." The high priest smiled in amusement. "With Claudius' popularity among the Etruscans and all his social engagements, he cannot depend on Palokart or his host to see him safely home. And Claudius uses his popularity to our advantage. The Etruscans talk in front of him."

He considered the characteristics he wanted in the slave. "I think an educated man can help me teach Claudius."

Abdmelkart nodded agreement. He thought his master tried to do too much. He always had, but right now, he must be prevented from overworking.

Sensing the Numidian's thinking, Hasdrubal's eyes narrowed, but a lively glint, full of laughter, escaped.

The slave market was bustling. A shipload of slaves from Athens had docked the night before. Hasdrubal recognized men he normally saw in the forum. Wealthy matrons in their litters were carried slowly from group to group. They searched for house slaves. Slaves who held positions of responsibility looked for kitchen help, gardeners, underlings. Haggling was sharp, on occasion strident. Physical deficiencies were argued against strength and age. The subdued hum and smell of sweat were not unlike the Carthage market, thought Hasdrubal as he looked around.

A muscular, clean-shaven man drew Hasdrubal's attention. "I will have a look at that fellow," he said to Abdmelkart.

The man returned Hasdrubal's look with anger in his eyes. "How old are you?" Hasdrubal asked.

"Thirty," sullenly.

"The best work years," said the slave handler. "He's solidly built and good for many years."

"I want that man," a woman's voice called.

Hasdrubal turned. A woman wearing too much expensive jewelry sat in a litter. Her finger pointed at the man he was talking to.

"Excuse me, my lady," Hasdrubal said. "I am bargaining."

"Flavius," the handler yelled to his assistant, "get the Celt for the lady." To Hasdrubal, he said, "He's smart, too."

"What's your schooling?" asked Hasdrubal.

"The usual."

Hasdrubal intently observed the slave. "The usual" could mean anything. Instinctively, he thought it meant much. He liked the aura of independence. "What is your price?" he asked the handler.

The man grinned slyly. "The woman will pay much."

"State a figure."

Flavius stopped at his side. He held one end of a rope. The other end was fastened around the neck of a broad-chested, blond man.

"I'll have him," squealed the woman.

Hasdrubal smirked. The handler looked irritated.

"Your price?"

"She'll pay plenty," the handler said under his breath.

Hasdrubal laughed. The handler laughed, too.

Walking home ahead of Abdmelkart and his new acquisition, Hasdrubal realized that he did not need to oversee the running of the house anymore.

Elissa is perfectly capable, Abdmelkart is my right arm, and— he turned.

"What name do you go by?"

"Lysander."

Hasdrubal finished his thought—Lysander is capable of handling Hanno. My trouble is, having run the temple for so long, I cannot drop the reins of authority.

"Now that you are in charge," he said, turning to Abdmelkart, "I expect everything to run as smoothly as usual."

"Yes, sire," said Abdmelkart who considered that he had already been in charge of his master's home for years.

Hasdrubal presented Lysander to Hanno. The slave bowed,

rather ungraciously to Hasdrubal's thinking. He called his nephew to him in secret. "Be careful what you say and do in front of Lysander. On the way to your dinner tonight, see what you can find out about his background."

The two left the house. Hanno, at ease and chatty, said, "I'll walk beside you since you don't know the city."

Lysander dropped heavy lids over sullen eyes and raised them again.

My uncle is right, thought Hanno. The slave is angry. Can he be trusted? Will he try to escape? "I understand you are to help my father with my lessons," he said. "That pleases me. I hope you will tell me something about your city and the way you lived."

Lysander glanced sideways at Hanno. To have a spoiled Roman boy show interest in his homeland, caught him off balance. "Whatever your father wishes, I will teach you." In a condescending manner, he added, "when you find time for studies."

Hanno bit his tongue. The fellow was surly, but a reprimand would only worsen the situation. They walked on, Hanno indicating streets, landmarks for identification, and corners they should turn.

Slave girls were still entertaining the guests, though the night was coming to an end. Before too long, streaks of morning light would creep up the sky. The excellent, overabundant food seasoned with garum, the fish sauce Hanno didn't like, had been removed, leaving only wine, always wine, and raucous laughter. A commotion in another part of the house caused the host to excuse himself. He returned with a furious, subdued Lysander in the grip of two muscular barbarians. An ugly red lash mark swelled across his face.

"Whose slave is this?" demanded the Roman host.

"Mine," Hanno said, jumping to his feet.

"He started a fight. Get him out of here. And if you take my advice," he said with disdain, "that one will need some harsh disciplining."

"My father will deal with him," said Hanno. In his most authoritative voice, he said, "Lysander, get your flare and escort me home. You will be punished for this."

Waving good-bye to his friends, he stalked from the room.

The blood had dried on the slave's face, but Hanno could feel his intense, trembling anger. "Lysander," he said, once they were walking along the dark, empty street, "Elissa is a physician and will treat your face. My father is a just man, but he will demand the truth, and you better be prepared to tell it. Why were you fighting?"

Instead of answering the question, Lysander burst out vehemently, "I was betrayed into slavery only weeks ago."

Hanno drew himself into stillness to listen attentively. It was going to bubble up first, then become a torrent of words. He slowed his steps to give Lysander time.

"For years," the slave began, "my people have been at war with the Aetolians. Cynaetha is a small island off the Peloponnesian coast. Some of the men ousted from power betrayed us to the Aetolians. I and three of my associates in the ruling council were in Sparta at the time, seeking help from the king. We heard what had happened to our people in Cynaetha and hurried home. We never got there. Very few escaped the massacre, but we met one man who did. He told us that we would die if we went home. My wife and children had all been slaughtered as well as my parents. All our possessions, our home, everything had been taken by the Aetolians. Some were living in my house as if it belonged to them."

Hanno found himself so caught up in Lysander's tragedy that he started to cry. Tears soundlessly streamed down his face.

Lysander stopped and laid his hand on Hanno's shoulder. "Thank you for your understanding."

Hanno brushed dry his face with the back of his hand. "How did you become a slave?"

"We were captured by some marauding Aetolians who did not recognize us as members of the council. Thinking that we were just Arcadian peasants, they announced that in their magnanimity, they were not going to kill us, but sell us into slavery. They sold me to Roman traders."

"You were fortunate to be bought by my father," said Hanno. "You must tell him what you told me. He will decide what is best."

Though the sky was bright with stars, the streets were so narrow that light only filtered in at intersections. Emerging into the Via Sacra at the forum, Lysander let out a deep gasp as the marble buildings shimmered in the starlight, ethereal and aloof, untouched by the many moving points of light on the Via Sacra.

"So this is the Roman forum!"

"Shall I point out the different buildings?" asked Hanno.

They made their way to the Vicus Tuscus, stopping every

few steps to discuss the buildings. As they neared home, Hanno said, "You can't go back, Lysander. You would be killed."

Lysander didn't say anything right away. When he did, it sounded very sad. "No, I can't go home."

In the kitchen, Hasdrubal and Hanno watched Elissa clean and treat Lysander's face. When she had finished, Hasdrubal said, "Lysander, you and I will go to my library."

Hasdrubal seated himself. Lysander stood modestly before him, without hostility, and told his story man to man, as in the days of his freedom.

The fight had involved the honor of his people. "A number of the Hellene slaves," he said, "started talking about the recent massacre and what they thought of our continuing war. The pain and horror of it is so close to me that I lashed out at them. I admit, sire, that the fault was mine. Rage blinded me."

"Your reaction," Hasdrubal said, "is understandable, but not to be tolerated in the future. I am sure you realize that."

"Yes, sire."

"You are a necessary and valued part of this household. We all do the best we can for the benefit of the others. You are expected to do likewise."

"Yes, sire." He bowed and backed out.

Fine, thought Hasdrubal. That bow was sincere, respectful and without servility. He will fit well here.

As though drawn by a magnet, Hanno checked every few days for any change in Aristide's household. His body had been thoroughly embalmed according to Roman custom and laid on a funeral pallet in the atrium for public viewing.

He mentioned it to Hasdrubal in front of Palokart. They were lying on couches in the dining room, just the three of them. Elissa had gone to bed.

"I shall go tomorrow and have a look," Palokart said. "Will you come with me, Claudius?"

Hanno was gracious, but declined, saying he didn't want to see someone that cruel adulated by mourners. Palokart found that funny. Hasdrubal, wanting to know the details of his son's funeral, issued a dinner invitation.

"Come and tell us about it."

"With pleasure, Paulus," said Palokart, rising.

After dinner the following night, they remained in the warm ambiance of the dining room. Palokart said, "Aristide lies in state. The head slave has done an outstanding job. He cleared the large foyer of statuary and benches. The pallet lies on a table in the middle. The undertakers were absolutely masterful with their unguents. He looks just as if he were napping; a handsome brute."

Hasdrubal, shaken, pushed aside his own feelings when he saw Elissa cringe. She wasn't close enough for him to touch, but when she raised her eyes to his, he smiled gently, his eyes filled with love.

"They dressed his body sumptuously. They even put a small coin on his tongue to pay the river-crossing fare," Palokart went on. "His body was surrounded by lamps and flowers. You really should see it. It's quite a show."

He turned to Hasdrubal. "I heard a slave say Aristide left the house early that morning and never came home. Nobody knows who stabbed him or why."

"It's a mystery I would like to be able to solve," said Hanno pompously.

Hasdrubal's eyes narrowed. Hanno wisely subsided.

In his innocence, Palokart laughed and said, "So would I."

A few days later, he reported that he had followed the mourners to the cremation grounds. "There were household slaves and a few neighbors. The procession to the funeral pyre was reasonable. The head slave hired a herald to go first, followed by pipers, flutists, horn players, torch bearers, and professional women mourners. I imagine he thought Aristide's father would approve. Aristide, himself, certainly would have liked the funeral."

"Did you stay for the whole ceremony?" asked Hasdrubal.

"Down to the cremation on the pyre. I saw them collect Aristide's bones to place them in honey. They are going to put his bones in one urn and his ashes in a different urn—to keep them, I guess, for his father."

They were all silent. Hasdrubal was thankful the whole thing was over.

"Well," he said, breaking the silence, "I have other news— disturbing news."

Hanno and Palokart were instantly attentive.

"The Roman forces have scored a great victory over Hannibal."

Palokart started. "No" escaped from him.

"The crowd at the forum was jubilant. Men were clapping

each other on the back, saying that the upstart Carthaginian would be finished in short order."

"He won't." Hanno stuck out his jaw.

"I do not think he will, either," said Hasdrubal. "We will wait to hear from my brother before we make any judgments on this."

Day after day, they waited. Hasdrubal began to fear that Bimilcar was dead and Hannibal in full flight. Hanno lolled on a chair in the atrium with his head thrown back and closed eyes. During a tutoring session, Lysander tried to draw him out. Hanno passed it off as being overtired.

In the privacy of his bedroom, Hasdrubal fussed and fumed. Would Hannibal attempt to recross the Alps with the remainder of his army? Elissa tried to calm him. She begged him not to mix so constantly with the crowds in the forum. He was adamant. For the sake of Carthage, he had to find out what he could and send the information to the Carthaginian senate.

At long last, a scroll came. Hanno, straight from the inn, burst upon Hasdrubal and Elissa eating fruit the dining room. He was jubilant. His father was alive. He rushed to Hasdrubal with the thick scroll and then, famished, flung himself onto a third couch and began stuffing food into his mouth.

Hasdrubal laid down his spoon and cracked the seal. Glancing rapidly over the beginning, he raised an eyebrow and cocked his head. Strange. The scroll began chattily as if nothing unusual had happened.

"What does he say?" Hanno could contain himself no longer.

"It can't be as much of a defeat as the Romans are making it," said Elissa.

Hasdrubal read aloud what all three were anxious to hear.

Hannibal has taken the town of Clastidium. He has not harmed the prisoners, though he paraded them. He wanted to show his mild policy. Also, he learned that some Celts who had made friendship treaties with him were also dealing with the Romans. Hannibal promptly sent a force of two thousand infantry and one thousand horse against them under raiding orders.

"Does he say anything about the battle?" Hanno held his spoon in midair.

"Not yet." Hasdrubal continued.

*Much booty was obtained. The Celts appealed to the Ro-
mans. That was the chance Longus was waiting for. He sent a
force of one thousand foot and much of his cavalry against us.
They crossed the Trebia where they engaged our men.*

Hasdrubal looked up. "Here is your battle, Hanno."
"It's not going to be much of a defeat," Hanno announced.
A wisp of a smile appeared on Hasdrubal's mouth.

*The Celts and Numidians fell back to our camp. Our troops
who were occupying forward positions understood what had taken
place and called for help. That made the Romans retreat to their
own camp. Longus then threw in more cavalry and javelin
throwers. They again turned the battle against our Celts who
retreated.*

"That's not even a real battle," said Hanno.
"I am not through reading, yet, son."
"Sorry."

*Hannibal never allows his forces to be drawn into a battle
unless by choice, and we were not prepared for a general battle.
So our troops were forced to turn and face the enemy. But rather
than let them close with the Romans, he sent out buglers to recall
them. This apparently surprised the Romans because they halted,
stood in formation for a while, then withdrew. We were fortunate
as we had taken some losses. A major battle might not have favored us.*

He stopped reading. "There is the kernel of the major victory
rumor."

*From what you say of Longus, we judged he would not let
things stand there, but be anxious to meet us in a general battle,
thinking that he could win himself a victory parade through Rome.
Accordingly, Hannibal mapped out his strategy.*

"I think the major battle is still to come," he said quietly and
unrolled more of the thick scroll.

Hannibal had noticed between the camps a flat, treeless area

crossed by a stream. Taking a few of us who are close to him, he
rode along the spot, looking for ambush possibilities. To our sat-
isfaction, we found the stream banks high, overhung by bushes,
and covered with matted, spongy, dead twigs and leaves. The
general consensus was that we had the perfect ambush spot. The
Romans would never suspect it because they only fear an ambush
where there are trees.

"How dumb," said Hanno.

"Have you seen sand and desert here? This terrain influ-
ences Roman thinking."

"If they start fighting other countries, they better learn,"
Hanno countered.

Hasdrubal smiled. That was probably more perceptive than
Hanno realized.

Back at camp, Hannibal picked one hundred infantry and one
hundred cavalry—the most daring of the troops—and asked them
to meet him after supper. At the appointed time, he sent for his
youngest brother who is with the troops and trained in soldiering.
He placed him in charge.

Each man of the two hundred was to pick ten from his own
company and report in two hours' time at the supply tents near
the baggage area. During the night, heavy rain started, the sting-
ing kind we get here in the north, which soaks everything. Led by
Hannibal, and with minimum noise, the troops left camp. They
carried with them dry clothing and food. Hannibal insisted on
that.

When he returned, I was waiting for him. He said that once
hidden under the bank, they were protected from the worst of the
elements and could find some comfort. He told them exactly what
time to attack, and left guides with them.

By dawn, the cold was bitter with gusts of snow. Hannibal
ordered the whole army to eat, dress in their warmest clothing,
and prepare their arms and horses for action. After issuing his
orders, he himself paraded the Numidian cavalry to draw out the
enemy before they had eaten or made battle preparations.

Everything worked out as he had hoped. Seeing the Numidian
cavalry, Longus sent out his horse to engage us. He dispatched a
large number of javelin throwers after the cavalry. And from what
happened later, we know that Longus was getting ready to move

his whole army out of camp. I suppose he thought the mere appearance of his superior numbers would cause us to withdraw.

"Carthaginians would withdraw!" cried Hanno.
Hasdrubal kept his eyes on the scroll.

Neither their men nor their horses were fed, so we found out. The troops threw on what clothes they could and rushed to the river. Because of the heavy rains, the Trebia was in flood. Crossing it was difficult. Many soldiers waded with water up to their breastplates.

The moment Hannibal saw that they had crossed the river, he ordered up pikemen and slingers. After advancing a mile, he drew the infantry into a single line made up of Hispanians, Celts and Africans; he divided the cavalry and stationed them on the two wings. The elephants were divided and placed on the wings in front of the infantry.

At this time, Longus called back his cavalry. The Numidians, dispersing and withdrawing, wheeling and charging, rendered the Roman cavalry useless. When the light-armed Roman troops opened action in the forward area, our troops proved themselves more effective. Fresh, warm, dry, and full of food, they beat back the Roman charge. As soon as the heavy infantry engaged, our cavalry assailed both flanks. The Romans fell back, exposing their infantry, whereupon our pikemen and Numidians attacked from both wings, causing heavy losses and hindering contact with the forward Roman troops.

"Hurray," yelled Hanno.

Their heavy infantry in the center fought courageously with no advantage to either side.

Just then, our ambushed troops attacked the Roman center from the rear, throwing the whole Roman army into disarray. Both infantry wings broke and the troops were forced back to the river. The heavy infantry in front found themselves pushed forward by the action behind. They managed to overcome the Celts and some Africans to break through the Carthaginian line. Seeing that both of their wings had been defeated, they succeeded in withdrawing to Placentia.

Because of the downpour, many of the Roman troops were

afraid to recross the Trebia and managed to reach Placentia. Like-
wise, our troops had no wish to pursue them across the river. So
when Hannibal ordered a pullback, we all returned to camp to
celebrate our victory.

Hasdrubal handed the scroll to Elissa to reroll.

"So much for their great victory," he said.

"Longus lied," blurted Hanno.

"Much good may it do him," Hasdrubal said.

"I can't believe the man is that stupid," said Elissa. "He must have said something slightly different, and maybe the public turned it into the rumor that is going around."

"From what I gather of him," said Hasdrubal, "what is more likely is that he claimed the great storm prevented him from having a resounding triumph, intimating that he had already won the battle anyway."

"What'll we do?" asked Hanno.

For a bit, Hasdrubal was quiet, looking into space. "There are good reasons to let the public think Rome has won a great victory. However, when the senate learns the truth, they will investigate. I think it best that they investigate. I leave it to you to tell as many people as possible that Hannibal still holds his camp while the Romans have abandoned theirs and taken refuge in the surrounding cities. That should soon come to the ears of the senate."

Rumors to corroborated facts! The idea delighted Hanno. Gleefully, he said, "My friends the Etruscans are good at spreading rumors."

Hasdrubal smiled ironically. "Claudius, you really are ingenious."

Hanno turned red in pleased embarrassment. He was off the couch and out the door, yelling for Lysander as the last word left his uncle's lips. Hasdrubal snorted, and Elissa laughed.

"He and Lysander are getting on beautifully," she said.

"And Abdmelkart tells me that he is cooperating well with the others—and he does not ask a lot of extraneous questions."

"You chose well when you purchased him." Elissa smiled at her husband.

"I think his brawl his first night and our discussions about it also had a lot to do with his present conduct."

"Possibly," she said, and dropped the subject.

Hanno returned to say that he had seen the Etruscans; they

had laughed and were already busy telling others what they had heard on good authority—elaborating it with great oratory.

In spite of his amusement Hanno seemed sobered. He met Hasdrubal's look with a troubled gaze. They were alone, walking around the atrium as they talked. Hasdrubal gave him plenty of time to initiate a conversation by stopping to gaze up at the sky before moving on, inspecting the overhang of the roof. Hanno made no attempt to leave his company, but volunteered nothing.

Finally, Hasdrubal said, "What bothers you, my boy?"

"On the way home, I went by Aristide's house. A carriage and four horses stood out front. A groom was unhooking the sweating animals."

"So—" Hasdrubal said and stopped. They walked again, at least twenty steps, before he continued "—Diodorus has arrived."

"Will he find us?"

"Probably. But not right away. He will have much to occupy him at first—handling the estate, putting out feelers, setting up a plan. He will question the slaves first. Aristide's closest friends will come next. Each one will lead him to others."

"What will we do?"

"Nothing. Wait."

Hanno seemed uncertain.

"After all, Aristide started this whole thing. He kidnapped, imprisoned and tried to seduce a married woman. The law is on our side. We did what we had to to rescue her. That is as much as he will find out."

Hanno looked relieved, but continued, "What if he finds out we killed Aristide?"

"We did not. Only one of us did. Four people know, and I do not expect any of us to tell. You said no one saw you when you dropped off his body. Aristide's slaves will testify that he was alive and well for two days after the fire, then he went out and did not return. The Etruscans are not involved. It could easily have been a robbery attempt."

Hanno had a strange expression on his face. His uncle surmised what was passing through his mind and said, "If anybody is to be blamed, I have the perfect reason for killing him. But let us not concern ourselves with that until we have to. That is not our main problem. If Diodorus attempts to prosecute and we are called to testify, the fact that we are Carthaginians will come out. We could be liable for treason."

"Why don't we leave Rome immediately?"

"I may very well send you, Elissa, and the baby home to your mother."

"You and Abdmelkart have to come, too."

"I am here to help Carthage. I stay. Abdmelkart stays with me. If I should die, you will be high priest of Tanit—at least until my son is old enough."

Hanno stepped in front of his uncle. The intelligent, strong, reliable man who was emerging from the adolescent body faced Hasdrubal.

"Then I will also stay," Hanno said.

Hasdrubal started to remonstrate, but Hanno continued. "If I am not able to protect you, I will become high priest of Tanit and train little Hasdrubal."

Much shaken, Hasdrubal hugged Hanno and kissed him on both cheeks. There was no need to argue the point. The future held the answer.

"Say nothing of this to Elissa," said Hasdrubal.

32

*B*imilcar sent word that the army was in Cisalpine Gaul and that Hannibal intended to remain there for what was left of the winter. Planning, he wrote, goes forward for the spring campaign, but in the meantime, the troops were tempering their constant patrol duty with a much-needed rest.

In Rome, despite the city's war preparation and panic, life settled down in the enlarged family. The baby grew chubby and daily more interesting. He recognized them all, cooing and crowing.

Hasdrubal regularly exercised his arm and felt confident that he would soon have full use of it.

Hanno became thoroughly Romanized. His speech lost its provincial accent; he wore the finest wool togas, fastened with a gold pin; he chatted the lingo of upper-class Roman youth whom he met through Palokart. And Elissa ran the household with such efficiency that Hasdrubal was amazed by her continually unfolding abilities, as the once-pampered Tyrian princess turned physician took up her duties as wife and mother.

In spite of the smoothness, Diodorus was an unsettling undercurrent. Every few days, Palokart reported. First, "He hired searchers today." Next, "He's questioning Aristide's Etruscan and Roman friends."

"Is the Etruscan who gave Elissa the ring among them?" Hasdrubal asked.

"Yes. He said they had only recently become acquainted and offered no help. He's gone to his family's estate in Tarquinia."

"Good. He did not implicate you."

"Diodorus has put the house up for sale and plans to put Aristide's slaves on the block."

One day, Palokart said, "Diodorus sent out word to look for Marita. He said she is young and valuable. He ordered that she be returned with an iron collar indicating her propensity to run away."

In the privacy of their bedroom, Elissa's fury exploded. "An iron collar indeed! She was bought for me. She is mine. Diodorus has no right to claim her."

"Keep her in the house until this blows over and Diodorus has returned to Athens," advised Hasdrubal.

"I will," said Elissa, "but it burdens the others with more work."

"Use Lysander for your errands. Anything to occupy him. He is too interested in Claudius' morning activity."

"He knows that you go out each morning. Abdmelkart doesn't follow you."

"He knows that I go to the forum. I am expected to go where business is transacted. Claudius is not."

"Clau - Claudius"—Elissa always stumbled over Hanno's Roman name—"could be learning the business."

"We do not go together. Lysander knows that, too. He has started to ask Abdmelkart questions."

Elissa's eyes widened. "Abdmelkart would never betray you."

"Of course not, but he has to be on guard."

Elissa pursed her lips thoughtfully. "I'll find things for Lysander to do."

Three days after that conversation, Hasdrubal found the Numidian squatted just inside the entrance door waiting for him. As the door opened, Abdmelkart sprang to his feet and bowed from the waist. He had become used to bowing rather than groveling. After considerable thought, he had decided that bowing showed as much respect, and he liked it better. It didn't get his short tunics dirty.

"What is the matter?" asked Hasdrubal, instantly alert.

Abdmelkart straightened up. "Oh, master, the whole marketplace buzzes like night insects. They are all talking about the amounts of money a certain Athenian trader is spending to search for Aristide's abducted mistress and for the baby he considers his grandson."

"If he is spending untold amounts, he is having no success. Let us hope his expenditures continue unabated." Starting toward his bedroom, Hasdrubal added, "Come help me out of this formal toga and then send Claudius to me."

"Claudius has not yet returned."

"Well, as soon as he does."

Elissa was also out; Hasdrubal had Abdmelkart bring his lunch to the library. He picked at the food distractedly.

It was not like Hanno, he thought, to stay away without informing them. Though Hanno often lunched with friends, he always left a message.

Unable to sit any longer, he got up to expend some of his nervous energy pacing up and down the atrium. Finally, he scolded himself: what he was doing was not helping matters one bit.

He returned to the library where he wrote at length to Elibaal. He was sealing the papyrus with soft wax when he realized that the hours were passing, and Hanno had not yet come to him.

"Abdmelkart!"

The slave was at his side as if summoned by magic.

"Where is Lysander?"

"On errands for the mistress, sire." Abdmelkart's dark, smooth face crinkled in worry. He had annoyed the Cook by seasoning everything she was boiling and standing in her way. Then, he had leaned against the library doorjamb where he could watch the main door as well as listen for his master's voice.

"And Elissa?"

"Out, sire."

"And Marita?"

"With my lady."

"With her! Why?"

"Lysander was busy this morning, and the mistress had a lot to carry, great lord." Somehow, he had done wrong. Marita had told him she was supposed to stay in the house, but Elissa had taken the girl. He was upset. Her action had made him disobey his master. He wanted to cry out, make amends.

Hasdrubal fumed. He would just as soon return the stupid girl. She adored Elissa and clung to her as to a mother, but was incompetent. He shook his head. If they were spotted, he would have to deal with Elissa's loyalty to the girl.

Someone knocked on the entrance door. The knock sounded loud and demanding.

Abdmelkart hurried to open it. He returned, a wax tablet in his hand.

Hasdrubal eyed the tablet—it meant disaster. Who and where would it strike? He ground his teeth and put out his hand. The tablet was from Diodorus.

"Sire, the messenger waits," said Abdmelkart.

Hasdrubal read the tablet's few words: Send my son's wife to me or be taken to court.

He required all his phenomenal willpower to collect himself.

"Send in whoever comes home," he said and sat back to think of what to write Diodorus. A court case was the last thing he wanted. He had composed two notes and erased both when Lysander slipped in and bowed.

"Sire?"

"Claudius has not returned. Do you know where he is?"

"No, master. It is late for him not to have returned." Lysander looked at the mosaic floor, studying one of the flowers as he turned over in his mind where his young master might have gone. When he looked up, he said, "I will find him."

"The city is large."

"I will find him, sire."

Hasdrubal dropped his head in acquiescence. Forgetting his position, Lysander turned on his heel and walked out of the room. Hasdrubal was too concerned with the wax tablet to notice that Lysander hadn't backed out.

He made up his mind to state the case bluntly.

*I can prove incontrovertibly that the woman in question is,
and was at the time Aristide abducted her, my wife.*

He drew a line under the word abducted.

He sat and reread the note many times before handing the tablet to Abdmelkart who delivery it to the waiting messenger.

Hasdrubal continued to sit, sunk in thought. Diodorus had not said anything about the slave or the baby. Undoubtedly, one of the Etruscans—in need of cash—had finally told of Elissa's rescue.

He must instruct Elissa not to let Marita leave the house under any circumstance, nor was anybody to take little Hasdrubal out.

Where were they, anyway? If anything happened, Elissa would more likely have to protect the girl than the other way around. Hasdrubal sighed. Fortunately, Marita had no responsibility for the baby.

Nobody could put a nose out of the house carrying the child. Hasdrubal would strictly enforce this precaution. Now that Diodorus knew where Elissa was, he might have the house watched.

That thought was like a knife going through him. Suppose he and Hanno were followed? Would Diodorus discover what they were doing in Rome? He would learn that the man he was having watched spent his days wandering around the comitium, listening. Diodorus couldn't make much of that. Hanno was another thing. Hasdrubal didn't really know how his nephew gathered information.

He stiffened. Had something happened to Hanno? Give Lysander a chance, he thought. But what did the slave know of Hanno's movements? Not much. Hasdrubal shook his head, ran his hand through his hair, and squirmed in the chair. Why didn't one of them come home? The day had been one disaster after another.

Elissa entered the library. How beautiful she looked. She wore a long pink gown and her hair was swept up in the style of a Roman matron. At her shoulder, a jeweled pin he had given her held her garment together. This lovely woman was his wife. Looking at Elissa, he never failed to ruminate on his good fortune. With a muffled cry of joy at knowing she was safe, he sprang up.

"You wanted to see me?" she said.

"Diodorus sent a messenger today demanding your return."

"No, no." She knelt beside him. "Please don't send me back."

"Send you back!" He stared at her in disbelief. "Of course I will not send you back. Whatever made you say that?" He drew her onto his lap. She snuggled against his neck, and he felt warm tears.

"You are crying, my darling." He tried to pull her around so he could look at her, but she kept her face buried in his neck.

"I'm afraid," she whispered.

"Yes," he answered softly. "One thing leads to another." He told her what he had written to Diodorus. "For the time being, you must also remain in the house. I want no risk of you being snatched from me."

She nestled closer.

"I must send word to Palokart," he continued. "If he has something to tell me, we will have to meet at the inn. Now that you are home, my main worry is Claudius."

Elissa sat up. "Hasn't he returned or sent word?"

Hasdrubal shook his head. "No. Lysander has gone to look for him."

"Claudius could be anywhere."

"I feel trapped in a narrow mountain pass like Hannibal's troops—the need to find him opposed to the possibility of arousing suspicion." He sighed. "Like Hannibal, I know what we have to do."

"We must find him," she broke in.

"Yes, we must find him."

Lysander didn't know the city that well, but knew where he intended to look. Even though he had never actually followed his young master, by accident, he had managed to accumulate a fairly good knowledge of his haunts. A slave he had met in the forum told of a boy who hung around a big house on the other side of the Palatium. During the discussion, Lysander realized the man was talking about Claudius. "He goes there regularly," the slave said. "He never speaks to anybody. And he hides if an Etruscan or a Roman walk along the street."

"What happens?" Lysander sounded eager.

"Nothing. Occasionally, an older man comes out and either gets into a chariot or walks down the street. Sometimes a slave stands at the door with the man and nods his head yes at whatever the man says."

One day, Lysander had been doing an errand for the mistress. He happened to see Claudius talking to some old men. He carefully retraced his steps so Claudius wouldn't see him.

What Lysander hadn't been able to figure out was why Claudius went to the house or why he sat with the old men. His mind worked at that, so far without result, but he headed directly for the house.

The street was empty. Lysander stared, planting both feet solidly on the ground in front of the house. No sign of life was visible anywhere. For a short while, he stood there, not sure what to do next. When nothing happened, he began to walk up the street, turned and walked back the other way. Then he ducked into the nearest doorway. The slave he had seen outside his master's house was coming down the street. Lysander peeked around the doorpost. He saw the slave go into the house. Hum, he thought. I'll just hang around a bit, but since I don't know what goes on here, I don't want that slave to see me.

Soon a chariot arrived. A distinguished looking, middle-aged man and a younger man got out. Lysander pretended to be casually passing by the house.

"Here, slave, hold these reins until I send someone out," said the older man authoritatively. He flung the reins at Lysander, then went into the house, followed by the younger man who carried a bag. Lysander caught the reins. Hum, he said to himself again. If I judge rightly, that is a physician and his assistant.

A slave appeared to take the reins.

"I hope nobody is ill," Lysander said discreetly.

"No. Some nosy kid who hangs around here was kicked by one of our horses. It's his own fault. He got too close."

He had found Claudius. Now, how could he gain entrance to the house and get his young master out.

"If the dead master's father weren't so generous," the slave continued, "he would have left the little beggar to die in the street. But since it was his horse who kicked him, he had the boy brought in and put to bed."

Lysander went home to report what he had learned.

"In that house!" Hasdrubal exploded.

"I will go to him immediately," cried Elissa. "It doesn't matter if the slaves recognize me. What's important is to help Ha— Claudius."

"Hold on, my sweet." Hasdrubal raised an arm for silence. "You are important here, too. You stay. A physician is already attending him."

"But we don't know how competent he is."

"Once Hanno is home, you can take care of him. Right now, we must make a plan. We do not know how badly he is hurt, or whether he will need our help to escape."

Hasdrubal turned to the slave. "Ask Abdmelkart to join us in the dining room. We must think of some method to get Claudius out."

Well after midnight, the four people were still in the dining room, Abdmelkart squatting on his haunches, Lysander sitting on the floor, his back against the wall, hardly able to keep his eyes open.

"Don't you think, dear," Elissa said to her husband, "that we have been talking long enough? Everyone is tired. We haven't made any new suggestions for a long time. Let's meet again in the morning when we are fresh."

Hasdrubal, used to working through the night, looked around. He couldn't tell about Abdmelkart, but Elissa had little drooping pockets under her eyes.

"All right," he said, "right after—"

A loud banging at the entrance interrupted him. "Oh," cried Elissa. She looked around at the others. The Numidian rose to answer the door, and Lysander trailed behind in case of trouble.

"Someone from Diodorus," Elissa said.

"About Claudius." Hasdrubal's voice was deep and troubled.

"Oh, dear." She gazed at her husband. His face was bland, his eyes downcast, but she knew he was worried. She stretched out her hand to comfort him.

Abdmelkart and Lysander entered, supporting a pale and wan Hanno.

"Claudius," exclaimed Elissa.

Hasdrubal flew from his chair. He took his nephew in his arms. Hanno relaxed against him and sighed heavily.

"Abdmelkart, get a blanket." Hasdrubal eased the boy onto a dining couch.

Elissa, kneeling beside him, felt his forehead and limbs.

"I was trying to get out of the way," Hanno mumbled. "The horses came too fast."

"Where were you kicked?"

"My right side. It wasn't really a kick."

"Does this hurt?" Elissa gently pushed at his flesh.

"The horse's shoulder brushed me—no, it doesn't hurt—and knocked me down. I remember a crack at my head and seeing all kinds of stars, and that's all. The next thing I remember is being in bed and hearing two people talking." Hanno swallowed hard. "One said, 'This is the boy who yelled "Fire" the night our mistress disappeared.' So I pretended I was still out and kept my eyes closed."

"Open your eyes now and look at me."

Hanno opened them slowly, making a face at the brightness of the room, and tried to focus on Elissa.

"His trouble is not the horse, but the fall," said Elissa, cautiously feeling Hanno's spine, up to his neck and the back of his skull. "He has a large bump."

"I'm going to throw up," said Hanno.

Abdmelkart rushed from the room.

"Lysander, hold his head to the side."

The Numidian brought back a small bowl. Hasdrubal took it and said, "Bring some warm water, too." He positioned the bowl under Hanno's face. Hanno vomited. Lysander slid his arm under Hanno's back to hold him up.

"When Abdmelkart comes back," Elissa said to Lysander, "I will wash his face and hands, then the two of you get him into bed."

The Numidian was quick. Hanno vomited again; then, exhausted, he rested against Lysander while Elissa cleaned his face. When she gave the signal, the two slaves picked him up. Hasdrubal hurried ahead to pull off Hanno's bed covers. By the time he was tucked in, Hanno was asleep.

Worried, Abdmelkart turned to Elissa. "Has he passed out again?"

"No," said Elissa, looking carefully at Hanno. "I think he is sleeping."

She addressed Lysander. "Sleep here on the floor beside him tonight. If he is restless or in pain, call me. We will keep him in bed for a few days. Since light bothers his eyes, don't open the door. Don't let him get up under any circumstances. Abdmelkart will relieve you in the morning."

She suddenly realized that she was appropriating Abdmelkart. "Forgive me," she said to Hasdrubal. "Is that all right?"

"Of course. I will also sit with Claudius. I have done it before—as Abdmelkart will remember."

"I do, sire. And the mistress nursed him."

Elissa smiled and, taking her husband's hand, led him to their bedroom.

As the bedroom door shut behind them, Hasdrubal muttered, "Thanks to Tanit, the war in the north is quiet. We do not need that turmoil right now."

"Has the panic calmed down?"

"Somewhat. The preparations the senate ordered go forward, but nothing new has been started."

All except the Cook and the baby slept late the next morning. The Cook prepared thin, hot cereal as usual. Nobody came. She poked at her bread every few minutes. It would be overdone or cold. She fussed. She went to the tiny room where Abdmelkart slept. The door was shut. Bravely, she ventured to the young master's bedroom door. It, too, was closed. She hesitantly walked across the atrium and looked at the master's door. Closed. Confused, worried, feeling very much alone, she stood by the dining room, twisting her skirt in her hands. What should she do? The master's door opened. The mistress, looking thrown together and tired, flew out, started at seeing her, waved a greeting and rushed to the kitchen, the Cook at her heels.

Elissa grabbed her red-faced, squalling baby and gave him her breast. His tears instantly dried. The red color on his little face disappeared, and he smacked away, his long dark lashes fluttering in slow motion. Only then did Elissa try to explain through gestures that the young master was ill.

The Cook did not really understand, but comprehended that something had happened.

In the evening, Hasdrubal took his turn sitting with Hanno. The boy was awake and had even taken a little food without throwing up. Elissa had told him in no uncertain terms that he was to lie quietly, and he was obeying.

"Would you like to talk, son?" Hasdrubal sat on the floor in the darkened room.

"Yes. I want to tell you what I heard them say. Are we alone?"

"Yes."

"They recognized me and connected me with Elissa's disappearance. I kept my eyes closed, but I'm sure it was Diodorus and the chief slave. Diodorus wondered if I knew something about the slave girl and the baby, too."

Hasdrubal whistled.

"He asked the slave if the baby was Aristide's. The slave said he assumed so since the mistress was big with child when the master had bought him. But he said Aristide never went near her room, and he always had prostitutes and young boys in the house. Diodorus let out a big sigh and muttered something about the same old pattern—I don't know what he meant." Hanno lay still. He could guess what use Aristide made of the young boys. Aristide had tried to kiss him, but he had sidestepped his advances. "Diodorus didn't ask any more questions about that, but said he would ask me about the baby. The slave told him he knew how to make me talk. I was scared. I figured they were going to torture me."

"And well they might."

"I didn't feel well and getting up made me vomit, but after everybody went to sleep, I let myself out and came home. I guess they thought I was unconscious so didn't leave anybody to watch me."

Hasdrubal patted Hanno's arm with great tenderness. "You have done well, son."

Hanno closed his eyes, a smile on his lips, and turned his head to sleep.

True to her abilities as a doctor, and being unusually cautious, Elissa kept him in bed until his eyes focused properly and the contusion on the back of his head had disappeared. It wasn't easy. As the weather improved, he became restless. The door to his bedroom remained open most of the time so he could see the sunlight dance in the atrium as the breeze ruffled the leaves on the young pear and cherry trees. He told Elissa he could almost see their green color deepen from day to day. She laughed. "If your eyesight is that sharp, you can get up soon."

She was as good as her promise. He ventured out one morning, Lysander beside him in case he stumbled. Elissa walked with them through the vegetable garden, where they commented on the little sprouts, and unlocked the gate. If the house were watched, they assumed that it was only the main entrance since this little back gate was rather hidden.

"Remember, she said, "this is to be a short walk. I don't want you to come back tired out." Hanno and Lysander nodded solemnly.

Elissa shut the gate tightly behind them, leaving it unlocked so they could get in. She returned to the house. It felt empty. Abdmelkart had gone to the market and Hasdrubal was at the comitium.

Crossing the atrium, she saw the Cook, little Hasdrubal in her arms, enter from the street. With a gasp, she rushed to the Cook and snatched the baby. Wildly, she gestured that the infant was not to be taken out of the house. The Cook showed that she thought Elissa was wrong—there was no reason not to take the baby out; besides, it had only been into the street, to look for the seller of cooking pots.

Elissa could find no way to express the danger to the deaf woman. Abdmelkart tried to explain when he returned, but the Cook only burst into tears. Thinking the reprimand unjust, she went to her room. Lysander, coming back with Hanno, told the mistress they had returned, and was surprised at her indifference. He took his young master to the bedroom and closed the door. In agony, Elissa waited for Hasdrubal. He burst in, kissed her and said, "Both new consuls have taken to the field; the spring campaign has started. Gaius Flaminius is camped before Arretium, after marching through Etruria. Gnaeus Servilus marched as far as Ariminium to oppose any advance by Hannibal there."

He was suddenly aware of Abdmelkart lurking in the background, and he noted his wife's stillness. Sharply, he said, "What has happened?"

Choking back tears, Elissa said, "The Cook took little Hasdrubal into the street. She's weeping now, probably afraid of being sold without knowing why."

Hasdrubal stood with bowed head, thinking. Elissa bent
toward him, her whole body stance a plea. He took her hand. "Let
us go sit in the garden to talk."

"Abdmelkart," Hasdrubal raised his voice slightly, "bring
lunch," adding to Elissa, "I will deal with the Cook later."

"I'm not hungry."

"My love, we carry on as usual while we wait for the next
message from Diodorus."

He led her to the area where he used to sit with Hanno near
the bedroom door. Elissa slowly regained her composure.

After they had finished eating, he said, pushing himself from
the chair, "I will find the Cook."

Hasdrubal entered her room. The Cook was lying face down
on her bed. Her crying had stopped. With all her heart, she had
been willing her master to come to her. She trusted him implicitly
and believed he would help her.

Hasdrubal did not want to startle her more than necessary.
Gently, he touched her shoulder.

The Cook raised her head, twisting her neck to see who was
beside her. Recognizing him, she scrambled off her bed and grov-
eled on the floor at his feet.

Hasdrubal motioned her to get up and follow him. In the
vegetable garden, he thought, they would be alone, and he would
have room to move around, swing his arms, pantomime. He
meticulously acted that men were watching the house to get the
baby. The people who had imprisoned her mistress and the baby
wanted the baby back.

With understanding came desperation. She could lose her
darling child. Never would she take him out again. Her tears
flowed, and she dropped to the ground.

"Come, come," said Hasdrubal automatically, as if she could
hear him. Leaning over, he pulled her up and led her back to the
kitchen. He indicated that she was to continue cooking dinner. Her
face was still wet with tears, but she smiled, looking to see if Marita
had washed and trimmed the artichokes for the vegetable stew.

The sun, at sunset, hovered at the horizon, hating to leave
the spring day. Hasdrubal sat in the garden where he could see
both the early spring flowers—pink, deep blue, and white—and

Elissa, through the open door of their bedroom, like a flower in her yellow gown.

He heard a knock and saw that Abdmelkart carried a tablet as he crossed the atrium.

Hasdrubal scanned the message. "Elissa," he said, his voice low and sympathetic.

She looked up, saw the tablet in his hand, and rushed out to stand trembling before him.

"Diodorus asks us about the female slave. He also asserts that the baby in our possession is the same age as his grandson, and he wants us to explain his presence in our house."

"Can we tell him he belongs to the Cook?" she suggested, fighting back tears. "It would be impossible for anyone to question her. She can't read or write."

"No." He shook his head. "They could make her understand that they were asking her if the child were hers. Having lied, we would be in an awkward position. No, my darling, you were pregnant when Aristide abducted you. The child is mine. I believe you when you say he never lay with you."

"I did not allow it." Elissa was her old fiery self.

"How do we prove that?"

"Marita slept in my room. He never came near me."

"That was while you were large with child."

"Or before either." She stamped her foot.

"It only takes once," he said sadly.

Elissa dropped her eyes, but he caught the tears in them.

"Give me your hand," he said, reaching toward her. She laid her hand in his, and his closed, holding her tightly. "We have each other, and we have our baby. We must cling together. I will tell him the truth about our child, and that Aristide gave you the slave, but if he insists on having her back, he may do so."

"Oh, no." Elissa tried to pull her hand away.

Hasdrubal kept her prisoner. "Even though the girl is yours, we might offer to pay for her. He would probably sell her anyway, as he has the others. If he accepts money, she would not have to hide any longer."

"And if he won't?"

"If he forces the issue, we may have to let her go," Hasdrubal said gently.

"She is so young. I would hate to see her branded as a runaway slave."

"I agree. Keep her busy in the vegetable garden or in the kitchen. Do not let her in this part of the house. I will see what I can manage."

Elissa nodded. "She loves the garden. Her people are farmers from way up north. And she is already doing some of the cooking."

"Really!" Hasdrubal's eyebrows rose. "The meals have been extraordinarily good."

Elissa smiled serenely.

"Well," he continued, "that should occupy her. If she stays inside, Diodorus' messengers will not come face to face with her by accident. There is no need to aggravate the situation, even though he knows she is here."

Hasdrubal was silent, thinking about Diodorus' third point. "He also asked if we knew the whereabouts of the young man who disappeared from his sickbed."

"What will you tell him?"

"That the young man he refers to is a member of my household. I will not say anything except he regained consciousness, rose, and came home."

"Nothing about Claudius being given the baby?"

"Diodorus may not have connected that yet, but he will. The slave who gave him the baby will undoubtedly tell him."

Hasdrubal reread the wax tablet. "I will write him that I was gravely wounded rescuing you and that I was bedridden for weeks. With that, I would hope he would look elsewhere for Aristide's killer."

Rising heavily, he went to their bedroom. Elissa followed him dejectedly. He took a stylus from the niche where he kept his writing implements. She sat on the bed beside him, watching every stroke as he wrote. Two or three times, he stopped writing and covered her fidgeting hands with his.

Finished, he ordered Abdmelkart to give the tablet to the messenger.

Dinner was not a lively affair. Elissa, Hanno and Hasdrubal lay on their couches, saying little. Abdmelkart, moving quietly among them, urged Elissa to eat.

"I can't," she said.

"Diodorus is getting closer and closer to accusing us of murder," said Hanno.

"Yes," said Hasdrubal. "It is only a matter of time before he announces that we killed Aristide."

"I killed Aristide," said Elissa.

Hanno's eyes slitted.

"We are in this together, Elissa," Hasdrubal said. She said no more, but shot him a defiant look.

"Claudius," said Hasdrubal, "You had better tell Lysander of Elissa's rescue. Tell him that an abductor took my wife and baby. The abductor died mysteriously, and now the man's father is trying to implicate us. Use your own judgment about how much detail you want to go into, including your own role in the affair."

"Thank you, sire," said Hanno. "Lysander is asking questions. I have had to be very careful."

"It is best he know. He may be called upon to help us and do it quickly. If he knows the circumstances, he will be able to act expediently."

Hasdrubal spent the following morning at the forum. On his return, he was met by a vivacious and smiling Elissa. "We had another message from Diodorus. You won't believe what he said."

"What did he say?" Hasdrubal put his arm around her waist.

"He says that I can keep the girl! We don't have to buy her again. He says it's because you have been so forthright in your answers, and Aristide did you a great wrong."

Hasdrubal narrowed his eyes. "That is surprising. It makes me suspicious. His demands are as abrupt and aggressive as a lion's. We reply truthfully, and he is as passive as a lamb. Either he does not question our statement, such as his first threatening court proceedings over you, or he acquiesces to our suggestion without so much as a 'but.' Most peculiar. What do you make of it?"

"I have never seen the man."

"True. But what do you think?"

"It's almost like indifference. He is doing the expected, proper thing, but doesn't seem to care one way or the other about the result."

"It is beyond me." He picked up the wax tablet and read it. "Obviously, he quizzed Aristide's slaves and knows how you were treated. At least he realizes that. I will erase this and write, thanking him for his gracious act. Abdmelkart can take the tablet back."

Hasdrubal hoped the exchange would be his last communication with Diodorus. To his disappointment, he received another message from the Athenian trader some days later.

"Will he ever stop this stream of accusations!" sighed Hasdrubal.

"My Etruscan friends say that he is at his wit's end," said Hanno. "None of them know anything about the murder, but Diodorus keeps pestering them. They think some robber did it even though nothing was missing."

Hasdrubal's eyebrows went up. "We made a mistake there. We should have thought of it."

"Apparently that's why Diodorus is sure there is another reason. And he thinks it's connected with Elissa's rescue. He's frustrated because he knows you were laid up and in bed, so he can't accuse you. He doesn't know what to do next."

"Well, let us see what he has to say this time." Hasdrubal sat down. Hanno stood by his chair, as his uncle read aloud:

"I am convinced you know something about the murder of my son." Hasdrubal looked at Hanno. "This is the turning point."

"We better be prepared to get away if we are exposed," Hanno said.

"Would you take that responsibility, Claudius? Find out what ships go where."

"Yes, sire."

"I say we have about a week."

"The courts here move slowly."

"We do not have to wait for our case to come before the courts for Rome to find out that we are Carthaginians. Diodorus would recognize me."

Hanno reared back and stared at his uncle.

Ignoring him, Hasdrubal picked up the tablet which rested in his lap. "All this just when the army is again preparing for battle, and Hannibal might need our help." He sighed and glanced over the wax. "This is rather lengthy."

The slave who was head of my son's house was not sold with the others. We have gone over the events in precise detail. Aristide knew that some of the men helping during the fire were Etruscan. After the fire was out, Aristide sent a message to his friend, a high-ranking Etruscan. Then, he paced the house in a rage. But no message came until late in the day. He read it, laughed wildly and shouted threats. The next morning, he left the house at dawn, returning that evening. He did the same the next day but never returned. His body was found in the street. The slave has no idea where he went or what he did. Did he come to your house? When

did he leave? You have dealt honorably with me so far. I assume
you will in this.

Hasdrubal let the tablet drop. "He is convinced we are involved."

"What will you tell him?"

"Only as much of the truth as I can."

Hasdrubal wrote the return message. Elissa stood at his shoulder.

Hasdrubal told her what he would say, writing in the wax as he spoke, "Aristide snuck into our home after seeing my slave leave for the market. He came into my bedroom where I lay helpless and attempted to strangle me. My wife forced him to stop. That is the last we saw of Aristide." He laid the stylus down and looked at Elissa.

"I'm so afraid that they will take me from you."

Hasdrubal set the tablet beside the stylus and pulled her into his lap. "Nobody is going to take you from me. Claudius is already devising an escape plan if we suddenly have to go."

She nestled her head in his neck and cried a little.

He held her tightly. "We will go home to Carthage where we can be Phoenicians." He felt her head nod in assent.

After a few minutes, she said, "Hasdrubal?"

"Yes, my love." Her tone was soothing, wheedling, even coy.

"Will you buy me some surgical instruments?"

"Will I—" He almost dropped her.

Elissa laughed shyly. "Not many, not major ones for amputations or anything like that."

"What do you have in mind?" Taking her chin in his fingers, he pulled her face up so he could look at her.

"Just one or two female instruments so I can help the young ones."

"Just the young ones? I thought you might be planning to set yourself up as a surgeon."

She evaded his eyes. "Would you object very much if I had a practice as a physician?"

He didn't answer. She looked at him sharply, "You would object, wouldn't you?"

"That is unfair, Elissa. You apparently have given this thought, but you are springing it on me without warning. It is an idea that is totally foreign to our customs. You must forgive me if it takes some consideration on my part. Allow me to reflect, and I will tell what I think."

"Yes, my lord."

Lysander was sent to deliver the tablet.

Late in the day, Hanno returned with news that ships frequently left Ostia for Sardinia. "From there," he said, "we can board a Phoenician trading vessel bound for Carthage."

Hanno also brought the first communication from Bimilcar in weeks. From talking quietly in the garden, they moved to their usual seats where Elissa joined them. Hasdrubal read aloud:

> The routes to invade Etruria are long and familiar to our enemy. The road through the marshes is short and contains the element of surprise. As Hannibal thrives on surprise, he chose the marshes. Before announcing this route, he had it rigorously checked. The water on the ground was shallow and the ground underneath solid. In the crossing, he placed all the best fighting men forward in the column, interspersed by the supply carts. The Celts marched behind them, and the cavalry was last.
>
> The Hispanians and Africans, who were in the lead and used to hardship, came through in good shape. The Celts, not used to physical hardship of this kind, suffered because the passage of so many men had softened the ground. The march was difficult as the mud sucked at them. If they tried to turn back,they faced the cavalry in the rear.
>
> Everyone suffered from lack of sleep as the crossing took four days and three nights marching through water. Many of the pack animals stumbled and died in the mud. The men piled packs on them and lay down, thus snatching a little sleep out of the water.

"Interesting," said Hanno.

> Hannibal rode our remaining elephant. We lost the others through cold and exposure. He suffered terrible pain from an attack of ophthalmia as it was impossible for him to halt and have it treated. As a result, he has lost sight in one eye. But that does not curtail his activity or his concern for the rest of us.

"That's sad," said Elissa. "It could so easily have been prevented."

"If I know Hannibal," said the high priest, "he will go on as if he had two good eyes."

Hanno vowed to himself that someday he would meet Hannibal.

"There is not much more," Hasdrubal said.

We pitched camp at the swamp edge to rest and reconnoiter. I write from that camp. Almost immediately, our scouts found the new consul Flaminius camped before Arretium. What is your opinion of him? The country offers much plunder, and Hannibal plans to try to draw Flaminius into battle.

Hasdrubal sent back word that Flaminius was a politician—a demagogue, who constantly played to the gallery, with no practical experience in war, but who had supreme confidence in his own ability.

An answer arrived within days. Hasdrubal read it to Hanno.

Many thanks. Your information was a major factor in Hannibal's decision about what to do next. Our strategy will be to march past Flaminius' camp, devastating the area as we go. This will irritate him. He will follow wherever we lead, having the desire to win glory for himself alone.

Within a fortnight, Hasdrubal wrote:

Flaminius has informed the Roman senate that he is being treated with contempt by the Carthaginians. He says smoke rises all around him from the depredation of the enemy; the situation is intolerable; and he intends to do something about this insult.

Some of Flaminius' officers have advised him against headlong pursuit, but he brushed aside their arguments and struck camp. In his stupidity, he has created so much confidence in victory among the populace that camp followers, as numerous as his army, follow in the hope of plunder.

"I discovered some things about Flaminius in the comitium today." He handed the scroll to Elissa to read. "There is fear among one faction in the senate that the gods will deny victory because Flaminius is not really a consul. He was elected, but not inaugurated in Rome."

"Must he return to Rome?"

"To be inaugurated, yes, but he is making no move to do so."

"What does the public say?"

"Their fears have been augmented by similar omens coming from various places. All have to do with fire. Some Romans said that the javelins of soldiers took fire. The truncheon of a horseman on night watch also took fire. And soldiers have been struck by lightning."

"The gods must be really angry."

"The Romans are busily placating their gods. A golden thunderbolt weighing fifty pounds was given to Jupiter."

Astonished, Elissa said, "That's a lot of gold."

"That is not all. Juno and Minerva are being offered silver. Each matron is being asked to give what she can afford to Juno Regina on the Aventine. You had better be prepared with a reasonable sum when the officials knock on our door."

"Oh, Hasdrubal, do I have to? I want Rome to lose."

"Yes, give them silver. As high priest of Tanit, I will perform a ceremony to counteract the efforts of Juno Regina."

"Very well."

They smiled, enjoying their collusion.

"I think," said Hasdrubal as he sealed his scroll, "that we will soon hear of a decisive battle that could very well mean the end of the war. And Rome will not win the battle."

He stood up. "Claudius can deliver that to the inn in the morning."

As was his habit, Hanno left with the scroll before dawn. Hasdrubal went to the comitium for the start of the day's business. Abdmelkart walked to the market. A uniformed man came to the house, asking for Elissa.

Lysander found her bathing little Hasdrubal. "A man dressed as a guard of the court, asks to see you," he said. "He is insistent."

She wrapped the baby. Terror in her heart, she said, "Lead me to this man."

The guard said, "You are Elissa, the woman from the house of the Athenian, Aristide?"

"Yes."

"You are to come with me to the court to answer charges of murder."

33

*A*s a startled bird utters a single cry before winging skyward, so one agonized cry escaped Elissa. Her world darkened. The bright, clear sunlight that had poured into the atrium dimmed and turned a misty gray. As she stared, the face of the guard crumpled. His eyes became sunken, his cheeks hollow, his jaw smooth and sharp. Death stood before her. No. Please. She had so much to live for. She tightened her grip on little Hasdrubal and swayed backwards.

Lysander, standing slightly behind her, saw the color drain from her face, giving her features the translucence of alabaster. Was she going to faint? He started to stretch his arms toward her, but she drew herself up regally and said, "I must dress for court."

The guard moved to follow her across the atrium. She pointed to the bench placed for visitors. "Wait there," she said with an authority that brooked no argument.

He opened his mouth, wiggled his shoulders indecisively, closed his mouth, and walked meekly to the bench.

She sped to the kitchen with Lysander right behind her.

The Cook's eyes buldged at their precipitous entrance. She laid down the long-handled spoon she was using to stir a pot of soup and wiped her hands on the front of her tunic. The slave girl, who sat on the floor cutting vegetables, stopped to watch.

"Marita," said Elissa over her shoulder as she handed little Hasdrubal to the Cook, "help me dress. I must go to the law courts."

"My lady," said the girl, suddenly assertive, "I will go with you."

"And I will come as far as the courts, then hunt for the master," said Lysander.

"He should be at the comitium." Elissa's speech was precise, her pallor the only telltale of her inner panic.

Marita began to wail the moment the bedroom door closed behind them. Folding Elissa's hurriedly discarded morning garments, she bewailed the unfairness of the judges. Totally ignorant of why her mistress was being arrested, she moaned about her lady's bad luck while she adjusted Elissa's dark blue wool robe.

Elissa snapped, "Stop it. Not another word out of you or you stay here."

Marita's smooth, pink brow knit in pain. The girl shrank within herself.

Tanit help me, thought Elissa. What a nuisance she could be. "Here, pin this brooch at my shoulder," she said.

The guard led them along the Vicus Tuscus and the Via Sacra, Elissa proud and composed, a beautiful Roman matron who turned many a head, backed by two servants ready to ward off any young man brazen enough to address their mistress. They reached the judicial square. The guard stopped before the open door of one building where he stepped aside and motioned Elissa forward. She hesitated. The stench coming from inside was unbearable, and the cacophony that reached her ears worse. Attorneys were trying to reason with clients who screamed as long as breath lasted, gulped and screamed again. Men unable to stay still, picked their way carefully around lounging bodies. Beggars, thieves, vandals; dirty, disreputable humanity sprawled on the floor, either indifferent to those around them or detailing their exploits—to closed ears.

Elissa still hesitated. Lysander said, "Come, my lady; I will make a place for you." With his foot, he shoved two men along the floor, pushing them away from the wall.

"A fine lady poisons her husband," jeered one of the men, but they sat up and moved together.

Elissa stood quietly. Men leered at her. Marita, unsure what to do if one of them approached, stationed herself in front of her mistress.

Lysander started to go. He said to Marita, "If anything happens before the master comes, go right home and tell Abdmelkart." He looked at her blank, scared face. "Do you understand?"

"Yes," she whispered, glancing at her mistress.

Stupid girl, thought Lysander. He ran to the comitium. He couldn't find Hasdrubal. He'd hunt for Abdmelkart in the market. The Numidian always knew the master's whereabouts. Hurrying along the market road, he spied Abdmelkart, laden with baskets, almost lost in the crowd.

"Thank the gods I've found you," he said when he reached Abdmelkart. "The mistress has been arrested." Abdmelkart lost his hold on one of the baskets.

"Here," Lysander cried, grabbing it, "let me help you."

"I have it," said Abdmelkart, trying to calm himself. "Where is she?"

"At the courts. I couldn't find the master."

"Return to the courts and stay with the mistress. I'll get him."

Abdmelkart searched in the comitium and along the Via Sacra without success. He couldn't understand it. Where was the master? Uneasy, he hurried to the law courts. He spotted Elissa, cool and majestic, her slave in a heap at her feet, Lysander close by.

"Go home," Abdmelkart said to the girl. "Try and make the Cook understand that it may be a long time before we come."

The girl objected. Her place was with her mistress.

"You are of no use here now. Your turn will come," said Abdmelkart. "You can be of more service to all of us if you go. The master will come home at the end of the morning."

She complied reluctantly.

Much later, Hasdrubal arrived. He found Elissa sunk to a sitting position against the wall. Lysander and Abdmelkart squatted close by, talking in low voices. Elissa was tiring. She had begun to feel deserted. The official who stood in the doorway and called names in a clarion voice had disappeared. Despite her efforts to remain composed, fear was asserting its sway.

To prevent herself from crying, she raised her eyes and looked around. Hasdrubal was at the door. She brightened and motioned to him.

"I must get you out of here," he said. "The courts are closed for the day."

"You mean—you mean—" she stammered.

"Hush. I will get you out."

Turning, he ran from the room. After what, to Elissa, seemed like hours, he returned, followed by a tall, thin, clean-shaven man with iron-gray hair. The blue eyes above his aquiline nose were kindly. Elissa noted the fastidiously elegant drape of his toga and the precision with which he analyzed the probable status of those still detained.

Gaius Aurelius' reputation went before him like a flaming sword. Several Romans recommended him to Hasdrubal as the finest advocate in the city. Usually, he rested in the afternoon, but at Hasdrubal's pleading, he agreed to see Elissa.

"You may go home, lady," he said. "Your husband has given his word that you will present yourself in court tomorrow morning. I will meet you here."

Elissa glanced distastefully around the noisy room.

Gaius smiled. "We'll find a quiet spot to talk. Maybe by the Temple of Vesta." He went on, "I will ask you many questions. Then we will see what is to be done. It may take weeks until your case comes before the magistrate."

Encouraged by Gaius' words, but subdued, Hasdrubal and Elissa, followed by Lysander and Abdmelkart, left the courts and walked home.

"How did he guess?" Elissa asked plaintively as they sat on dining couches.

"I was bedridden, so was not involved," Hasdrubal answered.

"Diodorus knew how cruel Aristide had been to you. He put everything together and guessed that you were the one who murdered Aristide," said Hanno.

Absolutely right, thought the high priest, nodding in approval.

The next morning, Gaius Aurelius heard Hasdrubal's version of the story first, then Elissa's, as they huddled in a corner of the forum far from the shouting and bursts of applause that greeted the appearance of celebrated advocates. He asked Elissa why she had murdered Aristide.

Her jaw dropped. "Because—because—" She stopped, collected herself, and said, "Aristide was throttling my husband. I heard him say, 'You will die.'"

Gaius agreed that she had acted to defend Hasdrubal.

"However," he said, "Diodorus has no proof. It is all supposition. We will admit nothing."

Gaius, true to form, prepared himself well. He tested witnesses, went over the scene, memorized facts down to the smallest detail. He wrote his speech, which he refined, practiced, and polished some more. He tried and cast aside various gestures and intonations of voice until he was satisfied. He also engaged some of his most influential friends to attend Elissa. The case finally came before the magistrate. Elissa walked into the open judicial square surrounded by Gaius, Hanno, Abdmelkart, Lysander, Hanno's Etruscan friends, and well-known Roman politicians.

A crowd gathered. Palokart stood among them while Hasdrubal prowled about, searching for a spot where he could hear and see to advantage, out of sight of Diodorus and the claque he had assembled.

Word had spread that Gaius Aurelius planned to defend a woman. Aspiring jurists, politicians, clients, aristocrats, and the general public converged to hear him. In the crush, Hasdrubal finally gave up trying to see and just listened. Diodorus' advocate asked for a list of witnesses. He asked for a recess to study it; he objected to three witnesses; he requested assurances that the defendant would be produced as needed; he begged the judge's indulgence on five days to attend to other business. Time wore on.

"They have nothing specific to go on," Gaius said to Elissa. "They are hunting, hoping for evidence to use against us."

"Do advocates find something when they do that?" asked Elissa.

"Not if you have told me the truth."

Elissa was silent.

Gaius Aurelius stood up and expertly countered everything the opposing attorney said.

Diodorus' advocate was still arguing at the time for adjournment. Irritated, the magistrate snarled, "Appear in seven days."

Once the case resumed, Hasdrubal spent his mornings running between the judicial courtyard and the comitium across the forum. He knew that the war in the north was heading toward a major confrontation. Hannibal's policy of burn-and-destroy in his march toward Rome would, sooner or later, seduce the new consul Flaminius into battle. Nothing of this had apparently reached the Roman public.

Elissa and her group of supporters had to appear again and again before the magistrate. The politicians stopped coming. Some of the Etruscans left to attend to other business. Witnesses were called and then called back again. Diodorus' lawyer went over and over the same ground: the fire, the mistress, the slave girl, the baby, Aristide's dead body; he had nothing to connect the body with the other facts.

"Tell your husband Paulus" Gaius said to Elissa one day, "that the judge is getting bored with the case. He is thinking of dismissing it."

Elissa's face glowed. "How wonderful."

"Diodorus' advocate will call your female slave, Marita, tomorrow. I think he will use her testimony to prepare a murder charge on grounds of cruelty."

"But that is still supposing I killed him," said Elissa.

"It is. And that will undoubtedly end his case—not a very persuasive presentation."

The slave girl was frightened. Elissa tried to calm her. "Just tell the truth, Marita," she said gently. "Remember, just tell the truth," she reiterated as the girl was led to the magistrate.

Marita did as the mistress said. She kept her head as Diodorus' lawyer asked her sharp, insinuating questions. She was very explicit about Aristide's cruelty.

The lawyer asked, "Could Elissa have stabbed Aristide?"

"Absolutely not."

"Why are you so positive?"

"Because I saw two men dump the master's body in the street."

Diodorus' head shot forward. Elissa gasped. Gaius went rigid. Hanno and Abdmelkart sucked in their breath.

Diodorus' lawyer took on the expression of a hooded cat. He had won.

"How did you happen to see that?"

The girl blushed and ducked her head shyly. Then she looked directly at the judge and said, "I was running away. I snuck out of the house late. But it was dark with only a little light from the sky. I was alone. I didn't know where to go, and I was scared. Even though I hated the master, I thought I better go back to his house. When I got near the house, I stood close to the walls, in the shadow. I saw two men carrying somebody. They dropped him in front of the master's house and left. I hurried inside and couldn't sleep—"

"Do you know who those two men were?" interrupted the lawyer.

The girl sat still. Nobody moved. All eyes were on her. As they waited, a transformation took place. Her mouth dropped open, amazement spread across her face, and she sat up straight.

"Claudius and Abdmelkart."

Blackness surrounded Elissa. She felt herself sinking in slow motion, unable to stop. When she opened her eyes, Hanno was kneeling over her, Gaius' face above him. Abdmelkart was on the other side. A crowd circled them. She tried to sit up. Hanno's arm went under her back and lifted her.

"I'm all right," she said.

"Abdmelkart sent Lysander to get my father," Hanno said. "He will take you home. The judge says he should. But Abdmelkart and I have to stay. We have been called to testify."

"I want to stay and listen."

"No." Hanno was firm. "We will tell you all the details."

Hasdrubal took Elissa home and made her lie down. He held her hand, sitting beside her. They talked quietly of Carthage; the Temple of Tanit; where they might set up housekeeping. He promised to buy her the medical instruments she had asked for. If she tried to speak about the trial, he gently placed a finger on her lips and shook his head. "Not now."

Hanno and Abdmelkart dragged in at midday. Everything had come out. Gaius had superbly outlined Elissa's defense. He argued that she had killed Aristide to defend her husband, and he begged the judge not to recall her. Her testimony would just be repetitious, and she was in no physical state to go through it again.

Diodorus' advocate countered that Elissa had taken the opportunity to retaliate against her protector for small affronts. He refused to acknowledge that Aristide had actually been her abductor.

Gaius thought the magistrate might render judgment the next day, but he didn't. He ordered Hanno, the girl, and Abdmelkart to testify again. And finally, he called Elissa. Hasdrubal hung around, fearful that they might call him. What would he do? What would Diodorus do? He had Abdmelkart reshape his beard to camouflage his features. To Gaius, he was a Roman and so was Elissa. But if he were called to testify, would Diodorus recognize him? Could they escape tonight or would he be immediately arrested on Diodorus' word? Even if they left Rome, how far could they get?

Hasdrubal kept a composed exterior, presenting a confident, calm front.

Gaius claimed his testimony would simply be repetition. Half unconscious from being throttled, he had neither seen Elissa come into the room nor seen her wield the knife. He had not been called to testify. Hasdrubal hoped it would continue that way.

While the case crept slowly along, he received an exciting letter from Bimilcar, indicating that the war might soon be over:

When Hannibal saw that consul Flaminius and his troops were nearby, he ordered a halt at a spot he had chosen.

We were in a level, narrow valley surrounded on both sides by hills. Lake Trasimenus was at one end of the valley. A steep cliff, where Flaminius would enter, was at the other. This restricted passage was the only access to the valley.

Hannibal led us into the valley at night. He occupied the hill end, with African and Hispanian men. Slingers and pikemen were stationed on the hills to his right; Celts and cavalry on the hills to his left. Celts and cavalry were also stationed in a continuous line under the hills and at the valley entrance. I was with those at the valley entrance, on level ground.

By morning, a mist, thick and white, lay over the lake side as Flaminius led his advance guard into the defile, followed by his entire army. The soldiers marched close together. Observing them, I could tell they were afraid as the mist made everything look weird and misshapen. The mist hung over the waters of the lake like a thick, soft cloud so the men couldn't see what was out there. They probably didn't know it was water. They drew closer together, a dark mass against the threatening white fog.

As the morning progressed, the mist lifted a little in spots, enough for them to see the lake and some of the hills. I could see them point and talk together. Flaminius is a stupid man. Even his rawest recruits apparently realized the danger.

Hannibal gave the signal for battle as soon as most of the Romans were in the valley. We struck from all sides. The majority were killed while still in marching order. Flaminius himself was killed. Many were herded into the lake where they either drowned while trying to swim in their heavy armor, or they were killed by our cavalry as they stood nose-deep in water.

About six thousand who had been near the head of the column managed to escape. From the opposite end of the valley, they reached an Etruscan village. Hannibal dispatched troops and pikemen to surround the village. The Romans surrendered without attempting to defend themselves, asking only that their lives be spared. All told, we captured about fifteen thousand men while our own losses were figured at one thousand five hundred, most of them Celts. Of the prisoners, Hannibal has sent all the allies of the Romans back to their homes and distributed the Romans among our troops.

As is Hannibal's wont whenever we have survived some diffi-

culty, he has ordered the troops to make camp and rest. We also need to bury our dead. We are all elated. The war should not last long.

By the time the high priest and Hanno reached the forum the next morning, the entire city knew of the Roman disaster at Lake Trasimenus, but not what had happened or how. Rumors were rampant. Silent, long-faced, milling people mobbed the forum, waiting for any tidbit of news, any glimmer of hope, concerning their defeated legions. People in small groups talked in low voices. Dazed, they couldn't believe that they had been defeated.

Matrons wandered through the crowd, demanding to know what disaster had occurred. Praetor Marcus Pomponius entered the comitium. In a choked voice, he said, "A great battle has been fought, and we were beaten." He turned and went into the senate house.

The praetors immediately busied themselves with the defense of Rome. Keeping the senate in continuous session, they sent word of the defeat to the other consul, Gnaeus Servilius, who had already dispatched Gaius Centenius with a force of four thousand cavalry to support Flaminius. Gnaeus planned to follow with the main body of the troops.

Three days later, news of another disaster reached Rome. Hasdrubal heard it from the crowds in the forum. The Carthaginians had attacked Centenius and his troops, killing half of them. The rest had fled up a steep hill, but the Carthaginians pursued them, and all were captured.

This time, the public erupted. The senate set aside the normal annual election of magistrates to adopt radical measures. The situation, according to the senate, demanded the appointment of a single, absolute commander. The public elected Quintus Fabius Maximus dictator for the second time. Though the first time had been fifteen years earlier, many Romans still remembered his term of office with respect.

Hasdrubal was certain that the war was over, all but for the signing of the treaty. He took long walks by himself so he could think without being influenced by those dear to him. He must extricate them from this murder charge. But how? Upon examination, each of his schemes had flaws. Finally, he thought of one that would work. He went over and over it. His plan seemed plausible. One or two weak spots presented themselves where he could fail. But he had to take the risk.

He wrote to Bimilcar, describing the senate's latest actions. He added a long personal section. He told him of the murder charge and of the decision he had made. Once he sent the message, he did not mention his intentions to anyone.

He requested a private audience with the judge. Condescending, the judge said the procedure was unusual. Notes went back and forth. He doesn't say no, thought Hasdrubal. A small token exchanged hands.

One day, while standing at the back of the crowd listening to Diodorus' lawyer, he heard a murmur. "Be at my judge's home as the sun sets tonight." The deputy who ran the magistrate's errands passed like a shadow behind him.

Elated but cautious, Hasdrubal made excuses at home. He went to the magistrate's luxurious villa. The judge stealthily opened the door himself. Hasdrubal slipped through sideways. There was no light, but enough came from the last rays of the sun for him to see a large garden. A fountain splashed; its water softly gushed and plopped. Nobody was about. The judge led him to two chairs placed under the portico's shadow. He motioned his guest to a seat, sat down himself, and listened.

"My wife is a princess of the royal house of Tyre. Since the war is going so badly for Rome, I wonder if you might agree that this is no time for us to stir up trouble with King Antiochus. I would be willing to take my wife out of Rome and out of any Roman territories. We would never set foot in them again. This would be a definite hardship for me, but as I am from the provinces, I could make do." He sighed at the great hardship he was offering to undertake. "I am prepared to adhere to the same rules as would be imposed on my wife."

"This is highly unusual." The judge shifted in his chair.

Hasdrubal wondered if this were the time to lay a small sack of coins on the judicial knee.

"I will consider your request," the judge said.

A soft leather money sack reached the knee.

The judge cleared his throat. "I need Diodorus' acquiescence. But I think that can be arranged."

At home, Hasdrubal dismissed Abdmelkart, then told Elissa and Hanno what he had done.

He turned to Hanno. "If the judge allows us to go, I will leave you in charge of our work as long as Hannibal needs you. You have a natural bent for it and are extremely competent."

Hanno beamed. "Many thanks, sire. I'll do my best."

"It won't be for long. Abdmelkart will remain to run the house—and Palokart can keep an eye on you."

"I am a man," objected Hanno.

"Not quite," said his uncle smiling. "But almost. I am very proud of you." After a minute, he said, "Lysander will be offered his freedom."

Hanno pulled at his ear. "I hate to lose him."

His uncle studied him for a long moment. Hanno and Lysander had become close. The slave could be given a choice. Hasdrubal had no idea what the situation was in Arcadia, the fellow's home. If Lysander chose to stay with Hanno, he would have to be told that they were Phoenicians. But that didn't seem important now with the war almost over. He certainly was loyal. Perhaps Hanno could bring him to Carthage. "Well, we will see."

Hanno asked, "Do you think Diodorus will agree?"

"He might. I just do not know, Hanno. He is a strange man. His responses to my messages have been so meek that I have been worried, wondering if some sword would fall."

The next day, the judge called a halt to the court proceedings. He claimed extenuating circumstances had to be resolved before they could continue.

Those in the house off the Vicus Tuscus hoped for success. With each passing day, success seemed more certain. Late in the afternoon of the fourth day, Diodorus himself knocked at their door. Abdmelkart answered the knock and announced the Athenian trader. Hasdrubal, with all the assurance of a man secure in his being, walked serenely forward to meet the rival whom he had not seen since he was seventeen. He carried the charismatic dignity of his position as high priest of Tanit. Behind him were Elissa and Hanno. Abdmelkart faded into the dimness of the portico where he could still hear and be immediately available in case of trouble. Lysander, unobtrusive but alert for danger, squatted at Hanno's bedroom door.

"You have the audacity to ask that the murderer of my—" Diodorus stopped short, ten steps from Hasdrubal. He shook his head as if to clear it and brushed a hand across his face. "Excuse me. These last weeks have worn me out. For a moment, I thought I saw my son's ghost. Be that as it may," he continued more forcefully, "I will not allow his murderer to go unpunished."

Again, he drew a hand across his eyes. "I don't understand.

I keep seeing Aristide." He stared, concentrating all his attention on the high priest's face. "Or else I've seen you before. My mind is playing tricks." He squinted. "No, it's not my son. I've seen you before. I never forget a face. But where?"

Hasdrubal remained silent. The aura surrounding him manifested his inner strength and his commitment to the safety of his family. He watched Diodorus, whose face became more intense as he sifted through events, reaching further and further into the past.

Finally, in a faraway voice, Diodorus said, "I was in Carthage once. Years ago." His face suddenly brightened. "Carthage! That's where I saw you." He laughed. "A pimply-faced boy, studying to be the high priest of Tanit. Your father was high priest."

Lysander straightened with a jerk. His mouth fell open. He glanced at Abdmelkart. Their eyes locked.

Lysander saw the warning, the veiled threat. His glance shifted to Hasdrubal. The man was a spy. Joy, wild, exhilarating glee, bubbled up in him. He looked back at Abdmelkart and grinned. Abdmelkart relaxed.

"I recognize you, even with your beard." Diodorus' eyes narrowed ominously. His lip curled in an ironic sneer. "You are a Carthaginian, living as a Roman. Very interesting. I'll bet you're up to no good. Let's talk about it." A cunning smile replaced the sneer.

So, thought Hasdrubal, he plans to blackmail me: get what he wants in exchange for silence. There will be no negotiations concerning Elissa. She goes free. Escape is—what was he saying?

"I would recognize you anywhere," Diodorus asserted flatly. "I only saw you two or three times, always in the company of my—" He stopped and squeezed his eyelids together tightly. A change took place in his expression as if Zeus were aging him. "You were—I'd forgotten—you were formally betrothed to Dido. That's why you look so familiar and why I keep seeing ghosts."

As the waterline drops in a leaking glass, the florid color of Diodorus' skin changed. A sickly white replaced the olive tone of his forehead, moving slowly down across his eyes, his nose, his mouth. Shock and disbelief followed.

"You are the father of my—of Aristide."

"Yes." Hasdrubal affirmed it quietly, without emotion.

Hanno's ears went back, and his mouth gaped. He glanced at Elissa. She looked at him warily. He made no sound.

What seemed a lifetime passed before Diodorus spoke, in

perfect control again. "The charade is over. All the pieces fit. We have come full circle, you and I."

A charade! Hasdrubal's mind turned somersaults. The instant Diodorus left, they had better leave Rome quickly—get out through the garden wall and grab the horses. He had no doubt the Athenian would expose them to the Roman authorities. Should they take a ship from Ostia? No. They would be too easily apprehended. North? Perhaps a small coastal port? That might give them a better chance of success—

Wait a minute! Had Diodorus said something about hate? The high priest turned his full attention back to the trader.

"It's true," said Diodorus, gazing blankly at the flower beds. "We hated each other. If it weren't for my reputation, I wouldn't be here. Certain behavior is expected of me. Aristide was a stone around my neck. A stone smeared in poison. Money was his god. Even if I'd given him mountains of gold, he would have demanded more."

His face became melancholy. "Aristide was a happy, affectionate baby. I loved him dearly. He was about a year old when Dido began to taunt me with the fact that the boy was not mine. I refused to believe her. She was already making my life miserable. I thought it was just another of her ways to hurt me. When I looked at Aristide, I saw no other man's features in his. I never thought of you. Of course, I would not have recognized you in him. By the time he was two, he was so fat, he could hardly walk, and his features were blurred. The fat seemed abnormal, but she spurned my every effort to have the child examined. She also began making excuses—he had a cold, he was sleeping, he was with my mother. I saw very little of him.

"He went to school when he was seven, but Dido persuaded the school to send him home every night. I think she told the lead teacher his excessive fat needed special food, but it was really to keep him fat."

Diodorus raised his eyes to look at Hasdrubal. "I began to receive reports about his behavior. He treated the other boys badly. So he was expelled." His glance swept around, focused on nothing, his eyes empty and desolate.

"Aristide's hatred became obvious. Dido was the source of that, I'm sure. It didn't take me long to figure out why she had married me. She destroyed my love for her and Aristide's love for me. I saw her deliberately destroy him. Why, I never knew. Her own perverse mind? Retaliation against you? The fact that I forced her to keep an Athenian household, which restricted her to the house?"

His words, which had gotten fainter and fainter, ceased. Diodorus slumped forward. Though no sound came from the others, Hasdrubal signaled them to be silent. No one moved.

Diodorus' glance stopped at each one before returning to the high priest. "She taught him to be a monster. He bought young boys and kept prostitutes. He never allowed me to arrange a marriage. He found marriage an abomination—perhaps because there was no happiness in our home. Dido was greedy and cruel. She goaded me beyond endurance. One night, I struck her. She fell and split the back of her head open on a bronze statue holding a sword."

Hasdrubal felt profoundly sad. His rival was beaten, his life in tatters.

Diodorus continued, "Some twenty-five years later, Aristide reversed her action. As your espoused wife, she left you. He stole your wife. I have no idea whether he knew what she had done— or whether Dido set him up to doing what he did."

"He did not know," said Hasdrubal.

"I will offer thanks to the gods of Mount Olympus for that. But what does it matter?"

Diodorus again looked into space. "This is a charade. I can't call it anything else. I only felt relief when I learned he was dead. It is best for him, for you, for your wife, and for everybody else."

Tears streamed down Elissa's face. The lonely, shattered man wrenched her.

"Our lives are in your hands," Hasdrubal said simply. "I am a Roman here."

"I will not push my case. You may take your wife to Carthage." Diodorus shook his head. "I plan to leave Rome tomorrow. You need not worry about your safety; I have no particular loyalty to the Romans. Whatever you are doing here will end when you go anyway."

Hasdrubal inclined his head, but said nothing.

"Your secret will leave with me."

In true Phoenician fashion, Hasdrubal bowed deeply and said he hoped Diodorus, too, would find happiness in old age.

The door closed behind Diodorus. The people in the house seemed frozen. No sound broke the stillness. Suddenly, Elissa sobbed and flew into Hasdrubal's arms.

"I'm free. I'm free," she cried between sobs.

"Uncle Hasdrubal," yelled Hanno. In his turn, he jumped at the high priest.

Abdmelkart was on his knees, striking his head on the ground, saying, "Master, master."

Lysander, completely caught up in the emotion, knelt before Hasdrubal with bowed head.

"There, there," Hasdrubal said, kissing and soothing his wife. He tousled Hanno's head and gave him a hug.

Still holding onto Elissa, he touched Abdmelkart's shoulder. "Stand up, my friend. You, too, Lysander. You have done well."

"Thank you, sire." Lysander bowed from the waist.

"Now, we must make our plans. I will take Elissa to my library. Claudius, come with us." His arm around Elissa, he led her across the atrium. She was crying quietly, her tension and worry gone in an instant, replaced by relief, and happiness at going home.

After discussing what had to be done before they could leave, Hasdrubal announced that he was not going to the comitium anymore. "From now on, Claudius, you collect the news and write the messages."

Hanno glowed. "I'll try hard to be worthy of your trust."

Hasdrubal smiled at him. He turned to Elissa. "You take charge of what has to be done in the house. I will sell two of the horses."

"Shouldn't we keep one for Lysander?" Hanno already had ideas in his head.

Hasdrubal surmised what those ideas might be, but agreed to sell only one horse.

"We will get rid of that unfortunate girl of yours," he said to Elissa.

"Poor thing," Elissa said sadly. "I never saw anybody so hysterical once she realized what she had done."

"A slave like that is no good to anyone. On the other hand, I do not want her mistreated. I will offer her to the vestal virgins. She can care for the little ones. The youngest is only seven."

"My dearest, how generous." Elissa smiled adoringly.

"Now, I must talk to Abdmelkart. He will run the house, oversee Lysander and the Cook, as always."

Elissa gave her husband a startled look.

"But Abdmelkart—" Hanno began.

Hasdrubal held up a silencing hand. "Claudius, invite Palo-kart to dine tonight."

"Yes, sire."

"Elissa," Hasdrubal said as Hanno left, "send Abdmelkart to me."

Abdmelkart fell to his knees before the high priest. Hasdrubal chided him. "What is this! On your knees, Abdmelkart! You have not yet left Rome."

"I hope to soon, great high priest."

"I prefer you stay with Claudius."

"No," wailed the slave.

"It will not be for long. The war is about over."

"Please, master." Abdmelkart's mouth drooped, and his brows puckered.

"You are the only one who can run this house." Hasdrubal felt awkward. He hated the idea of leaving Abdmelkart. He couldn't manage without him. But for Hanno and the Cook—

"Master, master, I'm your slave. I have to do what you say." Abdmelkart landed flat on the floor. "I don't care what you do to me. Where you go, I go."

Hasdrubal sat looking at his slave's outstretched body. The Cook was deaf, but not stupid. Lysander was efficient and helpful.

"How long," he said slowly, "would it take you to train the Cook to run the house?"

Abdmelkart sat up, a surprised look on his face. He stared at the high priest, his mind calculating.

"Six days. She wouldn't be perfect."

Hasdrubal's face remained immobile. "I will have a talk with her." He rose. "I will let you know what you are to do."

As usual, he took the Cook to the vegetable garden where he felt free to pantomime. He gestured that her mistress had been freed, but had to leave Rome.

Fear crept into her eyes. Were they all leaving? Would the master sell her? She would never see the baby again. She cried out. Tears rolled down her face, and she rocked back and forth.

Hasdrubal tried to distract her. Claudius was staying. Claudius needed her. Abdmelkart would teach her how to run the house. Lysander would help her. As soon as the war was over, Claudius would bring her to them, and they would all be reunited.

No need to tell her that they were Carthaginians. She would not be implicated if the Romans discovered they were spies.

Hasdrubal spent a long time with her. He emphasized that she would see the baby soon; that the war would be over soon. He repeated soon many times.

His appeal worked. Knowing that she would see the baby again, she calmed down. She started to ask questions about running the house. She was flattered that he wanted her to do it. She smiled, pleased that he needed her to take care of Claudius. She had never before been given responsibility, and she rose to the occasion.

Hasdrubal took her hand and led her to Abdmelkart. "Teach her everything you can," he said.

"Yes, master." Abdmelkart bowed low.

In the library, Hasdrubal collapsed onto his chair. He still had to talk to Lysander. Leaving Hanno would be wrenching. They were no longer uncle and nephew. They were friends, close companions. Never, he mused, have I had a friend on a par with me. Hanno is one of those rare people. He has matured, in many ways, far beyond his years; in other ways, not. Palokart and Lysander can be trusted to dampen down any youthful exuberance if it gets out of hand.

And Palokart. I must give up his companionship. Our life here has gone along so evenly, I haven't realized how much I depended on Palokart for company. To be going home is joy unfathomed, but part of me will stay here in Rome. I cannot help myself.

Hasdrubal didn't know how long he sat there. He saw Hanno and Lysander return. Later, he heard a knock and saw Abdmelkart go to the door. Palokart entered.

Hasdrubal went to greet him.

"Wonderful news. Claudius told me. I'll miss you, though." Palokart grabbed the high priest in a strong embrace. "But you'll see me shortly. I've already started to wind up my affairs here. I can't wait to get back to Carthage."

"That is good news." Hasdrubal clapped him on the shoulder.

During the evening, Palokart promised to spend time with Hasdrubal every day until they boarded the ship for home. In a private moment, he said, "I'll keep track of Claudius. And if it works out, I'll bring him with me when I come home."

That night in their bedroom, Hasdrubal said, "I cannot believe how well everything is going. Lysander remains to be talked to, and that is all."

"Is Abdmelkart staying?" asked Elissa.

"No. He flatly refused. I wondered what he would do if I threatened to sell him."

"Probably stare at you in disbelief."

Hasdrubal let out a long breath. "I did not have the heart to order him to stay."

"My dear," Elissa said softly, "the truth is, you cannot do without Abdmelkart, either."

"I cannot do without Abdmelkart. The bond between us is too strong," he said just as gently, and took her in his arms. "But you, my darling, are worth everything to me. And now we can go home."

"Yes." She clung to him.

Diodorus left Rome at noon the following day, after informing the judge that he had no objection if the Roman Paulus exiled himself with his wife.

Hasdrubal wrote to Elibaal, telling him that they would leave Rome in about a week. Depending on how soon they could find a ship in some neutral port sailing for Carthage, they should arrive about ten days after that.

He also wrote to Bimilcar, reassuring him that Hannibal could depend on Hanno for information in the future, that he was a capable agent for Carthage. Hasdrubal took his scrolls to the inn. In return, the innkeeper gave him one for Hanno. It had Saphonisba's seal. Hanno read it aloud to Elissa and Hasdrubal.

> Your grandfather and I were dining with Batbaal and Mago when a commotion in the entrance hall caused us to break off our conversation. A messenger from the suffete appeared, summoning your grandfather to the senate chamber.
>
> He demanded to know why.
>
> The messenger didn't know, but said that the suffete rushed into the senate building. Very excited, he said that communication had come from Rome—

"Palokart sent a message to his brother," Hanno injected.

> Your grandfather was flustered, but he rose and quickly rearranged his clothing, saying that the news must be something about Hannibal.
>
> Batbaal and Mago said at the same time that it must be a

victory—a great victory—or the senate wouldn't be convened,
then looked at each other and laughed.

Your Grandfather immediately became elated. too. Mago went
with him and came back to tell Batbaal and me. Soon the entire
city knew of the victory at Lake Trasimenus and headed for the
forum. Mago escorted the two of us. People with torches were
hurrying down the road, calling quietly to one another. Everyone
was smiling and talking of the victory.

Surprisingly, for all the emotion, everybody was subdued.
There was no shouting or loud laughter. But our joy was deep and
overwhelming. We think the war will soon be over.

Crowds packed the forum. Though night, light from the torches
turned it into day. The doors of the senate building were open.
People streamed in and out.

My dear Hanno, I can't begin to tell you how overjoyed we
all are and how I long to see you. I believe that time has come and
that I will be reunited with you and your father.

Hanno looked at his uncle. Hasdrubal said, "If Hannibal
moves quickly on Rome, the war may well be over soon." He
added, "But he does not seem to be taking advantage of his opportunity. If he allows the Romans to mobilize, it could drag on."
Hasdrubal threw up his hands. "Hannibal is the commander and
knows the situation in the north; I do not."

He got up. "Hanno, send Lysander to my library."

"Yes, sire. He told me he wished he'd known before that we
were spies." Hanno laughed. "The idea of spying on the Romans
sent him into wild fits of laughter. I've never seen him like that
before."

"Lysander may be a valuable ally for you. He keeps his head.
That pleases me."

Lysander entered the library humbly. Hasdrubal thought, he
is awed by the fact that I am high priest. If only he knew how
tedious it can get.

"You already know that we are Carthaginians in Rome to do
what we can for Carthage."

"I do, sire."

"You find that of interest to you?"

"I do, sire."

"Upon discovery, you will be subject to the same penalties as
Claudius. You understand that?"

"I do, sire."

"You are willing to take this risk?"

"I am, sire."

"Good. You have done well here, Lysander. I trust you to look after Claudius."

"I will, sire."

"At the end of the war, Claudius and the Cook will return to Carthage. You may come with them or you may have your freedom. The choice is yours."

"I— I—"

"You do not have to decide now. At the appropriate time, you will let me know. All communication to me should be sent to the temple of Tanit in Carthage. The Cook will run the house. Help her mornings while Claudius is away. She will shortly manage to do the marketing; she deals with the street peddlers now. In time, she will be efficient."

"Yes, sire. She is competent, sire."

"And Palokart is available."

"Thank you, sire."

The day before their departure, Hasdrubal called Hanno to his library. This interview was the most distressing of all.

"I shall miss you, Claudius."

"I'll be home soon."

"Take care. You are very dear to me . . . ."

Tears welled in Hanno's eyes. He ducked his head. He didn't want his uncle to see him cry. He'd think he was afraid to stay on alone in Rome and work for Hannibal. That wasn't true at all. He would miss him more than anybody else—more than Elissa, more than little Hasdrubal, more than Abdmelkart. He would miss their talks in the garden, riding side by side on the horses, knowing he was in the house to smile and joke.

Hasdrubal stood up and opened his arms. Hanno went into them. They stood together, each getting hold of his emotions. Hasdrubal released Hanno and nudged him gently under the chin with his fist. "Before long, we will be together in a victorious Carthage."

Hanno's eyes sparkled. "Yes, sire."

The following morning, Hasdrubal, still the provincial Roman, accompanied by his wife, baby, and one male slave, boarded the barge for Ostia. Knowing parting would be difficult, Hasdrubal had insisted that they walk out the door, leaving the others standing in the garden. They were silent during the trip down the river. Despite his desire to go home, Hasdrubal regreted leaving Rome. He sought Elissa's hand and squeezed it. She smiled sadly. They had been happy here. She would always remember these months.

In Ostia, they found a vessel bound for Agrigentum in Sicilia. After stopping at Cumae, the ship anchored in Agrigentum. A day later, two Phoenicians, with their baby and a slave, hired space on a commercial ship coming from Sidon sailing to Carthage.

Epilogue

*H*annibal did not march on Rome. Instead, he decided to plunder the countryside near the Mare Adriaticum. Fabius had time to mobilize and march north. The war dragged on for another fifteen years. After Elibaal's death, support for Hannibal dwindled as the Carthaginian senators and people bickered and divided into jealous and greedy factions. In 202 B.C., Rome defeated Carthage.

At home in Megara, Hasdrubal and Elissa had three more boys. Batbaal and Mago added two boys to their home. The family's succession to the priesthood was secure, though little Hasdrubal was a full-grown man with children of his own before he came into possession of the honor.

Hanno continued to live in Rome and spy for Carthage. Accompanied by Lysander, he made a daring trip to the territory of Hadriana, near the Mare Adriaticum, to see his father. There, he met Hannibal and fell under the spell of the great commander. After that, he made regular trips to see Hannibal and did much to help the fading Carthaginian cause.

In 207 B.C., old and tired, Bimilcar asked to be relieved of his command and returned to Carthage.

After their victory, the Romans demanded Carthage pay a huge war debt. To levy the funds, Hannibal restructured the finances of Carthage. He succeeded so well that the city once again became an economic threat to Rome.

The Roman senate demanded that Carthage surrender Hannibal. He fled to Antiochus. But the Roman clamor for a victory parade with Hannibal in chains, walking behind Scipio's chariot, never ceased. The Romans sent out spies to seek him in the far reaches of the lands surrounding the Mare Internum, wherever, for a few years, he managed to live before the Romans again discovered his trail. He finally fled to Bithynia, ruled by King Prusias.

In 183 B.C.—as Roman forces closed in on him—Hannibal swallowed poison, choosing death over captivity.